sting
of
ice

CLARA ELROY

Sting of Ice

Editing: Erica Russikoff
Proofreading: Nice Girl, Naughty Edits
Cover Design: The Pretty Design Co.

Revenge is a dish best served cold, and as a figure skating Olympic medalist, I couldn't agree more.

I thrived on the ice until the day my boyfriend cheated on me with my biggest rival, causing me to lose my job and tarnishing my reputation.

Seeing the two people you hate the most get everything you ever wanted hurts, but I'm not about to let them win.
In my quest for retribution though, I broke an unspoken family rule.

I kissed my sister's brother in law to make my ex jealous.

Killian Astor is everything I was taught to avoid. He is as gorgeous as he is dangerous. An anarchist and my unlikely ally.

He wants nothing to do with me, but giving up isn't in my nature, and I need his help. In order to keep my lies under wraps, I get him to agree to keep up this charade in front of my ex-boyfriend and his new flame, thinking my heart is strong enough to bear the burnt of his affections.

But the more we act like we're in love, the more I lose sight of my original plan.

And that can't happen because if this becomes more than a

fake relationship, we'll end up hurting the people we care about most.

NOTE

Sting of Ice is a full-length, interconnected standalone that features strong language, sexual scenes and mature situations which may be considered triggers for some.
Reader Discretion is advised.

I'd prefer for you to go in blind, but if you would like a detailed warning list you can find it by scanning the code below:

PLAYLIST

"The Color Violet"— Tory Lanez

"Oh My God"— Adele

"Atlantis"— Seafret

"Souvenir"— Selena Gomez

"Karma"— Taylor Swift

"Break My Heart"— Dua Lipa

"I Was Never There"— The Weeknd

"Love On The Brain"— Rihanna

"Heaven" — Julia Michaels

"Arcade"— Duncan Lorence

"Into Your Arms"— Witt, Lowry, Ava Max

"How Do I Say Goodbye"— Dean Lewis

For all those who dare to dream,
even in the darkest of times.

There is a charm about the forbidden that makes it unspeakably desirable.

— MARK TWAIN

PROLOGUE

KILLIAN

They said we had a devil on one shoulder and an angel on the other.

As it turned out, my angel had lost the route home after an extended vacation and had relinquished complete control to the devil in me for a hot minute now.

Greed, envy, pride, wrath... I was constantly playing spin the bottle with all the seven deadly sins. My most loyal companion was gluttony, believe it or not. Upon first glance, one wouldn't be able to tell I had such close ties with overindulgence. I was six foot three and two hundred pounds of pure muscle. There wasn't a blond strand amiss on top of my head, my teeth gleamed as if I solely survived off Crest white strips and charcoal toothpaste, and my stomach was dotted with abs girls loved to suck on, on their way to wrapping their lovely lips around my dick.

No one paid much mind to the glossy sheen over my blue eyes, the nervous drum of my fingers on smooth surfaces, and the bulge of my veins whenever I was having withdrawals. Addiction was as much part of gluttony as excessive eating was, but whatever didn't stand out could be buried. And it was fairly easy to distract myself from the ear-splitting screams of the vicious beast I'd locked in a cage in a dusted corner of my brain with the hit of a joint.

Unbeknownst to me, another game of spin the bottle had started, but when the bottle pointed at lust, it felt much more like I was playing Russian Roulette instead. Especially when the object of my desire was none other than my older brother's sister-in-law, whose pregnant wife I was tasked with driving around while he was away on a business trip.

Saint was clingier than a fucking cat in heat since he'd knocked her up, and it was getting worse the more she progressed into her pregnancy. Ariadne was seven months in and looked like she'd swallowed a watermelon. Driving was out of the question, and using a driver was also ruled out, but it wasn't because my brother wanted to entrust her safety only to me—quite the opposite.

I wasn't the one looking after Ariadne; she was the one looking after me.

It was the way it was when you were both the youngest person in the family and the most eccentric or kooky, screwy, freaky, wacky. I'd been called a variation of names in my life-time, and that list would only grow if one witnessed what I was doing at this moment.

I was sitting on a bench tucked under a blooming magnolia tree at the Fleurs' mansion, sucking on a cancer stick, when I heard it: the sound of a window cracking open. I'd parked my car on their sweeping drive as I waited for Aria to pick up some food from her mother. And naturally, I couldn't resist the upward climb of my irises, gliding over the crawling ivy and onto the first floor where the real-life example of the saying "curiosity killed the cat" materialized before my eyes.

She had the grace of a butterfly, all dainty, long limbs, and a lithe body honed to perfection after years of grueling training to keep up with her figure skating regimen. I usually liked my women with a bit more meat on their bones, softer. But it wasn't just looks that attracted me to this particular girl, although her strawberry blonde hair and ocean eyes certainly did not repel me either. It was that knowing glint in her eyes, the upward curl of her lips, and her inability to keep her mouth shut when I was around. To keep herself from fighting me on every little thing.

Whenever we were in each other's presence, an invisible melody played in the background. A semblance of a distance had to be kept between us before the lyrics started writing themselves.

I was fairly certain Irena Fleur couldn't see me when she filled the empty space of her bedroom window with the lack of light outside. Even so, her chin tucked slightly down, her top lip curled, and her nose wrinkled as if something about the view displeased her.

Now, I knew that couldn't be me because, for all my quirks, I was pleasant to look at, be around, and have inside. Not that she would ever get to know that particular tidbit.

"I can see you, you know." Her voice echoed into the dead of the night as she leaned forward, her hair spilling over her shoulders and eyes narrowing in my direction. A slight cough of surprise escaped me as I exhaled some smoke, and she elaborated. "And hear you."

Her bright blue gaze penetrated the gloom like a beam of light pointing straight at me. The safety of the darkness washed away, and I felt like I'd stepped into the limelight.

Fighting the urge to make myself small, I spread my limbs wider on the bench and smirked in response to her scowl. "I wasn't hiding."

"So you were just creepily staring at me from under a tree? Got it." It was a half-hearted lie, and she called me out on it. I didn't dispute her conclusion. In fact, I reaffirmed it by watching her some more through the haze of smoke surrounding my face. Watching her small tits press together underneath that tight black tank top she had on when she leaned forward more, asking, "What are you doing here?"

"Creepily staring at you from under a tree," I repeated, and the deeper the crease between her brows got, the broader my smile became.

"Killian," she hissed, exasperated.

"Irena."

"How is it that you get even more infuriating every time I see you?" She sighed, fingers toying with some of the vines below her windowsill. "I thought the older people got, the more they matured."

"Pretty sure that's wine," I countered, crossing my ankles.

Her contemplative gaze stayed fixed on my body for a few beats, and the muscles beneath my white tee flexed at her attention, a natural male instinct, like a peacock showing off his feathers in order to mate. I feared we'd turn into a Nat Geo Wild episode if she kept staring at me like that.

The cool spring air crackled with tension, and she shook her head ever so slightly, as if flushing whatever thoughts swam there. My tongue traced the edge of my dying cigarette as I readied myself for her reply. Except, it never came...well, at least not in the form I thought it would.

"Why are you waiting outside all by yourself? You can

come in. We don't bite," Ina said, abandoning our previous plight to see who could annoy the other more.

"Speak for yourself. I'm one wrong breath away from your sister chewing my head off." I took the last drag before dropping my cig on the ground and smashing it under the weight of my boot.

"Now, that's something I'd pay to watch." Irena laughed under her breath, as if the mere idea entertained her.

I let the sound of her laugh wash over me and put a fist over my heart. "You wound me, Lilith."

"You'll survive, Lucifer." She followed my lead by dropping my nickname.

I was the initial instigator of this all.

It happened during our siblings' wedding, when we stood across from each other. Her in her baby blue bridesmaid dress, and I in my suit and tie. She was just a sixteen-year-old kid then, an archetypal rebellious girl that I loved getting a rise out of, hence why I started calling her Lilith. That, and because of the slight twinge of red in her hair, complementing her defiant spirit.

"Are you avoiding me?"

The question hit me out of nowhere, and I shifted uncomfortably in my seat, my eyes drifting away from hers for a single second.

Avoidance bred nothing but more problems, but not when the biggest complication you tried to steer clear of went by the name of Saint Astor.

"Why would you say that?" I bit my tongue after asking the question because I hadn't made this self-inflicted game of cat and mouse a secret.

You see, somewhere along the line, Irena crossed the threshold of looking like a malnourished kid to a slightly fuller woman with sharp facial angles and a cunning gaze that woke Killian junior right the fuck up.

I had to stay away because being attracted to my brother's sister-in-law was the last thing I needed. Even though using her as a weapon to tease him was pretty satisfying whenever the occasion arose.

"Bea saw you at Café Nova the other day and told me as soon as she mentioned I was joining her after parking my car, you basically hightailed it out of there, left your blueberry scone half eaten and all." She tilted her head, baby pink nails clicking on the marble window perch. "You know, it's funny. I didn't think you were a blueberry scone kind of guy."

"Well, what kind of guy did you have me pegged for?" I humored her, mainly to give myself some time to think up a response.

"The kind that sacrifices neonates and consumes the hearts of puppies," Irena deadpanned, catching up.

"Very creative. You and that friend of yours sure have a wild imagination." My throat constricted like it did whenever I lied. It was odd since I should've been a natural at it by now, but I kept going. "Work is kicking up, so I don't have time—"

"For me." She cut me off.

"For anyone. It's nothing personal, Irena," I bounced back.

"Look at you, trying to bullshit a bullshitter, Astor." In an unexpected turn of events, she straightened up and sat on the windowsill before swinging her feet outside, three stories up from the ground, continuing as if this was the most usual position in the world. "You'll have to lie better than that if you expect me to believe you."

"What the hell are you doing?" I hissed, alarmed, when

she reached for some hundred-year-old vines on the wall next to her.

"Get off your ass and come help me, or you're going to be blamed if I plunge to my death," she ordered, or blackmailed —I couldn't tell—nonchalantly, and I felt compelled to do her bidding when she abandoned any stable ground and swung herself from a few fucking twigs.

She cursed audibly as her legs flailed in the empty air before she hooked them to the wall. I abandoned my post by the bench and rushed beneath her, hoping she could feel my glare penetrating through the thin material of her purple leggings.

"Piece of advice for the future, Lilith. Blackmail is not a great way to persuade someone to help you when you're at a disadvantage," I said, stretching my arms wide as if readying to catch her. She continued her descent unbothered, but my eyes bugged out of my skull when she almost mis-stepped, and I yelled, "Don't put your foot there!"

She put her foot there.

And on top of disregarding my advice, she scoffed—she fucking scoffed—and her ass looked surprisingly biteable as she peered down at me, a smirk etched on her lips when she saw my outstretched hands. "Relax, I've climbed down this wall like a thousand times. I know what I'm doing. You're just there for safety reassurance."

Feeling dumb, I let my hands fall by my hips, my insides churning at the excessive display of concern I was showcasing. So what if she fell and broke a rib or two? A fall from that height wouldn't be fatal. It would ultimately teach her a lesson.

"And why exactly are you testing your Tarzan skills and don't walk out the front door like a normal human being?"

"My grandma is in there, and I don't feel like seeing her again on my way out," Ina explained, stalling a little as she now reached the second-floor window, making quick work of climbing down, and I had to admit I was a little impressed. "As for why I've done this before, well..."

"Well?" I prompted, willing my eyes to move away from her ass. Alas, they were magnetized by her flexing muscles in those damned tights that fit over her legs like a second skin. The lower Irena went, the more my palms itched to touch forbidden territories.

Fuck, fuck, fuck.

This was precisely why I stayed away.

I didn't know what it was; I got laid on the regular, but one look at Irena's almost non-existent curves and I got a bigger hard-on than most teenage boys did when watching a Megan Fox movie.

"My dad tends to be a tad overprotective, and I used to be a horny teenager. Need I say more?" she inquired, but her question was rhetorical.

My awe of her climbing skills didn't take long to turn sour, although I didn't understand this weird tightening of my throat. I'd take an experienced woman over a blushing virgin any day, but I always had this view of Irena being too young, too inexperienced, needing to be sheltered by men like...well...me.

"Don't stop on my behalf," I commented drily, my throat closing up.

Why?

I knew there was a significant possibility she wasn't a virgin. I was friends with a tennis player during my brief stay at Berkeley, and he wouldn't shut up about all the fun they got to have at Olympic villages. Realistically, Irena Fleur had also participated in some fun of her own, seeing that she was decorated with three gold and two silver medals at the ripe age of nineteen.

Put a bunch of athletic, hormonal teenagers in one building, and you'd be handing out condoms by the bunch.

My fists curled by my sides, and I tried to swallow my bitterness as she threw me a glare over her shoulder, nearing the ground. "I think you can use your imagination to figure out what happened next, Lucifer. It's not something you probably haven't done a thousand times before."

"Thousand is a bit excessive. Let's stick to hundreds for the sake of accuracy," I said, shoving my balled hands in the pockets of my slacks.

Honestly, I'd lost count, but she did not need to know that, as I did not need to think about who had been inside of her at one point in time. We needed to stick to appropriate conversations, like the weather, but I'd never been one for idle talk.

"How reassuring," she sassed, letting go and dropping the rest of the way once a short distance from the floor.

She was less than a foot away from me, and this up close, I could see every tiny freckle on her face, a light dusting of reddish brown stretching along her nose and cheekbones. A particular few dotted over her full top lip taunted me, and her eyes, clearer than a spring, caught every emotion displayed on my face before I could hide it. Bury it with the rest of the unspeakable things that filled my head daily.

Irena remained planted in place, and I should've moved back.

But I didn't.

I never backed up from a challenge, and Irena Fleur was

dying to give me a good chase. Her words, posture, and the slight upward tilt of her chin all betrayed it.

"How about you? From what you're telling me, you started young," I continued, and the scalding look she awarded me made me think I should've put my foot in my mouth.

"That's not information I offer up willingly." She crossed her arms, and we both found ourselves leaning forward until the air between us compressed, and it was a lot harder to breathe when she followed up with, "Least of all to my sister's brother-in-law."

The title, the remembrance of where we stood, made my chest cave in, and my nose tickled from the force of a ghost punch. My brother's punch if he ever found out how close I stood to his sister-in-law. How tempted I was to lower my gaze to catch a glimpse of her cleavage pushed together in that black tank top.

"You don't trust me, Irena?" I raised a brow in question, fingers clenching and unclenching so hard when she pulled her glossy bottom lip between her teeth. "Whatever did I do to you?" I finished my questioning, but my heart wasn't in it when I got a whiff of her strawberry-scented lip gloss.

Irena leaned in closer, an apathetic mask painted on her face as she said, "It's what you haven't done."

Every part of my body locked up.

My stomach turned as rigid as a washboard, and I stopped my oxygen intake for a second to get her maddening scent out of my system and think clearly.

Had she said what I thought she'd said?

And did it mean the same thing I thought it did?

Surely not.

"What?" I asked.

"What?" she parroted, but for all her boldness tonight, her slender throat bobbed with a nervous swallow.

"What the fuck does that me—" I started, but I was interrupted by a voice floating over my shoulder.

"Killian? Irena? Is that you?"

At Ariadne's question, we jumped apart like we were burned. Not that we were doing anything incriminating to begin with, but we were standing a bit too close for societal norms.

Irena composed herself faster than me and sidestepped me as if nothing had ever happened, skipping over to her sister. I shook my head, hoping my brain slid to the right position again after that brief lack of judgment, and turned to join them.

The two sisters couldn't look any more different from each other. It seemed like Irena had fully taken from her father's French side, and Ariadne had that Greek goddess look nailed to a T, with curves in all the right places, luscious brown hair and eyes, and short enough that even with heels on, she elevated her status from a hobbit to a dwarf.

"Yes, sissy." Irena smiled, patting Aria's rounded belly once reaching her. "I was just asking Killian if he could drop me off at your place. I thought we could have a little sleepover now that your clingy husband isn't there to ruin our fun."

If Aria was mad Irena called her husband clingy, she didn't show it. Instead, she mirrored her sister's smile and negotiated, "Will you rub coconut oil on my belly?"

"And make some popcorn so we can watch the new season of *Selling Sunset* together," Irena answered diplomatically.

"It's a deal," Aria replied, and I almost rolled my eyes.

She was so easily impressed, and I was a little annoyed that I wasn't being extended an invitation, despite not being sure I wanted one after that disaster of a meeting with the youngest Fleur.

"I'm feeling a little left out here," I popped in, spinning the keys of my Dodge around my index as I walked up to them.

"Get used to it. It's the way it'll be when the baby gets here," Irena said in a sickly-sweet voice, her hand flying to her chest. "I, on the other hand, will be the cool aunt the small peanut won't be able to get enough of."

"Until he's old enough to understand the bullshit you spew on a daily basis," I chewed back.

"Asshole," she hissed, her cheeks growing hot.

"Bitc—" I tried to retaliate, but Aria cut in before I could.

"If I have to stand on these heels for one more minute, my ankles will explode. Save your bickering for the car, kids."

And so, we all piled in, anonymity thick in the air as Irena and I put on our best show in front of her sister. The one that didn't let on how quickly we'd go for each other's throats if given the chance and how we'd probably enjoy it afterward.

CHAPTER ONE
IRENA

"You're moving from one scandal to the next," Bea whispered feverishly. With the way her face was turning red as I took a bite of my hash browns before washing it down with a sip of my strawberry mimosa, I feared she might explode soon.

We'd been best friends since the day we were both forced to glide on ice at the age of four, and she has been the voice of reason since then, as well.

You see, while I was all too eager to take advantage of the responsibility bestowed upon me and "accidentally" skate over a little mean girl's fingers because she made fun of my non-existent lashes (I actually did have lashes; they were just blonde), Bea cut my plans short once aware of them by telling me I'd end up in juvie and there were even meaner girls there that would probably *wax* my eyelashes *and* eyebrows off.

"Whatever do you mean?" I asked nonchalantly, my heel tapping on the vinyl flooring in a staccato rhythm.

Ever since the *incident* two months ago, I'd never been fully able to relax in a public setting. I couldn't help but think I was the topic of everyone's conversation, that laughter was directed at me, or a camera I hadn't noticed had captured me mid-chew, or any other embarrassing position.

I was slightly more at ease, shoved into a corner table at Sorellina's, partially shielded by some huge leafy plants. No one seemed to be paying attention to us, and I preferred it that way. It was ironic, really. I rather enjoyed being in the spotlight.

I mean, who wouldn't?

I was an Olympic winner, daughter of the CEO of one of the biggest fashion houses in the world, which meant I got to wear the biggest trends first, and drop-dead gorgeous, albeit a bit lacking in the curves department. But oh well, I had a face that didn't need any reinforcement.

Narcissistic much, my subconscious whispered, and I didn't refute it.

For as long as I could remember, everyone either wanted to be me or fuck me...until recently, that was. Lust didn't just go away, but it was safe to say no one wanted my life anymore. It went from a fairy tale to a nightmare in the zero point one second it took to post a video to social media.

"It's *what you haven't done?* Really?" Bea repeated the words I'd said to my sister's brother-in-law last night, and a wave of heat hit my face at the tone she used. It made *me* sound so ridiculous, but at the moment, it felt right. "You can't afford any more bad press, Irena." She sat back in her chair, watching me through judgmental eyes.

I knew I couldn't, but I wasn't thinking about headlines at the time.

All I was thinking about was Killian avoiding me, elusive as ever, and infuriatingly detached, like always.

Our conversations were brief over the years. At first, we'd established a cordial friendship, and I thought we were on our way to becoming close. But something changed along the way, and every time we met, smiles got stiffer and words lessened, to the point where he was actively trying to steer clear of me.

I didn't know what I'd done to garner such a reaction, and it drove me nuts. I guess wanting to be liked by everyone was one of my major flaws, but I couldn't help it, along with pride. Of course, asking him what his problem was, was out of the question, so I went with the next big thing...sexual innuendos.

That would surely get any man's attention, and I would linger in his mind like he did in mine, driving me mad with all the possibilities of what I'd done wrong. I didn't like him like that. We were simply playing a game of *Why should I be the only one to suffer?* and depending on how bitter I felt in the future, this was only the beginning for the youngest Astor.

Telling Bea what happened was a testament to how little I cared.

If I was lusting after Killian, keeping it a secret would be the next logical step.

"Chill out. I was just playing with him, and I don't care what the press says." I waved my hand as if I were mentally shooing them away. "Those sexist assholes can go f—"

"You will when they decide to cut you off the next Stars on Ice season because of all the bad press," an intruding voice pointed out, and I remained silent as my manager stormed over to our table, looking like Cleopatra in the flesh, with smooth tanned skin, big brown eyes with blue eyeshadow complementing her turquoise flowy dress, and dark curly hair.

"Amani," I greeted her. Bea followed my lead as she settled in an available bistro chair on the round table.

I wrung my hands together in my lap as she gave her order to the waiter, and prayed she hadn't caught much of our conversation. While Bea was the voice of reason, Amani would bust my balls if she knew I was itching to give the world another show they hadn't asked for.

And she'd be right.

Sometimes I thought she cared more about my career than I did. After all, she was my manager and had helped me secure a place in Stars on Ice, a tour where fans got to see the best of the US figure skating team perform live. It was also a *Dance Moms*-style reality TV show, showcasing all the juicy behind-the-scenes stuff up until the day of the performance.

Truth be told, I wasn't even sure I wanted to be in another season, not when *he'd* be there, but I also didn't want *him* to win because my leaving meant my cheating ex won.

He was a figure skater, too, though fewer gold medals than me. Maybe that was what drove him to cheat with my biggest rival: feeling less than.

"How's my little star doing this morning? Hopefully, not making any more trouble for me." Amani gave me the stink eye, her pinky up, as she sipped on some water before addressing Bea. "Is she?"

"What?" my friend sputtered, pushing her scrambled eggs around on her plate to avoid eye contact. "Pshh, no."

"I'm not, Amani. I promise I'll do anything it takes to

make it back to the public's good graces." I reinforced Bea's half-assed answer, throwing her a side glare.

"You need to keep that attitude all the time, Ina. You need to look into manifestation. If you put the positive energy into the universe, you shall receive the good things in return."

"Riiight," I stretched out the word, not bothering to argue, and we all took a pause as Amani was served her breakfast sandwich.

I believed in manifestation as much as I believed in flying pigs. Whenever I came out of a test saying I did great, I always got the shittiest grades, and whenever I thought I did bad, I got the best. So yeah, manifestation wasn't for me, but I was sure if I said that, a lecture would soon follow on how it was much more than that.

"What do you have in store for me today?" I asked, my hash browns all but forgotten. I wasn't in the mood to eat anymore. "Are there any sick kids I need to visit? Charities of upcoming prominence I need to donate to, or any events I need to attend?"

Not that I didn't enjoy the first two parts of the equation titled *how to clean up your image*. In fact, I loved watching kids' faces light up with happiness and knowing I made their day just by visiting. Donating has also been a part of my life for as long as I can remember. Both my parents were big into giving back. I grew up volunteering in public soup kitchens and organizing fundraisers. It was one of the most gratifying things in the world.

But not when you did it for publicity because it left you feeling like a fraud.

Amani chewed thoughtfully as she scrolled through a list on her phone before hitting me with her plans. "We already visited two hospitals this month and three *Make-a-Wish* kids, so we don't want to overdo that. I've emailed you a list of some organizations you can donate to, and unfortunately, you haven't been invited to any events."

My eyes closed of their own accord. When I reopened them, I focused on a man a few tables over, checking for any food residue on his teeth on his selfie camera when his date left for the bathroom. I didn't want to look at the disappointment in Amani's eyes.

I was her greatest achievement. Everyone loved having me over, and I'd gone from being a breeze to work with to a perplexing mess.

"I heard Nicole invited Dumb and Dumber to her birthday party too and seeing as I haven't heard from her yet, I'm guessing we're both excluded," Bea chimed in, and a second pang of guilt hit. She was being caught in the cross-fire for simply sticking by me. "Daniel's father has an in with NBC's board of directors, and you know how badly she also wants to get on the show, so..."

"So she chose to advance her career over our friendship," I concluded, even though I was never sure there was much of a friendship between Nicole and me to begin with.

Both of us ran in the same social circles, but she was the type that loved befriending everyone, and in the words of Aristotle, a friend to all is a friend to none. It wasn't all that shocking to learn she had invited my ex and his new girl-friend after what they did to me. History is written by victors, and between the three of us, I was the sore loser, the one left in the dust and ridiculed.

Thinking about what happened made me sick. Not because I couldn't live without Daniel or anything like that. I was quite cynical, and him cheating with a hot Russian figure skater was nothing more than a little ego blow. The annoying part was finding out with the rest of the world and having them witness the massive meltdown that occurred afterward.

"There is a way to make this all go away, Irena," Amani cut off my train of thought before it could progress to me daydreaming about cutting Daniel's penis off and feeding it to him, like usual.

I was a deeply disturbed individual; I knew that much. But I couldn't put a cap on my lust for vindication. No matter how much I wished I could move on, it didn't work like that.

"If that way goes by the name of Jimmy Owens, then I don't want to hear it."

The asshole had actually invented a game on his show called the "Battle of the Girlfriends," where he used pictures to compare us. While Katrina Federova looked like a bombshell in her bikini photo, mine was a random paparazzi picture while I was having lunch after training, mouth full and with no makeup on.

It was safe to say I didn't win the popular vote.

Real fair.

"He's offering you an interview to help you explain the situation and clear your name," she countered.

"He's inviting me on his show to make fun of me, just like he did when the situation first broke out. I'll be damned if I help advance his ratings," I whispered back feverishly, hyper-aware of the tone of my voice, because that was what being humiliated in public and on the internet did to you.

You see, I didn't catch Daniel cheating on me by going through his texts or catching risqué pictures of other women on his phone—no. Ironically, it was on his birthday when dumb me decided to organize a whole-ass surprise party for him while we were on tour.

Obviously, the show's producers thought it would be a great idea to film the whole thing, "romance sells" and all, but as it turned out, drama sold way more. On the eve of Daniel's birthday, our viewership broke records unseen in the past when he waltzed into the room, his side chick and my biggest competitor, Katrina Federova, sucking his face like a squid.

My heart wasn't the only thing that got crushed. So did the three-tier birthday cake when I decided to throw it at them. Daniel and Katrina's photos of running for their lives while I chased after them turned into an overnight meme. While embarrassing, it wasn't too bad until I proceeded to dump his sorry ass, underestimating his ability to spin the story so well he turned himself into the victim and me into the emotionally abusive girlfriend he tried numerous times to leave but couldn't because I'd threaten to kill myself if he did so.

And that concluded the tale of Irena Fleur, the ice princess who turned into a raging lunatic. God, it felt demeaning knowing that a man had managed to *play* me, but with a touch of Greek stubbornness and a flair of French revolution, I'd find a way to bounce back.

Daniel Gregory hadn't seen the last of me just yet.

"You're that confident you're gonna get a high viewership?" Amani asked, and I grinned around my straw before answering.

"Of course. Dumb and Dumber might've trashed my reputation, but I'm the one with the gold medals, and all they have to account for is STDs."

Brunch was a disaster.

Amani and I had conflicting views on how to win back the public's empathy. It was hard to argue with someone who seemed to forget she managed only my career and not my life.

Perhaps the one thing we did find common ground on was me starting to get out there again. Posting on social media, going to lunch more (it turned out Bea felt severely neglected), and meeting up with other friends like we used to. All in all, it meant my period of hibernation had to come to an end. I wasn't the first or last person to ever get cheated on, and life went on for all of us.

Lost in my thoughts, I was searching through my bag for the keys to my apartment when suddenly the wind was knocked out of me, and I found myself disoriented and on the floor, piles of spilled groceries surrounding me.

Blinking rapidly, I groaned as a throbbing ache reverberated up my spine. Rubbing my lower back, I glanced around me and cringed when I witnessed the mess and a man sprawled across from me, he too wincing in pain from the fall.

"Oh my gosh, I'm so sorry, I wasn't paying attention," I apologized once I got my bearings straight and smoothed my facial expression because this guy seriously reminded me of Nick Young from *Crazy Rich Asians*. Picking up one of the bags near me, I said, "Here, let me help you with those."

"It's all right," he replied, as both of us started to pile in all the scattered items. "Good thing I decided to trip over you a few feet from my apartment; otherwise, it would've been a hassle carrying all these."

"You live here?" I asked, and my eyes widened when I spotted an XL Trojan box right next to my thigh as we knelt across from each other. I quickly shoved it in a paper bag before he spotted me staring at it.

"Yup, in number thirty-five," he professed, his mouth pursing in thought for a second. "Fuck...I guess I shouldn't have said that to a stranger." He smiled, shaking his head. "You're cute, though. I hope you don't turn out to be a murderer."

"Ted Bundy was cute, too; don't let looks fool you," I warned, my tone light and flirtatious.

God, what were the odds that a guy this good-looking and packing that much heat would be living right next to me, and I got to meet him on my official first day in my new apartment?

Suddenly, I wasn't all that bummed about crashing into him.

"There's also the fact that you're a girl and probably a hundred pounds lighter than me, so I'm not too worried."

"I'll have you know I'm trained in martial arts and a..." I was going to say an expert in yielding skates ever since I'd "accidentally" almost cut my annoying cousin's fingers off when we were young, but I'd rather not have anyone in this building know what I do for work. At least not at the moment. "And also, your new neighbor, so you *don't* have anything to worry about," I rectified.

"I know I don't. It was just an excuse to pay you a compliment."

A matching smile graced my lips when it finally clicked that he'd called me cute. I preferred smoking hot, beautiful, *unforgettable*, but I could swallow *cute* for our first meeting.

"I figured." I played it cool and held one of the bags when we got off the ground. "You're cute too, uh..."

"Colin," he filled in, content with idling in the hallway for a while longer.

"Colin," I repeated. "Even though I'm sorry for spilling your groceries, I'm glad we had the chance to meet. My name's Irena."

I extended my hand for a shake, and in a perfect gentleman move, he gripped it and pressed a kiss to the back of it. His black hair shone like onyx under the fluorescent lighting, and despite him being uber hot, he reminded me too much of Daniel, with a key difference.

Colin was *bigger*.

"Me too, Irena. Although, I do expect an apology in the form of a blueberry pie over the weekend. I'll bring the coffee." His straight white teeth remained a constant companion as he took the other bag from me, and I raised a brow.

"Is this your indirect way of asking me on a date?"

"Depends."

"On what?"

"If you're cool with that, then yes. If you're not, it'll be simply a *get to know your new neighbor* day." He shrugged, and his ability to not show a hint of bashfulness impressed me.

I was hit on constantly, so I'd become quite good at trolling (for lack of a better word) the desperate souls that tried to get with me. I'd also gained a nickname in the process—the bitch (very creative, I know)—but in a world where no meant yes for most guys, I found that undermining and outsmarting them worked better to get them to leave me alone.

"It's a date then, Colin," I agreed, feeling like he deserved a bone for keeping calm under pressure, and I deserved to get boned. My sister, the *wait until marriage type*, would surely have a blast when I told her I'd possibly found a fuck buddy on my first day at my new place.

"See you, Irena." He winked, and I waved bye as he disappeared inside his flat.

Trying to find those damned keys again, I looked around on the floor since I was certain they'd fallen out of my hand during the altercation.

"Aha," I murmured, bending over when something shiny and silver caught the corner of my eye.

A door opened behind me, and I thought it was Colin again, but the voice that followed had my insides turning like a pig on a spit. "Don't get too excited. Once he figures out you can't bake for shit, he'll send you packing."

"Holy shit." I sprung up, twisting at the waist. Killian Astor stood across from me, in sweats and a dark tee that left the various tattoos scattered on his arms on display, leaning against the doorframe, his face impassive, eyes inclined south. "Jesus, you scared the hell out of me." I fanned my face, although I wasn't quite sure why I was feeling hot all of a sudden.

Killian rolled his eyes. "Are you quite through with the dramatics?"

My hand fell against my hip, and I gave him my best blank stare, my brain doing the work while my heart lagged behind, my pulse thrumming wildly. "Were you eaves-dropping?"

I hadn't seen Killian since my famous parting line, and to

say I didn't feel the awkwardness of that decision would be a lie. He, on the other hand, seemed detached, so I played the part too, faking it till I made it, and placed my hands on my hips, my foot tapping on the floor.

"Hard to eavesdrop when you were being loud as fuck right outside my apartment."

"Your apartment?" I asked, shock flying through me as I tried to catch a glimpse over his shoulder.

"Did Saint or Aria send you?" Killian ignored my question, eyes shining with a cruel glimmer. "Why are you telling *my* neighbor you're *his* new neighbor? There are easier ways to pick up guys, you know."

"I wasn't trying to pick up anyone. *He* came on to *me*." As if needing to prove something, I pointed at Colin's closed door and then at me. "And I *am* his new neighbor. I just moved into apartment number thirty-six."

I waved my key in the air, and Killian's face dropped like I'd just told him he had to perform a surgical operation and lose his balls or suffer through unimaginable pain every day.

He sat upright, gaze zeroed in on the number plate next to my apartment, which was directly opposite his. "You're kidding, right?"

"Why would I be joking?" I breathed a little funny, the gravity of the situation hitting me all at once. I sometimes had these spurts of boldness, moments where it seemed like I'd consumed a mental Red Bull and words flew out of my mouth, but they always came back to bite me afterward. "Aria owns several apartments here. I imagine yours too. She reduced my rent."

For the first time since I'd met him, Killian looked stumped. His mouth opened as if he was going to say something, but then he slammed it shut again, staring at me like he was willing me to disappear.

It grated on my nerves.

He grated on my nerves.

I would have words with Aria for not informing me, but living opposite each other wasn't the end of the world. I would even try to stay out of his way, since he hated seeing my face so much.

"Yes, because you couldn't possibly afford to pay the normal rent." He settled on a response, his words slurred like it wasn't what he really wanted to say.

"Benefits of your sister being your landlord." I tapped my foot on the floor, refraining from telling him I actually didn't have to pay rent. The modest sum Aria and I agreed on was the only one she was open to accepting. It was peanuts for a place as nice as this, but at least it was *something*. "Are we going to stay out here for a long while? You can come in and help me set everything up if you want."

I extended the invitation, despite already knowing his answer. This conversation was a means to end before it got even more awkward than it already was, but it turned out Killian didn't care.

He clarified his disinterest by straightening up and shutting the door in my face. The loud bang echoed in the hallway, masking the shocked squawk that spilled from my mouth.

I was still there, wide-eyed, and more than a little mad when his head peeked out once more as if he forgot to tell me something, and announced, "Colin is too afraid to tell his parents he's gay, but they're starting to catch on and threatening to pull him out of the will, so he's trying to find a girl to pacify them."

In a matter of seconds, he was out of my sight again, and in a sign of silent protest, I gave him the middle finger.

"I saw that." His muffled voice floated through the thick wood of the door. So of course, I did it again, and I could've sworn I heard the faint lull of laughter.

Or it could've just been wishful thinking on my part that the guy I thought more about than was deemed normal wasn't totally averse to my antics.

CHAPTER TWO
IRENA

"He can't be gay, right? I mean, why would he need condoms if that was the case?" My unsure voice rang loudly in Aria and Saint's living room.

Despite the tumultuous start of their relationship, they were still living in their first home, but I understood why. It was like a giant, luxurious treehouse with wood accents, acres of land, and views of sprawling pine trees out of every window.

Their backyard had a firepit we were currently taking advantage of. Being late August didn't mean anything. There still was a slight chill in the air, and we chased it away with a glass of wine for *moi*, cherry juice for Aria, and some chocolate. New England summers, while hot and humid, were brief, and I was grateful for that. I did thrive on ice, after all.

Aria gave me a ludicrous look before shoving a piece of dark chocolate in my mouth. I choked at the surprise attack, pushing her away. She patted my back, saying, "There, there, eat some chocolate. It'll make you think better so you can realize how dumb that question was."

Sweetness exploded in my mouth as the bar melted on my tongue, and I groaned at my own stupidity. Condoms didn't solely exist to prevent pregnancies. They prevented all sorts of STDs too. I blamed Killian for my brief lapse of judgment and his harsh way of delivering information.

I didn't understand why he felt inclined to let me know that about Colin. We were certainly not friends. He had made that clear by how appalled he seemed to be when he found out I was his new neighbor. I hadn't seen him at all since last night. He didn't even bother to come visit me. You know, to welcome his sister-in-law to the building.

"That was dumb," I said, bitterness chasing away the sweet taste in my mouth after thinking about Killian.

"Indeed, it was." Aria nodded, her dark hair bouncing over her shoulders. Seeing if the baby had cute curls like hers would be interesting. I hoped so. I was a sucker for them. "Killian might be a handful, but he's not a liar. I believe him."

I believed him too.

Not because I thought him trustworthy, but because it seemed like petty lies were beneath him.

"Great, there goes my opportunity to start dating again." I swallowed a huge gulp of wine, moving on from Killian. He occupied enough of my thoughts as it was.

"Please." Aria's ruby engagement ring shone as she waved her hand dismissively at me. "I'm sure you won't find it difficult to find other potential suitors."

"True, but at least I knew Colin had a big di—" I smiled behind the rim of my glass when her eyes shone with warning. The baby wasn't even here yet, and my sister had every single family member adjusting their language so the kid wouldn't pick up on any naughty words. Apparently, it was going to help us slip up less in the future. I smelled a helicopter parent in the making. "*Dong* from the get-go."

She reclined back on the outdoor couch, propping her feet near the fire and wiggling her toes to warm them up. "It's not all about the *dong*, you know. Sometimes it's also about the connection you form with another person. Sex isn't the only thing that matters in a relationship."

"But it still ranks pretty high up," an intruder by the name of Saint Astor argued as he sauntered toward us, slipping past the sliding doors that led to the deck.

Clad in a suit and tie, he ruffled my hair before dropping next to his wife and kissing the welcoming grin on her face. Just a peck to not make me uncomfortable, but fierce enough to let her know he'd missed her while he was away at work.

An unknown feeling churned in my gut, and I wondered if I'd ever find someone that loved me as much as Saint Astor loved Ariadne Fleur. At first glance, they looked like polar opposites, but together they worked like a dream. He even tugged her feet in his lap, glamouring his overprotectiveness under the guise of giving his pregnant wife a foot massage, but both Aria and I knew it was because he wanted her away from the fire.

It was a win-win, though, so my sister sighed happily and let him get to work as he turned to me and winked, his amber eyes like molten gold under the light of the fire. "*Dong* size does matter. I stand with you, baby Fleur."

Aria rolled her eyes, nudging his fit stomach with her foot to get his attention. "You're only saying that because you have a big *dong*. Wouldn't you feel bad if you were below average and someone broke up with you over it?"

Okay...my sister needed to learn the definition of TMI, stat.

Another gulp and I was down one more glass. I refilled just when Saint kissed her ankle, and things got even mushier when he replied, "Well, good thing I'm above average, and the only one I care about breaking up with me is you."

Aria, who was already flushed, turned red as a poppy, and I coughed loudly when they started looking like they were about to go at it right in front of me. As if jolted back into the present, my sister gave me a rueful grin while an unapologetic Saint tugged her down, securing her under his arm.

"Can we please stop using the word *dong* and move on from this conversation?" I muttered. "I'm not looking for a serious relationship at the moment, anyway."

"My offer to beat that Daniel guy to a bloody pulp still stands," Saint stated, all businesslike. A devil in the skin of an angel, his blond hair like a halo over his head.

"Would you really risk going to jail and leaving your unborn child fatherless because someone cheated on me?" I raised a brow, swirling the liquid in my glass.

"My offer to *hire* someone to beat that Daniel guy up until he can't walk anymore, let alone skate, still stands," he reworded, his large palm coming to rest atop Aria's swollen stomach, rubbing against the blue fabric of her dress.

"We are not beating anyone up." My sister cut the cord. "Let Daniel have his moment. I'm a big believer in what goes around, comes around."

"He's had his moment for two months now. I don't want him to think he won, but I also don't think I can work with him *and* his side chick when filming commences in

November." It was three months away from now, and public attention would've likely died down by then, but still, he humiliated me, and that couldn't go unchecked. "The mere thought of sharing the same rink with them feels demeaning."

"That famous Fleur pride," Saint exhaled loudly.

"Ina, did you know back when we first got married, we used to sleep in separate bedrooms, but then *Sainty* over here would find any excuse under the sun to visit mine at night, never once admitting that he actually missed me, not even when I confronted him about it," Aria informed, directing a shit-eating grin at Saint, then turning to me. "Now, what do you call that?"

"Hmm..." I tapped my chin, my brows furrowing. "I believe it's a word that starts with P."

"The two of you together are unstoppable." I laughed when an exasperated Saint reached over to capture Aria's nose between his thumb and forefinger. She giggled, batting him away.

"Would you like me to call Killian to level the playing field?"

My stomach dipped dangerously at Aria's question, and I waited for Saint's answer with a bated breath.

"You know he always takes your side. It'll be three against one."

"It's not my fault I'm more likable than you are," she argued, and I changed the subject before they actually put the plan into motion.

Besides Saint and Aria, the rest of the Fleur and Astor family members didn't mesh well. Our mothers couldn't stand each other, and our fathers weren't any better. It was a rivalry that went back decades, when believe it or not, Saint's mother and our dad were betrothed to be married, and when that failed spectacularly, bad blood flowed.

The vein had somewhat stopped gushing the past few years but put Killian and me into a room together, and we'd paint the walls red.

"Can we focus back on the matter at hand?" I clicked my nails on the arm of the couch, feeling invisible in my corner. They were so disgustingly in love with each other they constantly forgot I was there.

I couldn't even be mad at them, though. It was nice seeing how close they were after all the trials and tribulations they had to work through to get to this point.

All I wanted was the best for my sister.

"Right." Aria sipped her cherry Capri Sun like it came straight from a hundred-year-old vodka bottle, rolling it in her mouth before hitting me with an idea. "You know, there is a way to leave the show without making it seem like you're chickening out."

I leaned forward, intrigued. "How?"

"By accepting a better offer." She bounced in her seat, but her excitement went down a notch when I didn't seem to get it.

"Do you know many other figure skating reality TV shows more successful than Stars on Ice?"

"Who said it had to be related to figure skating?" She answered my question with a question.

"I'm lost," I admitted, ditching the glass and going straight for the wine bottle.

"That would make two of us," Saint echoed and stole the bottle from me, chugging it.

"Have you looked in the mirror, Irena?" Aria barely elaborated. "You're a gorgeous 5'10" woman with piercing blue

33

eyes and weird reddish blonde hair that makes you stand out."

Her tone was matter of fact, and while flattered, I didn't dwell on the compliment for long. "Thank you for the confidence boost, but what does this have to do with ice skating? We don't get jobs based on looks."

"Nope, but there's a whole different industry that hires based on looks," she informed, eagerly launching to the heart of her argument. "Have you never considered working as a model? You have all the right connections, beauty that rivals the likes of Kate Moss, and a character that doesn't bend no matter what."

Modeling?

Me?

I'd considered it maybe when I was twelve, and Victoria's Secret fashion shows were still something to be admired, but it was superficial, a thing most girls desired at least once while growing up.

Skating was *it* for me, though. Something I couldn't imagine *not* doing, even for a second. The freedom you experienced on the rink or a frozen lake was unparalleled, and I wouldn't trade it for the world.

"That sounds suspiciously like nepotism," I argued, picking at the skin around my nails. Both of us were already seen as less than because we came from a privileged background, despite the hard work we poured into our craft. What she was suggesting would only fuel whispers.

"So? You wouldn't be the first model to have profited off connections," she dismissed my point entirely, and I saw the weak spots in my shield as opposed to hers.

Aria had always been criticized left and right for having a curvier figure, but had learned to tune out the noise and embrace her flaws. She even went on to launch a successful lingerie line, ensuring it was inclusive of all body types, a perfect *fuck you* to all those with something to say.

She knew who she was and didn't care about anyone else's opinion.

I wished I was more like that.

"It still doesn't *feel* right."

"The money that you'll make will. We pay some of our models gold." Saint nodded regretfully at her point, as if wishing he could find a way out of it. "Besides, I promise to go extra hard on you if it makes you feel better. I've been taking lessons from Saint." She patted his shoulder with a side glare. "Poor Killian took over managing the design and layout of our fashion shows at Falco, and I'm starting to think he wishes he hadn't."

My brows met my hairline, and I was glad they were too busy staring at each other to notice my piqued interest. I didn't know much about what Killian liked to do, but being near his family wasn't one of them. According to Saint, he even moved all the way to California for college just to be away from them.

"Just because he's my brother doesn't mean he gets a pass," Saint said, moving the wine bottle farther away from me when I made grabby hands.

Talking about Killian made me crave alcohol to erase our recent embarrassing meetings from memory. Still, I didn't want to be blackout drunk when I got home tonight, so I let Saint have it.

"Wait," I intervened. "I thought Killian was doing his own thing and didn't want to work at Falco."

"He does, but our parents were becoming relentless and pressuring him to find a '*real*' job because apparently interning at his friend's tattoo shop wasn't good enough for an Astor."

I could tell he disagreed with their judgments and had even put up a fight, but ultimately, it was Killian's decision. Having family members breathing down your neck wasn't pleasant. Sometimes it was just better to go along with the flow than listen to incessant chatter.

"Your mom too?" I asked. I expected this kind of behavior from his father, not his mom, though. She seemed more normal, even though she wouldn't win any mommy of the year awards any time soon.

"Spend enough time with someone, and you start to become them," he reasoned, unhappy with the outcome. Aria felt his discomfort and interlaced her fingers through his, holding on to his arm. "I much preferred it when she had no idea what went on in our lives."

Aria made eyes at me from beside him, and I got the memo not to ask any more questions. It was a sensitive topic better left for those at the center of it to discuss.

"Nevertheless, this sounds like a good job for Killian, since he likes to be challenged creatively," I acknowledged. If Saint had caught on to my poor attempt at changing the subject, he didn't let on.

"Indeed," Saint agreed, checking his smartwatch. "On that note, I'm going to leave you ladies to it. It's almost time for my workout. Spitfire..." He placed his palms on his thighs as he got ready to get up, but not before leaning in to whisper in my sister's ear, "Don't be long. I know how you like it: sweaty."

"Ew," I complained, my face scrunching up. I placed one of the throw pillows on my stomach, pretending to retch. "I did not need to know that about my sister."

Saint chuckled while Aria looked mortified, so I didn't grill her on any of the sexy details when her husband left and it was just us again. Instead, I commented on the awkwardness that plagued the air when Mr. and Mrs. Astor were brought up.

"That was intense."

"I know." She frowned, staring at the direction in which he'd disappeared. It was a no-brainer as to why he was in such a hurry to leave. "I thought our family was problematic until I met theirs."

Every family had their quirks, and no parent was perfect, but at the heart of it, ours always pushed us to pursue whatever we wanted and showered us with an abundance of love.

Some of the horror stories I'd heard about Saint's father, though... I didn't even want to believe them.

My sister's need to follow after Saint and make sure he was okay was palpable. So, I quickly addressed one more topic I had wanted to discuss since the beginning but didn't have the balls to, ripping it off like a Band-Aid. "Did you know that Killian would be my new neighbor when you suggested I move into one of your apartments?"

Aria turned back to me, taken aback by the question, but answered with a simple, "Yes."

"And you didn't think to tell me beforehand?" I inquired, harsher than intended, and a crease formed between her brows.

"You've always gotten along great with each other. I thought you'd be happy."

Right, a few passing conversations in public that lessened the older we got, and apparently, that meant we were best buddies.

Pinching the bridge of my nose, I let it go, choosing not to divulge all the recent happenings with Aria, and settled on saying, "I was just surprised."

A few beats passed before Aria asked expectantly, "Well? What do you say about the whole modeling situation?"

"I'll think about it, okay?" I mumbled, hitting the brakes when she got that glazed look in her eyes. "But don't get your hopes up because I don't want to give up skating."

"The way I see it, you can do both." She held her Capri Sun up in the form of a toast. "Hell, even buy a house with a skating rink."

CHAPTER THREE

KILLIAN

Usually, I'd be already blackout drunk by now.

Every 29th of August, I had a routine, and it started with some light drinking during the day and going all out when happy hour hit with Luca.

It was a tradition. One we'd started when we turned eighteen and discovered the wonderful world of fake IDs. This year, I was breaking it—half breaking it. I was still meeting up with him, but most of the day had gone by already, and I'd spent it tattooing yet another rose on some woman's ribs.

Ever since I'd started my apprenticeship at my buddy Ray's White Fox Tattoo Studio, I was primarily delegated to doing small stuff until I built up confidence. Hearts, waves, butterflies, inspirational quotes; I was surprised by how many people got the same thing over and over again.

It was getting pretty stale, but I was finally working on a big project next week and didn't want to bail today when Ray asked me to come in. It was a 3D design, and I was pretty damn excited, despite the fucking intense back pain I'd have to deal with after being hunched over for hours.

Small sacrifices.

Wendy inspected her tattoo as I hurried up and placed all the equipment back in place, her face lighting up with a smile. Even though I was a miserable bastard nine times out of ten, satisfaction rushed through my system when my clients were visibly satisfied with my work.

It made listening to my father's constant disapproval worth it.

"Oh, it's so beautiful! I love it! Thank you so much, Killian!" She squealed and pulled me into a tight one-armed hug when I tried to place some plastic wrap over her new ink. I cringed, but I couldn't very well push her away, so I just patted her arm awkwardly, my skin crawling from the unnecessary touch.

"My pleasure, Wendy."

After getting *that* out of the way, I launched into telling her about all the aftercare details, the weight on my shoulders lifting when she left. She was my last appointment of the night.

I had to cancel an Uber I'd ordered after Luca told me he would be picking me up. I wasn't sure what went through his mind because there was no way either of us would be in any position to drive tonight, but I was willing to entertain him.

"If I knew you'd draw in this many ladies, I would have hired you sooner," Ray barked from the back of the counter as I got ready to head out. His bald head was smooth and shiny like he'd waxed it.

"Poor judgment on your part," I boasted, staring at the logo of a running fox, stark white on the shop's glass display.

It was located on a shopping street in an urban area of Astropolis. Clientele was high despite Ray's complaints.

It was true, though. Most of the female customers tended to request *I* work on them. It wasn't my fault I was a pretty motherfucker.

"Are you coming in tomorrow?"

"I don't work on Saturdays, remember?" Not unless he wanted me to decorate his dark wood floors with puke.

"Ah, yes. You could always start if you wanted to. We'll talk about a pay increase sometime soon, as well."

I celebrated my upcoming promotion with a mental fist pump. However, the fact that I still had to work at Falco and Fleur put a damper on any excitement. I was currently splitting my time between there and here, and working *more* hours would cripple me.

Still, I didn't say no. I needed this apprenticeship if I ever wanted to open up my own shop, so I settled with a compromise. "I'll get back to you on that one. Good night, Ray."

I waved as I left, a car already waiting for me. As per the text I received, a Maybach was parked next to the curb, far fancier than any other vehicle on this street. People stared as they passed by, and the back door popped open for me once I got close enough.

My nose burned when I slid in.

Leather, perfume, and the stench of alcohol all blended together as Luca greeted me with a slurry smile. He wasn't the one driving, and while comforting, I had a few questions about how he went from broke to owning a Mercedes and hiring someone to drive him.

"Went all out and got us a driver for the night, huh,

Mietitore?" I asked, clapping him on the back. He followed suit, and my whole body felt the impact of his slap.

I was a big guy, but Luca Mietitore was *bouncer* big. He was over six feet tall, with gray eyes, slicked back brown hair and, as of late, a small scar running down his left cheek. We met when we were eleven, and I was aware that his father was involved in some shady shit. They used to live in Astropolis, but moved out a couple of years ago. We still managed to maintain contact, and I had an inkling as to what caused his injury. Luca never gave me a straight answer, though, and there wasn't much I could do to convince him to tell me. His newly acquired wealth spoke plenty.

He was like a modern version of Al Capone and made up for all the secrecy surrounding him with a pretty face. It worked in his favor, with women willing to overlook flaws for aesthetics.

"You remember that promotion I was talking to you about?" he asked after we pulled apart. I acknowledged the driver as the car started cruising down the main street and focused back on the conversation at hand.

My memory flashed briefly to the last time I saw him and his answer when I tried to pressure him into telling me what he did for a living. A smirk pulled at my lips when I remembered his response.

"The one where you go from doing shady people's dirty work to doing *more* of their dirty work?"

It was as vague as could be, and the average person would've cut ties, but Luca and I already shared secrets big enough to change the trajectory of both of our lives forever. I trusted him, perhaps more than anyone else in this world.

"That one!" he went on, excitement prominent in his voice as he reached for the mini-fridge nestled beneath the cream armrest. He pulled out a chilled bottle of Dom Pérignon, filling up two champagne glasses until foam touched the brim. "Welp, I got it, and Jerry over here is my permanent personal driver."

I took one of the glasses, and Jerry looked none too pleased when Luca patted his arm from behind. I pulled him back to prevent an accident and *tsked*, "You're going to get in trouble one day."

Not that he wasn't already. I preferred Luca alive, but I understood why he went down this road. His childhood was rougher than most, with a father that got rich *too* quickly and didn't know how to properly manage his finances or protect his family. Hence, the reason his mother passed (or was murdered, depending on which rumor you believed) when he was barely eight.

This was all he knew.

"So be it. I'm not particularly attached to my life," he admitted.

I wasn't shocked. The morbid energy wasn't anything new. There used to be a time when I thought the same way, but life had gotten better and less empty through work. I stared at the blinking city lights from my window. The drinking, the drugs—it was all a gateway for the people not brave enough to slice their wrists or pull the trigger, one that led six feet underground.

"Yazmin wouldn't be happy," I reminded him.

Unlike me, Luca had someone to take care of. His half-sibling was still too young to take care of herself and had no other living relatives except him. And fine, maybe I liked having him around too.

"I've assured Yazmin will be taken care of in the event of every scenario," he replied, and of course, he had. Luca maintained tight control over his ship after having none for the first few years of his life.

"You know best," I gave up, knowing he wasn't selfish enough to go through with it.

"I do." The glassy eyes and fake smile returned as he extended his left hand. "Here, let's start with a toast."

"To the bitch's death." I took the lead, and we clinked glasses, champagne spilling on the couple hundred-dollar floor mats. I caught Jerry's brows furrowing in the mirror, but didn't supply any context. We took an oath years back that we would never say anything to anyone because it wasn't my story or Luca's story.

It was *our* story.

And it would stay between us.

"To the bitch's death!" Luca wished back jovially.

I was pretty sure I'd stepped in shit.

Or it could be mud.

Either way, coming to the cemetery after it rained for almost half an hour straight was not the wisest. We tested our luck every year and saw how long we could keep trespassing without consequences. So far, we were on a winning streak, and this time was no different, as the guard we passed on our way in had been dead asleep.

"Did you make any progress with that psychologist you told me you started seeing last time?" Luca asked as we stumbled past rows of gravestones.

"She was paid off by my father. What do you think?"

My mother had the fantastic idea to see a specialist for all her problems (after fifty years on this earth, I could see how they'd piled on), and daddy dearest thought it appropriate to ship me along with her, too, to fix my *troubled* ways.

I could've technically said no, but that meant he'd just bust my balls for months to come. So I did go, and after a couple of visits, the psychologist deemed me *untreatable*, and I was off my merry way again. Safe to say, he didn't suggest anything similar again.

"God, that asshole is a world-class cunt," Luca said, and even though I agreed, I also had a rule. I only talked shit about my family *with* my family.

"Can't be any worse than your father," I jabbed, and Luca snorted as if in agreement.

"That was insensitive." His tone was businesslike, fucking around. He wasn't offended, not when even in death, Luca still blamed him for everything that had happened, and he had every right to.

"What are you going to do? Hit me?" I taunted.

Luca took my mocking to heart and tried to swing his fist at me. Keyword: tried...*and* failed miserably. He crashed against a tree and huffed and puffed as he supported his weight on the trunk in order for the world to stop spinning.

"You're pathetic," I commented, which was ironic as I'd propped my hands on my knees, also out of breath. I could've sworn this cemetery could rival Central Park in terms of size. Between all the sneaking around, walking for ten minutes straight with no end in sight, and alcohol taking a hit at my system, both Luca and I were panting like dogs.

"I'll hit you tomorrow," he promised.

"You won't remember any of this tomorrow."

"I will." Luca slid down the tree, and just when I was about to tell him to get his ass up because we still had some way to go, he pointed behind me and said, "I always do when it comes to her."

There was no enthusiasm in my movements as I turned to look. My jumbled brain would've kept walking until I reached the other end of this garden chock-full of dead people and who knew what else.

Farah Mietitore.

Even in the dark, her name popped out against the white marble. Underneath the much ironic epitaph, *Beloved mother, wife, and friend. Gone but never forgotten,* was written.

At least they'd gotten one part right. The wounds she inflicted had never properly healed and turned into scars. There wasn't a day when I wasn't reminded of how raw they still were.

I found myself stumbling back in the dark, my feet getting caught on some overgrown roots until I mirrored Luca's pose, squatted on the moist earth, my back against the few thousand-year-old red maple tree. Every time I came here, the urge to bring a hammer against her undeserving plaque hummed in my veins, no matter how trashed I was.

"Would you erase the first ten years of your life if a neuralyzer actually existed?" Luca distracted me with a random question, and I didn't have to think too hard to answer.

"No. Hidden traumas are worse than actual traumas. Some part of me would remember, and I'd go insane trying to figure out what was wrong with me." I twisted some overgrown weeds between my fingers, the liquid they released turning my skin sticky. "You?"

"I think I would."

"Why?"

"For her," Luca said with a sigh, and I understood he was

talking about his half-sister even before he clarified. She was the only woman in his life he cared enough to talk about. "For Yazmin. She deserves a father figure in her life, but I can't, I *can't* take on that role. Not when I remember where the other half of her comes from." He shook his head, staring at Farah's grave with haunted eyes. "All I can do is provide for her and hope one day she forgives me for being a shitty older brother."

At least he didn't abandon her. Considering the convoluted past with her mother, I was fucking dumbstruck by Luca's decision not to drop her off at the nearest foster home after their father offed himself, too, a few years after Farah.

He did more than most people would've done in his situation, but if I pointed that out, his fist would be on a straight trajectory toward my face. Unlike his father, Luca was fiercely protective of his family, friends, and sometimes virtual strangers. Since the circumstances under which we met were horrific, to say the least, I knew this firsthand.

"She looks nothing like her mother," I offered half-heartedly, attempting to pacify him. I hadn't seen Yazmin since she was a little girl. Still, despite inheriting her mother's deeper complexion, her button nose, hazel eyes, and full lips came from her Italian side of the family.

"She has her quirks. She likes to eat dessert before her meals, loves wearing red, and rubs the side of her neck when she's lying." Luca released a bitter laugh, throwing some unfortunate dandelions at her resting place in protest. "God, sometimes it feels like the bitch passed down only a few traits she knew would drive me crazy."

"That would be very on-brand for her." The tendons in my neck stretched with a swallow. Luca was a better man because I could never see myself caring for *her* offspring.

"I don't think I could've ever gone through with it."

"With what?"

"Exposing her," he explained, and my brows shot up in surprise.

Being two years older than me, Luca was the one hell-bent on dragging her name through the mud when he found out he wasn't her only shiny toy and eventually roped me along. Two testimonies were stronger than one.

I still remembered the anxiety coursing through my system, like mucus dripping down my lungs, turning breathing into a difficult feat when I thought about the rest of the world learning what I considered to be *my* personal failure. Though, as it turned out, I was agonizing over nothing when whatever upper force existed decided to take matters into its own hands, and Farah passed from a sudden cardiac arrest.

"Yes, she might've gotten jailed, but you and I both know public opinion would not have been favorable," Luca clarified, wiping away my staggered expression.

"Maybe not at the time," I agreed, and he gave me a look that said *definitely not at the time,* but I continued, undisturbed. "But it would've gotten better."

Luca shrugged as if to say, *Sure, Jan,* and I bit back any more responses, not sure if I even believed myself. People seldom accepted what they deemed unconventional. That's why everyone tried to blend in.

"Let's agree to disagree," he said, scratching his back against the trunk with a contented sigh, scurrying to change the subject when he asked, "So, any ladies in your life you need to talk to me about?"

"None memorable enough to remember their names." I tried to sound confident, but my words overlapped, and

Luca's nose twitched like a bloodhound catching on to a scent. I blamed it on the high concentration of alcohol in my blood because there truly was no one beyond some random hook-ups.

"You're lying." He wasted no time calling me out, but I kept calm.

There was no one.

"I am not."

"I can see it in your eyes. There is someone," Luca baited, and I chuckled...or, well, tried. It came out more like a choke.

"When did you start part-timing as a mind reader?"

"Changing the subject, avoiding eye contact." He made a *hmm* sound, grinning like a fool. "Man, this girl, whoever she is, has you hooked in deep."

A picture of crushing sea waves underneath a blood moon flashed behind my eyes when I closed them, but I ignored its meaning, steering the conversation back to a safe topic.

"How do you know it's a girl?" I asked, hinting at the rumors that were whispered about me. I never bothered to correct them.

"So there *is* someone!" Luca exclaimed enthusiastically, bumping his shoulder against mine as if to say, *"I knew it."*

"No, I'm just teaching you not to assume people's sexual orientation."

"Should I remind you what happened the last time I visited you in California?" he inquired flatly, and I grinned.

California was a part of my life better left undiscussed. Luca was impressed by the stories I kept telling him, so one day, he decided to come see what all the hype was about for himself. I ended that weekend with more weed than white blood cells in my system and waking up on the coast by the turbulent ocean with no idea how I got there in the first place.

"No need, I was there. Good times."

My eyes sliced to the tombstone once again, and I felt proud of myself for the first time in a long time. Proud of pushing through when I thought I'd never make it.

"How would you feel if someone made a pass at Yazmin?"

My question came out of the blue, the thought of losing that feeling of being at peace with myself for an itch I wanted to scratch, cutting off my air supply. It wasn't worth it, but the temptation of defying a direct order never stopped thrumming in my veins.

"I'd cut his dick off and then feed it to him," he answered simply, face devoid of emotion. "Proceeding with his hands to make it difficult for him to even touch her, and then his feet so he can't even physically get near her."

I snorted. "Why don't you go all out and just kill him?"

"'Cause I'd want him to suffer," Luca replied in a voice that deemed my question stupid like I should've already known the reason why.

"You are a twisted man, Mietitore," I coughed out, relating to this topic to an uncomfortable degree. Nevertheless, I told myself it was nothing to be wary of. Saint's obsession had started rubbing off on me, and I needed to sever all ties with a blade sharp enough to slice through steel.

A shiver made the hair on my nape stand to attention, but I played it off with a shake, rising from the floor with sloppy movements and extending a hand to Luca. "Ready to take a piss?"

"I'm winning this time." He took my assistance, and we

walked to *Farah Mietitore*, ready to end this day of the year like we always did. Determining who had the best aim by shooting for her picture, standing a few feet away, and seeing who could pee on it first.

So far, I'd only lost once.

Was it childish? *Maybe.*

Did we care? *Not so much.*

She deserved a fate far worse than the one she got. Urinating on her grave was innocent compared to her acts.

"In your dreams, you're a terrible shot." I unzipped, a cocky smile hiding the unpleasant emotions this woman inspired in me. "I'll be surprised if you don't piss on yourself."

CHAPTER FOUR

IRENA

The sound of jingling keys and an angry mewl woke me up at an ungodly hour today. I'd mastered the art of ignoring my nocturnal cat's little nighttime zoomies in my living room, but he was insistent today, so blurry-eyed and more than a little annoyed, I shot up to check out what had piqued his interest.

Dusty stopped patrolling the entrance when light flooded the living room, and his yellow eyes pinned me with a glare over some cardboard boxes that said, *took you long enough.*

"What is it, Dusty?" I sighed as I made my way to the tuxedo cat, and he gave me a long meow, rubbing his furry body on the door. Obviously, whatever disturbed his nighttime routine was outside the apartment.

Claws hooked into the delicate material of my lavender nightie as I tugged him against my chest and bent forward, looking out the peephole. It was pitch black, but even in the total absence of light, I could see an even darker blob moving strangely in front of Killian's door.

I clutched Dusty uncomfortably tight when my brain jumped to the conclusion that someone was trying to break into his home, and he left fine scratch marks on my neck in protest. I hissed, but let it go as I focused on the matter at hand.

My panic subsided when I caught a familiar glimmer of gold on the intruder's head along with a straight Greek statue-like male nose when he cursed, hitting the door with as much force as he could muster...which wasn't that impressive.

"Ah, ah, ah!" I shrieked when Dusty had had enough of being held and decided to climb on my shoulder and jump back to the ground. Startled by the noise, the guy outside turned in my direction, and relief and embarrassment battled for dominance inside my head.

Relief because that was Killian, and mortification because he'd clearly caught me snooping on him. I couldn't make out his expression, but the step he took toward my apartment betrayed his curiosity.

My throat dried at the thought of talking to him again after how disastrously our last meeting ended. I couldn't escape it, though, or he'd think I was a spying creep, and I didn't want to give him more ammunition to use against me. Heaving a sigh, I went ahead and opened my door, giving Dusty the stink eye in the process because he was the one that got me in this predicament.

I was swift, trapping my little escape artist inside and hitting the light switch next to my doorbell. The dark freaked me out—being confined in a dark hallway with Killian Astor even more so.

"Holy shit." His voice came out squeaky, and he obstructed my view of his face by throwing his arm over his eyes, shielding them from the light. Killian's legs twisted, and he came down like a house of cards, his back slamming against the wall. "Fuuuck!"

I tugged up the strap that had slid down my shoulder as I looked down the long hallway, hoping he hadn't woken up the entire building.

"I would say I'm sorry for startling you, but that would be a lie," I said, and he grunted as he sat on the carpeted floor like his legs couldn't hold up his weight.

Served him right.

This was like déjà vu, except the roles were reversed.

"Technically, you already did, Fleur." He rubbed his face with his hands, then peeled his fingers back. That piercing blue I'd eagerly anticipated every time he looked at me was underwhelming tonight, overpowered by the black of his pupils.

His misstep and struggle to enter his apartment had already clued me in that something was amiss, and his glazed eyes gave me the final stamp of approval. Killian was so hammered he'd likely spent the whole night in the hallway if I hadn't stepped out.

"Must everything be difficult with you?" I blew out a breath as I stared down at him. Even drunk, he managed to come up with a response that infuriated me.

The smile that took over his face was wonderfully chaotic, as if he enjoyed ruffling my feathers. I tried not to ogle, but he was at his best when he set his inner heathen free, that roguish grin of his making parts of my body stand to full attention.

Killian studied me in return, and in case he had a recollection of any of this tomorrow, I kept my face stern, even as I brought my arms over my chest, disguising my erect nipples.

It had been some time since I'd gotten the uninhibited side of Killian, and the lack of anonymity and unwanted formality was refreshing.

God, I should be ashamed.

While I found it difficult to muster up empathy for anyone outside my immediate circle, my family was always at the forefront of my mind, but with the way I was entertaining the dangerous thoughts that entered my head, one would think otherwise.

"You look cute when you're irritated," Killian finally said after looking his fill, and I flexed my toes in my slippers to keep them from curling. He pursed his lips, reconsidering, "No, hot. Like a scorned Lilith. A hot, scorned Lilith."

Heat scattered across my body, traveling to places it had no business being at.

I couldn't remember the last time a man had called me hot. Beautiful, pretty, and elegant were the adjectives most commonly thrown my way. While endearing at first, I'd grown to hate them when the majority threw it away for one night with the supposed gauche women they claimed were beneath them.

"What is it with you and calling me Lilith?" I didn't acknowledge his compliment. It was the alcohol doing the talking.

His eyes rolled back in his head, his voice barely above a whisper when he answered, "She-demon and butterflies."

She-demon?

Well, that did sound like me. I wasn't sure where the butterflies tied in, though.

"Butterflies?"

"Pretty blue butterflies," he confirmed like that made any sense.

"How much have you had to drink?"

"Just this little." He held up his hand, his thumb and pointer finger barely an inch apart.

I made a noise of disbelief, and it brought him out of his drowse. Killian grinned up at my scowl, a whiskey-sipping, skinny-dipping smile that made me forget why I came out in the first place.

The scratching on my door brought me back to the present, though, and I extended my hand to Killian. "Give me your keys."

He looked to his right, as he'd dropped them a few inches away from him, and barely stretched before flopping back against the wall, exhaling like he'd run a marathon.

They don't say if you want a job done right, do it yourself in vain.

With a severe frown, I bent over to get them myself, but right when my fingertips touched the metal ridges of the keys, a hand enveloped my wrist, warm and unexpectedly calloused. My gaze snapped to his, and I sucked in a breath when I noticed how close he'd suddenly moved.

Note to self: Drunk Killian is a sly little shit.

"Wha—" My question got caught in my throat when he clamped down harder, and I was forced to kneel next to him.

The scratchy carpet rubbed against my bare knees, but I was too distracted to pay it any mind. Goose bumps traveled up the length of my arm, and the scent of bourbon and rum singed my cheek, followed by the featherlight touch of his nose trailing a path from my jaw to my ear.

"You smell like cookies," he muttered, fingers sliding between my hair and gripping tight, controlling the position of my head. Chills at a hundred degrees covered every inch of my skin, and my sense of self gradually scattered the harder his hands pressed against me.

This wasn't happening.

It had to be a hallucination or a dream.

My sister's brother-in-law was not, in fact, *smelling* me in a super intimate way, and I was *not* enjoying it. Certainly not wishing for this to progress any further than it already had.

"Aria brought me some earlier today."

Dumb.

I was dumb for entertaining this, but I could barely string two sentences together as I tried to make sense of what was happening. And what Killian said next detonated any chance I had of wrapping my head around my current reality.

"I wonder if you taste like them, too," he rasped, and my eyes rolled to the back of my head. His mouth subsidized his nose, and the rough contours of his lips had me clenching his shirt with my free hand.

To push him away or pull him even closer, I didn't know yet.

He is hammered.

The voice of reason managed to squeeze past all the hormones declaring dominion over my brain, and it felt like a shot of clarity straight to my heart.

Killian didn't have any sense of what he was doing or, more accurately, *who* he was trying to do. It was weird. We were weird. We didn't make sense, and he knew that... when he was sober. I wasn't Irena Fleur to him at this moment. I was just an available girl like any other.

And while I usually wouldn't mind our current predicament, as I wasn't opposed to casual sex with someone as hot as him, the fact remained that he was Killian Astor, and I was Irena Fleur.

We couldn't sacrifice our families' sanity to satisfy our needs.

Listening to the voice of reason, I freed his shirt, and my knuckles brushed against his abs as I made my way to his neck, wrapping my palm around it. My intentions were pure, but my mind was clearly set on taking the scenic route.

My mouth dried when a rough noise that sounded suspiciously like a growl came from the back of his throat. In all my years of dating, I'd never met a man that liked that particular move. It was too possessive, too aggressive for a girl. We were simply supposed to look good and moan at all the right times, never overpower or fragile masculinities would suffer.

Trying to ignore all the ways Killian drove me mad, I pushed him back, and he fell flat against the wall again as if he weighed nothing. Blurry eyes sought mine out, blinking like he'd lost all sense of self and was trying to re-acclimate himself.

I cleared my throat and dusted the skirt of my nightgown to get rid of non-existent wrinkles and distract him from the fact that my face was most likely red as a poppy.

"You'll have to keep wondering for quite some time, Lucifer," I spoke, and his brows jumped at the nickname. I didn't use it often, but it felt necessary this time.

He had that sandy blond hair that gleamed with an angelic sort of glow and blue eyes as deep as the pits of hell. A smirk that spoke of wickedness, set on a face that was godsent. Killian Astor was the perfect combination of all things divine and unholy.

"How long?" he asked, his jumbled brain unable to distinguish the sarcasm in my voice.

Taking advantage of the fact that he wouldn't remember any of this tomorrow, I crawled his way, my neckline dipping dangerously low as I did so. Killian could be unpredictable, but at this very moment, he acted the way any other hot-blooded male would. He admired the view as I got within inches of him and whispered, "Eternity."

A spark of awareness zinged through his eyes as he took his time to meet my gaze, memorizing the dips and valleys of my chest and face, before biting back with a, "We'll see about that."

There was a promise somewhere in there that I chose to ignore because acknowledging it meant obsessing over it.

Rolling my eyes, I got off the ground, trying to mask how my fingers shook as I unlocked his door and got him inside. I chose not to linger and settled him sideways on his couch in case he puked sometime throughout the night. I felt uncomfortable leaving him to fend for himself, drunk out of his mind. But if there was one thing sober Killian didn't backtrack on was keeping me at a distance, and getting kicked out first thing in the morning like a cheap whore wasn't on my bucket list.

He was out within a few seconds of lying down, and I thought that was for the best as I slammed his door shut on my way out.

"I can't believe I'm doing this. It feels like I'm giving up," I expressed, examining my eyeliner in the well-lit mirror in front of me, wondering why it never looked that good when I applied it myself.

Despite my mixed feelings about partaking in one of

Aria's shoots for her next campaign, at least my makeup had never looked this good before. The artists came in with three bags worth of product, and after almost two hours of sitting on a set chair, in addition to a sore ass, I got to look like a goddess, too, with soft chocolate brown eyelids and nude glistening lips.

"This is just a trial run. Cool it with the dramatics." Aria whooshed in the dressing room, carrying a dress taller than her and hanging it on a silver rack next to me. "Besides, look at it as diversifying your portfolio, not a career change. Tons of ex-figure skaters have gone on to become NBC commentators and all sorts of other things."

I gave her the stink eye when she made to crouch to unzip the cloth protecting the outfit I was set to wear and shooed her away. She settled on the chair I'd just vacated with a heave as if merely walking had exhausted her, and I got it with a belly of that size. She seemed to forget she was hauling around another human into her sixth month and still working, much to Saint's dismay.

"Yes, but none of them got it the easy way because they were basically *born* into the business," I said half-heartedly, my attention enraptured by the expensive fabric spilling from the garment bag.

The cream silk corset and draped skirt gown had my mouth dropping open and Ariadne smiling with pride at my reaction. I'd seen it before. She always asked for my opinion on her designs, but seeing something in real life versus a picture was different.

"You don't know all of them, so never say never. I'm not treating you any differently than any of the other models, Ina, and besides, even if you weren't a Fleur, it wouldn't have been too difficult for you to have gotten a modeling gig. I mean, look at you." Her eyes examined me much like I imagine a casting agent's would, and even though her next words were positive, I shifted uncomfortably. "You could have walked into any modeling agency, and they would be begging to sign you."

"You really think so?" My voice came out embarrassingly squeaky, and I didn't realize where the sudden bouts of insecurity stemmed from. I was *the* Irena Fleur, after all. One thing I never questioned was my appearance, but I'd fallen into the nasty habit of doing it more and more lately.

Aria's expression mirrored my confusion. Seeking validation was a first for me, but before she could say anything, a third person intruded into our bubble, her voice stern and authoritative.

"No, they would've screamed in horror and chased you out by throwing tomatoes at you." Mom sauntered into the dressing room, her dark hair pinned up in an elegant bun and face devoid of any heavy makeup save for some eyeliner. She was like an older version of Ariadne with an Audrey Hepburn flair today, going by her form-fitting black pantsuit and a string of pearls on her neck.

"Mom!" I complained at the mocking tone of her voice once I got over her surprise appearance, clutching Aria's dress tightly.

She chuckled, slapping me on the cheek lightly as she passed by me on her way to Aria, saying, "Stupid questions demand equal answers. Stop fishing for compliments, Irena."

"What is she doing here?" I turned to Aria again while they greeted each other with a kiss on the cheek. I had nothing against my mom, but I was planning on keeping this first photoshoot as intimate as possible. Mom could be unnerving with her various *suggestions* and supposed expertise on any given topic.

My sister's sympathetic expression as she waddled over to me wasn't enough to ease my nerves, but I found another place to exert them as she removed the vice grip I had around the dress I was supposed to already be in if the rapid knocking on the door was anything to go by.

"When I told her what we were doing, she kind of invited herself," she explained, trying her best to smooth out the wrinkles I'd created.

"I couldn't miss my *skatouli's* first photo shoot," Mom justified, hanging her Prada bag on a metal coat rack.

"I told you not to call me that, Mom. I'm not little anymore." I cringed, the pout on my face contradicting what I'd just said. My nickname in Greek was *little shit*, and I despised it. I much preferred Killian's *Lilith* to it. "And this isn't my first photoshoot. I've done promotional campaigns before for the show."

"Good." Anastasia Fleur shrugged as Aria snapped her fingers, urging me to take my clothes off and change already. "Then this should be a breeze for you."

Difficult and awkward would be a better way to describe how my first photoshoot went, rather than a breeze.

And it was no one's fault but mine.

"Do we have anything?" Aria asked the photographer dejectedly. Though they were partially hidden behind a monitor, I didn't have to read her expression to realize she was disappointed in me.

"It's going to be difficult, but I'm sure we have some good

shots. Her face is too photogenic for all of them to go to waste."

In his defense, he tried to be quiet, but seeing as I'd already left the scene of the crime and ventured closer to them, I heard everything. My morale was already at an all-time low, so the comment rolled off my back. At this point, I was simply wondering if we were done because, with the way the walls seemed to be closing in on me, I didn't think I could go through one more round of uncomfortable poses.

My face was too tight, spine too rigid, chin too low, and there was no fluidity in my movements. Every time I tried to fix one problem, another arose until I got overwhelmed, and the end result was an epic flounder.

Heat flowed from my chest to my neck and face, followed by a restrictive tightness that made my breaths deeper and slower. I knew if I looked down, I'd see stress hives on my skin, a telltale sign of my embarrassment.

This wasn't me.

I didn't fail.

I didn't second-guess myself.

But most importantly, I didn't know what was wrong with me.

I wasn't lying when I said I'd done this before, so my lackluster performance didn't make sense.

"All right, thank you, Alen," Aria said, dismissal clear in her tone as she clapped his back and gravitated toward me, looping her arm through mine. "I'll catch up with you later."

"Thanks," I said as quickly as I could as Aria started dragging me out of there before I could hear the whispers of how I didn't deserve to be there from the rest of the staff.

Mom abandoned her post by the wall and followed us, and the fact that she hadn't spoken once during the whole ordeal unnerved me. In fact, everything unnerved me. Like remembering that most of these people probably had social media accounts, and my name could be dragged further down into the mud.

"The undeserving bitch with no talent. I guess Daniel knew what he was doing when he dropped her."

"Katrina is so much nicer and comes from a humble background, unlike that Fleur girl. She had everything served on a silver platter."

I'd stumbled across the latter comment on a gossip column after googling my name one fateful afternoon and promptly puked my guts out when I realized history was repeating itself.

"Well, that was a humbling experience," I got out through the panic, squeezing my throat.

Recognizing my rising hysteria, Aria drew calming circles with her thumb on the back of my hand. "It gets better with time."

"And practice," Mom chimed in, throwing herself on the terra-cotta sectional once inside the dressing room again, doing nothing to quell my deteriorating psyche. "I've already enrolled you in some classes that will help you perfect your poses and walk. Oh, and I talked with Amani about signing you with the right agency."

Amani?

Classes?

No wonder she hadn't talked the entire time. She saw what a wreck I was and immediately got into disaster control mode.

"Whoa, what happened to this being just a trial run?" I untangled myself from Aria, pacing the room.

"Mom, Ina is right. Let her do this at her own pace."

"Please, I'm your mother. I know what you want better than you do. Just like you were obsessed with pins and needles since you were in a diaper, Irena was obsessed with hogging the spotlight and taking up the frame of every home-made video all the time." Anastasia bit back and pierced me with her gaze. "Don't lie to me now, *gape mou*. Haven't you always wanted to try modeling?"

Something about her calling me *my love* soothed me a little bit, and I breathed in deep before replying. "Well, I'm not repelled by the idea of having my picture taken for a living." They both gave me the stink eye, and I bit my lip, throwing my hands up. "Fine, yes, I like being the center of attention more than I care to admit."

Lord knew I'd always been, but for once, I wanted it to be for all the right reasons.

"Then why all this resistance?" Aria asked, exasperated.

"Your sister may put up a strong front, Aria, but deep down, she is just as sensitive as her father." Mom scooched next to me, tucking a ginger lock of hair behind my ear. "It's not easy being cheated on and feeling like the whole world is against you. It's understandable your confidence took a dive."

Holy unprepared for what she had to say, my eyes watered on their own accord, and before I could stop them, a few stubborn tears rolled down my cheeks. Dealing with one negative comment in a wave of positives was hard, but being constantly ridiculed with no way out but to lean on those that profited off your disposition was like swimming in shark-infested water and hoping you made it out alive.

I wouldn't wish it on my worst enemy—

Okay, I'm not that benevolent.

I would totally wish worse on my enemies.

"Oh, honey. I'm sorry." Aria patted my head. "You always act so tough. I never thought about how big of a toll this must've taken on you."

"It's fine." I cracked a sad smile, wiping my face. I wasn't used to crying with an audience, even if that audience was my mom and sister. "I hadn't connected the dots myself until Mom pointed it out. I mean, I feel uncomfortable in public a lot, but I hadn't really realized how much it had impacted me either."

"It's okay not to be okay all the time, Irena," Mom intervened. "You will face many challenges in life and will have to rebuild yourself from the ground up multiple times. That's why I got so excited when Aria told me about getting you to try modeling. It's a cutthroat world, but also the perfect medium to help you rebuild your confidence and love yourself again."

"As long as you choose the right brands to work with," Aria muttered but shook off her skepticism in my favor, ever the loving older sister. "You're going to do perfect, *skatoula*. Don't listen to what the people with no life have to say."

"But aren't I too muscular for this job? I've seen plenty of modeling TV shows where they even judged a girl's calves—her *calves*—for being too manly!" Years of figure skating had left me with more muscle tissue than was *normal* for women. "Do you think that's why Daniel cheated on me? Katrina *is* curvier than me, that's for sure."

Because even though we had the same profession, she somehow managed to look like femininity personified.

"Representation is bigger than ever. Whoever judged that girl's calves must have been a bored asshole looking for entertainment. There is no standard body in this industry.

We're past the stick-thin model phase. You're perfect the way you are, Irena." Aria settled on the makeup chair as it was higher, determination swimming through her eyes as she looked at me. "And Daniel cheated on you because he's an insecure, short-dick man. I had my doubts about him from the start."

I couldn't help it; I cracked a smile.

The only time I ever heard my sister curse was when she got really heated over something. I shouldn't be so surprised at her ability to shoot down my argument in seconds. She was a big advocate for body positivity, having struggled with image issues herself.

"Truth be told, he was on the lower end of the inch spectrum," I admitted as I toyed with the dead skin around my nails.

"Irena!" Mom gasped, as if scandalized.

"Oh, don't act shocked, *Mama.*" I rolled my eyes. "You took me to the gynecologist to get on the pill as soon as I got my first boyfriend."

Aria's face reverberated with shock. She clutched her swollen belly as if unable to believe our mom, a devout Orthodox woman, would ever be fine with her daughter having sex before marriage. "Excuse me, why did you never do the same thing for me?"

"You had your first relationship after you graduated from college, plenty old enough to give me a grandchild." Anastasia waved her off as if that made total sense. "Besides," she continued, all sly, "I was just going to say to never settle for anything smaller than seven inches."

My ears rang, and I felt the need to bleach my brain when I thought about how she must've adhered to the same rule with Dad.

"Mom!" both Aria and I yelled, but she didn't pay us any mind, giggling like she'd said the funniest joke ever. Eventually, we started laughing too, and despite this being a shitty day, I ended it feeling grateful.

For my family.

For the only people capable of bringing me back from the precipice of a breakdown. We had our quirks, but we were always there for each other. I needed to do a better job, and I'd start with not resorting to old habits and seeking out attention for all the wrong reasons anymore, least of all from Killian Astor.

CHAPTER FIVE

KILLIAN

"Could we add some more shading around the tiger's eye?" Brenda breathed over my head, and with the way my teeth clenched with annoyance, you'd think I had misophonia.

But I knew the truth, and it wasn't her breathing that annoyed me. It was *her*.

Her coming into my office during every lunch break after she found out I also part-timed as a tattoo artist, pestering me to design something for her. Obviously, I didn't mind at first. I even found it fun, a happy escape to what I really wanted to do while working at Falco, but after her fifth-hundredth correction, I was starting to lose it and realize that she was wasting my time.

"If I add any more, the blue is not going to be as vibrant as you wanted." I stopped sketching, pen paused an inch away from my iPad. She wanted a tiger's face with bright blue eyes tattooed on her back to reflect her inner tigress. Or so she said.

"It looks vibrant enough."

Her necklace brushed against my shoulder, and I leaned to the side as she tried to get closer. Brenda was a beautiful woman with a fit body and a cute accent betraying her Argentinian roots, but I wasn't a big fan of touching. Not unless I instigated it.

"That's because this is an iPad screen. It'll look different on your skin," I explained.

"Oof," she huffed, rounding my desk and resting her hands on the metal, giving me a front-row view of her rack in her low-cut turquoise dress. "Can we take a break? All these choices confused me."

That *was* what I was trying to do before she burst into my office like she had for the past week. This was turning out to be a lengthy process, and I was super close to starting to lock my door.

Making friends at Falco wasn't of importance to me. I kept my circle tight-knit, and I didn't feel the need to add to that list. Finding a fuck buddy or girlfriend, even less so when I was a phone call away from getting some whenever I wanted.

We can take a break separately, I thought, but didn't get the chance to voice it out when someone else entered my office. "Careful now, don't overwork yourselves *too* much."

My eyes flicked to the entrance to discover the owner of that sarcastic-filled tone, who was none other than Noah Astor. My father.

Surprise whipped through me for barely two point five seconds when I remembered that he liked making little unannounced visits. Retirement didn't suit him since he had no one to torture with his demands, so we—Saint and I— were the only ones left for him to annoy. That is, until Saint had enough and banned him from showing up here until

Mom begged Saint to give him another chance because he was driving her crazy at home.

It was a nasty cycle, and our father was operating on borrowed time.

"Mr. Astor." Brenda's spine went ramrod straight as she turned to greet him, a fake smile plastered on her face. Noah gave her an appreciative once-over despite the fine lines decorating the skin around his blue eyes, betraying that he was more than twice her age. They were the only sign of aging on him since he had his brown hair colored regularly.

My pen clattered on the desk, creating a loud enough noise for both their heads to snap to me. I stretched my legs underneath the table, crossing my ankles and arms, a crooked smile pasting on my lips as I made no move to welcome him. "Now, now, Brenda, he doesn't pay your bills anymore. You can cool it with the over-the-top politeness."

My father's nostrils flared, and he decided to cross the threshold anyway. "Some people consider manners a part of their daily lives."

"I guess their parents did a better job raising them then," I said simply, watching the tendons jump out of his stiff neck.

He had an accident a few years back, and ever since then, he'd been unable to move his neck much. I felt bad for him initially, the blood in my veins doing its thing and caring for its own, but that stopped the second his detestable self woke up in the hospital.

Brenda shifted from foot to foot, sensing the animosity in the air, and excused herself as she sidestepped my father. "Um, if you'll excuse me, I need to head back to work."

None of us spoke as she left, locked in a staring contest until my father had had enough and proceeded with his routine of staring disapprovingly at the tattoo peeking under my shirt as he said, "It's good to see some work ethic still exists around here."

"Some would say even more than since you were CEO, seeing as profits have quadrupled ever since you left," I shot back, my voice impassive. He used to be better at getting a reaction out of me when I was younger, but over the years, I became better at pushing *his* buttons.

My father shrugged, examining the art I'd hung on the beige walls. It was mostly black and white figures hiding or crawling beneath layers of gray smoke, symbolizing the many hidden facets of a person's personality. The acts depicted were macabre, some would say, even inappropriate to hang at your place of business, but old habits die hard, and garnering strong reactions was one of my favorite pastimes.

"Yes, I raised Saint well," he answered, and it seemed like a dig at me.

"I think his father-in-law also had something to do with it. A lot of the employees look up to him. He has a sharp eye for business," I replied gleefully, knowing that the one person he hated most in this world was Aria's father. There was a lot of bad blood between them, but the details were lost on me.

He paused in front of a shadow girl holding what suspiciously looked like a dripping heart as he smoothed his palms down the front of his navy suit, an act I perceived as calming himself down before answering. "And that's why you're stuck with an entry-level job while your brother inherited the family business."

"Saint inherited the business because he was the only one old enough to marry off for your interests at the time."

Although Saint never admitted it to me, it didn't take a genius.

He and Aria barely knew each other when news of their engagement spread like wildfire. Even though my now sister-in-law once tried to convince me otherwise, she was a terrible liar. It was incredibly unbelievable when you factored in how much pussy my brother used to go through at the time.

And then, the merger between Falco and Fleur became known shortly after. There was no doubt in my mind that this was my father's idea. Combining the two biggest fashion houses in the world was the type of shit he would cream his pants for, even if it meant marrying off his son to a person he didn't love.

It did work out in the end for Saint and Aria, but that didn't mean I couldn't use their relationship as ammunition against our father.

Noah turned slightly red and a lot unhinged when he finally gave me his full attention as he marched to my desk and slammed his palm on it. "I regret the day I listened to your mother and didn't send you off to that teenage correctional behavior facility in Utah when I had the chance."

My blood strummed under my skin, but after being involved in fights left and right for most of my teenage years, there'd come a time when I needed to learn control. Channeling my anger through more productive ways, like boxing, helped, so I wouldn't let him ruin my *near-perfect* track record.

"You can bet I won't skimp on the first chance I get to lock you up in a retirement home for the senile if you continue bothering me for much longer." Showing no emotion, I straightened some Post-it notes that had dislocated during his temper tantrum, not fucking around anymore. "Is there a reason for your unsolicited visit?"

Whether he believed my threat or not wasn't clear. What was clear was that I'd managed to raise his blood pressure, and for a man his age, that wasn't advisable, so he took a deep breath, fixed his tie, and decided to pick his battles. "Your mother is throwing a fundraising party to honor your grandfather's passing from leukemia in two weeks. She wanted me to tell you before you made any other plans."

"Couldn't you have called me for that?"

"I would've if you ever bothered to answer."

Right, I'd changed my phone number a while ago and conveniently forgotten to inform him.

"I'll be there. If that is all..." I motioned to the door, having gotten the daily quota I could handle from him.

He looked me up and down twice, and just like he hadn't bothered to say hello, he didn't bother with goodbyes either. And after managing to keep my temper under control, I finally lost it when he slammed my door on his way out, the way a teenager would after locking themselves in their room.

My hand curled around the unreasonably priced Apple pen, and I hauled it at the door as if I wanted to stab through it, my arm arching so far back it sent a jab of pain down my spine. After bouncing on the door, it clattered on the floor with a disappointing thud. Ultimately, no harm was done, but imagining the pen had gone to the back of my father's skull did help subdue my fury.

Blowing out my nose, I rubbed a palm down my face and picked up my phone to warn Saint. That had to be his next destination, and I'd rather spare my brother all the fuzzy and warm feelings our father inspired in people.

Killian: Daddy dearest is on his way to your office.

I laughed when a response came through a few seconds after.

Saint: What a coincidence, I was just on my way out.

Killian: Lucky bastard. Are you free later tonight?

Saint: No, Aria and I are flying to Crete for two weeks to visit her grandparents. Why?

Killian: On any other occasion, I would've been jealous, but I remember how her grandpa loves to shit on you for not being a "real" football player, so good luck, brother. I'll miss my favorite sparring partner.

Saint had managed to play pro American football before an injury took him out of the game, and let's just say Aria's Greek side of the family enjoyed calling him a rugby player more than an author loved coffee.

Saint: Thanks, I'll need it. You could always ask Ares.

Ares, as in Saint's friend and our occasional workout buddy that recently had twins...yeah, his hands were plenty full already.

I scrolled through my contacts before deigning him with a response, my finger perched over Mia's name. She was a girl I knew from high school. We'd hit it off at the time and still talked regularly. She was off traveling the world, but whenever she was in town, she was sure to stop by.

I hadn't gotten any action in August, so hard and fast were the way to go. Mia enjoyed both of those things.

I shot her a text and went back to Saint.

Killian: It's okay. I thought of another way to get rid of all my pent-up energy.

Saint: Spare me the details.

After missing the one and only lunch break I got all day, I stopped at the break room on my way out. It was usually stocked with snacks, and I needed a pick-me-up before heading to Ray's.

Fridays were brutal. I had to work two shifts, one in the morning and one at night. White Fox was a block away from a trending bar street, so Ray preyed on people too far wasted to realize getting a drunk tattoo was a bad idea. He didn't have the best business practice, but I wasn't planning on working for him for long.

The saying, *when you make plans, God laughs,* echoed in my mind as I rounded up the corner to the break room, fully equipped with a coffee machine, snacks of all kinds, and even a blue ping-pong table. There were no people at this hour, so I made a beeline for the Snickers bars neatly lined up on the counter, but stopped midway when something —*someone*—snagged my attention.

I dragged my gaze from the laminated floor to purple, crystal-embellished pumps, boyfriend jeans wide at the bottom and tighter up top, and a white crop top revealing a sliver of skin, partially covered by a wave of strawberry blonde hair. A faint, heartbeat-like sound started strumming in my ears like it commonly did when Irena Fleur was around.

My jaw tensed as I considered ignoring her. Irena's neck was bent, and even though I could see her face, her eyes were solely focused on her phone, all consumed by whatever she was reading, and not so happy about it either if her white knuckle grip on it was anything to go by.

"Be careful," I spoke before I could think about what I was doing.

Irena jumped in place, but her surprise was short-lived. We were getting used to each other's sneak attacks. Wasn't that cute? She tipped her chin up, giving me a quick once-over before asking, "What?"

I walked closer, noting how her mascara was smudged at the edges, and her bottom lip looked raw, like she'd chewed all the dead skin off. Sensing something wasn't right, a part of me only Luca and occasionally Saint had seen before came forth. The one that could smell pain in the air and tried to distract the other person as best as they could.

"You're also staring at your phone like you're willing it to go up in flames, and it's a Samsung one. That's a recipe for disaster," I noted, forgetting about the Snickers bar and plucking some grapes from the plate in the middle of the granite island as I stood before her.

She shut the screen off, propping her hip on a stool, and raised her brow as she said, "You're an Apple fanboy, Astor? I knew there was a reason I didn't like you."

"You don't like me? Well, that just hurts my feelings, Lilith."

"Why do I somehow doubt that?"

"I like *you*," I admitted, and the little mix of a gasp and a moan she produced made it worth running my mouth. I wasn't lying. I *wished* I was, but the fact that I wanted that sound as my new ringtone only served to restate my point.

77

She blinked, and when her eyes reopened, it was like she poured ice-cold water all over my fantasy. "Spare me the hot-and-cold game, Lucifer. I'm not in the mood today. Get what you need, and please leave. I'm waiting for my dad."

"Why?" I asked simply, deterring her from shutting me out.

"Why what?"

"Why aren't you in the mood?"

"Since when did you start taking such an interest in my problems?" Irena scoffed, mistrust clear in her gaze.

I popped a few grapes in my mouth, stalling. I didn't know why I was pushing it, why I didn't make myself scram after what I did to her when I got home yesterday—yes, I remembered, despite wishing I didn't. Maybe I wanted to see if she would treat me any differently, or perhaps a dam had broken, and I was failing miserably at patching it up.

"You're my brother's sister-in-law. I *have* to care," I replied after swallowing the juice from the grapes, sweetening the otherwise bitter taste of my lies.

Irena's already sour expression dropped further, if that was possible, and she slid her phone into her back pocket as she took a step away from me. "Wow, I'm sorry for being such a burden, but don't worry. If that's the case, I'm releasing you from your duties. Feel free not to fake any concern for me anymore."

Like a moth to a flame, I followed, catching her wrists in my hands and caging her in against the counter. Her swift inhale punched me straight in the gut as the thought of how *she* would like it if I choked her as she had me plundered through my mind.

"You're not a burden. You're a pain in my ass."

Truer words had never been spoken.

Here I was, in my early twenties, obsessing over my brother's sister-in-law when I should've been lusting after anything with a skirt. It wasn't normal, and my increased day-to-day exposure to her was affecting me negatively. It was like trapping all your forbidden thoughts and emotions in a chrysalis. There'd come a day when it would bust.

"Why do you care?" she pushed, her eyes so strikingly blue and angry they made the rest of the world turn gray.

"The same reason you almost melted in a puddle when I touched you a few nights ago," I retorted, my voice loud in my ears. Like a stroke of lightning had gone through her, her mood shifted from enraged to stunned, and she stopped fighting for a single second. "There's something about you. Something that makes me want to light our already fragile familial bonds on fire."

My admission was met with a drop of her mouth, and I rubbed my lips together, as if preventing myself from saying anything else that would place me in an even more precarious position.

"You remember." Her voice was baby soft this time as she slumped against the island. I had no reason to still be holding on to her, but I was riding this moment of weakness until the end.

"Unfortunately," I replied. I didn't have everything jotted down to a T, but what I did remember was enough to have me rubbing one out when I got home every night to the imagination of how it could've ended if our siblings had never met each other. "Don't worry, it won't happen again. I was drunk."

"You just admitted you're attracted to me, and now you're telling me not to worry." She pursed her lips, and I didn't miss how it was out of disappointment.

I didn't need her to confess to anything. Her body already spilled all of her secrets for her.

"You're not the only woman I find attractive. You're just the only one I'm not allowed to touch," I stated simply, praying on the fact that I'd hit a nerve because this day, while enlightening, didn't change a thing.

"You're touching me right now." She served me some sass, not taking the bait.

There was no hint of humor in my smile as my thumb caressed her inner wrist, feeling her pulse accelerate with each passing second. "Come now, Lilith, I'd like to believe you're smart enough to figure out the kind of *touching* I'm talking about."

"You're a horrible human being." She shook her head, raised her hands, and pushed against my chest in order for me to release her.

"I'm simply playing along to the game you started, sweetheart." I retreated, seeing her eyes light up with recognition.

It's what you haven't done.

She'd started the cat-and-mouse chase. Now it was only a matter of settling who was the hunter and who the prey.

I let her chew on that, turning my back on her as I walked to the fridge. I was running late, as per my watch, but I was willing to put in a later shift if it meant finding out why she looked like the world had turned upside down when I first came into the room.

I skipped the coffee and went directly for a chilled can of Red Bull for that extra boost of energy. It was seven PM, and I was about to work until three. The only saving grace was that tomorrow was Saturday, and I had a meeting, and I didn't get to work again until Monday.

"Now, back to the original question," I stated, the drink

sizzling after I popped it open. "What's going on?" Irena trailed my movements with high brows when I turned to her again, in disbelief that I was able to move on so quickly after what'd just happened.

She looked frazzled as she thought over her reply, but ultimately settled for moving on as well. "Don't you have to work or something?"

"Nope," I informed happily. "I'm done for the day, and from the looks of it, you're stuck here until Darian comes, so humor me."

Her cheeks puffed as she held back an exhale, swallowing it down. She strode in my direction, heels clicking on the floor, and once she was in front of the fridge didn't bother telling me to move. She simply hit my shoulder with the door, so I got the memo.

I chuckled, and she glared at me before reaching for a banana—*fuck me*—and said, "I just got off a phone call with my agent where she duly informed me that I'd been dropped from the second season of Stars on Ice."

My amusement was cut short, and I stared at her as if she was an alien. "You were fired?"

"Well, yeah, that's what being dropped means."

"Why? You're one of the best figure skaters I've ever seen."

God, I really needed to put a cork in it today, but it was true. Every time I watched her perform, it was like she flew on top of the ice. There were no missed steps, and she always adopted a specific expression that had you captivated from start to finish.

She stopped peeling her banana, eyes blinking rapidly up at me, wonder in her tone as she inquired, "You've watched me perform?"

"It was a one-time thing. I was at Saint and Aria's for dinner, and they had the TV set on your show. You were great..." I scratched the back of my neck, finding a speck of dirt on the floor fascinating as I rephrased, "Good, I mean. You were really good, not just another ice princess with vacant eyes. Watching you was actually entertaining."

"That might be the nicest thing you've ever said to me."

A cool touch on my forehead made my head snap toward her, and I almost dropped my drink as she felt me up.

"What are you doing?"

"Checking to see if you have a temperature," Irena explained flatly and giggled when I swatted her hand away. "Thank you, but we all shine in different areas. Those so-called ice princesses have gone through years of grueling training to get where they are. Stage presence is not as important as technique."

"Yes, but you have both the artistry and the talent. Weren't you one of the very few people to land a quadruple jump at the Olympics? At least that's what Aria said." I added the last bit as an afterthought, and she took a bite of her banana, looking at me through narrowed eyes.

There wasn't anything sexual about the scene, just a girl eating a snack, but my brain definitely took it there. We men were so predictable sometimes. I'd give that one to the girls.

"I guess it wasn't *enough*," she replied after a while, picking on the flailing parts of the banana's skin as she pleaded with me. "Please don't make me say it. It's not like you don't already know why I got fired. The video has over ten million views."

My brows bunched, and I set my drink down, having no clue what video she was talking about, but jumping to the worst conclusions immediately.

"I *don't*. I don't have any social media accounts. I don't go out of my way to learn what other people are doing unless it directly impacts me."

"Spoken like a true narcissist." She snorted, darting around me to throw the reminders of the banana into the trash. I shrugged, and she gave me the full force of her puppy eyes as she said, "Do me a favor, don't look it up."

"Why?" I didn't confirm or deny.

If it was what I thought it was, I wasn't even sure whether I wanted to watch it, but I'd have to in order to cause some serious damage to the other party involved.

She shook her head, avoiding my gaze. "Because if one more person gives me a pitying look, I'll lose it."

CHAPTER SIX

KILLIAN

P ity.
  It was definitely an emotion my FBI agent felt
  for me after watching me scour the internet for
information on Irena's so-called scandalous video that had
garnered millions of views.

The search affirmed a few things:

My imagination was too wild for my well-being.

Her ex-boyfriend was a piece of shit.

People loved to tear down successful women.

The comment section was pungent with hatred and jealousy, even though Irena wasn't the one at fault. She reacted exactly how anyone in her position would have (okay, maybe it was a little much for the average person, but still less than I would've done); standards were different when you were a public figure, though. There was no room for flaws. One mistake defined your whole being.

I usually kept my word, but Irena's father barged in at the right moment yesterday, and I was saved from making a promise I would break. She'd piqued my interest, and even the possibility of being traumatized wasn't enough to deter me from clicking link after link.

Like a creep, I'd spent the better part of my morning obsessing over all the details of this story, so much so I was running late to my date with Mia—if you could even call it that; we just fucked occasionally.

My hair was wet, cologne still drying on my blue button-up shirt, when I heard knocking. Confused because I wasn't expecting anyone, I headed to the door. Save for my family, no one else had my address, and if I could've had it my way, my family wouldn't either. Since my father was prone to sneak attacks and was undoubtedly plotting a way to get back at me after our last encounter, I looked through the peephole first, in case it was him. I wasn't embarrassed to admit, I've pretended I wasn't home before to not deal with him.

Imagine my surprise when I ended up wishing it was Noah.

It turned out there hadn't been anyone knocking at my door, and soundproofing sucked on this building. It also turned out I was in big trouble when my hands turned to fists against the dark wood. A feeling akin to jealousy coursed its way down my veins when I watched Irena open the door and welcome Colin into her apartment with a warm smile and a hug.

In a knee-jerk reaction, my hand slammed against the door when they both disappeared from my sight, releasing multiple frustrations at once. Like why the fuck did I care who she invited to her home, and why the fuck couldn't I stick to my original plan of pushing her away?

Yesterday was bad enough, and here I was today, reconsidering going out with Mia at all. The past few years of effort on my part to not see her as anything more than a problem that would go away if I ignored it for long enough was crumbling right before my eyes, and I wasn't doing anything to stop it.

But I wasn't lying when I said Colin was probably just using her. We weren't the best of buddies, but we had been neighbors for a good part of the year, and unfortunately, when people saw you every day, they felt comfortable enough to unload their life problems on you.

And when remembering that Irena had just gotten out of a shitty relationship, and she didn't need to deal with another one, I was exiting my house before I could really even think about the consequences of what I was about to do. It was a recurring theme where she was concerned.

Air whooshed across my face, and an irritated Irena greeted me, stopping me from ringing the doorbell for the third time since she didn't answer on the first two. The way her eyes studied me told me she liked—correction, loved what she was seeing, and wished she wasn't. They crawled from my black loafers to my form-fitting striped pants and got stuck in a bit of traffic on the part of my chest that was exposed, since I liked wearing my shirts with the first few buttons undone.

I cleared my throat to get her attention, trying not to linger on the fact that she also looked fucking phenomenal in a light pink spaghetti strap sundress. It was mostly the idea that she dressed up for Colin that I couldn't shake off, despite him batting for the other team.

Her cheeks flamed when she realized I'd caught her ogling me, and she hissed out, "What do you want?"

I opened my mouth, then shut it again. If I really told her why I was here, there was no way she was letting me past that threshold, so I bit my cheek as I thought over my answer.

Her brows shot up as she waited for me to find my words, so I settled for, "I'm all out of sugar, and I was wondering if I could borrow some."

"Sugar?" Irena repeated, sounding suspicious. "What do you need sugar for? Don't you order like every other meal?"

Every meal.

And a grossly overpriced Starbucks cup a day.

I'd become too addicted to the luxury of never having to fry, boil, or bake anything and spent most of my salary on food. Growing up, I didn't really have anyone to teach me life skills, not when my supposed role models couldn't survive without a personal chef.

"Coffee," I explained, squaring up my shoulders, not ruling out the option to barge in uninvited. "Now, can I get some, or do you have any more questions?"

Her unimpressed stare was hard to miss, but she let this one slide, thinking she'd win me over with her next words, "Wait here, I'll get it for you."

She shut the door in my face.

Or at least she tried to.

All the apartments in the building were equipped with soft-close door hinges, so she didn't notice when I stopped it from slamming completely shut by sliding my foot between the small crack at the last minute. I waited a few seconds until I was sure Irena had disappeared and then slipped in.

Noticing her shoe rack right at the entrance, I decided to take mine off before going in. It was an unspoken Greek household rule, and I'd learned it the hard way.

The house was separated by the hallway running down the middle. Two bedrooms and the kitchen sat on the left side, and the living room and bathroom were on the right. Thankfully, there was no open floor plan here, so I was able to sneak into the living room, where—for his sake—I hoped Colin was.

There were still some boxes piled one on top of another in every other corner, but for the most part, the basics were out, except without a hint of decor. The house lacked a soul, but there was a TV, a dark blue sectional, and windows as tall as me, flooding the space with tons of natural light while overlooking The Promenade, Astropolis's riverside park. It was like an orange maze from above as fall started slowly rolling in.

I didn't notice him at first, sitting there crouched on one end of the couch in his preppy getup; that's how unassuming he was. I didn't have any time to digest my feelings. I had to set this plan in motion before Irena got back.

"Colin?" I asked, and his head snapped up at the sound of my voice.

"Killian?" His eyes widened, and the smile on my face was so fake it was painful.

"Hey, man."

"Hey." He got up, and I patted his back, skipping the whole awkward half hug he went in for. "What's up?"

"Needed to borrow some sugar from Irena real quick. What are you guys doing?" I asked, like it wasn't obvious. There were two bowls of popcorn on a glass-top coffee table, and the television was paused on some Tom Cruise movie.

It was a date, but of course, Colin couldn't admit that, not to me, unless he wanted a good lesson for stringing Irena along.

"Oh, nothing. We both had no plans for tonight, so we decided to watch a movie together."

"Did you, now?" I stared harder at the TV, trying to figure out what they were about to watch, then pinned him with a stare and said, "Is that the new *Top Gun* movie? Damn, I've wanted to watch it for a while but never found the time."

He blinked awkwardly at me, but it didn't take him much time to say exactly what I wanted him to. "Well, if you're free, I don't see why you can't watch it with us."

"Really?" I clapped him on the shoulder, and a genuine smile spread on my face when he grimaced at the excessive force. "Thanks, man."

"I hope Irena's cool with it." He tried to backtrack.

"Oh yeah, I'm sure she'll be on board." I sat in the middle of the couch, spreading my arms over the sides. "Our siblings are married, so we're practically family."

You usually didn't fantasize about putting your dick in any of your family members. I didn't bore him with the details, though. You usually didn't cockblock your family members either, but this was for her own good.

Colin took to the light pink beanbag on the floor, and I bit my lip to stop myself from laughing as he tried to sit on it without falling. If I was a better man, I would've made space for him on the couch.

Footsteps drew near, then stopped. I felt a burning on the back of my neck like someone was trying to glare a hole through it, and a few seconds later, Irena stormed over.

"I thought I told you to wait outside," she accused, nostrils flared and knuckles white around the cup of sugar I'd asked for.

"I got a cramp in my leg, and I needed to sit down," I reasoned. "Besides, Colin here just invited me to watch the movie with you guys, so I guess I'll stick around for a little while."

Colin half winced when Irena turned her accusatory gaze on him and stumbled to explain himself, "Um, yes, he mentioned how he was waiting to watch it, so I thought, why not join us?"

"Because—" she started, all fired up, but I cut her off.

"And who's this little girl?" I pointed to the black and white fluff ball, who jumped on the couch, her feline eyes homed in on me. Pointer finger extended, I brought it to its nose, and it gave it a good sniff before rubbing its face against my hand.

"He's a guy, and his name is Dusty," Irena corrected.

"Dusty?"

The name gave me a pause because, seriously, who fucking named their cat Dusty?

"He was the oldest cat in the shelter where I adopted him from; the name felt fitting." She rounded the couch, leaning down to take the purring cat from me, but he gave her a warning growl and climbed into my lap.

"Well, she's obviously not happy about it," I remarked, scratching just behind his ear. He slowly blinked at me as if in agreement. "Yes, I know she's a mean mommy," I told him, and Irena's shoulders sagged when she finally realized I wasn't leaving any time soon.

"Stop misgendering my cat and scoot over," she ordered. I happily obliged, sliding closer to Colin, who was probably feeling a little left out. "The other side," Irena grumbled.

"Ah, ah," I breathed through clenched teeth, clutching my calf. Dusty, who had found the perfect laying spot, meowed in protest at all my wiggling around.

"Are you okay?" Colin reached for me, but I leaned back.

"That cramp is persistent," I complained, and Irena rolled her eyes, abandoning the sugar-filled cup on the table and dropping on the spot next to me with a huff.

I had nothing against Tom Cruise. The opposite, really. I admired him for doing all his own stunts, but somewhere along the two-hour movie, I drifted off for a few seconds and woke up just in time to hear Colin excuse himself.

"I should get going. It's pretty late."

I kept my eyes closed, curled up with Dusty as I heard him pant while trying to get out of that bean bag. It was one of those low-quality ones that acted like quicksand. The more you struggled, the deeper you sunk.

"Yeah, I am feeling pretty tired myself," Irena voiced, and I felt her sharp elbow jab digging at my ribs as she got up to escort him out.

I didn't budge, and my face remained neutral until the next time I heard him speak, their voices fainter the farther away they went.

"We should go out some time, though, just the two of us."

My face scrunched as I waited for her reply.

"I don't see why not."

She didn't see why not?

That just meant I got to have a one-on-one chat with our dear Colin and hopefully get him to open his eyes and see why they wouldn't work. If he didn't, slamming them shut would also work.

Inciting violence had stopped being my thing when I

grew out of the attention-seeking teenage phase, but I was no saint either.

This was only for Irena's protection, of course. We lived next to each other, and I couldn't let something like this slide.

"You can get up now. I know you're not sleeping."

I was so consumed by my thoughts, I didn't hear her come back. I masked the slight jump of my shoulders by slowly extending my hands over my head and pretending to yawn.

"What?" I straightened my back as she got into my field of vision again, understandably furious. "What time is it?"

"Time for you to drop the act because you're not getting an Oscar anytime soon," she seethed, and the cat scampered off my lap and out the room.

"Dusty doesn't like it when you yell," I pointed out.

Irena pinched the bridge of her nose, her tone of voice much lower and speech slow like she was talking to a baby, as she inquired, "Why did you barge in like that today?"

I shrugged, resting back on the couch and manspreading as if I owned the place. "I thought I told you Colin just wants to take advantage of you."

"Yeah?" she goaded, her arms falling to her sides. "Well, so does every other guy. One way or another, you all have something to gain and very little to give."

Oh, I didn't know who she had been with, but I always made sure to give plenty. Climaxing by yourself was overrated when you and your partner could do so together. One-sided satisfaction wasn't my thing, and even though her statement wasn't just about sex, that was where my mind flew. I shouldn't be surprised. I'd been in a constant state of horniness for some time.

"Judging by your ex, I do get why you feel that way. Wasn't much of a giver, huh?" Trying not to sound judgmental but failing, I went straight for the kill.

Her eyes grew perplexed, her entire demeanor shifting at the reminder of him. Irena's hands shook a little by her sides, making me want to swallow my tongue and never utter a word again. I didn't take pride in hurting her. I only did it to push her away, though this time, it was a miscalculation on my part.

I could almost see her anger toward me disappearing like a dark cloud over her head as she focused on the matter at hand. She flopped back on the couch as far away from me as possible.

"You googled it, didn't you?"

"Guilty," I stated, and she buried her face in a throw pillow, releasing a muffled groan. I slid closer, getting ahold of her arms, and tugged her up again. "Hey, if anyone should be embarrassed, it's him. He looks like he's trying really hard to keep a fart in, in most of his pictures, and could honestly be Lord Farquaad's twin."

"He does have a pretty long face." She cracked a smile, but it vanished as soon as it appeared. "I should've seen it coming. I'm turning twenty-two in December, and his dating history consists of girls only twenty-one and under."

I scowled, my hatred for this guy running even deeper. The time crunch could be coincidental, but when you were this much of a conceited piece of shit, I didn't think so.

"Must be getting his dating tips from Leonardo DiCaprio." I released her and tucked a strand of her hair that kept getting in her eye behind her ear. I didn't move away immediately, just to see that little hollow on her neck get deeper with a nervous swallow.

On my way up, my gaze got fixed on her lips, and God, what I wouldn't give to be anyone else at this moment just so I could've licked that shiny lip oil off and bit that plump bottom lip until she allowed me inside that mouth of hers. There would be no need to talk in riddles or tiptoe around topics.

Embers flared between us the longer we went without speaking, a palpable tension growing until she cleared her throat, and I subtly shook my head to refocus, dropping my hand from her face like a hot potato.

"So you don't find me weird?" she questioned.

It was the first time I'd heard Irena sound anything but confident, and I didn't know how to deal with the vulnerability of her question in any other way than to crack a joke.

"You mean more than I already did?" That answer got me a punch in the stomach, and I wheezed out a laugh, rephrasing, "Ouch, okay, I don't. There was nothing unusual about your reaction. In fact, it was quite entertaining. Cheaters deserve to have cake thrown at their faces."

"Right? That's what I said, but I was vilified instead." Irena threw her hands up in the air. "Everyone was saying that I should've been madder at my 'man' than the girl he cheated on me with, which I was."

"Maybe it's because you mostly aimed for her."

"He hid behind her. What was I supposed to do?"

What a fucking bastard.

There were only a few short clips online, so you didn't get a clear picture of what went down, but I knew enough to want to break his legs so he could never skate again.

"There's still time to rough him up, you know. I, for one, would take great pleasure in it," I offered, sitting back once my ass got sore in one spot. Her strawberry scent got weaker, and I distracted myself by staring at the dark sky out the windows.

Really?

Her scent?

Was there anything about this girl I didn't like?

And why was I still sitting here acting like her fucking therapist for a second time when Colin had already left? I needed to go too and possibly start searching for a new apartment, because living across her would be my undoing.

"You and Saint are very similar in some ways," Irena mused. "He also offered to take care of him, but excessive violence is what got me here in the first place. I need to be smart about it."

Of course, Saint had offered to beat him up. He wanted to do the same to me for far less. I didn't think it was because he had an attachment or fondness for Irena; Aria did. And whatever Aria loved, Saint protected.

An awkward silence wrapped around us like a suffocating blanket in ninety-five-degree weather. I had to physically bite my tongue to keep from responding because the more I talked, the harder it got to just get up and walk out, and there was no way I was spending the night.

Red spots bloomed on Irena's neck from my lack of reaction. I bet this seemed like another hot and cold game to her. I could see the gears shifting in her eyes, trying to make sense of what this meant. When she finally had enough, she raised her head—a move I noticed her doing whenever she felt insecure—and looked toward the empty bowls and soda cans on the table.

"All right, I need to clean this up and head to b—" She got on her feet and suddenly hissed, her face a picture of pain. "Ah, fuck."

"What?" I was instantly on alert mode, scanning her for any hidden injuries. I stood by her, and she hooked on my arm as I helped her lie down completely. "What's wrong?"

"An actual cramp. I've been taking catwalk classes all day yesterday and today. My feet have been killing me. Six-inch heels are no joke." Eyes closed, she nodded toward the table. "I'll clean this up tomorrow. If you could let yourself out, that would be great."

Well, there was my out, so why was I hesitating?

I towered over her, planted in place as I watched her try to flex her toes ever so slightly, and they barely moved. She cracked an eye open as if to ask what I was still doing here, and I wondered the same thing.

The resounding answer? I was stupid.

Indecisiveness battled inside of me, but when I saw her try to move her foot again and fail, it was all over.

"Kicking me out so soon, Lilith?" I *tsked*, and in one fluid motion, I gathered her legs and settled beneath them, spreading them over my lap.

As expected, she didn't just settle in like Dusty or purr at first contact. Instead, she got on her elbows, eyebrows meeting as she tried to regain control of the situation and failed. "Hey, leave my feet alone. What do you think you're—"

I slid her back down, and she fell with a pained squeal, huffing at the ceiling. Using my two thumbs, I worked my way from her heel bone to the base of her toes, gently spreading the tissue. I watched the harsh expression on her face melt, giving way to tranquility.

"For once, can you just relax and stop talking?" I teased, kind of liking my current position of power. She went from wanting to chop my head off to being putty in my hands —literally.

"I'm a Sagittarius. We're known for excessive talking," she argued, voice faint. Irena released the tiniest whimper as I spread her toes, her chest rising slightly off the cushions, and I immediately repeated the action just to hear the sound again. "Oh, that feels so good, thank you."

As I was working my magic, I moved her feet as far away from my crotch as possible. Her dress's skirt had bunched up and cut off a few fingers away from her knees. One wrong move and it was game over. Half of her hair spilled from the side of the couch like dark honey dripping on the floor, eyes shut, and pink lips half parted as if in total contentment.

"How come you're taking catwalk classes?" I launched into a conversation, trying to keep my mind at bay.

Her shoulders came up and down again. "I'm out of a job and decided to explore a new career path. Although, I tend to choose professions that destroy my feet."

I turned my eyes to them, and even though her nails were painted a milky white color and they were well-taken care of, her toes were pretty busted from being cramped in skates for so long, and there was a faint scar along the side of her foot like she'd undergone a bunionectomy.

Finally, this woman did have imperfections as well.

"Not going to lie, they are pretty ugly, Lilith," I joked.

Irena made a noise of displeasure, wiggling her toes freely now. "I'll have you know, I've been offered a ridiculous amount of money for pics of my feet, and you get the privilege of rubbing them for free."

"They probably asked for a refund once they saw them." I chuckled, and having had enough of my mocking, she tried to retract her legs.

I didn't let her and *oomphed* when I got kicked in the gut. It was accidental, judging by the horrified look on her face, but I still didn't let her get away with it. I paid her back in the form of tickling her soles, and she giggled like crazy.

Somewhere in all of our struggle, she'd migrated closer to me, half on my lap, head thrown back in laughter, but close enough for me to lean forward and bruise that long neck of hers with my teeth if I wanted to.

I stopped my torture, causing her to glance at me, and in a fleeting moment, the humor in the situation was gone, absorbed by other emotions our proximity sparked.

"I didn't know you felt that passionately about finishing your massage," she said with a tremble in her voice.

The space between us faded ever so slowly. It was as if she was a magnet whose pull I couldn't fight, and before I knew it, my nose was brushing against hers, fingers digging into the flesh of her thighs as I hugged her legs to my chest. My cock was stiff as a pole in my pants, ready to fucking go.

"Irena," I spoke, and her name tasted like bourbon spilling down my throat. "I should leave."

"Mm-hmm." She nodded, burrowing even closer as she did so. "You really should."

We were both in agreement, yet instead of leaving, I angled my head, my lips inches away from hers. There would be no turning back from this if neither of us were strong enough to resist the temptation.

I didn't know if I could stop at just a kiss. I hadn't wanted someone so badly since I first discovered that sex wasn't all bad.

Her breath coasted over my lips like oil igniting a fire even further. I was seconds away from obliterating the joke of a gap that remained when a divine intervention happened.

The doorbell rang.

Everything froze for the few seconds the noise took to travel to us. We were both stuck in our positions until we weren't, until we scrambled apart, chests heaving like nearly crossing an imaginary forbidden line was acute to running a marathon.

Irena's blues were horrified, hair askew on her face and dress almost riding past her panties. I tore my gaze away, running my hands down my face and breathing hard.

What the fuck was I about to do?

I could be a piece of shit, but this was on a whole other level. I couldn't risk losing my brother, the only normal family member in my life, for a girl.

That damned doorbell rang again, and I dug my fingers into my scalp, elbows resting on my knees, as I said, "Go get the door, Irena."

Because thanks to male anatomy, walking was a bit difficult at the moment.

Out of the corner of my eye, I saw her break out of her trance and smooth her skirt down as she got up and walked away in stiff, robotic movements. Shock reverberating through my system, it took me a while to gather my thoughts, and I was thrown into another unpleasant situation before I could even process what was happening.

"May I help you?" Irena's question traveled all the way to the living room, which told me she didn't know the person on the other side.

"Hi." My ears perked up, and I cursed, punching the couch's arm when I realized who it was. "I'm looking for Killian Astor. I thought this was his apartment."

"Um, no, it's not." I could picture Irena's confusion as I willed my dick to go down. "What do you need him for?"

Thankfully, the unexpected turn of events helped accelerate the process, and I was up and flying down the hall just as Mia started her next sentence.

"We had a date today, but he didn't show up or respond to any of my calls, so I got worr—" Round brown eyes narrowed in on me from over Ina's shoulder, pausing her explanation midway to utter my name. "Kill?"

Both of them faced me, a different set of expectations written on either of their faces. Mia scanned me from head to toe, making sure I was okay, and I mentally kicked myself for not informing her I wasn't going to make it. She seemed so short next to Irena, her complete opposite in terms of looks, with tan skin, soft features, and a more demure character.

Because one thing was for sure, if Irena was in her place, I'd have my balls handed to me by now.

"Mia, I'm sorry," I apologized, because she at least deserved that. "I was helping my friend get settled because she moved in a few weeks ago, and I lost track of time. I'm really sorry."

Irena sucked in a sharp breath, her fingers turning ghost-white around the door's handle, and if looks could kill, I'd be ten feet under. Her expression twisted several times, her brows meeting her hairline, then diving down again, her lips set in a grim smile.

For a second, I thought she'd throw me out kicking and screaming, but she surprised me by exercising control.

"Right, that he did, helped me get all moved in. Killian's very helpful like that. Doesn't know when to stop," she said, sickly sweet, but the hand she hooked around my bicep told a different story. Her fingers dug into my skin as she pushed me toward Mia. "But since you're here now, feel free to take him with you. It's gotten pretty late."

One second, I was by her side, and the next, by Mia's.

"Irena," I called out her name, not knowing what else to say. She hesitated for a little bit, waiting for an explanation, but I couldn't push anything out but a simple "Good night."

Irena just nodded, and not at me, but Mia, who had witnessed our exchange with poorly veiled amusement. She wasn't dumb and most probably was able to sniff out my lies the minute I uttered them. Mia didn't get attached and wasn't prone to jealousy, which were some of the main reasons why I kept her around.

Irena's silence was so loud that even the soft click of her door echoed in my ears long after I disappeared into my apartment.

CHAPTER SEVEN
IRENA

He went home with another woman.

My lungs burned as I skated from one end of the rink to the other. There was no method to my madness. I needed to feel the wind on my face, the ice particles melting on my skin, and the adrenaline thrumming through my veins. Other people were skating about, but they all blurred in the background, my thoughts taking precedence.

Not only that, but he invited her to his home five minutes after he almost kissed me.

God, how I wanted to punch him in the face. How I wanted to claw at his skin for making me feel special and then ripping it all away. But that was how Killian operated. One day, you could talk to him like you were best buddies, and the next, if he saw you on the street, he'd act like that was the first time he was ever meeting you.

I spun in place, regaining some energy, before sliding back out again, taking it a bit more leisurely. All this anger that had been boiling up inside of me came to a crescendo after last night, and I needed an outlet to let it all out.

Were all men cheaters?

No, a better question was, were all men hypocrites? While he crashed my date with Colin—whatever his reasoning—it was all good for him to find solace in Mia's arms afterward. Why not, right? Men were allowed to fuck anything with a skirt, and women were branded as whores the moment our body count rose to four.

I did two toe loops in a row and thought I heard some aws around me. I couldn't be sure, though, over all the different thoughts buzzing in my head like a swarm of bees.

What happened to staying away from Killian? If I kept my heart out of reach, no one would be able to break it. And as much as I hated admitting it, it was still sore after the last round of beating it received.

I dry-heaved as I leaned against the railing. It had been almost three weeks since I last skated—the longest time ever since I first started. Detach from a sport, even for a short amount of time, and you'll have to work twice as hard to get back into shape.

"Got it out of your system?" someone questioned behind my back, and I smiled when I recognized the voice.

Bea was here. Her hair, an assortment of tight curls, framed her heart-shaped face perfectly as she grinned back at me. She was wearing a pair of blue tights from a start-up brand we both loved (so much so I probably owned these tights in every possible color but had chosen black today to match my mood) because they made our butts look perky and had pockets.

What more could a girl ask for?

I flew to her, and she laughed when we collided and spun around.

"Not even close." I hugged her tighter, missing her after not seeing her for a week.

"You're out of shape, Fleur."

"I blame that Italian restaurant you took me to. I've been ordering from there three times a week." I pulled back to get a good look at her.

I felt like a fish out of water whenever Bea or my sister were away from me. They always gave the best advice, but because I couldn't talk to Aria about Killian, Bea had the misfortune of listening to me ramble.

"You should try to actually go there. The waiters are even more delicious than the food." She winked, throwing my fishtail over my shoulder. "It's a family-owned business, and the owners' sons do most of the work."

"I do have a weakness for Italians." I looped my arm through hers as we made our way down the ice.

I liked having peace and quiet while practicing. I wanted it to be just me and the music, but today we were just skating for fun. The ice rink was full enough that I didn't get to miss out on entertaining slips and tumbles but not so full you felt suffocated by people.

"If that was so, then you would've joined me when I offered you an all-paid vacation at Lake Como for a week," she argued, and I rolled my eyes at her.

Her parents owned a vacation home at Como, but she flew there a day after my move, and I couldn't very well abandon my stuff in boxes (although I was slow in sorting all of them out), and I couldn't leave Dusty on such short notice.

Cats didn't like it when their environment changed. I knew from experience. The first few nights after I'd adopted him, he'd pee anywhere but the litter box, even though the shelter claimed he was trained.

"The timing was off, Bea. Otherwise, you know I would've jumped at the chance. Who says no to Lake Como?"

She shrugged, a smirk forming on her face. "Anyway, I found a way to keep myself amused."

I raised a brow, and she gave me that little smile that told me the tea was piping hot. Bea had this annoying quirk where she'd never share her news over the phone and saved everything for when we met because she loved seeing my reactions live.

"Oh my God, you slut." I let her arm go, circling around her and poking her ribs. "Tell me everything."

"He's six feet tall, has curly hair, dreamy eyes, and plays soccer." She listed before she, too, started gliding backward as we neared the end of the rink. "He stopped in the middle of the road and offered me a ride home when I found no available taxi," Bea sighed dreamily, but I frowned at her gullibility.

Never get in a stranger's car.

That was like common sense 101.

"Girl, what happened to ordering an Uber or Lyft? Anything but getting in the car with a stranger?"

"Hey, I'm here, aren't I? I wasn't kidnapped." She zigzagged past me, throwing me a Cheshire grin over her shoulder. "Although, I do admit I wouldn't have been that mad if he kidnapped me."

I was sure I had the phrase *I think you're stupid* written all over my face, so I simply said, "Do you need me to say it?"

"Let me just say he knew how to use his dick—"

Bea's comeback was cut short when we passed by a horrified woman and her child. We both smiled apologetically at them, but she huffed at us like we were a bunch of hussies and pulled her kid along.

"That certainly changes things," I teased, a little jealous but mostly happy she had a good time during her vacation.

Bea gave me a rundown of everything that went down, from him giving her flowers every morning that one week they spent together, to the multiple Os he gave her every night.

I was so touch starved, I was eating up all the details.

During round number *I lost count*, around the rink, and after sharing her news, she asked, "What's up with you? What was that hysterical phone call in the middle of the night yesterday?"

Not one of my greatest moments.

After I barely pulled myself together in front of Killian and Mia, who had infuriatingly symmetrical features, I called Bea, fed up with all of my life's bullshit. I didn't have to give her many details for her to cut her trip short by a week, but they spilled out of me like a fountain now. Sentence after sentence, I told her what she'd missed and waited for her verdict with bated breath.

"What an asshat," Bea said, her face blank as she tried to absorb all the information I'd shoved down her throat. She shook her head, trying to catch my eyes, but I stared at my skates as she continued. "But fuck, Irena, maybe it was for the best that things didn't escalate more. You can deny it all you want, but I know you wouldn't be satisfied with just a kiss when it comes to Killian Astor. You've been crushing on him for forever now."

"I have not," I denied, even though my throat closed up.

I...liked him when I was younger. He was kind to me then. But I liked a lot of people. It didn't mean I had a crush on them.

"Really?" Bea asked, unimpressed, hair flying forward when someone whizzed past her. "Weren't you the one obsessing over every single word every time you guys talked, and weren't you also the one constantly complaining about how he stopped talking to you after your eighteenth birthday?"

I still remembered that day as if it was today, my eighteenth birthday. He texted me even before coming to my party and told me not to go too wild because I could actually go to prison now.

I'd worn a custom piece created by Aria for me that day. It was made to look like my skin, with strategically placed beads and crystals. It was quite the coming-out dress, but still tasteful, the perfect amount of sexy and elegant. His smile vanished the second he laid eyes on me in that dress. They darkened as if I'd somehow hurt him, and I felt the wall of frost building between us from that moment on.

"I wouldn't say constantly, and obsessing is a bit of a strong word, don't you think?"

"What I think is you should let this matter go." She suddenly stopped by rotating in place, her blades digging in the ice. Bea clutched my shoulders, needing me to understand her. "I don't want to see you hurt again. There's plenty of other fish in the sea. Why are you set on just this one?"

A question I asked myself every day and came up with no concrete answer.

I could sit around and list Killian's attributes all day. He was handsome, had that rugged bad boy persona that promised you a good time, but he was also intelligent, hardworking, and kind—when he wanted to be. Any girl would want him.

"It's human nature to want what you can't have." The lump stuck in my throat made it difficult to swallow, but I agreed with Bea. I needed to keep my distance and set my sights on someone else. Perhaps that would help. "But you're right. After last night, I'm not sure I ever want to see him again. I felt like I was transported back to that dressing room with Katrina and Daniel for a split second and barely held myself together."

My eyesight fogged up, and I blinked rapidly, willing the wetness that had gathered in the corners of my eyes to evaporate. Bea's concerned gaze was justified, because in all the years of our friendship, I didn't think I'd cried once, but lately, it was as if someone had poured a bunch of hormones in my food, and I couldn't stop the waterworks.

I didn't like crying in front of people. There was something so vulnerable, so weak about letting them witness what truly haunted you. Ever since I was a kid, I locked myself in my room whenever the urge to cry washed over me.

I heard a thump next to me, and I swiveled just in time to catch a young boy trying to hold on to his father as he fell, but ultimately, they slipped together. The dad knocked another person down before being spread on his back, and so forth, a mini domino chain of people unable to keep their balance formed.

I couldn't help it, I giggled as I watched them struggle to get up, dropping like flies again and again. I'd been there so many times in the past. Eyes all dried up now, I glanced at Bea, who was also trying to hold back her laughs because she was the type of person that didn't like putting people in awkward positions.

Tugging on her arm, I nodded toward an empty part of the railing where we could talk in peace. My feet were hurting from the skates, but I wasn't ready to leave yet. This place, the cold, it felt like my second home.

"Enough about him." Clutching the metal tight, Bea tried to change the subject, and I was grateful. I'd gotten what I needed to say out of my system. "What do you say we go out next Saturday? We're two hot, available girls in our early twenties. We should be partying it up every other night."

"Weren't you just gushing about the guy you met in Italy?" I raised a brow in question.

"I'm not averse to having a guy in every continent," she said with as much seriousness as she could muster. The joke went unmissed, but at the same time, Bea wasn't into lengthy relationships, and I guessed she had a point. We were young; now was the time for exploration, not getting hung up on one guy.

I shrugged because why the fuck not? I needed a night out. "All right, we might as well go out. I owe you a drink after getting you thrown out of Nicole's guest list. She didn't invite you because you're close to me. That's not fair."

"And you think I care about some dumb party?" She popped her hip, crossing her arms.

I mirrored her stance, not wanting her to hide her true feelings to make me feel better. Our entire circle of friends was invited but us. "When they're as outrageous and over the top as Nicole's, yes. She had actual elephants there last time, so people could take pictures with them. Who else does that?"

"That's not cute, that's animal abuse," she challenged.

"Besides, I heard she's keeping it small this year by renting out half of Marquee."

"Marquee? That's like the hottest nightclub at the moment." I frowned.

Only in Nicole's world would renting out half of a club like Marquee be considered "keeping it small."

Bea opened her mouth to reply but never got the chance when the sound of blades breaking the ice overpowered whatever she had to say. Not long after, we were sprayed with a wave of ice. It was an asshole move, one kids did for shits and giggles.

Bea gasped, hands flying to her hair to dust off the ice particles because it was prone to frizz, and I growled under my breath, turning to the perpetrator and yelling, "Hey, watch it!"

Once the snowy dust had settled and my field of vision became clear again, the hair on the back of my neck rose when I saw her.

Silver-haired and with eyes as blue as the arctic tundra, Katrina Federova looked every bit of the cold-ass bitch that she was. Her body was straight, like someone had shoved a rod up her ass, and she had a shit-eating grin on her face as she hooked her dead eyes on mine.

"Irena?" She clutched her chest, feigning surprise. "Sorry, I didn't see you there."

The world disappeared for me as I focused on my enemy since day number one. Her fucking my boyfriend was only the tip of the iceberg when it came to all the unpleasant experiences I had with this girl.

Ever since she'd moved to town at ten years old, I haven't known a moment of peace. From her tripping me up when- ever we practiced together, to stealing my clothes at a trip our trainers had taken us in a geothermal pool in Iceland, to claiming bribery was the only reason I'd won gold in the Olympic ladies singles category and so many other things I needed an unlimited supply of paper to list them all.

And here she was, yet again, ready to go again. I couldn't say I was a saint and hadn't done a single thing to her. Still, I never initiated, only retaliated, because I refused to be a doormat.

Shaking off Bea's hold on my arm, I glided toward Katrina, glancing at the small horizontal scar under her eye, and smiled. I'd accidentally given it to her with one of my blades after another one of her trips. She stiffened when she noticed where my attention strayed.

"I sincerely doubt that." My whisper was anything but soft.

"Do I look like I care?" She tried to sound nonchalant but failed, a tremble of excitement entering her tone.

"Actually, you do. Otherwise, you wouldn't have gone out of your way to get my attention." My eyes drifted over her shoulder to find some of her friends watching us with rapt attention. I looked back at her, relishing at the thinly veiled contempt I found burring into me. "What's going on, Katrina? You miss me?"

She'd had no access to me for a few months. I learned the hard way that the more you fed a snake, the bigger it became, so I stopped responding to her pettiness a while ago. Katrina lived to antagonize me. She was so obsessed with me that she couldn't go a day without seeing me, thinking about me, and plotting against me. It was like she was my ex and not Daniel.

Now that she stumbled across me, she couldn't let this opportunity go to waste.

"You always think so highly of yourself. The world only revolves around you, in that little head of yours, doesn't it?" She tried to provoke me, but I simply shrugged.

"Why shouldn't it? After all, I am your world."

She blinked at my response, like she didn't see it coming. A second of weakness was all she allowed, though, before laughing at me. "What the hell are you on about?"

"Come on now, Katrina, do you really think you would've gotten this far if it wasn't for your insatiable desire to best me in, well..." I slid even closer, enjoying the doubt blooming in her eyes. This wasn't going how she'd planned. "Anything?" I finished with a sarcastic taunt. "You're obsessed with me. Admit it."

Her answering glare could melt the ice beneath us. Still, she only allowed her unadulterated hatred to show for a mere second before feigning confusion like a skilled actress. "Ah, poor, Irena. I understand your words are coming from a place of hurt. I would be sad too if my boyfriend chose someone else over me."

The change of subject went unmissed. It was sloppy at best.

"Honey, I wouldn't consider spreading your legs for my sloppy seconds an achievement. By all means, have at him. I know what he has to offer, and it's not much," I said, lacing my tone with enough false sympathy to drive her up the wall.

Her nostrils flared, which looked funny because she had such a small nose. I bit my grin back as she attacked with no tact, purely looking to hurt me. "And yet, you're the one whose hole is dug deeper as the days go by. You lost your job, you lost your friends, and no one wants to be associated with you."

"Don't worry, I'll cry myself to sleep while hugging all my gold medals tonight." I refused to let my temper flare. "You think you've won because you stole what once was mine, but one thing you can never steal is talent. As much as you try, you'll always be second."

Her façade cracked like a rotten egg, showing me all the ugly emotions festering inside her when she rushed forward. I braced myself for a hit, but she pulled short when Bea appeared by my side, staring her down like she'd crush her in two seconds if she got any closer.

"Irena, let's go." I looked at her, but she kept her focus on Katrina as she spoke. "People are watching."

Katrina cackled. "Your friend is right. Hide like you've done the past several months."

"Enjoy your time in the spotlight, Kat," I warned, even as Bea started dragging me away. "It won't last long."

CHAPTER EIGHT
IRENA

"Irena, we need to leave."

As expected, Bea started protesting the second she discovered where I was taking her tonight. She thought I was keeping it a surprise to build up excitement but was sorely disappointed when she got out of our Uber and saw Marquee's sign a neon purple, illuminating the shadowed pavement with its brightness.

The only thing that got her to agree to at least go in was when I mentioned that her boobs looked phenomenal in her red bodycon dress and that it would be a shame to let such an outfit go to waste. Yet, the second she figured out why I wanted to come here, she started freaking out again, ever the non-confrontational person.

Half the club, my ass.

Nicole Ivanovksy didn't do anything half-assed. She'd rented out the entire VIP section and left some space for the rest of us mortals to worship at her feet. Quite literally, they were in an elevated part of the club. People from my social circle were packed in the space around the DJ's booth, most of them lounging in black leather couches in their thousand-dollar outfits, showing off their pearly teeth while fake smiling to each other and flashing their expensive watches and jewelry with exaggerated hand gestures.

Nicole wasn't the best skater, but she was the biggest attention whore.

Everything was so neon here, my head hurt.

There were tiny squares with neon blue and purple lights on the walls and ceilings, the chandeliers were grand and probably a hundred pounds each, and there were girls with nothing but oversized T-shirts and super, *super* short shorts dancing provocatively on stage.

The interior was as exaggerated and over the top as Nicole was.

I hadn't spotted her yet, but I was sure she'd come out of the woodwork soon.

"You can go if you don't feel up to the task, Bea," I egged her on after posting a selfie of myself, making sure the club's logo could be seen on the bar behind me. It was my first reappearance on my socials after months of silence, but what Katrina had said motivated me.

I was done hiding and letting others tell *my* story with their skewed narrative.

"What is the task exactly? What are we doing at Nicole's party uninvited?" Bea tugged my hand down, forcing me to look at her.

"Stealing her moment. Besides, she rented *half* the club. We deserve to be here as much as Scarface over there."

How did you get through to a person with narcissistic tendencies? Make them feel neglected and forgotten. This was her party, but I would be the star of it. Everyone would be talking about me tonight, and I'd come prepared in my

August Getty gold mini-dress. It elevated my tiny chest from barely there to *hello there*, made my legs look even longer, and shimmered like crazy in this kind of lighting.

I'd raised the bar and hem tonight because while Nicole's only sin was abandoning me to play nice with my ex, he was also here, and I'd show him just how little I thought of him. Killing two birds with one stone.

There was only one hitch to my otherwise carefully curated plan. I was yet to find the stone that would help me take them down, i.e., a guy that would turn everyone's heads.

"You know they won't see it that way, and that's a rude way to address a stranger." Bea glanced at the guy I'd called out, intending to have him face me so I could get a better look.

He was situated a few stools down from us, conversing with an equally hot friend of his. They were both buff, tall, and dark and had an aura of danger that reeled you in. This guy's biggest selling point was the scar running across his left cheek, an imperfection but one that added to his allure and memorability.

Sometimes you had to be rude to get what you desired, and he proved my theory right by scanning the crowd around him to get to the source of the voice.

"I don't care how they see it," I spoke louder than usual, aiding his process of locating yours truly. His head snapped in my direction, and his thumb ran over his lips as he studied me. I held his gaze for longer than socially acceptable before addressing Bea again, hoping he took the bait. "There's nothing they can do to me anymore, but plenty I can do to them."

"Like what?" she scoffed.

"Hitting them where it hurts most. They are motivated

by fame and fortune. Take the spotlight away from them, and they have nothing left."

"And how do you plan to do that?"

"By making the night about myself," I replied with a healthy dose of self-assurance. I'd had enough of deflecting, and Amani had signed off on it too. Albeit reluctant, I was handling things alone. She preferred me getting myself out there rather than doing nothing.

"I don't like this." Bea frowned, leaning against the bar and opening up my field of vision. Scarface had finally gotten off his ass and was moving our way with a swagger in his step, stopping to greet the people who talked to him along the way. All he was missing was a cigar because I swear he had the Al Pacino look down to a T in his white dress shirt and black slacks.

"You're about to." I leaned in, nodding my head over her shoulder ever so slightly. "Scarface and his friend are headed our way."

"Really?" She perked up, fixing her dress lower and squeezing her tits together.

I gave her an envious once-over and whispered, "Slut."

She smiled sweetly at me. "You're just jealous because your tits are the size of a slightly overweight pubescent boy."

She wasn't wrong.

Still, that didn't mean I'd let her insult my girls. At least they were perky. Using the pointy end of my silver heels, I hit her shin lightly, but she took it there by complaining loudly.

"Ow!" she whined, hitting me right back.

"Ow!" I couldn't help but mirror her whine as pain spread up my leg.

And at precisely that moment, the highly sought-after

Scarface showed up next to us, a smirk plastered on his full lips as he glanced between us. He seemed more formidable up close. One of his biceps was thrice the size of mine, and his gray eyes held a coolness that sent shivers springing down my arms despite the easy-going stance of his body.

The other man bumped up behind him, his light-colored hair taking on a blue hue when he stood directly under one of the neon light squares. I didn't pay him any mind, keeping my focus on Scarface. I'd had enough of blond men traipsing over my heart like they owned it.

"Ladies, ladies." His lips split with a smile as he placed a large arm on each of our shoulders, glancing between us. The scent of cedar wood overpowered my nostrils as I was brought closer to him, a welcome break from Killian's milder colognes. "There's no need to fight. There's plenty of me to go around."

"Cool it, Don Juan," I scolded light-heartedly, shaking his hold off despite enjoying the heaviness of it. He slipped his other hand off Bea, waiting for further instructions, which I provided. "Buy us a drink or four, and then you may touch the goods."

"You hear that, man? She's not drunk enough to lower her standards for you." The blond guy laughed, swooping in for Bea with a charming grin and extending his hand. "I'm Nicolas."

"Bea," she replied, going in for a handshake, but of course, he was having none of that and brought the back of her hand to his lips.

"Extremely pleased to meet you, Bea," he said to my rosy-cheeked friend, fitting himself on the empty stool next to her as they launched into a natural conversation.

In the meantime, Scarface followed Nicolas's lead, and

together they showed their expertise in the divide-and-conquer technique by keeping us individually entertained. This was their shtick, I could tell. It went far too smoothly for them to be doing it for the first time.

"Is my friend, right, *piccolina*? Am I not to your liking?" Scarface asked as he twisted my stool to face him in one smooth move.

He had somehow managed to signal the elusive bartender over while I was too busy watching the exchange between Bea and Nicolas. I let him order for me as I thought over his nickname.

It seemed like God had listened to me rave about Italians. Yet, when comparing it to being literally called the Queen of Hell, I found it lacking. It was infuriating how even when Killian wasn't here, my brain found a way to remind me of his existence.

"I don't judge people based on looks." I focused on the matter at hand.

There was no more Killian for me.

He'd knocked on my door every afternoon for a week straight, and I managed to stay put even when he threatened to break it down if I didn't open it. I pretended not to be there, and he ultimately settled against the destruction of private property, though I'm sure if he was certain I was on the other side, he wouldn't have given a shit.

He seemed hell-bent on talking to me, but I was holding on to my promise this time.

No more Killian.

"Based on what, do you fuck 'em?"

I was so deep in my thoughts, I couldn't manage to control my reaction to Scarface's question. I choked on the first sip of the whiskey sour the bartender had dropped off seconds ago, and he smiled, pleased with himself at catching me off guard.

Bea threw me a glance over her shoulder and I nodded at her, my answer that I was all good. I cleared my throat as I held Scarface's amused gaze. "Now, if I answered that, it would make it too easy for you."

Impressed by my not shying away like a blushing virgin, he scooched my chair forward, bringing me closer to him, and said, "I like you, *piccolina*. You have a mouth on you."

"I'll like you more if you stop calling me *piccolina*. It's creepy," I volunteered.

"You know what it means?" He raised his brows, impressed.

"Little one, of course, I do. I prefer *bella, tesoro, cara*." I flexed my Italian, my sister's mafia romance book recommendations coming in handy for once. Going in for the kill, I leaned in and whispered conspiratorially, "Especially in bed."

The buzzing in my purse told me that my post was published, and Daniel and his ass kissers would put two and two together and realize I was here in about five minutes.

"*Cara mia.*" He tested the words on his tongue, which sounded divine with the right accent. The corners of his eyes crinkled. "The nicknames I reserve for the bedroom aren't so...PG-13."

I stumbled again, blinking several times to ensure I'd heard him right.

The twist of his lips told me I had, and I exhaled, wondering why the fuck the tingle I'd just felt was so minuscule. If *he who shall not be named* had said this to me, I would've been trying to convince myself why jumping his bones would be a bad idea.

Yet here I was, wanting to get this show on the road just to extract my revenge.

"Color me intrigued." I pursed my lips, not knowing what to call him by, and asked, "What's your name? I've been calling you Scarface in my mind for a while now."

"Mietitore. Luca Mietitore." He smiled with all his teeth, as if pleased that I had noticed his scar. It was probably a big selling point for him with the ladies. He did a little bow. "Happy to satisfy your *aroused* curiosity anytime."

"Irena," I offered in return, sans my last name, because this wasn't a Bond movie.

"Pleasure to make your acquaintance, Irena." He licked his lips, staring at my legs when I uncrossed them like he wanted us to be way more than acquaintances.

"I have a feeling we're going to be much more than that," I commented, downing my drink to help make this easier, and looked toward the direction Bea had disappeared in. A Rihanna song blasted from the speakers, one of her favorite artists, so of course, she dragged Nicolas over to the dance floor.

I had to get out there too.

I could see some of my ex-friends gossiping with each other and scanning the crowd, but none of them had spotted me.

Luca didn't seem like the type to hit the dance floor, but I tried my luck. "Do you want to dance—"

"Much more than what?" someone interrupted, and the hair on the back of my neck raised. A shiver of awareness worked its way down my spine, and I slammed my mouth shut as disbelief hit me.

CHAPTER NINE

IRENA

I t couldn't be.

Killian Astor was not, in fact, standing right next to me.

Astropolis was fucking big. Stumbling across someone you knew in public was a rare occurrence.

Were the stars aligning in order to annoy me? Or was Killian Astor the one behind everything? After all, we lived next to each other, and Bea and I got ready at my place. How difficult could it have been for him to find out where I was going tonight?

Eyes narrowed, I swiveled in place, directing all the heat packed in my eyes at him, hoping that I was somehow mistaken and Killian wasn't here. But, of course, why would God go easy on me? Not only was he very much present, but he was also seemingly furious when he had no right to be.

And at the same time, he was as handsome as the prince of fucking hell in his all-black outfit and shiny silk shirt, half buttoned up as if he was debating going out without one at all. I didn't blame him. Girls and boys alike stopped to stare at the rigid muscles and colorful tattoos peeking out underneath—ones I actively tried not to pay attention to because Lord knew I'd start obsessing over their meaning, and there was enough about this man that had me hooked already.

"Are you following me?" I seethed, and my body wound up as tight as a knot. Luca's gaze bounced between us, confusion evident between his knitted brows, his fuckboy persona coming to a pause.

Killian gave me a look so cold it could freeze over hell, and my heart picked up its pace. Whether it was in excitement or fear, I wasn't sure. I was only certain about the anger pumping through my veins.

A vein popped on his forehead as he answered through clenched teeth. "I should be the one asking you that question. You're the one that keeps showing up where I'm at, not vice versa."

I exhaled in an attempt to remain level-headed.

Of course, he'd deny it.

"Trust me, you're the last person I want to see," I retorted, and before this could go any further, Luca cut in.

"You two know each other?"

Our connection broke as we averted our eyes to him, and I was secretly thankful because I could breathe more easily. I opened my mouth to tell him Killian was a crazy stalker because Scarface looked like he could knock him down, and maybe I wanted to see him hurt, but Killian beat me to it.

"She's my—"

"Neighbor," I finished for him, giving him the side eye. No one tonight could find out who he was to me. "I'm his neighbor, unfortunately," I repeated.

Killian's face hardened as he gravitated toward me,

pinning Luca with a glare, and added, "And also off the market."

My eyes widened as surprise shot through me at his statement. He raised a brow at me as if willing me to dispute it. The pendant around his neck shone under a beam of light, and I felt the urge to squeeze the chain around his neck.

How dare he do this to me again after fucking Mia?

"Says who?" I gave an uppity sniff and turned back to Scarface, determined to simply ignore Killian's existence because, if anything, he was persistent. Whatever. He could stare while I acquainted myself with Luca's body. "I'm very much single and ready to mingle."

Luca, who had been watching our exchange with an amused grin, tilted his head at Killian in a *well, what do you have to say about that?* manner. I bristled at his lack of care and reconsidered *mingling* with Scarface. He seemed way too at ease with letting Killian stake his claim on me, and well, I liked my men a touch on the protective side.

"Remember what you said about Yazmin?" Killian asked, and the familiarity with which he addressed Scarface had me straightening. *They'd talked before?* Killian rolled his shoulders back, widening his stance, and went in for the kill. "I'll go the extra mile and break your legs before cutting them."

My nails dug into the edge of my seat as questions swirled in my brain.

Who the hell was Yazmin? How did they know each other? And why the fuck did a shudder work its way down my body at the threat?

I was so bemused I chose to stay out of it, observing as Luca raised his hands in an *I surrender* motion and held my breath at his following conclusion.

"So she's the one you wouldn't talk about," Luca told a stone-faced Killian, and my brain was stuck on the fact that Killian had mentioned me to someone as Luca grabbed his beer and hopped off his stool, eyes sparkling like he'd discovered the cure to cancer as he bid me farewell in his own unique way. "I'm sorry, *Cara mia*, but I don't fuck with my friend's girls."

"I am not his girl!" I yelled in a knee-jerk reaction, but the music was so high it was akin to speaking at a normal volume. Scarface didn't linger to listen to me, though, and slapped Killian's back on his way out.

I gritted my teeth, shutting my eyes to regain my cool.

There was so much to unpack, I wasn't sure where to begin. Or if I even wanted to. I came here with a purpose, and I was being majorly side-tracked by none other than Killian fucking Astor, who, up until two months ago, would've fled the premises if he caught word of me being near.

He sighed as if waiting for me to get over my tantrum, and I finally met his magnetic stare, drilling holes into the side of my face before taking a detour downwards. It was as if he was actually noticing me for the first time tonight now that he'd gotten what he wanted, running his gaze leisurely over my body like taking the time to map out every cutout and crease of my dress.

"He's your friend?" The interest lacing my voice concealed the storm that was yet to come.

"Known him since elementary school," he confirmed.

It was just my luck to attract one of his closest friends.

I blew out an angry breath, throwing my head up to the ceiling, and let my frustration at his surprise appearance bubble to the surface and into my voice. "I hate you. I truly hate you. You cockblocked me twice in a week. What is your excuse this time?"

He glowered at a man that bumped into him from behind before explaining, "Luca is not the man for you. He's dangerous."

Tired of hearing excuses, I jumped off the stool. My feet hurt from the pressure applied to them by my heels, but the anger at his desire to control me overshadowed all else, and my claws came unsheathed in an instant.

"What's dangerous is you believing I'll allow you to police my life for one second longer. Last I checked, you're nothing to me. You can't tell me what or *who* to do like I never told you!"

A muscle in his jaw flexed as I pointed at him. I was so done with his shit he sensed it and caught my elevated wrist, pressing it against his partially bare chest before I had a chance to run off. I tried to pull back, but he wouldn't allow it, his tone too obscure to read as he continued pestering me.

"Is this about Mia?"

My lips turned down at the mention of her name, and I was pretty certain I looked like I wanted to strangle him, judging by the dark laugh he released.

I wouldn't feed into his plan, though. He couldn't get through to me in my apartment, so he followed me all the way here. Well, he'd be sad to find out I wasn't willing to listen to him anywhere else, either.

"Let me go. I want to go dance." I ignored his question.

"Then dance with me," he offered.

I had to snigger. "In your dreams."

"You either dance with me, or you don't dance at all. Which one is it going to be, Irena?" My heart beat in my ears when he nodded toward the VIP section after I remained silent. "I can cause a hell of a scene, and I don't think you want that right now."

I discreetly glanced beyond the frenzied crowd to the elevated area and noticed my plan had worked like clockwork. Whispers and looks flowed in my direction like booze at a frat party. Obviously, I wasn't the only one who'd detected the increased attention I was getting.

On top of everything else, Killian also had to be hyperaware of his environment. It surprised me, and it didn't. According to old rumors, he used to get into fights nearly every day when he was younger. Looking out for danger had to be second nature to him.

I sucked on my teeth, realizing that I was surrounded by enemies on both sides, and Bea was off somewhere with Mr. Hot and Mysterious.

I had to pick a lesser evil to be civil at, and while it hurt my pride, I had no other option but to reason with Killian.

"I have a plan, and you're hindering it," I whispered through a painful-looking smile.

"What's the plan?"

I rolled my head, straining my neck from side to side. "Make Daniel think I've moved on and am deliriously happy."

That would get them talking.

"Then include me in it. I can help out with that."

I laughed, but it turned sour when he didn't crack a smile, his blank face telling me he was serious.

How could he believe I could fake being happy with him when he made it a personal goal to anger me all the time?

"No." My voice came out high pitched.

"Yes," he insisted.

I considered denying him again, but I knew he wouldn't

give up. If anything, he was persistent. He'd just tell me no again in that lord-and-master tone of his, and I'd just be wasting time.

I had to get this show on the road, and if that meant having to endure Killian's touch one more time, so be it.

He recognized the second I gave in, self-satisfaction sitting atop his proud shoulders when I flattened my balled-up palms on his chest. I leaned into him, our noses almost brushing as I whispered, "If you ruin this for me, I swear I'll hurt you, Killian."

His arm migrated around my waist as he ushered us to the dance floor, his mouth at my ear as he said with a chuckle, "Darling, that excites me more than it frightens me."

I let him lead me, yet held on to that thread of irritation. We found a spot in the crowd, and Killian's stiff front pressed against my back, both his hands grabbing the sides of my hips as we began moving with the music.

Dancing with an audience wasn't anything novel for me. Figure skating was like that, along with some added tricks. The pure attention was exhilarating, calling to my lack of modesty, and right now, I could feel a thousand pairs of eyes on us burning with jealousy as I dropped my head on Killian's shoulder, my hair brushing his cheek as I taunted him. "What happened? Did Mia not satisfy you enough, now you're back for round two of humiliating Irena?"

Pleasure and pain battled for dominance on his face as our bodies swayed to a pop song I couldn't even name. It was like I was here, but also so attuned to all the spots where Killian and I connected that I couldn't function properly on my own.

My pulse leaped when he traced the curve of my cheek-bone with his lips, his words sinking into my skin. "Irena, that wasn't my plan. I didn't know she was going to show up. I forgot I was even supposed to go out with her."

"But you didn't miss the opportunity to fuck her." I kept my voice soft, taking a good look around us. There were plenty of beautiful women here tonight, some with their partners, others dancing provocatively in order to find a partner. Killian would have his pick of the litter. "I wonder who you'll take home after I get you hot and bothered again. Tell me something. Did you imagine you were fucking me when you had your dick in her?"

I was so hell-bent on putting him down, I didn't realize I'd crossed an imaginary line between us until it was too late. We were already teetering on the edge of not coming back. Still, words held power, and I'd just voiced out a hidden aspect of our relationship that shouldn't fucking exist.

Killian froze at my choice of words like he was physically holding himself back from blurting out something he really wanted to say for the sake of keeping his cool.

"Is that jealousy I smell in your tone, Lilith?" He bunched the front of my dress out of frustration when I thoroughly rubbed myself against every part of him but made sure to keep my ass from fully pressing against his crotch, instead teasing him with accidental brushes and prolonged touches.

The placement of his hands haunted me.

I was torn between wanting him to go higher and relieve some of the tension that was building under my chest the longer we danced, like we were one step away from tearing each other's clothes off or lower to ease the heat pooling between my thighs.

"Hardly, it's pity. I have you wound up so tight, you have to get yourself off to the idea of me," I spat out my venom, enjoying this more than I thought I would. "Do you think I'm stupid, Killian? That I didn't notice how hard you were simply by being near me. I've seen some erections in my life, and yours isn't anything to write home about."

I was lying, but he deserved it for the steamroller approach he'd adopted as of late. Another song began to play, the beat of the music doing nothing to mask Killian's thoroughly entertained chuckle and my annoyed sigh. It was almost impossible to get through this man's skin, and not for my lack of trying either. He was so confident. No matter how hard I tried to make him mad by insulting him, it didn't work.

"I don't think you're stupid. As a matter of fact, I have no problem admitting I'm hard as a rock right now." He twisted me around, his lower abdomen squeezing against my navel and his indeed hard dick digging into my stomach. My breath left my body in a shattered gasp, and his polarizing blue eyes missed nothing as his fingers eased over the arch of my ass. "But let's not pretend like I wouldn't find you soaked for my *less than impressive erection* if I slipped my fingers underneath that pretty dress of yours, Irena."

I swallowed when his thigh settled between my legs, so hot I feared I was coming down with a fever. He had shifted the tables, and I was straining to keep up as our bodies crushed into each other like violent waves, proving that the length of his cock was nothing short of impressive with how much of my stomach it covered.

If this was how he danced, I could only imagine how he fucked.

"I might like you. I might like toying with you. I guess you'll never find out," I breathed.

"Is that a challenge?" He purred, and I looked around us,

noting that he'd somehow maneuvered us into the edge of the dance floor. We were the farthest you could get from the VIP area, but I still had a very clear view of my ex-friends over Killian's shoulder, watching us with thinly veiled interest every so often.

"You wouldn't dare do anything here." I rolled my eyes, dismissing him.

"Do you put it beyond me?" His question was a growl that lowered into a threat. Those clever fingers of his were on my thigh now, his other arm wrapped around me like a steel band, eradicating any space between our bodies. Every twist of my waist hiked up my dress, and he took advantage of it, caressing the crease right below my ass cheek. My breath hitched, and his knowing eyes missed nothing as I ceased moving, paralyzed by his touch. "How little you know me."

I jumped when his whole hand made its way beneath the fabric covering my pelvis, thumb running down the front of my panties before stopping right over my clit. A wicked smile ignited on his face when he noticed how damp the material was under the pad of his finger. Pins and needles ghosted over my skin when he continued to stroke my hyper-sensitive flesh through my underwear.

"Killian," I warned when I found myself unable to close my legs so he wouldn't be able to move his hand.

A fire had already begun stoking inside me, and as much as my head tried to tell me that we were heading in the wrong direction, my body was enjoying the ride to the fullest.

"Weren't you the one that called me Lucifer?" Killian's gaze darkened, and the cool air that suddenly flooded my pussy when he pushed my panties to the side was replaced by his fingers in mere seconds, touching and prodding like he was an actual demon doing very fiendish acts in public. "I think it's about time you learned how evil I can get, especially if you keep pushing me."

My nails dug so hard into his shoulders I was surprised his shirt didn't rip. I barely managed to keep a guttural moan from escaping my throat when he gathered some of the wetness that had pooled between my thighs and smeared it across my folds, paying special attention to my little bundle of nerves.

I hissed at the pure pleasure that rained over my body like a scalding shower, and it was hell trying to keep my composure when Killian Astor, the man that had owned my mind and was the frequent star of my sexual fantasies ever since I first met him, was fingering me in public, a few feet away from my ex.

"You need to stop." I strung my sentence together half-heartedly, which he regarded with little interest, continuing to drive me mad with his slow exploration of my private parts. His thumb kept torturing my clit while the rest of his fingers teased the edge of my entrance, circling around it but never going in. "P-people are watching."

"Your asshole of an ex can only see my back, the people around us are higher than a kite, and there's nothing but a wall behind you. The people that *are* watching are seeing exactly what you wanted them to."

He tore down my argument and left no crumbs. I flicked my eyes to the VIP section again, noting that Daniel had moved closer to the railing, Katrina talking a mile an hour next to him, but his eyes kept venturing down toward me. How Killian knew what was going on behind his back was a mystery to me, but I didn't question it.

The rush of feeling their envy lick at my skin made it even harder to control my ecstasy, and I finally let a moan rip free when he pushed a finger inside me and then a second one immediately after stretching me so much it burned. It got lost in the hum of the crowd, but soon thereafter, more strained sounds followed as Killian began moving his fingers in and out of me.

I was so wet my arousal trickled down my thighs and clung to Killian's knuckles, but he didn't seem put off by it. On the contrary, he groaned under his breath and pressed a kiss on the side of my face like he needed more physical contact in order to keep his urges down, speaking in hot, dark words against my skin. "Just like I thought, as wet as the motherfucking ocean, even after I left you and ran right into Mia's open arms...*and legs.*"

At his statement, the last bit of my withering control snapped in place again like a rubber band, recuperating after getting stretched out. I clawed my way up his neck, grabbed a fistful of his hair in my hands, and pulled until he cried out in pain.

God, how I despised him and his ability to flush my brain by simply pestering me until I gave in. But I didn't stay with Daniel even after he begged me for days on end to take him back, and I wasn't going to start anything with Killian if this was how he treated me from the start. No matter how much my knees went weak for him, I'd always place self-respect above all else.

"Let me go." I wiggled in his hold, and even though I wanted to feel nothing but disgust, I couldn't when I inadvertently caused his fingers to drive deeper into me.

I paused my squirming almost immediately, cursing him for his long digits because they were so far inside me, I was close to throwing up. Not out of nausea, out of the pure bliss only an orgasm could provide.

And I couldn't let that happen.

I *wouldn't* let that happen, not after he'd bragged about fucking Mia.

I pulled his hair again, and he growled so loud I thought a dog had broken into the club. "Cut it out. Nothing fucking happened with Mia."

I instantly stopped, yet the war of emotions still waged in me. My fingers flexed in his hair, and I massaged his scalp absentmindedly as my brain tried to play catch up. "But you just said—"

"What you *believed*. The worst, of course." He punctuated the sentence by inserting a third finger, and I gasped so loud I captured the curiosity of the man standing closest to us. With one glare from Killian, though, he was off, disappearing into the throng. Killian turned back to me, his possessive gaze making his eyes burn as blue as the hottest fire. "I invited her in because I owed her that much, but if you'd spied for a little longer, you would've seen her leave five minutes later, and I'm pleased to announce that I last a lot longer than that."

He penetrated me after every word, *in, out, in, out, in, out,* and I was barely holding on. If it wasn't for his arm supporting me, I would've melted into a puddle on the floor. It was like a huge weight was lifted off my shoulders, and simultaneously another one was building low in my belly, the early licks of an intense release. There was music, flashing lights, laughter, shouts, and talk all around us, yet all I could focus on was Killian Astor and his magical fingers. There was no ounce of fear about being caught in my mind, and that should concern me.

Nothing happened between them, and that knowledge made me so happy I could kiss him.

Correction, I *really* wanted to kiss him.

"I don't spy," I protested, biting my lip while doing so when he rolled his thumb up and down my clit with the perfect amount of pressure and speed.

"Are you sure you want to lie to me right now? I hold your release on the tips of my fingers, *literally*." He hooked them inside me as if to make a point, and white dots spread in my vision.

"Whatever, as—" I started, but had to take a moment to breathe when his light scruff scratched against my jaw as he traced my earlobe with his teeth. A low chuckle escaped him at my responsiveness, and even though I was almost at the edge of coming, I got what I wanted to say out. "As if you don't do it too. You always seem to know when Colin is near, and don't tell me you being here is a coincidence. It's like having my own personal stalker."

"If you're this eloquent, it means I'm not doing my job well enough." He glossed over my accusation, and despite his words, his pace was fast enough to get me going, but not rough enough to take me there.

I had a feeling it was intentional.

Like he liked seeing me at his mercy.

"Killian, being thrown out for public indecency is not my idea of a good time. Make it quick," I panted, and then appealed to his gracious side by adding, "I'm begging you."

His chest shook with a rumble when I implored him to make me come. My legs were nothing but jelly at this point, I'd lost count of how many songs had changed, and his arm had to hurt from holding all my weight. Even my head was getting heavy, and my mind, hazy by the sensations.

"Perfection takes time," he spoke into my ear. "You just need a little more patience."

"Perfection is unattainable," I goaded him, and for all his intelligence, he was still a man, and rising to challenges was his second nature.

He upped the strength with which he penetrated me, hooking his fingers again in a *come hither* motion, putting them directly against my G-spot, and that was all I needed to explode. To keep myself from letting half the club know what we were doing, I shoved my head into the crook of Killian's neck, biting my tongue so hard I tasted blood.

The music's beat and my body's pulse became one and the same as noise distorted in my ears, giving way to an all-consuming pound that made my body quiver as I rode through the waves of my orgasm. It felt like betrayal and destiny at the same time, two wrongs coming together to make a right.

"You were saying?" It was his time to gloat over me, and the only answer I could give in return was a pitiful moan when he removed his hand from inside of me, fixing my panties in place at the same time. "Yeah, that sounds about right."

"Quit taunting me," I ordered weakly after regaining some of my strength back. My very core missed him, even though he'd stripped me of his touch mere seconds ago. I raised my head to catch him already staring at me like he, too, was ready for a second round, but I shook my head, the gravity of what could happen if we allowed our emotions to control us hitting me all at once. "This is so wrong, Killian."

"I know," he murmured, smoothing the hand he used to hold me down my hair, yet he didn't sound regretful, and that knowledge filled me with so much elation.

It could be the aftershocks of my orgasms influencing my thinking, but would it be so wrong to fool around with Killian? Get this crazy lust that drove us mad out of our systems?

No one would have to know.

No one but us.

I opened my mouth to voice my thoughts, but movement from beyond Killian's shoulder distracted me, and I slammed it shut again as I tried to see who was making a beeline for us. Nervous butterflies swarmed my belly when my vision focused enough for me to realize who it was, and I immediately looked at a confused Killian again, who'd caught my momentary distraction.

"I'm about to make it a little less right," I whispered enthusiastically.

"Wha—" The space between his brows creased, but I didn't give him any time to process before I grabbed his face and brought my lips to his.

Killian was stiff at first, disoriented, but I kept up the pace, and he gave in with little effort, taking over the kiss like pirates raiding a ship and causing havoc on board. His taste, a mix of bourbon and mint, bloomed on my tongue when he pried my lips open, making me drunk on the feel of him. All that hard muscle of his torso rubbed against my chest, making me press in closer, giving in to what I'd been craving for so long it seemed like forever.

The kiss started out slow at first, like the shimmer on the water in a river of moonlight, and gradually turned frenzied, like a falling star burning through the night sky. I couldn't get enough of him, the way his tongue caressed mine like we were old lovers reunited after years apart. I nipped his bottom lip when he didn't let me come up for air, and in a move that left me breathless, he slapped my ass. I squealed in his mouth, and he swallowed that sound down too.

"Irena? Irena?" An intruding voice broke through the haze, and I gulped in mouthfuls of air when Killian released my mouth. His forehead was an assortment of perplexed lines, but realization dawned on him when I mouthed Daniel's name.

For the first time in a while, I saw his character change right before my eyes, his eyes growing heavy, mouth upturned on one side, and body bulking up. He looked like vengeance personified, and I was grateful it was him sharing this moment with me because if there was anyone that could put Daniel Gregory in his place, it was Killian mother-fucking Astor.

A question lingered in Kill's eyes, and I let my hands fall by my sides, nodding once. It was all the confirmation he needed to draw me under his left arm as we both slowly faced the bane of my existence.

The reason I'd lost my job.

The reason the world was laughing at me.

He stood there in all of his asshole glory, clad in a pastel green tux, the color complementing his tanner skin tone and black hair impeccably well. Vanity rolled off him in waves from the way he positioned his body, and while his personality was shitty at best, it was his looks and arrogance that had reeled me in at first.

Nicole was the one that'd called out my name, though. She'd accompanied him on his trip down to peasant level, it seemed, her monogram Christian Dior dress sticking out like a sore thumb amid more modestly dressed individuals.

Her eyes widened when they fell on my face and then the arm over my shoulders. Interest sparked in her browns, and a fake smile graced her lips as she stripped Killian in her mind and repeated my name again. "Irena! Oh my God, I knew it was you."

"Nicole." I acknowledged her, noticing the way Daniel stiffened at the sound of my voice. "What are you doing here?"

Her head snapped in my direction as they both stepped closer to avoid getting trampled by the horde of dancing bodies behind them. "You mean, you don't know?"

"Am I supposed to?" I raised a cool brow when they got a mere three feet away from us.

A frown marred her face at my aloof stance, and I wondered if she believed I was so much of a doormat I'd worship at her feet when she quite literally cast Bea and me aside for clout.

"It's my birthday," she said purposefully. "I'm celebrating it at Marquee as a favor to the owner. He's my dad's friend, and obviously, a day like this is guaranteed to receive a ton of press."

"Ah," I exclaimed, not bothering with any birthday wishes, instead looking up at Killian, who was too busy shooting glares at Daniel with a warm smile on my face. "Well, we're just here because I was in the mood to dance, and even though this is not my boyfriend's scene, he can never say no to me."

Killian shook his head at me with a strained smile as if saying, *what the hell are you involving me in,* and I flashed my teeth, replying, *you better play along if you know what's good for you.*

"Was that what it was? Dancing?" It was Daniel that spoke up this time, his questions directed at Killian as if he was the one he had a bone to pick with. "'Cause it sure as hell looked a lot more than that."

Brief surprise registered on Killian's face at Daniel's British accent, and I remembered I'd failed to mention that Daniel was originally from the UK but had moved to the States five years ago to advance his career.

Before Killian could undoubtedly rip into him, though, I acted as if I'd lost something, patting the front of my dress and scanning the floor as I worried, "I think I lost them."

"What?" Daniel took the bait, and my lips tipped with a grin as I pinned him with a stare.

"All the fucks I give about your opinion."

Nicole rolled her eyes at my antics, used to them, but Killian laughed out loud, and warmth unfurled inside my chest at the joyful sound.

Daniel didn't let the moment live on for long, though, and addressed Kill through strained teeth. "And who might you be?"

Unbothered, Killian dragged me along as he extended his free hand to Daniel for a handshake, saying, "The lucky bastard who got to *more than dance* with a beautiful girl."

I marveled at his friendly greeting, and not one to miss an opportunity to establish dominance, Daniel took his hand, probably planning to squeeze it to the point of causing nerve damage. It never got to that, though, because a few beats after their hands came together, Daniel's face twisted in disgust, and he retracted his as if he'd been burnt.

"Ew," he whined, shaking out his palm. "Ever heard of washing your hands, mate? They're fucking sticky."

My shoulders snapped at that, my spine jerking upright when I put two and two together and worked out *why* Killian's hand was sticky...because it had been shoved three fingers deep in my pussy not too long ago, and I was soaked like crazy. My cheeks burned with a fierce blush, and I pinched Killian's back to get his attention, but he paid me no mind as he went for the jugular.

"Maybe you should've gotten yours dirty more often. You know, actually kept your girl satisfied instead of making up for your lackluster sex life by hooking up with randos for a cheap thrill."

Everyone went silent after Killian tore into Daniel like that.

Even I held my breath, and I wasn't even on the receiving end of the fire. What I was, though, was extremely turned on because, except for my father, no other man had gone to bat for me like that before.

Killian jumped at the chance, though, and enjoyed the interaction a whole ton if the avenging grin on his lips was anything to go by. He was begging for a fight and all to aid my cause.

But I'd gotten what I'd come here for tonight, and satisfying Killian's bloodlust wasn't part of the plan. I'd planted the seeds, and now I—we needed to leave on a high note.

I patted Killian's stomach, resting my hand on his tight-as-a-drum abs as I said, "Let it go, babe. He's not worth it."

Disappointment emanated from Killian when he grasped that I wasn't going to let this get out of hand, and he made sure to curl his lip at Daniel as he started for the direction of the bar with me under his wing.

Daniel jumped in before we could be on our merry way through, desperate to get a word in with me.

"Irena, wait! I need to talk yo—"

Killian pushed on his chest when he got in too close, and we attracted the eyes of at least a dozen people around us with the commotion. Nicole gasped when Daniel flailed back as if Killian had punched him instead, no doubt one of the craziest things to ever go down in her prim and proper life.

"What you need to do is disappear before I make you wish you were never born," Killian threatened, the veins on his neck jumping out and his broad shoulders spanning out even more. He looked so formidable, I got a flash of me on my knees, sucking his dick and him staring at me from above like that.

It was a quick thought, a dirty fantasy, but nonetheless served its purpose of making me horny again.

When Daniel stood back, Killian grabbed my hand, breathing hard through his nose as we navigated through bodies. I smoothed my thumb over his knuckles, trying to ease some of his tension, and also my way of thanking him for, well...a lot of things tonight.

The severe lines around his mouth smoothed when he peeked down at me, and said, "I feel used, Lilith."

A reasonable distance away from a reeling Daniel and Nicole, I simply told him, "You wanted to be included in my plans."

And I'd gotten more than I bargained for, but I wasn't complaining.

He licked his lips when we came to a stop in front of the bar, no doubt thinking the same, and a blush exploded on my neck and cheeks when he traced the decolletage of my dress with invested eyes, almost undressing me with them.

The gravity of what transpired would no doubt hit me in the morning, but for now, I let myself enjoy this rare moment of freedom. I took a step forward to do—I wasn't sure what, when I heard my name being yelled for a second time today.

"Irena!" Killian and I jerked apart when an irritated Bea joined us, holding two handbags in her hands as she seethed. "What were you thinking?"

My eyes turned into tiny moons when it registered that she'd probably witnessed us doing some freaky shit. How much I didn't know and was now upholding the promise I couldn't keep to myself.

"Bea—" I tried to explain that Killian hadn't actually done anything with Mia, but she snapped at him before I could.

"Take your hands off her," she commanded, and I realized that Killian was still holding on to me. I swallowed, deciding to do the work for him when he clenched his jaw stubbornly, glaring at Bea like she was a bug he wanted to squash.

She pointed at him as she essentially got between us, her low tone piercing through Killian's armor and the haze in my brain as she said, "Irena might be too far gone to resist your charm, but I see you for what you truly are, Astor: an opportunistic pig. This story can never have a happy ending, and the last thing she needs right now is more heartbreak."

Killian opened his mouth to spit his own venom back, but Bea whipped in my direction, shoving my bag in my chest and nodding for me to walk in front of her. "Let's go. We're leaving."

CHAPTER TEN
KILLIAN

I could still taste her blood on my tongue and smell her cum on my fingers as I splashed my face with ice-cold water the following morning.

After she left, it was all the same. I was already buzzed, put a few more drinks in my system, and I was straight on the highway to hell. I also took some funny-looking pills Luca's friend, Nicolas, offered us when we switched clubs because I couldn't stand breathing the same air as Irena's pompous ex. The aftermath was waking up with my head in the toilet and retching my guts out.

I was so fucking mad at that mouthy Bea for all of last night. It seeped out of my pores. Once the booze didn't influence my thinking, though, her words seemed all the more like the voice of reason and not ones that had stolen something precious from me.

She had riled me up so bad, I'd fingered her in public. It wasn't like I hadn't done worse before, but usually not with someone I was supposed to keep away from, and the worst part was that I wanted to do it again and again and again. I wanted to do more than that.

Taste her on my tongue.

Feel her on my dick.

Have her scream my name without worrying someone might hear.

The Irena Fleur virus was real, and with each passing day, I embraced it a little more.

I looked in the mirror after brushing my teeth twice and using mouthwash three times to get rid of that god-awful acid-like taste in the back of my throat. I still looked like death personified, though. My blond hair was shaggy, strands sticking up on every side, and the black circles under my eyes looked like bruises.

Ever since the first innocent crushes in elementary school, I hadn't had a girl linger in my mind as much as she had. I was too...tainted to act on them back then, and Irena was too out of my reach for me to act on them now.

It was driving me crazy, wanting what I couldn't have for a second time due to outside factors, putting me back in that fucked-up mentality that led me to become who I was today. Chasing the high only drugs and alcohol could provide to forget what I was and *who* made me like that.

A figure appeared next to me in the mirror, leaning against the bathroom's opening. It was Luca, the bright smile on his face hiding demons similar to mine. Everyone dealt differently with their trauma, and Luca's way of dealing with depression was trying to look as not depressed as possible.

He had a short fuse when it came to sympathy and hated when people considered him weak. He'd never admit it, but I'd been in his life long enough to know him better than his own self.

"Morning, sunshine." He raised his coffee mug at me, already having helped himself to the pot I'd brewed before retiring to the bathroom to puke my guts out at the scent.

Bastard didn't pour me a cup either after I let him stay over and would give him a free tattoo once I regained some of my energy, the whole reason why he was back in town so soon.

Typical.

"Why are you so chipper?" I groaned as I tried to comb my hair, but eventually gave up when it got even worse, turning frizzier by the friction the comb created.

I let it clatter in the sink, hearing the soft click of the outside door as I did so, and had my *aha* moment. Just because I was going through a period of self-imposed celibacy didn't mean the people around me were doing so, too.

After I'd warned him off Irena, he found someone else to bring over. It wasn't difficult for him. I was impressed he'd managed to get the girl to leave, only clad in *my* boxers (ew, those would have to go straight to the trash), his abs on full display. Even I admired them because no matter how many hours I spent at the gym or tires I flipped, I'd never get that buff without the help of roids. I lacked the necessary genes.

Saint had stolen all the muscle mass in the family. While I wasn't skinny, I *was* more on the lean side.

"I get to finally make fun of you about last night," he quipped and followed in my footsteps as I brushed past him, heading for the kitchen.

I had to have been pretty out of it if he fucked a girl in the same apartment as me, and I hadn't heard shit.

"Go ahead. I have no recollection of it, so it's not going to be as enjoyable."

You couldn't really get embarrassed over things you didn't remember. That philosophy had carried me through many low points in my brief stint in college, where, I could be honest, my major had transitioned from architecture to partying 101 somewhere along the way.

"Oh, I beg to differ." Luca circled around me like an eagle eyeing its prey as I put some bread slices in the toaster because, of course, he couldn't even get me coffee, but I had to make him breakfast. I gave the stink eye when he propped his hip on the counter, his smile stretching to the point of appearing painful. "I'll never forget how you called up Saint to tell him how you would fuck his sister-in-law—just your neighbor, my ass—if you wanted to, and if he tried to stop you, you'd punch him in the dick so he could experience how bad *your* case of blue balls had gotten."

I froze in place, the coffee pitcher scalding my palm as I had a mini panic attack. My case of blue balls was bad, but not bad enough to risk getting estranged from my brother.

Right?

Or had Irena's tight fit enticed me more than I initially deemed possible?

She'd been soaked enough to take three fingers, and I couldn't help but imagine it was my cock that had painted that expression of pure bliss on her face as I moved the digits inside her.

I shook my head to focus on the present and mumbled, "Tell me you're lying."

Taking pity on me, Luca nodded yes, and I scowled at him as I ran the tap, holding my hand under the cool stream to ease some of the burn. When I went back to the jug, I made sure to use the fucking handle.

I blamed Irena, as always. She was so far deep in my mind I'd forgotten how to function like a normal human.

"Relax," Luca said, sounding like a New York crime lord for a second. "I'll never forget how you punched me in the mouth so I wouldn't traumatize poor Yazmin on her birthday. It was the perfect time to get my revenge and shut you up at the same time."

When he'd first seen her snacking on cake before her birthday celebration had even started. It was something Farah always did. Eating dessert before a proper meal and watching his half-sister do the same had triggered him out of the blue.

I had to physically intervene before he ruined her day.

It wasn't Yazmin's fault a monster had birthed her. I understood that better than anyone with my father. Luca always kept his cool around her; that was the first time I'd seen him lose it, and I had to get it under control before it did some irrefutable damage to the girl.

I left my mug half full, glancing at my reflection in the kitchen's glass cabinet doors. The bruising wasn't necessarily severe for a black eye, but it did look like I hadn't slept in a whole week and then some.

"You cunt, those *are* bruises under my eyes, aren't they?" I asked, but Luca remained cool as mint.

"What did you think they were? Dark circles?" He snorted, stealing a piece of bread that popped out of the toaster. He took a bite, chewing leisurely as he mocked me. "You can't be that stupid."

"You're dead," I promised and lunged for him.

"Hey!" Luca sidestepped my uncoordinated self, like I was a leaf in the wind. "I shut you up, didn't I? Otherwise, you would've blabbed to your brother about what you would've *loved* to do to his sister-in-law's mouth every time she sassed you. You got as far as calling him before I hung up for you."

Holding myself against the fridge to overcome the queasiness that overwhelmed me after my sudden move, I cursed myself for running my bloody mouth about Irena.

Don't get me wrong, I wasn't against dirty talk *with her*.

Telling other people what I wanted to do her, though, was a big no, no in my book. It was disrespectful, one, and it made me want to crush their brains to bits for visualizing her the same as I was, two.

"Did he answer?" I straightened once the urge to reacquaint myself with my best friend, the toilet, wore off.

"No, dumbass. He's out of the country, in case you've forgotten."

I hadn't, but knowing my brother, he was working even while on "vacation." He probably had some mobile plan that allowed him to receive and make calls even while he wasn't in the US.

Luca took another bite of *my* fucking toast and chewed it as if it was popcorn as he watched me with renowned interest. It was like I was a dolphin at an aquapark doing unseen tricks for a mesmerized audience to marvel over.

"What?" I bit out as I grabbed some berries from the fridge, too tired to prepare anything to eat.

We sat at the kitchen island, and he splayed his palms on the black marble, puffing out a long breath. "You've got it bad for this girl, huh? Is that why you wouldn't speak about her, too afraid I'd realize how lovely she was and steal her from you?"

A sharp laugh pierced the air—*my* sharp laugh. It echoed like a warning around us, and I inhaled five blueberries at the same time to tone down the jealousy. "Not even in your dreams would that happen," I retorted whilst chewing. "But yes, I did find the least available woman to get constantly hard for."

"Why?" Luca grilled a simple question with a complicated answer. "What's stopping you from pursuing her? She's single as far as I know, and even if she wasn't, that hasn't stopped you."

I shuddered at the sharp turn toward memory lane, dropping my raspberry back in its plastic container.

It was a long time ago, but one of the many times I'd gotten suspended in high school was when a classmate learned that in addition to cleaning their pool when my father forced me to take on a summer job before my senior year, I was also cleaning his stepmother's pipes when her husband was at work.

In my defense, she was young enough to be his sister, and his father was a creep for marrying a girl four decades younger than him. It was my way of regaining some control I was stripped of and make an adult my own personal bitch. She enjoyed it, though. I made sure to provide the pleasure I wasn't given.

"My homewrecker days are behind me. I'm a better man now," I stated, wiping the precipitation from the fruit off my fingers on my white sleep shirt.

"Cut the shit," Luca commanded, fed up with my skirting around the subject.

"You cut playing dumb." I met his gray gaze head-on, and despite having very little to eat, my appetite ceased as I delved into the Irena topic for what felt like the thousandth time when it was just the first I was discussing it with anyone other than the voices in my head. "What part of she's Saint's sister-in-law don't you understand? I'm not scared of him, but I respect Aria too much to fuck Irena and cause problems in their marriage."

"But why would they have such a big problem with the two of you getting it on?" Luca questioned, not getting it.

"Because it would never go beyond that. You know I'm not the relationship type, and it would get awkward because I'll keep having to see Irena even after I tire of her, since our families are intertwined."

And more awkward tension was the last thing that we needed. Our parents already despised each other, and extended family gatherings were a shitshow, to say the least. I wasn't going to add more fuel to the fire.

"How can you be so sure she wouldn't tire of you first?" The rhetorical nature of the question made me take a break from twisting my mug around in my hold and strive to find a response that would shut his argument down, but I came up empty-handed, and he took it as his sign to keep going. "Has it ever crossed your mind that she might not be looking for a relationship right now, either? She just got out of a pretty bad one. A rebound might be all she wants, a fun time with no ties attached."

"No—" I tried to break apart his argument before it had time to fully form in my mind, but he spoke over me.

"Why not? Is your ego so big that you can't think of yourself as disposable?" He scoffed, inching the container with the berries his way once it was clear I wasn't interested. "My advice is, *talk* to Irena. Explain to her how you'd like things to operate. The worst that can happen is she says no. Saint and Aria never even have to find out."

I tried.

I tried really hard not to blurt out what hid in a small

corner of my mind like an annoying splinter I couldn't pull out. Always there, tormenting me with its presence. In a society where men weren't allowed to show any weaknesses because it made them less of a man, it wasn't normal to talk about your feelings or open up about problems beyond how much of an asshole your boss was at work.

Being vulnerable wasn't my cup of tea. However, when someone knew every detail of my life and had never abandoned me despite witnessing all the fucked-up things I had done over the years, it made talking about it feel like piercing your finger on a prickle instead of falling through a thorn bush.

It was painful, but it could've been worse.

"What if she finds out? What if I lose control around her and talk?" I blabbed on my internal fears, and Luca's eyes fogged at the remembrance of our history.

"Ah," he exclaimed. "So there lies the problem. You don't really give a shit that Saint would never approve of this relationship. You're afraid she'll dig too deep."

"You understand me better than anyone. You can't ask me to risk it all like that. She's too close to my family. If she finds out, then Aria finds out, Saint, everyone!" I threw my hands in the air, panic gripping my throat in a vice grip, and the thought, *I can't let that happen*, repeated in my head over and over again like a broken record.

Luca shook my shoulder as if to snap me out of it, and I focused on his words as he said, "I'm not asking you to do anything, Killian, but I won't pretend to understand why you'd be so opposed to Saint finding out. From what I remember, he always looked out for you."

"He'll feel responsible." It had nothing to do with shame. I'd crossed that threshold a long time ago. "He was a better father to me than our own ever was. He'll blame himself for not *sensing* something was wrong, even though it was nearly impossible with how tongue-tied I was."

After what I'd admitted, the silence was heavy because if there was anything he related with me on, it was him not letting his sibling bear the burden of what happened to him. He couldn't in good conscience give me advice that he, himself, couldn't follow.

He did try, though, forever hoping that I would have the courage to do what he couldn't because if one of us won, it was considered a victory for the both of us.

"I say don't let your past define your future, Kill. She has already taken more from us than we'll ever be able to reclaim; don't allow her to take any more on the far-off chance that you'll lose control." He squeezed the back of my neck.

Far-off chance or not, it was still a possibility, and that was all I needed to keep torturing myself in my personal kind of hell, limbo.

I broke off Luca's hold, all but shut down for the day, and it was only nine. I should've been in the office about an hour ago, but I allowed myself to be laxer now that the big boss was missing.

"Whatever, I'm not making a decision about it now," I said, stealing the food back from him, and he swore as he tried to snatch it again.

"You're such an asshole sometimes. I don't know why I'm friends with you," he complained.

"It's what attracts the ladies." My voice was muffled as I rearranged the contents of the fridge.

"For a night, because if they stuck longer than that,

they'd go crazy." He slapped the countertop as he chuckled like he'd said something ingenious.

"Keep talking and I'll tattoo a dick on your back instead of the insignia you requested," I threatened, reluctant to do it in the first place.

When I asked what the symbol of a key with a snake slithering on top of it meant, he'd clammed up big time. I would've gotten offended if I didn't know he wasn't giving me the details for my own good.

"At least make it big to reflect the size of mine," he yelled as I disappeared down the hall to get ready for work, hoping for no more surprises after such an eventful wake-up call.

CHAPTER ELEVEN
IRENA

"Are you a virgin?"

My brows climbed to my hairline when the lady sitting next to me in the waiting room addressed me. She had to at least be in her mid-forties, a mom judging by the three names tattooed on the side of her arm. One of the cool ones that got Botox treatments and covered every available inch of her skin with tattoos.

"Excuse me?" I asked as I glanced around, wondering if she had talked to someone else. But no, there was only one other person at the tattoo parlor with us, and he was currently behind the counter, flipping through a car magazine, bored out of his mind as he waited for his shift to be over.

I went back to the woman, and she laughed as she clarified. "I meant a tattoo virgin. Have you had any other tattoos before?"

"Ah, no." I gulped, stilling the repeated wringing of my fingers on my lap. "This will be my first."

And probably the only one with the way I kept rethinking it.

I didn't know if it was because I was unsure about getting tattooed or facing the person who would be tattooing me. Probably a little bit of both. I'd always toyed with the idea of getting one, and Killian was a damn good artist, so I thought, why not?

Because you'll seem like a desperate bitch, showing up in his place of work, that's why. The logical and slightly pessimistic side of me screamed in my head until I got anxiety pangs for the second time. It wasn't a good take, especially since I was making my debut at the New York fashion week on Friday after Amani pulled a few strings and got me in several shows by mostly emerging designers.

I was opening for Falco and Fleur, though, and that meant I'd have all eyes on me for the remainder of the week. I already had an influx of messages asking me if the rumors were true, and letting my dad, Aria, and Saint down was my biggest fear.

But the tattoo I'd picked was small; it wouldn't be all that visible. I worked my ass off on those catwalk classes to the point where I couldn't feel my feet after a while, and I was about to meet some of the biggest names in the industry.

I had no reason to worry.

"Don't worry, hon. It only hurts momentarily, and depending on where you get it done, it might not hurt at all." The woman gave me a sympathetic smile, her hazel eyes crinkling at the corners, and despite possibly having more ink than all the pictures on the walls of this shop combined, she seemed incredibly kind.

Don't judge a book by its cover and all.

That wasn't the reason why I was fretting, but I smiled back because it was nice of her to sense my nervous energy and try to calm me down. "Thank you."

"Of course." She abandoned her Kindle, ready to strike up a conversation with me. "I'm Kim. What's your name?"

I was about to respond when a teenager came from one of the back rooms and read my name off a list in her hands while smacking gum obnoxiously. "Jane Foster?"

Well, technically, my other name. The one I used to sneak into bars when I was underage, and as of late, to have Killian accept me as a client. I wasn't sure what his reaction was going to be when he heard that I'd specifically requested him after the way we parted, so I chose to be safe rather than sorry and hand out my fake ID card.

I could claim I simply confused them at the end of the day. It looked very realistic.

Keep fooling yourself. That annoying voice struck again, and I ground my teeth.

"That's me," I told the girl, but she'd already moved on, and I took it as my sign to just go in. So I turned to Kim and gave her a last wave as I got up on shaky feet. "Sorry, I gotta go."

"Good luck in there," she wished, but her face said that she didn't have much faith in me. She most likely was betting on me fainting and being wheeled out, and it was confirmed by her following words. "Holla if you need me to hold your hand."

"You got it." I gave her a thumbs-up, not opposed to the idea in case Kill kicked me out.

The hallway leading to the design room had big leafy plants on either side, and it gave me the vibes of walking into a tropical forest late at night because of the textured black wallpaper.

I didn't let myself think twice as I twisted the handle to the room, but my anxiety plagued me for a little longer when I found his back was to me. He was seated in a little spinning chair printing out the design I'd provided in my consultation with one of the store's staff. I'd come at specific hours I knew he wouldn't be at Falco and Fleur.

Killian seemed totally in his element here. Relaxing music was playing in the background, and he was wearing a black pair of jeans and a sleeveless T-shirt, allowing for the ink on his body to be displayed freely. He was bobbing his head along to the song playing in the background and even mouthing the lyrics when he turned his head a little to acknowledge me.

"So, Jane Foster..." He whistled, laughing to himself. "Big Thor fan, huh?"

I got to the tattoo bed, walking as if I was stepping on eggshells, and played along. "He's got the best abs in the MCU, and I support no one but the greatest."

Killian stilled at the sound of my voice, recognizing me immediately. The head bobbing stopped, and the music somehow got fainter as a ringing sound enveloped my eardrums while I waited for a reaction.

Save for the loss of his grin, he didn't give me one.

He recovered quickly and began cutting the parchment-like paper he was holding into a round shape, his back still to me as he remarked, "Captain America would like to object."

I sighed before I could stop it, but I was so damn relieved I couldn't hold it in. I'd imagined several ways he could've responded to me being here, all ranging from bad to horrible, so it was a welcome surprise when he didn't tell me to get the fuck out when I sat down.

"His are artificial," I countered.

"And Thor is literally a god, so he has an unfair advantage," he argued back, finally spinning on that chair of his and setting his eyes on me. The greeting was a familiar one. His gaze crawled up my legs slowly like he was admiring them, then got hooked on my chest for a second or two before meeting my face at last. His rounded eyes told me he couldn't believe I was actually here, despite having already surpassed the initial shock.

It was weird, though. I wasn't exactly the normal tattoo candidate.

He licked the inside of his lip as if debating what to do with me. I clutched the edges of the bed while my mind conjured a few ideas. Some of which wouldn't leave my mind after he made me come with his fingers alone. Something no man had managed to achieve before. They usually couldn't even find the clit, and got mad when you tried to aid them along.

Taking a deep breath, he moved past my antics, going straight for the meat of the matter. "Why did you use a fake ID, Irena?"

"Would you have accepted me if you knew who you were taking on as a client?" I asked, unsure, and bristled when he snorted.

"Yes, and I probably wouldn't have charged you either."

"Probably?" My eyes narrowed.

"Yeah, it would've depended on how nice you were to me."

"Then change my name back to Irena Fleur in that little sheet of yours. I don't mind. I'll be the most delightful client you'll ever have to work with." I swung my legs in the air, but he shot me down.

"It doesn't work like that. You're Jane now."

"Jane would like to have a word with you."

"The only thing Jane and I have to talk about is her tattoo, and since you already submitted a Pinterest picture of what you want to get done, there isn't much left to say." He picked up the paper again and held it up to the light, examining it. "A snowflake? To symbolize your generation, I'm assuming?"

I rolled my lips in my mouth, not allowing the feelings of dejection to take over. "You're part of the same generation, so you're essentially roasting yourself."

He shrugged as if holding himself to a higher standard than the rest of us and motioned for me to lie down. I did, the chair squeaking under me, and took a deep breath when he wheeled closer, delighting myself in his scent. It was so characteristically male it made my mouth water.

His face appeared over my head, those crystal blues as clear as the Mediterranean Sea on a sunny day. "How did you know where I worked?"

"I pulled some strings." I shrugged.

I was cautioned not to say anything.

The bird that had gotten me the intel I needed went by the name of Luca, or as I liked to call him, Scarface. We stumbled across each other on his way out of Killian's apartment last night, and after hearing him roast Killian and me for our very obvious desperation for each other for what felt like an eternity—I let him have it, but he was reduced back to being called Scarface to his face again—I asked him where Killian worked, and because he was such a little matchmaker at heart, he texted me the address.

"Are you actually getting a tattoo because you want one, or are you just here for me?" Killian questioned, examining my every tell in case I thought to lie.

"Both." I sat unnaturally still in response, my body locking up from the added stress. "I came to a decision yesterday, and I want to remind myself to stick to it no matter how hard it gets every time I look at this tattoo. Plus, I'm kind of anxious and I wanted someone I trust to do it. And also, if you fuck up, I know where you live, so..." I trailed off, letting him fill in the blanks, and an antagonizing smirk took shape on his lips.

"So what? What could you possibly do?"

I flicked some non-existent dirt from under my nails as he kept busy setting up the tattoo gun. It clattered on his portable metal table when I said, "Fuck Colin against your door."

His head whipped in my direction so fast I feared he'd crack his neck. And if I was ever having doubts about Killian's attraction to me, all I needed to do was bring up other men, and they would be cleared right up.

"I'll tell you once again threatening me while I hold your fate in my hands is not a great idea." His lip curled in a snarl, and he gave the tattoo gun a little buzz as if to restate his point. "Taking someone else down with you too, disastrous," he added, voice dropping even lower.

Heat curled low in my belly, and I put on my most innocent smile as I replied, looking at him through lowered lashes, "But getting you all riled up is so fun."

Realizing he'd gotten played, he released a long puff of air, shaking off his shoulders to release some of the tension. Approaching me with a printout of the design, he asked, "All right, where are you getting this done?"

"My inner arm. I want it to be visible, but not *too* visible," I instructed, holding my hand out on an armrest, and he hovered the paper over my skin so I could pinpoint the exact placement. When he stopped right in the middle of my arm, I nodded, giving him the green light. "Perfect."

I let him get to work, afraid to distract him now that we were getting to the actual tattooing. My stomach gave a nervous flip after he finished pasting the design on my skin, and started up the tattoo gun, the low whine of the machine giving me a mild headache.

Killian's eyes flicked up at me when my hand started trembling, and I took in a stuttered breath as I watched the needles move up and down at rapid speed. His gloved hands fiddled with the cord of the machine, and I followed his every move like a hawk, my insides twisting and turning.

I should've predicted this would happen, that fear would hit me at the last moment. I'd avoided overthinking about the process of getting my fine-line tattoo and focused solely on the end result.

I was so consumed by the sudden burst of uncertainty that I didn't notice the noise had ceased until Killian's warm fingers grasped my chin, and he pulled my head up, ensnaring my gaze with his. His thumb left a trail of heat as he caressed my jaw, and the speed with which the direction of my thoughts changed almost gave me whiplash.

"Why are you looking anywhere but me when I'm so handsome to look at?" he joked, but I was too overtaken by panic to laugh or even smile. Giving my chin a reassuring squeeze before removing his hand, he instructed, "Keep your eyes closed or only on me. Those are your only two options. Okay?"

I nodded, honing in how the light reflected over his

sandy hair, and focused on the music instead of the low whine of the machine this time, repeating the lyrics with fervor as Killian's wrist settled on the inner part of my elbow right before he began.

"You didn't tell me what you decided." He spoke, and I was unsure what he meant until I put two and two together in my muddled brain and realized he was talking about the reason I was getting inked for the first time.

"I'm not giving up on figure skating," I said as if in a trance, waiting for the pain to hit, and when it did, I hissed out my protest at the ache that spread all over my arm.

"I thought you'd try out modeling first." Killian kept up the conversation, but I couldn't reply immediately.

Squeezing my eyes shut, I breathed through my teeth as I tried to adjust to the constant pricking sensation. Even though the needles were concentrated in one place, it felt like fire ants were marching all over my arm, and the pain was blinding for the first few minutes.

Killian continued without giving me a break, though, and the more he went on, the more familiar I became with the sensation. The hurt became more bearable, and after a while, the vibration in my body convoluted the pain.

I breathed in deep, trying my hand at talking again. "I will—for a year or two until I have a sufficient amount of funds to create my own elite figure skating group and go on tour. I don't want to give up on my dream because of a handful of mean people. Somewhere along the line, while filming Stars on Ice, I lost sight of what was truly important. Not the fame or the money, but simply doing what I love."

Ironically, it was my talk with Katrina that forced me to make some tough decisions. I hated seeing her gloat over my demise, but most of all, I hated myself for allowing it to get that far.

Modeling wasn't bad, but figure skating was where my heart lay. Even if *I* wasn't the one performing, I'd be training and directing a team, which to me, was equally as enjoyable.

I mean, who didn't like ordering people around?

"Mimicking the people around you is normal if you start spending a lot of time with them," Killian theorized like he'd personally gone through it. "I'm glad you're not giving up on your dream; you're too talented to do so."

I opened my eyes to look at him again, and that intense need to puke had waived a little. He was hunched over, his tongue peeking out a tiny bit as he worked with precision.

"You sound like you're speaking from experience," I noted, and his answer came late as he balanced working and talking.

"The whole reason why I went to college despite it not being my plan initially was because my father had brainwashed me enough for me to follow along with his plan. When I finally dropped out and pulled my head out of my ass and realized I wasn't living out *my* dream, it was the most relieved I'd felt in a while."

"*This* is your dream?" I studied the room where he spent hours creating, and it was a dingy little thing filled with age-old equipment that had seen better days.

I was sure there was worse out there, but claiming it was his dream wasn't true, so I called him out on it.

"It's a step to get to my dream," he clarified. "I want to open my own tattoo shop and better vet my clients, but it will take some time to get there."

"Aren't you exhausted? Working two jobs at the same time?"

"Aren't *you* after a whole day of training?" he bounced back, pausing the tattoo process to wipe at my arm before starting all over again.

I clenched my teeth, feeling the needles twice as much after a brief period of rest. "Yes, but the suffering makes the win all the sweeter."

"Exactly." He said it like I'd reached the conclusion he wanted, and I crossed my legs while trying to keep the upper part of my body still.

Finding people that loved the grind and the hustle was rare enough. Finding them in a society where most of them were already richer than God due to their parents was like searching for a needle in a haystack. Killian could've simply borrowed money from Saint at the end of the day and had his own tattoo shop within a week, but he didn't because he didn't want his success to be attached to someone else.

Of course, he had privileges—we both did—that the average working person could only dream of, but that didn't make his accomplishments worth any less.

"You know, Killian, even your parents don't realize how hardworking you are. It doesn't matter. You're a big inspiration to all of those that actually *see* you," I pointed out because I had a bone to pick with his father for judging him so harshly. "My dad couldn't stop raving about the set you'd put together for the New York fashion week, and it shows that you give your hundred percent in any project you take on. Darian is not one for empty words. I believe he likes you more than Saint."

"Everyone likes me better than Saint. I got all the charm in the family. He's too abrasive," Killian joked, but I caught the slight crack in his voice he tried to mask.

I was blessed with beyond-supportive parents, so I

couldn't imagine how having a father like Noah could be. Killian could pretend it didn't affect him, and I'd let him have it because tearing down someone's coping mechanism was never the answer.

"And the humility, too, I see."

"Ah, Lilith, that's something we both lack," Killian *tsked* and stopped tattooing long enough to meet my eyes, his shining with something I couldn't quite name. "You trust me enough to let me add my own twist to this? I promise, nothing too crazy."

I peered down to get a glimpse at how far along we were, but he *had*, shaking his head and hovering his free hand over the tattoo, intending it to be a surprise. I shifted on the bed, my back lifting as I weighed my options.

He did say it wasn't going to be anything crazy, and I believed in creative freedom, so why the hell not?

"Okay," I sighed, wishing to heaven and back I didn't regret this.

His head tilted a bit like he couldn't fathom that I'd agreed, and he said, full of wonder, "You *are* being uncharacteristically agreeable today."

It was true for several reasons. For one, I wanted to prove to both of us that we could talk without arguing in every other sentence. Two, I was to blame for what Bea had said. And three, I had a motive and had to ease him into it, so I started slow.

"Indirect apologies are kind of my thing; the actual words somehow get stuck in my throat whenever I try to say them." I cleared said throat, and he chuckled.

"What do you have to be sorry for?" he inquired as he kept busy dipping the tip of the tattoo gun in a plastic cup full of water, and filling a smaller cup with a beautiful pale blue color, before dipping the needles in there as well.

"What Bea said..." I stopped my eyes from migrating south again because seeing the color was unsettling. God, I really hoped I wasn't making a mistake in trusting him. "It was rude, and she only said it because she was fueled by my words. She regretted it after I explained what really went down."

Admitting that I'd talked about him with my best friend was bad enough, but his following words definitely took it there.

"And also true."

"Excuse me?" I moved my arm when I jostled in place, and he gave me the stink eye as he was getting ready to start inking again.

Killian was so close I could see each individual lash on his eyes, and despite him being blond, they still looked full. I despised how perfect he was. He had no texture whatsoever on his skin, and his pores were so tiny it made you question if he had any. His lips were pouty and red and oh so inviting they could corrupt an angel.

I watched, magnetized, as they twisted up on the corners while he aimed straight for my heart. "Come on now, Lilith, I'm a warm-blooded male, and you needed my help to show your ex you'd moved on. Of course, I took advantage of the opportunity to get my hands all over you."

Of course.

I mean, I couldn't judge him. With the way my hormones were going wild for this guy, I would've done the same.

"What if I told you I need your help again?" I eased into it as he pivoted back to my arm, the torture starting up all over again. My throat hurt from having to speak louder than usual to be heard over the buzzing sound.

"You'll have to give me more than that," Killian remarked, intrigued.

"I want to make Daniel and Katrina feel insignificant," I began, the crazy idea that had taken shape in my mind right after Bea and I left Marquee coming to fruition as I voiced it to Killian. "Especially her. She always went to great lengths to hurt me, and there's no doubt in my mind she doesn't actually like Daniel. She just went after him to get to me."

Don't get me wrong, I had it out for Daniel as well for spreading false rumors about me, but I knew he wasn't bright enough to come up with those on his own.

"What do you need from me?" Killian spoke, unable to discern how he could be of help.

Since my only options were looking at him or closing my eyes, I opted for the latter in order to avoid facing his reaction to the absurdity I was about to spew. I'd given it a lot of thought—specifically a day's worth, so there were still some kinks in my plan, but I was too high on Daniel's disbelief when he spotted me with Killian. And his face after Killian confirmed his hand was sticky because it was coated with my cum—priceless.

Nothing would bruise his ego more than slapping my new relationship across his face.

"Pretend to be my fake boyfriend a few more times," I said quickly, ripping any hesitation to shreds. "I don't want to be in another relationship so soon, but I also want to show the world and them how moved on I am, and unfortunately, they'll only understand the *show, don't tell* way."

I felt his shock and skepticism when he pulled back for a few seconds, as if to avoid making a mistake. I bit my tongue for choosing this particular moment to break this to him. I couldn't wait any longer, though. I wanted to get this show on the road as soon as possible and embark on my new job without the past holding me back.

"In case you've forgotten," he spoke carefully, spelling out every letter. "Our siblings are married. I will be the cause of more problems if anyone finds out who I am."

"They won't," I replied, enthusiasm blooming inside of me at the fact that he hadn't outright denied me. "I'll be careful. I'll make sure your face is never fully shown on social media, and I doubt anyone from my social circle will recognize you. They won't hang out with anyone that doesn't at least own five different colored polo shirts and two pairs of Gucci loafers. I'm sure your paths have never crossed."

Killian snorted, and I flushed. "Man, those are some great friends you used to hang out with."

"I won't lie, I'm embarrassed, but I was blind to so many things back then..." I trailed off, reconsidering. "Or well, I forced myself to be, to fit in."

"Don't be," he exhaled. "We've all done embarrassing shit to fit in before, whether we care to admit it or not. The main thing to remember is to do things because they make *you* happy, not because you want to get back at anyone."

Doing you would make me positively ecstatic.

The thought was sudden and potent, and when Killian coughed out a laugh, I realized I'd failed at keeping it in.

"I said that out loud, didn't I?" I groaned, covering my face with my free arm.

He chuckled. "It's all right. It's not groundbreaking information. Your pussy *was* squeezing my fingers to death not too long ago, anyway."

"Killian." I turned to him sharply, but he simply gripped me harder, annoyed by all my moving around.

"If you want me as your fake boyfriend, you're going to have to put up with my crass mouth, Lilith," Killian affirmed, and I held my breath, stopping the butterflies in my belly from talking flight without his explicit confirmation.

"So you accept?" I almost bounced up and down, but he shot me a look that told me not to get too excited *too* soon.

"I'll have to think about it." He wiped down my tattoo one more time, and I deflated like a balloon. "All done."

"That didn't hurt much," I noted, even though I'd acted like a drama queen at first.

The pain honestly got much duller as we went on. It was like sinking in ice-cold water; my body felt like it was burning in the beginning, but with time it became nothing but a minor ache. I supposed placement was also important. Pain tolerance was lower in other areas of the body.

Killian poured some water on it with a pipette bottle. "'Cause you were preoccupied while going through it... First rule when getting a tattoo for minimal pain, have someone with you that will distract you until it's done."

"Well, thank you for the tattoo and for distracting me."

I didn't believe it would have gone over so smoothly if anyone else had done it.

"Don't thank me without having seen it yet," he said as he dried the water off, and I could finally look at it.

My skin was red and inflamed, but the tattoo itself was nothing like I'd ever seen. The design was the one I'd originally presented, a beautiful snowflake with elegant fine lines, and within those fine lines, Killian had created magic. I gaped over the magnetizing blue, white, and slightly green shades that blossomed within the rounded edges of the snowflake, and in the middle, he'd added a rhombus that looked like a jewel come to life.

"Killian, it's beautiful," I gushed and looked up at him through fluttering lashes, amazed by his talent. "It looks like the snowflake is filled with sapphire gemstones."

"It is." His eyes lit up at my reaction, and my heart thundered in my chest at what he had to say next. "To remind you of your worth. You're too good for men like Daniel or friends like Nicole, and you should never forget it."

My throat closed up, and it was difficult to get any words out when his handsome face shone with a sincerity that backed up his statement. It was one of the sweetest things anyone had ever done for me, and what made it even better was that it wasn't premeditated.

My bruised ego soaked up all the love it was getting, and I managed to croak out, "Thank you, I love it so much."

"Better than some Pinterest copy and paste design, huh? I hate it when customers come in with pictures from the internet," he noted, moving on, but I couldn't. I was consumed by thoughts of how badly I wanted to break apart the halo we constantly clung to and carve the two halves into thorns, if that was what it took to have Killian Astor.

I was aware that complicating matters between us wasn't for the best, but I wasn't going into it expecting a fairy tale-like love. I wanted him to pull my hair, slap my ass, and whisper filthy things in my ear while he took me from behind.

It could be for one night, two, or three, as long as it took to tire of the forbidden apple that was being dangled over my head daily.

"Stop looking at me like that, Lilith." The tendons in

Killian's neck bulged when some of my thoughts translated into my expression.

"Like what?" I asked, my voice all but innocent as I got on my elbows.

He wheeled closer on that chair of his, eyes a mosaic of opposing emotions. "Like you want a round two of what happened at Marquee."

I lifted a shoulder, running my gaze down his body. "Maybe I do."

He lowered his head so it was level with mine, those sharp angles on his face and harsh lines of his shoulders making him look formidable as the war within himself waged on. "Be careful what you wish for, Irena."

I smirked, ready to tell him that I was done being careful, when the door to the room swooshed open, and the moment fizzled out like a dream fading away as you slowly regained consciousness.

"Killian, are you almost don—" The bored teenager that read out my name barged into the space but stopped before her sentence was even done when she looked up from the list in her hands and noted the minimal distance between Killian and me. "Oh, was I interrupting?"

I cleared my throat, beyond annoyed at what felt like our thousandth interruption, and wondered if maybe the universe was trying to show me that Killian and I weren't meant to be, as I said, "No, we just finished." Which overlapped with Killian's, "You clearly are."

The girl popped her gum in her mouth as Killian's glare turned to me, clearly unimpressed and too bored to deal with us. "Whatever. You have another appointment in five minutes."

"It's all right, Killian," I assured when she shut the door

behind her. "Let's wrap it up. I have an early flight tomorrow."

And wrap it up we did, unspeaking, but I could feel something left hanging between us, something his parting smirk told me would be resolved at a later date.

CHAPTER TWELVE
KILLIAN

Golden birds dangled from invisible strings over a red runway.

There wasn't a particular theme for the night. Still, I was told the recent collection screamed quiet luxury—in other words, old money—and you could never go wrong with a bit of red and gold action.

They'd kept the venue low-key, so it was up to me to make it memorable, and so far, everyone was gaping at the phoenix-like, gold-coated creatures hanging from the ceiling with open mouths. Crystals also hung sparingly between them to break up the monotony and fill the atmosphere with enough white light to balance out the yellow.

It was an intimate setting, and judging by the satisfied smile on my brother's face as he settled in a clear bistro chair, I was sure I'd nailed New York fashion week. His face was tan after soaking up that Mediterranean sun for the past week, and there were a few added wrinkles between his brows that told me putting up with Aria's grandma and grandpa wasn't his idea of fun.

"I thought you were sitting this one out." I smirked as he sat next to me.

We were by the end lines of the front row, overlooking the exact place where the models were instructed to stop and strike a pose by a tiny white dot on the ground. It was just like Saint not to inform me that he was coming.

"So did I." He clapped my shoulder in a greeting. "But Aria wanted to be here for Irena."

Right, Irena.

Whether I cared to admit it or not, she was the only reason I was sitting here as well, amongst all these pretentious, so-called fashion experts. Most of them were dumb celebrities that would wear a trash bag if it was deemed the next big thing.

"I imagine you got her quite a large present to express your gratitude for saving you," I commented drily.

He straightened up his jacket, crossing his ankles. "I'm treating her to dinner at La Perla tomorrow night. I imagine dropping more than a thousand dollars on food is good enough."

"In that case, can I come? Since you're paying and all."

"Sure, you earned it for putting together a beautiful set." He gave me a side glance. "Anything breaks, though, and you're eating the leftovers."

I was about to reply when Aria breezed in, in her cream pleated dress, barely stopping to salute the people that tried to capture her attention along the way, her gaze homed in on us. Her breasts were barely contained by the low-cut decolletage, and with the way Saint was undressing her with his eyes, it told me their second child wouldn't come too long after the first.

"Stop messing with him." She whooshed in, pinched his

side, and leaned over him to kiss my cheek, then pat it. "You've done an amazing job, Killian."

I preened under her praise and said, "I know I talked shit about you in the beginning, Aria, but rest assured, you're my favorite now."

Her face screwed up, and she jerked back. "You talked shit about me?"

"Umm, no?" I backtracked, but the truth was, I didn't hesitate to run my mouth about my doubts on the validity of their marriage way back when.

"You can't take it back now. What did you say?" she asked, and when I hesitated, she turned to a squirming Saint. "What did he say?"

It was fascinating, really, how she was the only person that could get my eloquent brother to lose his words. The low beat of the music heightened, though, and the projectors beamed at the start of the runway, signaling that we were saved by the bell.

"Shh, babe." Saint looped his fingers through hers and pointed at one of the side openings. "The show's about to begin."

"You're safe," she grumbled and pressed deeper into her seat, not before pointing at me with a threatening finger and adding, "For now." A few seconds later, though, she'd forgotten all about her grudge and bounced excitedly. "Oh my God, I'm so excited. This walk will set the stage for the rest of her career."

"No pressure, huh?" Saint scoffed.

"It's not gonna be a long one, anyway," I mumbled, resting my ankle on my knee.

Irena's sharp gaze met mine, and she frowned. "Why would you say that? That's so mean."

"I didn't mean it like *that*," I objected. "Irena told me so herself that she wasn't planning on doing this for the long run. Only until she gathered sufficient funds to create her own figure skating team and go on tour."

She blinked at me, her face going blank. "This is the first time I'm hearing of this."

"It was a recent development."

"And you know how?" Saint questioned.

"We're neighbors, and I see her every day?" I replied, and his brows climbed up. Aria made some weird facial expressions behind him, ones I couldn't decipher. I was about to ask her what was wrong, but Saint intercepted.

"Your *what?*" His voice was so loud some of the people around us turned to look at the commotion, and I stared at him blankly, our faces mirroring each other.

We were both confused, but I didn't get why *he* was confused.

After all, it was Aria that had suggested Irena stay at that apartment. How come Saint didn't know? They told each other everything.

"Shhh, look," Aria intervened, and he reluctantly let go of the situation.

The lights went out, a gentle breeze sweeping up the room before they opened again, and a shadowy figure appeared at the start of the runway. It was merely her silhouette, but my body turned tighter than a drum while seeing her run her hands down her hips seductively. She was instructed to do so, to add to the experience and show the lines of the dress, and it was certainly enriching my world.

When she stepped into the light, I held my breath as I appraised her. No inch of her body was left untouched by my eyes, starting with her red toes peeking out of stiletto heels to her shiny legs before a sheer black dress broke my uninterrupted view of her silky skin.

If I had difficulty breathing before, I all but lost the ability to take in oxygen as she powered down the runway, her eyes laser-focused on the camera, face blank but with a hint of a smirk. The dress was so sheer and tight, her alabaster skin was on display for everyone to see, and the feelings that arose...well, let's just say they weren't ones a platonic friend should possess.

On the areas of importance, though, the material thickened, and I wasn't sure whether that made me happy or mad. She zipped past us, her perfume invading my nostrils—strawberries, like always, making me want to cling to summer as it made way for fall. There was gold detailing on her shoulders, and I didn't know what bra they'd put her in, but it did great things for her tits and horrible things for my dick as it strained in my pants.

Even with my brother next to me, I couldn't contain my attraction to Irena, and he gave me an inquisitive look when I readjusted my weight on the seat for the hundredth time.

"Holy shit, she looks like a goddess in that dress," Aria echoed, and I had to fucking agree.

She looked like Lilith, with her softly curled hair that glimmered with blonde and red hues, that dress that screamed queen of the underworld, and her gait so full of confidence a lesser man would've never dared talk to her.

When she turned around, I almost passed out when I saw that the thick material on private areas did not extend to the backside, and I had a full view of her ass with a measly thong covering it.

I set my foot down, crossing my legs, and Saint shook his head at me, all caught on to what was troubling me. I couldn't care less. I wasn't the only man in this room with a hard-on, and it annoyed me immensely, but it helped my case. He mouthed, *"Stop looking"* at me, and I nearly gave him the finger as I went right back to looking my fill.

If only he knew I'd blown past that rule ages ago.

"Black is her color," I quipped because I meant it, but also to get on Saint's nerves.

"It really is," Aria muttered back, and once her sister disappeared behind the wall at the end of the stage, taking her lovely ass with her, Aria turned to us, awe on her face and voice. "Did that just happen?"

"That did just happen." Saint gave her a proud smile. "Baby Fleur killed it. I never doubted her for a second."

Aria's lips pulled down, and she gave him a huff as she faced the direction Irena had disappeared in and from which more models were pouring out. "I'm going to let that fly since I don't want to ruin Irena's big day."

Saint rolled with it, eager not to linger on whatever comments he'd made behind the scenes, and went right back to what had previously triggered him. "What was this talk about you being neighbors?"

"Ask your wife. She's the one that set it up," I answered simply.

"And didn't tell me anything? Yeah, right," Saint scoffed before taking it up with her. "Ariadne?"

Full name.

Ouch.

It seemed Aria understood the gravity of his anger, too. Hence, she pretended to be fully engrossed in the rest of the clothing line and didn't pay him any mind as she struck up a conversation with the guest next to her.

"Does she tell you every time she goes to the toilet too?

Obviously, she doesn't share every detail of her life with you," I interfered on her part, taking on the full force of his glare. Normally, I would've stayed just to spite him even more, but I wasn't in the mood to deal with him today. "Now, if you'll excuse me, I have to go. Enjoy the rest of the show yourself."

"Where are you going?" He gazed around as if to say it wasn't normal to leave a fashion show midway, but I couldn't give less of a shit.

I only came for Irena. I saw Irena, and now it was time to leave.

"I have a backstage pass, and there's a room full of gorgeous models waiting for me," I lied, removing myself from the situation before I could see the approval on his face.

Saint couldn't care less for my manwhore ways. He was the biggest one to ever exist. He was only content because it proved that I wasn't as hung up on Irena as he initially believed, and that was precisely why I'd said it.

But I only cared for one, namely Irena Fleur.

I had solid intel that Irena was on her way out. And by solid, I meant a mini army of paparazzi stationed outside the hotel door waiting to get a good shot of whoever was coming in or out.

I should let her have her fun.

I shouldn't be outside her hotel door waiting like a lovesick fool for her to come out. And I shouldn't have flirted with the receptionist to find out her room number.

But Saint, Luca, and Irena's words all blended together until I wasn't sure what to think anymore. To give in or not to give in—in my head, the question had turned as polarizing as God's existence. No amount of logic could solve the riddle I was plagued with. Still, emotions sure had a funny way of manipulating my thoughts until I felt like standing here was the right thing to do.

It wasn't, but I'd held myself back for so long, there was no stopping me now.

Ironically, it was Saint and my spirit of defiance that had made me pull the trigger. His lack of faith had irked me enough to want to shove his stupid rules up his ass. Not that he was wrong in believing the worst in me, anyway.

I heard some shuffling behind the door before it clicked open, and she appeared fresh-faced and appetizing as ever in a mini pink skirt that looked more like a belt than anything else and a bedazzled silver backless shirt that could be removed with a snap of my fingers.

"Killian." Her eyes widened when she spotted me, but I didn't give her much time to think it over.

Grabbing her by the chin, I basically shoved her backward, barging into the hotel room as if I owned the place, a smile reigning over my lips, when she choked out, "What the hell?"

"Hello, Lilith," I said, kicking the door shut behind me.

Her face was a picture of confusion and surprise. She hadn't even greeted me at the show, probably too sore from my indirect rejection of her proposal.

Her foot tapped on the carpeted floor as she said, "What are you doing? The girls and I are going out for celebratory drinks."

Oh, I was aware.

As I was also aware, no man in their right mind wouldn't hit on her after tonight. She'd painted her face as well. Any hint of pores showing was gone, her eyelids were a smokey black color, and her lips the perfect nude, a light pink color I longed to see rings of on my dick.

"Cancel it," I answered simply, shoving my hands in my pockets to hide the tenting in my pants.

"I can't cancel it, we—" she rattled off, but I spoke before she could finish.

"Do you still want me as your fake boyfriend?"

Her teeth clinked as she slammed her mouth shut and stared at me with a blank look, a slight tinge of red coloring her cheeks.

"Yes," she answered hesitantly.

I took a stroll through the room, letting my gaze roam over the messy vanity mirror, her suitcase open on the floor, clothes half spilled out.

If there was one thing to know about Irena, it was that she didn't have a single bone in her body that cared enough about organization. She thrived in chaos—her natural habitat. It had almost been a month now since she'd moved in, and there were still boxes in her home, and even though she'd had her driver's license for a few years now, switching lanes without a turn signal was the norm and grazing random cars while parking was an everyday thing.

I rotated in place, her bed behind me, as I asked, "How badly do you want it?"

She bit her lip, scanning my face for any hints as to where this was heading, but I held on to my neutral expression. "Pretty damn bad."

I grinned, giving up the fight and letting my eyes roam south. "Prove it."

That gave her pause.

"How am I supposed to do that?"

"You're an experienced girl, Irena. How do you usually win a man over?"

Her gaze instantly fell to my crotch, and I wanted to punch myself in the mouth for putting that picture in my mind.

"I don't think you want to find out."

"Oh, but I do." I pressed forward, my blood pumping thick and hot in my veins. I wanted everything I'd held myself back from taking.

I reached her in two strides, and her mouth parted with an exhale as I came within inches of her.

"But—"

"Favors come at a price, and I'm afraid all the money in the world cannot cover my retainer."

Catching on, Irena trailed her fingers up my chest, watching me through her long lashes, a vision of innocence wrapped in sin. "Do you accept sexual favors as payment then, sir?"

She pretended we were in an actual business transaction, and that word, *sir*—it did wonders for me. I was sure she could feel my erection poking her lower belly if her breathy giggle was anything to go by.

I held her arms as they circled my neck, clearing something up before this could progress any further. "As long as we're both on board with them having an expiration date, all forms of sexual favors are accepted."

The light in her eyes dulled at my terms, turning my

insides upside down, pulling my breaths through a diaphanous haze of misery.

Hurting her didn't give me pleasure, but I was too lost in my selfish needs to put everything into perspective.

Irena cleared her throat, though, and hid those conflicting feelings of hers behind sarcasm. "Should I get my strap-on, then? We could begin with some light pegging."

I slid my hands down her arms and to her waist, my thumbs nearly touching on either side, and pulled her body flush with mine. "Getting on your knees would work just fine too."

"So cliché," she simpered before hooking her claws on my nape and bringing me eye level with her. The pain traveled all the way down to my dick, and I resisted the urge to groan against her lips as she said, "There is no going back from this, Killian. I'll forever remember what you taste like on my tongue."

As if to commemorate her words, her hands slipped over my face, holding me to her as she hunted down my tongue, caught it, and tangled it with hers. I let her lead, cupping her ass with both hands, squeezing her flesh, and eating up the pained whimper she released in my mouth.

I walked us backward, and we both stumbled to the bed when the back of my knees hit the frame. I didn't let her break the kiss. In fact, I deepened it, pursuing her with my teeth, silently demanding she took everything I'd held back for so long.

Her fingers started pulling the buttons of my shirt apart as she tried to break the kiss to breathe, but I held her in place until her lungs shrunk from all the air she'd lost. She took in hungry gulps of oxygen, her exhales cooling my damp lips when I broke away with a cocky grin.

"Then perhaps"—I ground her cunt against my cock, paying her back in her own coin—"you should get to work, so I'll forever remember what your mouth feels like on my dick."

"So impatient." She threw her head back when I did it again but contained herself seconds later, not one to give it. Her hair tickled my face as she ripped me apart with a wicked grin. "You should know I'm not good at following orders when it comes to anything sexual."

She traced my abs with her gaze the second they became visible. I went to the gym five days a week for the same reason most guys did as well—to get laid, and seeing her interest in my body made me want to go even more often. She reached out to touch my abdomen, but I captured her hand in mine, forcing it behind her back.

Her jaw dropped in a soundless gasp as she rushed forward, almost faceplanting against my chest. It looked like she was about to curse me out, but I cut her off, asking, "Do you want to come?"

Frustration crinkled her brow. "Is that a rhetorical question?"

I glided my hands down her thighs, gathering her skirt in my fists and inching it higher and higher and higher until I reached bare skin. Goose bumps prickled beneath my fingers, and I didn't give her any time to adjust before letting my hand fly, the slap echoing through the hotel room.

She bucked in place to escape the assault, but the only thing she accomplished was to align her pussy with my dick better, her legs resting on either side of my hips.

There was an essence of disbelief thrumming through my veins.

That this was actually happening.

That I was massaging Irena Fleur's heated skin, and she was grinding on my lap with nothing but a thong on.

"When I ask you a question, I expect an answer." Enlarged pupils met mine, and a wave of warmth circulated through me at the desire I saw there. "Do you want to come?"

"Yes." Her lashes fluttered down as she answered, nostrils flaring with long, deep inhales.

"Yes, *sir*," I corrected.

"Excuse me?"

"You're excused since you didn't know, but next time I won't be so lenient."

"What if I like having my ass slapped?" she challenged in a haughty tone. "What will you hold over my head then?"

I thumbed the string of her underwear, hooking my finger under the bottoms of the lacy edges, and dragging the material upward, pulling the tiny scrap along her crack to expose more flesh. Her legs trembled at the touch, sending a thrill through me. "Your release, Lilith."

"That's not fair." She pouted.

I reached up and captured her bottom lip between my teeth, stretching it out before saying, "It's a cruel world."

I tried to put a cap on my eagerness, but having her bare neck right in front of my face, I couldn't help but peck every inch of available skin and slide my tongue up her jawline. I wanted her, and that need was an endless throbbing beat, banging against my chest to be set free.

She moaned, angling her head to give me more space to explore. "I'm surprised you're this eager, Lucifer. I thought you'd grown attached to your blue balls."

I worked my fingers down to her hole, probing her

through her underwear. She jerked up, and I chuckled at the dampness staining my skin.

"Decided your cunt was a better alternative," I jibed, but she gathered my face in her hands, forcing me to look up at her.

"Did something happen that I should know about?"

"Yes. It hit me how I couldn't go one more day without your thighs warming up my ears."

She threw her hair over her shoulder, giving me a sultry look. "My thighs warming up your ears or my mouth on your dick? Which one is it gonna be?"

"Why not both?" I flattened my legs on the bed, gripping her thigh, and in one swoop, flipped her so her ass was pointed at me and my erection was poking her face. She squealed at the shift of gravity and did it once more when I slapped all the expansive skin suddenly at my availability.

Any previous doubt about where I was taking this shifted into pure lust as the intoxicating scent of her arousal made my brain turn into mush. Conviction hardened my gut. With one swift tug, her panties were lying discarded somewhere at the head of the bed, and red, engorged flesh greeted me.

"Killian, no...I don't...I've never..." She struggled to form a coherent sentence, and I helped her out, the pulse in my veins going wild as I held myself back from burying my face in her cunt completely.

"You've never sat on anyone's face before?"

Her unsure blues met mine over her shoulder. "Well, no. What if I suffocate you?"

I had to laugh, and her lips pursed as I made fun of her. "Death by pussy doesn't seem like a bad way to go."

"Killian, it's not funny."

This was the longest I'd conversed with a girl before

doing anything sexual, but God, if I wasn't enjoying the hell out of it. Irena Fleur was entertaining even when she wasn't trying to be, and the assurance that I'd have first dibs at showing her something new had my mouth salivating.

"If you knew how many times I've imagined this—you riding my face, your fucking hair in my fist while I fuck you from behind, and every other possible and *impossible* position—you'd laugh too."

She already had an inkling of how deep my obsession with her ran. Now she got the full picture.

Her gaze grew heated, and she nibbled on her bottom lip, revealing her truth reluctantly. "I've imagined you too."

Fuck.

I let my head fall back as an image of Irena in bed with her fingers spreading her wet folds and sliding inside her cunt to the thought of me arose in my mind. My grip turned white-knuckled on her thighs when her wandering hands unzipped me, her touch splaying over my cock. She yelped in pain as I looked up again, more determined than ever, and for all her confidence when it came to sex, she liked being guided. I saw it as she waited for further instructions.

"Then relax, scoot your ass up, and sit on my face," I ordered harshly, and whatever she spotted on my face told her to simply follow along.

She shimmied up my torso, and when she straddled my head, I was floating on a cloud of unparalleled lust. When my tongue came out for a taste, a deep rumble filled my chest in response to her essence working its way down my throat. She made a strangled noise, a loud one, and I chased it again, swiping through her slickness a few more times to better acquaint myself with her flavor.

It burst along my taste buds, sweetness mixed with a

tinge of salt, and within a few seconds, joined the top ranks and knocked down some of my other favorite drinks. I was fucked, because I didn't know how long it would take for me to get over *her*. I was being offered a sample and found out I wanted to claim the entirety of Irena Fleur.

My arms turned into concrete around her hips, holding her in place when she wiggled around as I went to town, grazing my teeth over her clit before clamping down on it and sucking it in my mouth. Her trembling limbs and husky moans sent scorched heat through my cock, engorging it to painful steel.

"Oh my God, Killian. This feels unreal." Her hair tickled along the small of her back as she turned to get a view of me. Irena's eyes were hooded with desire as she subconsciously glided over my mouth in tune with the movement of my tongue.

"Tell me about it," I mumbled against her.

"Better than you imagined?" She grinned, getting more comfortable.

I gave her a languid lick from the hilt to her hole, wanting to see how she would react as her juices glistened on my tongue. Her answering whimper didn't let me down, and her lashes fluttered as she struggled to keep her eyes open at the sensation, not daring to miss the view.

And I was certain it was a glorious one.

I was many things, but modest wasn't one of them. Irena's reaction only served to solidify my lack of humility.

"By a mile," I rasped, and she responded by sweeping down my body as if wanting to see if I lived up to her expectations as well.

I nearly thrust in her mouth when her firm fingers curled around the thick base after pushing my boxers down. She gasped, and damn if that didn't make Killian junior stand to attention even more, and my balls tingle as they underwent her appraisal.

"Shit, of course, it always looked like you had a semi. Your dick is huge," she exclaimed, her warm breath coasting over my nether region. I felt the nervous bob of her neck on my lower stomach, but she played it off with a laugh. "This is gonna be hard."

Irena gave me an experimental pump, resulting in the involuntary upward movement of my hips, and I gritted my teeth. "Already is, sweetheart."

"Shut it. You know what I mean." Another nervous giggle plagued the end of her sentence, and I could sense all those anxious thoughts brewing in that head of hers.

To erase them, I buried my face between her legs again, curving my tongue through her folds, and licked her in long, wet strokes. Her aroma was driving me insane; it was the kind I wanted to bottle up and bring everywhere she wasn't so I always had something of hers to jack off to.

Irena heaved, and her soft startled cries were ones I was becoming consumed by. She sounded like a wounded animal, and the more she called out, the more it ignited my hunger.

I ate her pussy like I was starving. I licked, nibbled, and thrust my tongue inside of her. Then I slid my fingers in, too, because I needed to refresh my memory of how she felt gripping my digits. She scooted up at the unexpected penetration, but I didn't let her escape my warpath.

"Your taste has me so worked up, all you'd need to do is wrap those pretty lips around my head, and I'll come," I panted, hardly able to control my own breathing.

My heart had picked up its pace, my skin was burning,

and my cock was begging to find out how the back of her throat felt like. I was giving her just enough to drive her wild, but not so much she'd come without me. We were getting there together.

"I don't half-ass anything." I felt her grin on the head of my dick. "You best believe I'm not gonna start with sucking your cock."

Sucking your cock.

Those three words in Irena Fleur's mouth sounded like heaven had descended on earth. And when she actually put them into effect, it very much blew my perception of both heaven and earth.

Pun intended.

She thumped the tip against her lips before the little vixen tasted the collected precum against her tongue, lapping it up like it was an ice cream cone. My exhale shuddered out as her hands attacked my balls, squeezing softly while she worked my dick with her mouth.

She progressively got bolder, teasing the ridge between the head and the shaft before closing her mouth over the whole head and sucking until white dots filled my vision. A groan escaped as I forgot about my mission for a few seconds, letting my head drop on the soft cushions below me.

I couldn't connect the dots of how all the emotions I tried to keep contained for two years unraveled within the span of a month, but I wasn't regretting it.

The only thing Irena Fleur sucking my dick was making me regret was not giving in sooner.

I hissed when she started bobbing her head up and down on my cock, taking me as far as she could go, coating it with her saliva. Simultaneously using her hands to stroke the part of my shaft she couldn't fit past those talented lips.

Red-hot pleasure buzzed up my spine, and my balls tingled in warning as I laced my fingers in her hair, urging her to go slower, and breathed out, "Fuck, Irena, I don't want to come until you do."

"Then get me there," she dared, and that brief pause gave me back some of the energy she was intent on hoovering out of me.

Keeping a steady pace with three fingers inside of her, I stretched her out, and when she cried out, I shoved my cock back in her mouth, holding her head immovable as I plowed in and out of her, fucking both her mouth and pussy ruthlessly while sucking her bundle of nerves with newfound urgency.

Over and over, I stabbed my cock past her lips, not allowing her to make a sound. My release was building block by block, but I kept my focus solely on her pleasure, putting mine on the back burner so I wouldn't come.

The way her wetness dripped down the sides of my face told me she loved being dominated, and her porno of choice was probably double penetration. While sharing wasn't my kind of style, I could sure give her the illusion of being worshipped twice, and that's exactly what I set out to do.

Irena gagged against my cock, and her spit slid down my balls as she lost any bit of control she had left, and fuck if that didn't expedite my orgasm.

I nipped her clit, as I let her come up for air while doing the same, and she squirmed in delight, stumbling over her words, "G-god, do that again, please."

I let my five o'clock shadow rub over her sensitive skin as I asked, "Are you forgetting something?"

"Sir." Her husky voice sent a zing straight to my dick,

and she licked another drop of precum that formed and gave me what I needed to hear. "Please, *sir*."

"Good girl," I praised, and did what she'd asked for, enjoying the way her moans vibrated against my length as she set her own pace this time while I rolled my hand down her back, grabbing a handful of her pert ass and spreading her cheeks apart so she'd be able to take my fingers deeper.

I stretched her clit with my teeth again, holding it hostage as I applied a rolling pressure on it with my tongue. Her inner walls convulsed around my fingers, and I almost breathed a shout of relief when she finally came, her cunt adopting a second pulse.

I was barely holding on as it was, so it didn't take long for me to follow suit. My mouth was occupied, so I couldn't warn her, but it didn't seem like she minded when she kept her lips wrapped around me, swallowing down every last drop of my cum.

With every bit of my energy spent, I let her go, and she flopped on her back next to me, dry heaving, as she said, "I can't believe we just did that."

Me neither.

For the longest time, she was an unreachable dream, but now that I'd gotten a taste, you best believe I was going back for more.

Her forehead was shining with sweat when I turned to face her, and I tucked away some strawberry blonde strands that were stuck to her face. She leaned into my touch, those sparkling blues homing in on me.

How could something supposedly so wrong feel so right?

"Well, believe it 'cause it's gonna happen again," I

replied with determination, watching my thumb glide over her jaw.

"This is risky, Killian." She shifted closer.

"We'll be the only ones that know. How much of a risk can it truly be? No telling Bea either."

She bit her lip, thinking it over. "Or Luca."

"Luca would never betray me," I shot back instantly.

"Bea would never betray *me*," she answered in kind, her pupils taking on that stubborn glint.

"Fine. I'm not telling Luca," I relented with a sigh and asked the much-dreaded question, "How long do we have to keep up the charade for?"

She recoiled a little bit at the recollection that this was temporary—or at least, that's what I would like to believe. It could be because I reminded her of her ex.

"End of November, when the show is set to air again. I have until then to put a crack through the perfect couple's façade." She gnawed on her bottom lip, her face swimming with uncertainty.

Two months—*I could do that.* A good enough time to get my fill of Irena Fleur but not nearly long enough to get attached.

I smiled, feeling myself getting hard again at all the things I had in store for her. All the things that now were an actual possibility instead of a far-off fantasy.

"Your vengeful mind is one of the things I find most attractive about you," I thought out loud, rolling on top of her.

With my weight fully on her, she sucked in a sharp breath when my erection poked her lower stomach. I slid my forearms on either side of her to take some of the pressure off, and she asked in wonder, "You're hard again already?"

"Better get used to it." I laughed into her skin as I kissed my way from the side of her face and hovered over her lips. "It takes a lot to tire me out."

The satisfied gasp mixed with a sigh she released when our mouths connected told me she appreciated that. A slow sizzle started building in my veins again as I stroked my tongue with Irena's, and her fingernails dug into my back, underneath my ripped dress shirt. I nudged her knees open and positioned myself, so my dick rested on top of her cunt.

This wasn't the way I'd originally planned this going down, but I didn't have the patience to wait until we were back in Astropolis.

We both held our breaths at what was about to happen, but as I reached between us to tease her clit with the tip of my dick, a few rapid knocks at her hotel door gave us both a pause.

"Irena?" a female voice spoke, and I disconnected my mouth from hers as we listened intensely as she continued. "Are you in there? Are you coming? The rest of the girls already went out, but I thought I'd swing by your room first to check on you."

Irena's head fell back on the mattress, and she closed her eyes as she said with a pained groan, "This needs to stop happening to us."

Fuck.

I was half tempted to ignore whoever was on the other side. She was so wet and so warm, and I was inches away from sinking inside of her.

I buried my face in her neck, and her hands tightened around me. I'd bet my left kidney she'd keep going if I did, but I wanted her to enjoy this day with her new friends. Lord knew she needed them.

"Go. I shouldn't have sprung this on you today." Breathing her scent in deep one last time, I rolled off her, tucking myself in before helping her straighten her clothes.

"I don't mind. Actually, I love that you did." The disappointment in her eyes as I fixed her skirt, then her rumpled shirt hit me straight in the dick—*yup, that's right, the dick.* "Are you leaving tonight? If not, we could go out tomorrow and explore some of the city together."

I watched her smooth her hair down and run a finger along the corners of her mouth to fix her lipstick. It didn't matter how well she managed to touch up, she still looked like she needed...well, me, inside of her.

"Let's not turn this into more than it is," I cautioned, and her face soured as she got on her feet.

"Irena." The voice came again, sparing me from some very colorful language, I was sure.

"Coming!" Irena yelled toward the door, then pointed at me. "You're my fake boyfriend, no? That entails going on dates so I can post cute pictures of us on social media, faceless, of course."

I pretended to think it over, but the truth was, I didn't need much convincing.

"In that case, I'm down." She beamed at me and started to turn, but I called out her nickname and hooked my finger at her. "Lilith."

She came rushing back, and our mouths crashed as we reveled in our newfound freedom and surrendered to the intrusive thoughts.

I pecked her lips twice and held her head to mine as I informed her, "Fake relationship or not, my stake on you is very real until this is all over. So if anyone gets close to you when I'm not there, you knee them in the balls for me, okay?"

"Does the same apply to you?" she asked haughtily.

"The women I usually go for don't have balls."

"Then punch their boobs." She smiled, and I couldn't keep my laughter in any longer.

It was ironic how I'd laughed more the past hour while doing something I wasn't supposed to than I had this whole month.

"Okay," I confirmed, and she returned the sentiment.

"Okay."

CHAPTER THIRTEEN
IRENA

A piece of steak was lodged in my throat, and I was buzzing with nervous energy, unlike Killian, who sat beside me cool as a cucumber, cutting into his filet mignon with surgeon-like precision.

I liked spending time with Saint and Aria, but add Killian in the mix, and I had a permanent blush on while constantly stumbling over my words. I was trying to appear as normal as possible because Saint acted like a hound that had caught a whiff of a suspicious scent.

From the cringe on Killian's face, I understood I was failing miserably. Coming to dinner with them wasn't the wisest choice after everything that had happened over the past forty-eight hours. Still, I couldn't very well say no when they wanted to congratulate me for doing well on my first show.

It had been thirty minutes in now, and while the place's ambiance was warm and welcoming with the soft yellow lighting and neutral tones, I couldn't shake off this anxiety that plagued me.

"So, Irena," Saint started, his gold hair the exact same shade as his brother's shining whenever he turned his head. "I heard that you and Killian are neighbors now. How's he treating you so far?"

"Terribly," I replied, finally putting a crack through Killian's carefully curated image when he choked on his bite. "Didn't even help me with my boxes when I asked him to."

With two pairs of eyes on him after an unexpected attack, he struggled to contain his cool and chewed as fast as possible to blurt out, "I was busy."

"Yes, *busy* with Mia." I swished some water in my mouth, pretending to give him the side eye, when in reality, I was urging him to play along.

He raised a brow at me like we were having a silent chat, and a smirk took over his lips like he understood exactly what I was trying to do. Bantering was natural for Killian and me in front of everyone. We had to play it like we normally did.

Killian sat back in his chair, abandoning his food, and I stiffened when I felt his hand snaking up my thigh. My eyes immediately flew to Saint and Ari, but they were both engrossed on Kill's face, waiting to hear his explanation.

He shrugged, digging back at me, "What can I say? Some of us have active love lives."

"Oh, please," Aria snorted next to Saint, ever my protector. "The word *love* isn't even in your dictionary."

"Was it in my brother's dictionary when you met him?" Killian argued, those fingers of his inching underneath the skirt of my chiffon dress, despite me clamping my legs tightly closed and clawing at his hand as subtly as possible.

"No, but he was thirty. His prime time was coming to an

end," Aria said with a sly smile, picking at the berry sauce on her plate.

Saint snorted. "Thirty is the new twenty. My life was just beginning."

"Well, I swooped right in time and took your best years." My sister batted her lashes at him, and he all but melted on the spot.

"I'm not complaining." Saint leaned in to kiss the tip of her nose and then transferred some more food from his plate to hers.

I didn't have the time to feel that familiar jealousy swooping in because the touch on the apex of my thighs shocked me to my core.

I couldn't believe what he was doing.

Right in front of our siblings.

I tried to get him to look at me, but he was focused on his discussion as if he wasn't delving between my folds at this very minute. And to my great horror, it simply took a minuscule touch from him to get me wet and ready. The sole sign that betrayed what he was doing was the upward tilt of his mouth.

"I am," Killian cut in, and I pressed my lips tightly together to keep in a wrangled moan when he gathered my wetness and swirled it around my clit. "Has anyone ever told you how annoying it is when you guys always find a way to make every conversation about you?"

I tried to close my legs again when Saint pinned him with an unimpressed glare, but he pinched my inner thigh, and I masked my squawk by shoving a piece of bread in my mouth.

"No, they usually admire us," Saint answered, and Killian scoffed.

"You're so conceited."

"It's in our gene pool," the older Astor retorted, swirling the wine in his glass. "I thought Mia moved away."

"She comes and goes whenever she pleases." The pressure with which Killian was rubbing on my bundle of nerves upped as if punishing me for putting him on the spot, and goose bumps spread up my arms. "By the way, I'll be handing in my resignation by the end of next month," Killian added, shocking us all into silence.

"What?" both Saint and Aria blurted after taking a moment to collect themselves.

Killian had to have some kind of superpower for being able to still converse normally, and I had to have had some sort of brain deficiency from almost coming at such a time and place.

"I found an investor that was interested in the plan I presented, and I'll be opening my own tattoo shop by New Year's." Killian downed his second glass of whiskey on the rocks in one go, showing off his expert multitasking skills as he rubbed faster.

I was so close to squirming in my seat, and it was pure torture to have to sit there dead faced and pretend I was engrossed in whatever they were saying.

I was so paying him back for this.

"If you needed funding, I could've helped," Saint offered.

"I didn't want *your* help," Killian replied abruptly, and I was able to breathe properly for a minute when he paused his movement as hurt flashed in Saint's eyes. It was a rare display of emotion from my brother-in-law, and one that vanished as soon as it appeared as he clarified, "I already have more connections than people can dream of. The least I can do is put some work in myself."

"I see." Saint pursed his lips, and Aria's gaze bounced between them, looking like she knew something I didn't. "Who's the investor then? Did you do your research? There are a ton of ways you could get screwed over."

"It's Luca. The plan is to pay him back within a year. I'll probably be able to do so within five months."

I clutched Killian's wrist under the table when he went ham again, urging him to stop with this slow torture, but when he didn't listen, I decided to antagonize him instead.

"How are you so sure you're gonna succeed?" I raised a brow at him.

He grinned in my direction, some of his previous intensity gone as he cocked his head. "Failure also isn't in my dictionary."

Just as he said that, his middle finger entered me, and unable to control my reaction, I scooted my chair back accidentally. Aria looked at me curiously, and I gave an uppity huff even as the muscles in my lower stomach tightened, readying for my release.

"Conceitedness really runs in the family," I commented.

"I call it confidence." His gaze sliced to where his fingers were entering me for one split second, and he fingered me harder, rolling his hand, so his knuckles brushed against my sensitive folds, and my mouth dropped a little when a myriad of colors burst behind my closed eyelids.

My joints hurt from how hard I was clutching his hand, but he still didn't stop, even as an orgasm burst through me. Heat traveled to every corner and crevice of my body, lingering for a few maddening minutes that I wished lasted forever.

I bit my tongue in my mouth to keep from making a sound and to distract myself from the bone-shaking pleasure that filled my veins.

I bet a part of Killian delighted in this. Defying his brother right under his nose. He really did not play by the rules, and enforcing them on him, led you...well, with his fingers shoved in his brother's sister-in-law's pussy underneath the dinner table.

Finally, I got him to remove his hand with one more push, and I couldn't even dispute his last sentence with a straight face as the lower half of my body quaked from the intensity of the orgasm he had given me.

I threw my hair over my shoulder and faced forward as I tried to calm down, and for the first time during the whole night, I was grateful to Saint for intervening.

"Either way, I'm proud that you're following your passion," he said, and you could actually hear it in his voice.

"Father is gonna freak," Killian said as he used the cloth paper towel to wipe my cum off his fingers. I blushed even more as a result.

With each passing day in Killian Astor's presence, I became more reckless.

He made me lose all common sense, and all it took was a few touches.

"Leave him to me," Saint assured and glanced at me curiously. "Irena, are you okay? You're sweating."

My hand flew to my forehead, and indeed precipitation dotted the space between my brows. I fumbled to find an excuse but settled for one that made men uncomfortable and, therefore, would put an end to the questioning.

"Y-yes, just a hot flash. I got my period today," I explained. If Aria caught on to the tremble of my voice, she didn't say anything, though her expression grew confused.

"TMI, Lilith." Killian's amused voice grated on my nerves.

"It's a natural bodily function, Lucifer. What are you, five?" I retorted.

He shook his head. "Nope, I'm a ten."

"You're insufferable." I let out a long sigh, though I didn't continue playing into his hand.

It had been enough excitement for me for one day, and I was content with taking a back seat as the rest of them steered the conversation and we finished our meals.

CHAPTER FOURTEEN
IRENA

An hour later, I could finally breathe easy again. The rest of the dinner went great, I got to talk about my plans to produce an ice-skating show of my own and shared how exhilarating walking in my first show was, but in the back of my mind, I couldn't rid myself of the guilt that blanketed me for the rest of the evening.

It was one thing going behind my sister's back, but what I *allowed* Killian to do was disrespectful. I made sure to let him know when we met up at the Grand Central Terminal half an hour later.

"Are you out of your mind?" were the first words I spoke to him as he pulled me to the side so we wouldn't get trampled by the onslaught of people that went about their night. "How could you do that?"

He leaned against a pillar, resting his hands on his elbows, and I willed myself not to look at his bulging biceps. He had somehow managed to find the time to change from his suit and tie to more casual attire consisting of a short sleeve blue shirt that did wonders for his body type.

"You'll have to be more specific." His blues took on a devious glint that told me he knew exactly what I meant but got off on hearing me say it, and like the fool that I was, I fed his fantasy.

"You fingered me in front of *your* brother and *my* sister!" My voice was loud enough to pull some judgmental stares from passersby, and his mouth turned into a thin line. He draped an arm over my shoulder, pulling me to his side so not many people had a clear view of my face.

"I helped you loosen up. You looked like you had a stick up your ass the entire time." His excuse was half-assed at best, and he didn't even put any effort into altering the sound of his voice from bored beyond imagination to try to convince me.

"Killian..." I pinched the bridge of my nose, unsure about how to continue.

He blew out a frustrated breath, took my face in his hands, and forced my head up, his eyes boring into mine and nearly giving me third-degree burns by how unnaturally icy they seemed at that very moment. "Did they find out?"

My forehead bunched at his question, but I humored him. "No."

"And did you come?" He raised an eyebrow, and I squirmed.

"Yes," I answered simply.

"Then I don't see what the problem is." Killian shrugged and dropped a peck on my lips that left me craving for more as he blazed past the topic at hand. He let go of my face, only to grab my hand and start ushering me toward a platform. "Now, come on or we're gonna be late."

With my thoughts all over the place, I let him have this one as I battled with the morality of the deal we'd agreed on and tried to stop his advance by saying, "But the Broadway show doesn't start until eight."

I'd booked us tickets to watch *Hamilton*, even though he told me he was more interested in *Moulin Rouge*. I'd texted him back asking if he was willing to take me to a *Magic Mike* show then, and he wasted no time agreeing on *Hamilton*, so I was surprised by this turn of events.

"Yeah." He sucked air through his teeth as he said regretfully, "I'm not sitting through that."

My eye twitched because the tickets were non-refundable, but Killian seemed hell-bent on his plan. He was quite literally dragging me along like dead weight because I refused to comply.

"Then where are we going?"

"Have some patience, Lilith. I promise it's gonna be worth it."

I let out a disgruntled sound but went on with his plan anyway. We only had one more day left in New York, and I wanted to spend it with him. The cranky, sarcastic Killian that always managed to make our time together memorable, despite the circumstances.

The way to his destination was a blur as he asked me not to look at any of the signs because he wanted to surprise me. I agreed reluctantly, pretending I actually knew my way around the city despite being mostly driven around every time I visited in the past.

It was chaos inside the train, but we were oblivious to all the noise around us—the sweaty bodies brushing against us, the overabundance of coffee cups despite the late hour, and takeout bags containing greasy foods with an unpleasant aroma. It was just the two of us.

I usually always planned my days. I was an organized

mess, and that also played a role in my relationships in the past. Most of the guys I'd dated were too indecisive to think of something to do when we went out, so it was always up to me to pick. And when it came to tonight, I hadn't even thought about asking Killian if he would like to do something else and had simply sprung my ideas onto him.

I couldn't blame him for wanting to do something different, especially when he told me he hated musicals because he was forced to watch *West Side Story* all the time when he was a kid because his father was a fan. It seemed anything associated with that man, Killian hated.

I also liked that he'd taken charge. It was nice not being in the driver's seat for once and having someone else take care of you—although he could've saved both of us some money by telling me sooner.

Much to my dismay, he legit used the tie he'd worn earlier today to blindfold me when we got into an Uber after exiting the subway because, apparently, this place was quite a distance away. No matter how many times I asked where the hell he was taking me, he wouldn't give in. I had half a mind to peek when he left me alone for a little after we got out of the car, doing Lord knows what, but didn't, even though I probably looked stupid.

"All right, you can take the blindfold off now," he said as we came to a stop.

We had to be in an open field, judging by the onslaught of cold wind that made my hair dance over my shoulders.

I undid the hasty knot and blinked as I focused on my surroundings and realized how wrong I was. This was no open field; it was downtown Manhattan, and we were surrounded by water and skyscrapers on a runway that had helicopters parked on either side.

I opened and closed my mouth, trying to figure out something to say, when I put two and two together and realized what we were about to do.

"Killian, no way." I clutched his forearm, turning toward him for confirmation.

"Yes, way. You said you wanted to explore the city, no?" he confirmed, and I couldn't contain my squeal.

Killian was spooked by the high-pitched sound, but I didn't give him any time to make fun of me—I was sure he would compare me to something akin to a rat getting stepped on—and kissed him square on the lips.

He didn't respond right away, surprised by my excitement, but definitely took it there by cupping the back of my head and deepening what started out as an innocent peck by sucking on my tongue hungrily. He was about to cup my ass when I pulled back and gave him a stern look.

This man was a ball of raging hormones. Not that I was any better around him, but we weren't alone and I didn't want to put on another show.

He still clutched my butt for good measure as he ushered me toward a black helicopter. While these suckers looked small in movies, I was barely half its size while standing next to it. It had no doors in the back, and there were harnesses resting on the leather seats.

"I haven't been in a helicopter in forever. Are we taking a tour of NYC from above?" I asked, resting my palm on his neck and staring up at him.

"Mm-hmm, and I'll be flying us," Killian informed me happily, and hell if that didn't put a damper on my enthusiasm.

I looked at the helicopter again, at all the weird switches

and buttons and different kinds of levers, and then back at Killian.

I'd misheard him, right?

"What?" I took a step back, but he didn't let me get far.

He seemed amused at the sheer terror that took over my face and simply said, "Oh, don't look so scared, Lilith. You're not dying on my watch. I'm too attached to your ass to let that happen."

He gave it a squeeze as if to reiterate his point, and I elbowed him in the gut to break out of his hold.

"Because that makes me feel so much better." I tucked my hair behind my ears, but it was no use. The wind took the strands again. I rubbed my hands down my arms now that I wasn't burrowing into Killian's heat. I certainly wouldn't have worn a strapless mini-dress if I knew we'd be spending so much time outside. "How did you even manage to find a helicopter? I wasn't even aware you could rent one without a pilot. Aren't they worth millions or something like that?"

"I have over fifteen hundred hours of experience, so I am a pilot. I got my license at nineteen." Killian regarded my shivering form with little sympathy but ducked for a back-pack resting on the helicopter's floor and pulled out an over-sized gray jacket that he draped over my shoulders. "It *is* tough to rent one, but not when one of your buddies owns a helicopter tour agency. I greeted him while you were blindfolded. We got our licenses at the same time."

I pushed my hands through the sleeves, and the material swallowed me whole. It was his jacket, judging by the fresh pine scent, and I burrowed my nose into my shoulder and breathed in deeply like a creep while he rummaged through the bag again.

For some unexplainable reason, my mind kept

repeating the word *pilot* over and over. I never expected this from Killian, and there went my hopes of losing interest once I got to know him better, because all I could think about right now was jumping him in a pilot's uniform.

"I have so many questions." I gulped when he came to stand behind me with a hair tie. He had really thought of everything.

Killian gathered my hair with one hand and dropped a kiss where my neck met my shoulder, and shivers rushed down my body from the sensation. "Let's get in the air, and we'll clear them all up."

I twisted my head while he was tying my hair, making his work harder, and said, "I'm trusting you, Killian."

"Famous last words," he mocked.

"Stop it." I pinched his side, and he ducked away, laughing boisterously as he headed for the helicopter and motioned me closer.

I was all strapped in and given a safety briefing by Killian after I sat on the co-pilot's seat, but I was too excited to pay any attention to anything he was saying, so if this thing went down, it wasn't looking good for me.

Killian knew what he was doing, though, as he fiddled with the instruments on the panel, and I simply watched on, taking pictures here and there to post later because I couldn't lose sight of why we were actually doing this.

We both had our headphones on, and I was tongue-tied as the engine buzzed loudly and the blades started spinning, washing away any other sort of noise. The wind picked up, and I let out a startled gasp when we wobbled, an indicator that we were in the air.

Killian had no time to make fun of me, though. With his hand on the cyclic, he steered us forward and talked to the radio before taking off. "Lining up on the runway. Lights are out, RPMs are good, temperature pressures are in the green, sufficient fuel."

He then nodded after receiving the all-clear from the other line, peeked at me to see how I was holding up, and fought a smile at my green face.

"And we're off," Killian confirmed, and we started climbing in altitude, the numbers on the radar on top of the controls rising.

The urge to puke became more intense the farther up we went. Sitting in the cockpit gave me a complete bird's-eye view, and it felt like I was going to plunge to my death any second because the glass extended so far down. The wind was howling like crazy behind us, but I barely felt the cold with all this adrenaline running through my system.

A mix of fear and excitement clashed inside me, but when the skyscrapers that once towered over us sprawled beneath us, they gave way to awe. I couldn't even open my mouth to reply when Killian's voice fleeted through the headphones, asking me if I was okay.

I was fortunate enough to experience many things and visit many places, but this would be a memory I would cherish forever—that is, if I didn't die.

The city lights pulsed beneath us, and I could see why Killian had opted for helicopter lessons. We were pretty high up, but not disconnected from the world. I often found flying boring—save for take-off and landing—because you were basically stuck in the clouds for hours on end, but this was different.

You had millions of people stretched underneath your feet, a skyline that lit up the night sky with its brightness, and the ocean that gave the air a hint of saltiness, making you nostalgic for hot summer days spent at the beach.

My worries suspended.

I was a tiny blip in the universe, and all that had me lying awake at night seemed so trivial up here.

"Wow, this is surreal," I marveled when Killian repeated his question.

"It's beautiful." Even though the headphones amplified our voices, his came out surprisingly soft. Eyes bored into my cheek, and I met his gaze, catching an emotion he was quick to hide by looking away. "The freedom you get up here is unlike anything else."

"Is that why you got your license?"

"Yes. As soon as I turned seventeen, I began taking flying lessons."

"To get away from your dad? I know you guys don't have such a good relationship with him."

"That's an understatement." Killian released a sharp laugh. "But yes, among other things."

"Like what?" I probed because while most of his problems were in the light, he carried a sort of weight on his shoulders that indicated the well went deeper than one could see.

"That's a can of worms you do not want to open, trust me," Killian answered, and just when I was about to oppose him, he pointed at something in the far distance. "Look, that's the Statue of Liberty."

I followed his finger, and indeed, Lady Liberty was

standing proud on her island as a bunch of ferries and boats, mostly chock-full of tourists, taking pictures passed by. I wasn't any better than them and whipped out my phone to shoot a video as Killian told me this was the closest we could get. Apparently, it was prohibited to fly directly over it.

"Oh my God, she doesn't look all that big from up here," I mused, remembering how on top of the world I'd felt when I was a kid and we'd taken a tour of the inside.

Killian angled the helicopter left, and I shut my phone as we got farther away. "She was actually transported to the US in individually packed pieces that took up more than two hundred cases. It was a gift from France."

I ran my hands down my bare legs to warm them up because the cold had started affecting me. "You're a history buff as well? What else don't I know about you?"

Killian took my question in stride and gave me the rundown. "I'm lactose intolerant, half vegetarian, and have a handcuff collection."

A handcuff collection?

Of course, that's where my mind lingered.

The city view didn't hold a candle to him, and I missed the landscape as I studied his strong profile, the scruff on his jaw that would mark my skin every time he leaned in for a kiss, and those full lips I craved to feel everywhere on my body.

I was willing to do a lot of things. I'd wanted him since I was sixteen, for fuck's sake, but control... I liked having control after losing every bit of it for the past year.

"Vegetarian? You literally had a steak for dinner," I scoffed, ignoring what inconvenienced me.

"Hence the *half*. I crave meat sometimes, but I'm mostly

disgusted by it," Killian explained, eyes flicking to mine. "You're not touching the handcuff comment, eh?"

I fidgeted with my seat belt, sensing a deal breaker. "I don't like being restrained. Being at someone else's mercy doesn't sound pleasurable to me."

"What's my name?" he inquired, throwing me for a loop.

"Huh?"

"What's my name?" he repeated louder.

"Killian Astor," I indulged him after a moment of hesitation.

"Exactly. I'm not just *anyone*." The way he uttered the last word made it sound like a curse, and my throat tightened as he went on. "You *will* be at my mercy, and you *will* like it because, in my world, a woman's pleasure always comes first."

The straps I was holding dug into my palm so hard I had to loosen my hold when it started to hurt. I was both intrigued and terrified, but I kept my cards close to my chest as I asked, "How do I know you're not just telling me what I want to hear? You're a notorious womanizer, after all. You must have picked up a thing or two over the years."

He grinned to himself, and even though he was flying a fucking helicopter, he looked me dead in the eyes as he said, "Well, I believed I'd already proved it by now, but I'd be more than happy to refresh your memory."

An uncomfortable ache developed between my legs, but I set my mouth in a firm line. "Keep your eyes on the...*sky?*"

I was going to say road, but clearly, there were none. My command lost its punch after my hesitation, but Killian shook his head and let me have this one. It was far from over, though. That much was clear as his determination flowed in the air between us.

"What about you? Tell me some things I don't know about you."

I was pleasantly surprised at his subject change and compiled a list as we whizzed past some of what had to be the tallest buildings in the world. "I love cheese—I eat almost all my meals with feta cheese, and my fridge is always stocked with Parmigiano Reggiano, so I couldn't imagine being lactose intolerant. I probably own more than fifty skirts, not including my ice-skating ones, and I like making fun of Aria's love for smutty books, even though I occasionally borrow some of them without her noticing."

"I, for one, am extremely grateful for your love of skirts." I stretched my legs when he glanced down at them, giving him a little show, and he shook his head. "And why don't you want Aria to know that you also enjoy them?"

"'Cause then I can't tease her anymore, duh." I rolled my eyes, chastising him for not putting two and two together on his own. We neared a dark patch of land with shifting trees and a few people making their way through. "Is that Central Park?"

"Yes," he answered.

It usually had more people while it was still light out, but it wasn't recommended to go after dark. It had a serenity about it, though, one that only the bare eye could capture, despite me trying my best, a thousand pictures and videos later.

"Everything looks so beautiful," I sighed.

Our flight wasn't even over yet, and I was already thinking about begging Killian to take me on another one again soon.

"Sure helps that we're far enough away that we can escape the stench of piss, overcrowding, and rats."

"Don't rain on my parade, spoilsport."

"All right, all right, the city has its charm..." He relented, but it didn't last long as per the Killian way. "When you're not being yelled at by randos on the subway."

"I take it big cities are not your thing?" I asked, because this was not just a New York problem. I'd lost count of the number of times I'd gotten yelled at in Athens for standing on the wrong side of the escalator or witnessed a robbery in London. It was crazy everywhere, even Astropolis, though the gated communities sure helped keep it to a minimum.

"I prefer something more contained, not one million people per block. That's stifling."

"What if I happened to be one of those one million people?" I raised a brow.

Killian wrinkled his nose, hitting me with a dose of sarcasm. "Then I'd immediately drop everything and move there, obviously."

"I'd make it worth your while." I bit the inside of my cheek when his fingers flexed on the cyclic and his jaw squared.

"For that, I have no doubt." His tongue passed over his bottom lip.

Killian had managed to shift my view of him so much within a couple of weeks it wasn't even funny. Now I didn't only want to ride his dick. I also enjoyed talking with him.

It was tragic.

And bad news for me.

I managed to get through the rest of the flight without betraying the second thoughts I was having about our little arrangement. Killian Astor could only hurt me if I let him, and this wasn't my first rodeo. I wasn't allowing him to get that close.

Besides, I was gaining way too much from this to abandon ship so early on. I hadn't even properly put my plan into action, and I was already getting calls from Daniel after that day at the club. Well, *call*, just one, but it didn't take a genius to figure out there would be more after I plastered my fake relationship with Killian everywhere.

I couldn't share his face, and that was a strength as much as it was a weakness. People would go mad trying to find out who he is, and from the bits that I *could* share, they would be able to tell that Daniel could never compare.

We landed after an hour-long flight, and I was so wind-blown my hair was sticking in all sorts of different directions. My legs were numb from the cold, the tips of my ears burned, and my nose was so red I could give Rudolph the Reindeer a run for his money.

Still, it was an experience I'd remember forever. Who would've thought Killian Astor knew how to fly a helicopter? It was an expensive hobby, and Killian, with his bad-boy persona, didn't fit the bill.

I sometimes forgot where he came from.

"I'm sad it's over. This was incredible, Killian," I said as I fumbled to undo my seat belt. There were like four different ones, so Killian reached over, batting my hands away and unstrapping them for me. Of course, copping a feel in the process too.

"You're welcome, Lilith." His pearly whites made an appearance when his palms brushed the sides of my thighs, and I made a sound of contentment at the heat of them.

"I didn't thank you yet." I pushed him back in his seat before the situation could escalate. It was my turn now. I looked around the utterly dark heliport before asking, "How many minutes do we have until we need to be out of here?"

His forehead wrinkled in question. "Five, give or take. A van is coming to pick us up. Why?"

"More than enough time for me to show my gratitude." I leaned over his lap.

"Fuck." His head fell back as I unzipped him and took his engorged dick out of his pants. It barely fit in my hands, and I never thought I'd say this, but it was the most aesthetically pleasing cock I'd ever seen.

"Have I told you I love the way your cock looks? Perfect amount of girth and length," I shared as I pumped him, my mouth ghosting over his slit.

He shook his head, staring at me in anticipation. "No, but since this is only the second time you're seeing him, I'll forgive you."

"Hmm," I hummed, languidly licking the top and grinning up at him. "Tastes perfect too."

"Stop torturing me, Lilith," he pleaded.

"But isn't that what the Queen of Hell does best?" I giggled before taking him deep in my mouth again. There would be plenty of time to torture him later, but I was working against the clock and needed him to come fast.

"Goddamn." His hand fisted in my hair as I started bobbing up and down. "You're the best risk I've ever taken, Irena Fleur."

CHAPTER FIFTEEN
IRENA

"Wait for me, I've got little legs." A struggling Amani wobbled behind Bea and me on the ice, her legs sliding in all directions but forward.

I'd gotten back from New York late last night, and she said she needed to speak with me at my earliest convenience, so I thought, why not invite her to practice with Bea? We got free entertainment while we trained.

Technically, I was retired, so I didn't have to practice, but I didn't do it out of obligation. I did it out of necessity. Skating was too embedded in my blood for me to go long without visiting the rink. Even just driving by soothed my nerves sometimes.

Bea and I slowed down, skating circles around her, willing to lend the helping hand she clearly needed, but ever the independent woman, she shooed us away, going at her own pace.

"I don't think your height is the problem," I commented with a snicker.

"You know this all could've been avoided if you just

answered your damn phone." She huffed and puffed, her tight jeans certainly not aiding her at all.

"Where would the fun in that be?" I skated backward, pinning her with a stare. It was my time to gloat. "I needed to see your face when you finally admitted that you were wrong and I was right."

"About what?" she scoffed.

"Really?" Bea came to my rescue, raising a brow at Amani. "I was there, you know. She has witnesses."

She was referring to the argument we'd had a month ago over breakfast. Amani's doubt cut me deep because I always delivered until that one incident. Did every job she threw on the table with a fucking smile on my face. I think she low-key believed some of the stuff Daniel had spewed, and if she did, I didn't entirely blame her. Daniel was a great bullshitter. I'd learned firsthand how good of a deceiver he was.

I didn't usually take the petty road. I had this view of being vindicated without having to say a word. Still, I realized that would never happen, or more accurately, Killian helped me understand it. The content I'd shared of our date had done the job, and an hour or so afterward, I had a call log full of missed calls from Daniel.

He'd taken the bait, and Killian primed me up for a direct hit. I didn't see how posting screenshots of all the missed calls could help. However, he told me if I was as emotionally abusive and crazy as Daniel claimed, then why was he still trying to contact me when he was finally free?

I liked having my privacy, but this was a game I was forced to play, and unfortunately, the grand prize was regaining my career, so I had to go all in, guns blazing. There was still plenty of room for Daniel to defend himself. He did, saying that he was only contacting me because I still hadn't returned some of his stuff, but the seed of doubt was planted, and that was good enough for me.

People needed to look into the shades of gray that stood in between the black and white, and Killian gave me the courage to press forth. I couldn't pinpoint why, but I felt like the world couldn't touch me when I was with him. I got this weird knot in my stomach when he dropped me off at the airport, and we had to go home separately.

"Look, it's too early to tell." Amani didn't back down. "Yes, you've gotten some good press, but in the grand scheme of things, you were still dropped from Stars on Ice."

"I don't care about Stars on Ice anymore. I'm getting my own show," I was quick to rebuke, and she gave up her failed attempts at skating, her tongue poking out in concentration as she looked up at me.

"Did I miss a couple of chapters?"

I nodded, and when Bea bid us goodbye because her trainer called her, I launched into explaining my idea. There were plenty of similar TV shows out there. Late-night television was basically the same, full of middle-aged white guys whose names started with a J, and I'd lost count of how many dating shows copied each other.

Basically, originality wasn't the root of success in films and TV. It was charisma, especially in reality. The audience forms emotional attachments to the talent, and they watch on, interested to learn what happens next.

I'd been in this industry for so many years now I knew the ins and outs like the back of my hand. I had already compiled a list of all the figure skaters I wanted in my cast, and I emailed it to a stone-faced Amani. She was the type that only said *job well done* after plans were finalized. Even showing excitement beforehand was bad luck for her. She was superstitious like that.

"Sting of Ice?" She clicked her tongue after I told her the title. "Why Sting of Ice?"

I popped my hip, resting it on the railing, and observed Bea pull off a triple axel jump flawlessly. She was one of the skaters on my list, but I hadn't told her anything yet. She was offered to be on Stars on Ice, too, but declined. She was pretty camera shy, but with a little convincing from me, she would get on board.

"Because both excessive heat and cold burn. And my skaters will be so good, they could melt the ice if they wanted to."

She scratched her chin, thinking it over. "I like the name, but we're gonna work on the delivery."

"So you're on board?" I asked eagerly.

"Yes, I'll start pitching to some networks." She whipped her phone out, ready to start working already, and I did a little shuffle with my skates, sliding them on the ice and prompting Amani to point a finger at me. "Don't get too excited. We still don't know if anyone's going to want to pick it up."

"Well, what can I do to up our chances?"

"What you've been doing." She finished typing something and crossed her arms, pinning me in place with her gaze. "Who's the new guy?"

I didn't give into her intimidation technique and shrugged. "If I wanted people to know, I would've posted his name already."

"I'm your manager," she said, as if that made her privy to anything in my life.

It kind of did, but not this once.

I pretended to brush away some fuzz from my polo shirt, and like clockwork, a dry-heaving Bea took a break right when Amani was about to pressure me into answering. She placed her hands on her knees, wisps of curly hair escaping her tight bun as she asked, "What did I miss?"

Amani took the opportunity in stride and gave Bea a *help me out here* smile. "You wouldn't happen to know the identity of the guy she's dating, would you?"

Bea glanced at me. I shook my head ever so slightly and pretended to glance at a spot in the ceiling when Amani caught what I was doing. It was enough for Bea to get the message, though. As per my agreement with Kill, I hadn't told her anything about what went down in New York, but I didn't have to. She was a smart girl.

"Actually, I'm not privy to that information either." Bea blinked with utmost innocence, stepping up her lying game.

It wasn't good enough for Amani, though, whose expression soured like spoiled milk. "I doubt it."

"I'm sorry you feel that way." Bea bit the inside of her cheek to keep herself from cracking. Having had enough of our antics, Amani straightened, almost slipping in the process.

Both Bea and I rushed to help her maintain her balance, and this time, she fought us off.

"Just keep out of trouble," she cautioned as we each hugged one of her hands and escorted her to the rink's exit. "I have enough on my hands already."

"Sir, yes, sir," I mumbled, tired of hearing the same advice constantly.

So what if I got into a little bit of trouble? That was what I paid her for, to solve my troubles for me.

Bea's knowing gaze haunted me over Amani's short

build, but she wisely kept her mouth shut until my manager was out of our sight. Once we were alone, though, she held no punches. "Did you just agree to stay out of trouble while also promising to keep dating your sister's brother-in-law?"

I wasn't surprised she had caught that. She'd seen me struggling to answer the question, and that's why she swooped in.

"How-What?" I acted clueless, albeit half-heartedly, and slid down the nearly empty rink. It was early morning, and the space was reserved for a closed practice. "I'm not."

"You're insulting my intelligence, Ina." She followed close behind me, and we began with a few warm-up laps around the arena.

No telling Irena or Luca. That was what I'd agreed on with Killian, but *I* hadn't told her anything. She'd figured it out. How was that my fault?

I chewed on the dead skin on my lips because no matter how much Chapstick I put on, they still dried out at this temperature.

"Fine," I finally said, a little too loudly, and my voice echoed. Some of the other skaters that were also training glared at us for breaking their concentration. I gave them an apologetic smile before continuing on with a lower tone. "But we agreed it's just something short-term. I *am* keeping myself out of trouble."

Bea scoffed. "How well you lie to yourself. I'd pegged you as smarter than that, Irena."

"I guess my smarts were tossed out the window the second I thought about *him* pegging me." I made light of the situation, and Bea snorted out a laugh.

"You dirty ho. I didn't know you were into that shit."

"I like to keep an open mind."

The atmosphere lightened considerably, but the voice of reason, aka Bea Murphy, had to put her two cents in.

"I'm not going to fight you on this because it seems like you're set on your decision, but just be careful. Don't forget that it's all temporary, and don't start thinking you can change him." She air quoted the last two words.

"Of course not," I agreed, and my insides churned. "We're both young and ambitious. A serious relationship doesn't make sense for either of us. We're just—"

"Fucking?" she finished for me.

"Pretty much..." I confirmed, then rethought my answer. "We actually haven't even gotten there yet."

Much to my regret. We'd gotten stuck at simply fooling around. I hadn't waited this long to have sex with someone since fucking high school. I wasn't complaining about the foreplay—that would be dumb of me—but I was dying to actually feel *him* inside of me. Not his fingers, not his tongue, his dick.

"What's holding you back? I thought you would've jumped his bones already."

"Our schedules are not aligning," I said regretfully. We'd been back in town for one whole day and hadn't even seen each other. I'd texted him if he wanted to meet later for lunch, but he was working until the AM, so tonight wouldn't be the night either.

Part of me considered waiting for him until he got home, but I had an early morning photoshoot that required my face to be devoid of any dark circles. And I didn't want our first time to be rushed.

"You know what that calls for?" Bea wiggled her brows.

"What?"

"Some lingerie shopping, so you're finally motivated to find the time."

"Weren't you the one saying that this was risky?"

"Yes, but you're gonna do it anyway, so I might as well aid you along." She did a little spin in front of me, showing off after deeming me a lost cause. "Besides, as much as Killian rubs me the wrong way, he's a fine piece of ass, and I live for the juicy details."

My limbs were screaming for some downtime, and I forced Bea to stop at the nearest Sephora to spritz myself with some of the tester perfumes before she dragged me along on a shopping trip. I'd sweated my butt off, so I couldn't find it in me to care about the judgmental side-eyes the store clerks were showering me with.

Bea had never been to Aria's new boutique in upper Astropolis, so we decided to go. My sister was the best designer in the world, in my opinion at least. It was a new store, and Aria liked spending time there when Saint wasn't home, finalizing all the last details. My sister had started working ever since she was a teenager, so maternity leave would take some getting used to.

The lingerie room was bright and airy, shielded away from the glass windows at the front. The walls were white with a grayish tint, and there were elegant crown moldings on the ceiling and over the built-in racks. There were royal purple sofas for that pop of color and leafy plants in every other corner. It was lunchtime, but plenty of people were still browsing through the shelves and looking at clothes.

Aria was one of them, volunteering to help us when we

stepped inside. I gave her a heads-up before we came, and she was excited to see Bea. Me, on the other hand... Well, let's just say her feelings weren't all that warm and fuzzy after I failed to tell her I was going on a date after leaving dinner and having to find out online.

"The family's abuzz about your new beau, Irena," Aria said, scanning a line of lingerie and refusing to look at me. "A beau that I, your sister, had to find out you were dating *from* social media."

"Mom and Dad know?" I walked up to her, my throat closing up from panic. It was all getting a little too real now. "How? They don't even *have* social media."

"Mom has some fake accounts sprinkled here and there to keep up with...she says the 'current state of the world,' but in my opinion, she just wants in on all the latest tea."

"Great." I threw my hands in the air before dropping into a lilac armchair.

"Dad is already buzzing about meeting him."

"You mean intimidating him," I corrected, and she narrowed her eyes at me.

"He doesn't want to see his little girl getting hurt again."

As if. Even when I hadn't gone through an excruciating public breakup, my dad was all up in my business, scaring every guy I brought home. When he openly threatened to break my prom date's legs if he tried any funny business, I learned my lesson and never introduced anyone to them again.

"Well, they can keep dreaming. It's not going to happen. It's too early to bring him to meet the family."

"I agree." Aria surprised me, then gave me a sleek smile. "But not too early to meet the sister, right?"

I twisted my fingers in my lap. I doubted she would be

this eager if she knew who we were actually talking about. "I want to keep this on the down-low for a little while, Aria."

I used that low tone of voice that told her my decision wasn't up for further discussion, and she went back to angrily swiping through the rack of clothes. Even though her movements were sudden, her ecru tunic dress flowed gracefully. I hadn't noticed it before. She was glowing lately. Her olive skin seemed healthier than ever, and her makeup was on point. Her lips were fuller than mine, painted a dark red that brought her features to light. She had a tough time during the first six months of her pregnancy, but now it seemed like it was getting easier.

"Whatever. Keep your secrets," she said with a smirk that promised repercussions. And indeed, they came when she continued on. "You're paying full price as a punishment, though."

My mouth dropped, and she nodded as if to say, *yes, that's right, you little shit.*

Bea, who had been pretending to be interested in some crotchless panties, but in reality, was eating up the show that was my family drama, piped in, "Does that include me too?"

My sister swiveled to her, grinning from ear to ear. "Of course not. It's on the house for you, honey."

Bea matched her smile. "Thank you, Aria."

"You bitches," I muttered under my breath.

"That's what you get for keeping things from me," Aria argued, holding out a lacy three-piece, and asked, "You can't go wrong with red, right?"

The underwear was gorgeous, with little black chain details here and there. Still, I was solely interested in one particular color. They said drunk words were sober thoughts, and I occasionally wondered what Killian meant by *pretty blue butterflies* when I helped him get inside his apartment.

It could've been nothing, but I still wanted to pick a blue set. And while I loved red, it would blend in with my hair. It would look amazing on Aria, who looked like the epitome of a Greek princess.

My father's French genes were more prominent on me.

I let Aria know what I was searching for, and she returned to work, showing me two more options.

"Ocean blue or navy blue?" She dangled the two sets in front of me, but just as I was about to reply, she cut me off and decided for me. "Navy."

"Definitely," Bea seconded, and Aria shoved the lingerie in my chest in an attempt to mobilize me.

"So much for freedom of choice," I grumbled, but didn't protest because the set was amazing. The bra was made out of shiny silk with lace details that created a beautiful trail of winding florals, revealing the skin beneath. It also had a front-opening clasp for easy access. What more could a girl ask for?

The padded cups even gave the illusion that my boobs were bigger than they actually were, pushing them together so they looked perky. Now that was miraculous, seeing as I barely had anything to begin with. For all of our differences, that was a characteristic both Aria and I shared, so she understood the importance of making clothing that flattered all body types, especially flat-chested girls.

There were matching Brazilian panties as well—thank God, because I couldn't stand the ones that went up your ass —and a garter belt that fell from the waist in striking panels and finished in a delicate scalloped edge.

It was an instant buy, even if it cost me a whopping eight hundred dollars.

Aria kept to her promise, and after trying it on, she watched me pay with a serenity that rivaled my reluctance as I handed over my credit card. I was used to doing some damage on shopping trips. After all, I came from a family that had more money than they could ever count, but when you were spending *your* hard-earned money, it hurt no matter the bank balance.

When we were done, Bea went to get her car, but Aria urged me to stay behind. I did because it had been so long since I last talked to my sister alone. Also, I took over folding some new arrivals and nearly screamed at her to sit down. I'd never met a more stubborn woman in my life. She barely let the staff do anything, and she was supposed to be on maternity leave.

An onslaught of new customers came into the store, the bell on the door chiming every few seconds, but even amidst all the chaos, Aria's soft-spoken words captured my attention.

"I need you to realize that you can always open up to me, Ina." Aria ran her hands down her things, looking at me through earnest eyes. "I'm not clueless, you know, and I'll always be there for you, no matter what."

I paled. "Not clueless pertaining to what?"

"Little girl crushes that transferred into adulthood," she answered simply, as if she hadn't just put into question everything I thought I knew. "I married mine, however unconventionally, and while he can be a hardass, he always comes around eventually."

The shirt I was holding fell on top of the rest of the pile as I stared at her. The knowing glint on her face told me I was a fool for trying to hide something from her. My breathing got quicker when my lungs constricted, not letting any of the air in.

"Aria—" I started, but she held up her hand and shushed me.

"See where it goes." A pang of shock hit me when she gave me the go-ahead. "There's no need to cause havoc if your heart is not set on it."

CHAPTER SIXTEEN
KILLIAN

The top broker in town sure didn't play around when it came to his own home. It had a sweeping driveway and receiving court, twenty-foot ceilings, and it exemplified modern architecture with meticulously appointed finishes. An abundance of glass let in a ton of natural light inside the open design, and it integrated the vast landscape with the sophisticated interior detail.

Ares Alsford had made it in life, but not because of the two-plus acre property or the presidential-like office we were currently sitting in. He had been brought up in the lap of luxury and always had the best homes and vehicles, but never the kind of happiness present in his eyes whenever he looked at his family now.

He had two beautiful twins, Alexander and Penelope, with the most sultry woman I'd ever seen. Serena Alsford had dark hair and curves in all the right places, and I'd literally taken a minute to collect myself when I first met her—okay, maybe I'd exaggerated my reaction a bit to get a rise out of Ares, and thinking back at the shiner I sported for about a week afterward, it probably wasn't my smartest idea.

"What do you think about this one?" My phone lit up with a notification as Ares sent me a link to a commercial property.

The plans to open my own tattoo shop had already been put in motion, and I thought there was no one better than Ares to help me find the perfect place to buy. I'd saved quite a bit of money over the years, and with Luca as a partner, it shouldn't be too hard.

I swiped through the available pictures, and while it was a nice place, it wasn't quite what I was searching for.

"I like it, but the location is a no. I need something more central."

Ares scrubbed a hand down his five o'clock shadow and flicked the pen he was holding on the steel and rosewood table. "You're making my life difficult."

I caught it mid-air when it bounced on the surface and then rushed toward my face. Twirling it between my fingers, I said, "Show me better listings for it to get easier."

The gold in his eyes flared, and he set his palms on the table. "Let's get the facts right. You want a store located in the upper Astropolis area, with good lighting, renovated, and on a main road, all for under five hundred thousand?"

"That sounds about right," I informed. It sounded crazy, but he got where he was today by making the impossible possible.

"You're being unrealistic. All these places sell for millions," Ares argued, his tone incredulous.

I sighed, twisting the pen in between my fingers.

I was willing to make a compromise. A mortgage was much better than rent. At least you got to own the place.

"All right, I'm willing to up the price to six hundred K."

He scratched the back of his head and refocused on his computer screen. "We need to up the price to one point two mil, minimum." I opened my mouth to shoot him down, but he kept going, giving me no time to respond. "Look, I know some good creditors. I'll set you up and make sure you get an excellent interest rate."

Reaching over to the whiskey neat I'd treated myself with when I walked into his office and spotted a fully stocked bar cart, I let the liquor warm me up as I took a couple of sips, thinking it over.

If Ares was saying it, it was probably true.

So, I would have to cut back on some of the other ideas I had for spicing up the shop. Marketing would fall entirely on my shoulders as well, but that wasn't something I was concerned about. All it took was getting a couple of celebrities to get there, and the word would spread.

I had about a dozen numbers shoved down my pockets from models at fashion week, but somehow the thought of calling one of them up didn't sound so appealing. They expected something in return, and I could give it to them. Yet, I wasn't the slightest bit excited about it as any other man in my position would have been.

"Fine," I echoed to stop my thoughts from venturing down a path I didn't want them to.

Ares didn't appear any more pleased than he was ten seconds ago, and he went back to typing on his keyboard with a little more force than necessary. "Good. Now I need to start the search all over again because you were refusing to compromise the first time around."

"Well, what do I pay you for?"

"You don't," he deadpanned. "I can't even force you to babysit the kids 'cause I don't trust you around them."

"That wounds me," I drawled, downing what was left of my drink.

"I can tell you're really broken up over it." He ran his gaze over me. Before this could go on any further, though, the door to his study cracked open, and Serena walked in.

She'd changed from that vomit-stained shirt she was wearing when I first came in to a white sundress that contrasted against her tanned skin. Apparently, there was such a thing called baby reflux, causing them to puke after feeding, and I added it to my long list of reasons to never have kids.

There were matching dark circles under her and Ares's eyes. I imagined having twins would do that to you. She had a baby monitor in one hand and a tray filled with cold cuts in the other. There hadn't been one time when I visited the Alsford house and left hungry, and even on challenging days like today, Serena made sure to bring a snack.

Ares flew out of his seat when he saw her arm shaking, trying to hold the wooden platter, and took it out of her hands as she gave him a grateful smile, asking, "What are you two doing in here?"

"Killian is being a brat as usual," Ares answered his wife, setting the food on the table.

I smirked at her and got up to peck her cheek when she got closer. "Your husband is just mad that you bring out all the good snacks when I come over."

Ares gave me an unamused raise of his brows as I squeezed Serena in a side hug, and I challenged him by tucking her under my arm.

"Oh, I get to have the best snack every night." He

dropped back in his seat with a self-assured shrug of his shoulders.

Serena rolled her eyes at the pissing contest and pinched my side for me to let her go. "Not that I don't agree with me being a whole snack, but we shouldn't share that information with our guests."

She dropped the baby monitor on the free leather chair next to me and instead rested her hip on the table. Ares didn't miss the chance to admire her ass, even tilting the screen of his computer so he could get a better view.

"Killian is family," Ares stated his excuse.

"Which is even worse." I scratched the back of my neck.

"I'm helping you for free," he reminded me.

"Sexual innuendos that make people uncomfortable are the most normal thing in the world," I taunted, as if reading off a script at gunpoint.

I couldn't go acting like a hypocrite. I did love them myself occasionally. How they made Irena's permanently flushed skin in my presence turn scarlet.

"That's what I thought." He nodded.

A faint buzzing noise ate up my reply, and both of us looked around to find where it was coming from. It was the third time it happened tonight, and it was driving me insane.

Serena shifted her legs, but I paid her no mind as I stared at the massive arched windows and onto the shifting tree branches beyond. My family was a bit paranoid regarding our security, and I followed in their footsteps on this one thing. The abundance of stalkers was never ending when you had more money than you could blow in five lifetimes.

"Who's Lilith?" It was Serena who asked, and my blood ran cold in my veins, snapping me out of locate-the-danger mode.

"What?" My voice almost broke, so I cleared my throat, feeling Ares's attention on me.

"Someone named Lilith is texting you. Your phone is on the floor."

Even though she pointed out where my phone was, my first instinct was to check my pockets. When I indeed found them empty, I glanced down and cursed my tendency to leave my phone on vibrate. Serena was still squinting at the phone, trying to make out what the text said, but I was quick to grab it, so she didn't get her answer.

I tapped on the notifications, and Irena's messages expanded. The first text had come at five forty-five, an hour earlier.

Lilith: Can you come pick me up, please? I'm at Astro Studios and will probably run into Daniel. I don't want to deal with that.

Then half an hour later.

Lilith: Killian?

Lilith: Never mind.

The last text had come just now, and I fought with every-thing I had in me to take it easy and not burst out of Ares's house right this second. I'd been itching to have a real one-on-one with her asshole of an ex who deserved to die a slow and painful death after what he put her through. Irena was by no means my girl, but she *was* my responsibility, and what could I say? I always got a little trigger-happy when someone hurt the people I...*cared* about.

Fuck me, I did care about Irena Fleur.

It started as purely physical, but I'd grown to enjoy her unfiltered mouth, unwavering ambition, and refreshing honesty. The fact that a man so far below her caliber had managed to get his hands on her made me want to slice his limp dick into tiny little pieces.

Killian: Sorry, I didn't have my phone on me. Are you still there?

My fingers flew over the keyboard as I wrote back, and I balanced on the edge of my seat when she started typing a few seconds later, sending a rush down my spine when the green bubble came through.

Lilith: Yes. Are you coming?

Consider me already there, baby.

Killian: I'm not passing up an opportunity to put that tool in his place.

I pressed the power off button and was about to announce my departure. When I whipped my head up to do so, I found two fascinated gazes looking at me like I was levitating.

Ares worked a hand through his brown hair and chuckled. "Figures that a girl named after a she-demon would be the one to capture his attention."

"It's a nickname, no?" Serena, clearly the smarter out of the two, connected the dots faster, examining me for any hidden clues. "Aria mentioned something about how you call her sister that because you never get along."

"Irena?" Ares latched on, unabashed interest shining behind his question. "Then why do I remember you getting in fights with Saint because she and you got along a little *too* well?"

My molars hurt from how hard I ground them together. It seemed like none of my friends and family knew how to mind their business. Still, I was neither confirming nor denying anything.

"Schizophrenia could be a likely cause." I stretched my arms over my head as I got up, then stole a cold cut from Serena's platter as I gave him further instructions. "You can email me anything you find worthwhile, and I'll get back to you. Something came up."

Ares shook his head. "You're playing with fire, Killian."

"Maybe I want to get burned," I replied, realizing for the first time that I'd grown a little too accustomed to Irena's blazing heat.

CHAPTER SEVENTEEN
KILLIAN

After giving the stationed guards my name, I rolled through the studio's gates approximately thirty minutes later. It was an hour drive here, but I'd broken some speeding laws along the way. I was currently texting and driving—something I did not recommend to even the most experienced of drivers, but my blood was boiling. I was itching to get in on the action.

Killian: I'm here.

The security guards told me Irena was most likely in building ten, so that's where I was heading. Every studio was mostly the same from the outside. They were designed in boxy brown shapes, and so spaced out, some of the employees were using golf carts to get from one place to the next.

I didn't know what Irena was doing here since she was dropped by the show, and I didn't think she came because she missed the fucking place. Obviously, it had to do with her limp dick of an ex and his bitch of a girlfriend. Irena wasn't without support, but she thought she could take on the world by herself and hated asking or accepting help. And while her wits and guts were admirable, people like Daniel needed a heavy-handed approach she was unable to provide.

My phone pinged with a notification as I was parking, and I did a haphazard job at it as a result. Taking up two parking spots was a pet peeve of mine, but I couldn't give less of a shit today as I put my car in park and read Irena's reply.

Irena: I just got out of a meeting with some show executives. Wait for me at lot ten. I'll be there in five.

Yeah...fuck that.

I wasn't waiting in the parking lot like a dirty little secret, even though that was what I technically was. Still, we'd agreed to this so I could help her clear her name, which was exactly what I was about to do...help. Whether she wanted me to or not.

It was starting to get dark out, and the streetlamps were too far apart to provide any significant amount of light, so I walked to the entrance of building ten, partially covered in darkness. People that filtered out didn't give me a second glance, and I managed to squeeze in without anyone noticing. There weren't many employees left at this hour anyway.

A little too late, I realized I might've gotten in, but I had no idea where to go. There was a vast opening with a Starbucks positioned right next to the entrance and a recreational area to the far right. At the very end of the room, two hallways led in two different directions. There were no signs indicating where to find what, so for the fuck of it, I decided to go right.

A wall filled with numbered doors stretched as I made

my way down, but I figured Irena had to be on her way out because she said she'd meet me in five minutes. And indeed, as I rounded the corner of the hallway, I stopped dead in my tracks when I heard a heavily accented voice say, "Was getting humiliated once not enough for you? You're back for round two?"

"Leave me alone, Katrina," replied a second person, her tone like hard candy, sweet but rough enough to break your teeth when you bit into it.

I immediately recognized her as Irena.

I extended my upper body to peek out the corner, and the sight was enough to send my body temperature upwards of a hundred degrees. Irena's coat was flowing beside her, her hair lightly waving over her shoulders as she rushed to get away from the determined blonde that was following her.

"Scared?" Katrina asked, and Irena missed a step as a result.

"Of an insecure little bitch? I think not." Her words rang true as her cavalier attitude got the worse out of the other woman, and she sprinted forward, arms poised as if she was about to push Ina.

I snapped back into action, not above hurting a female, but it turned out I didn't need to. Irena knew this girl quite well, so as if she could foresee her reaction, she twisted around at the last minute, grabbed Katrina's wrists, and pinned her in place.

I couldn't see Irena's face, but I imagined her teeth were exposed as she threatened, "You try that again and I will slap you with a lawsuit so big, you'll have to get on food stamps to pay it off."

My dick stirred in my pants, to my surprise, and I held back a laugh as I watched her handle it. I'd come to save her, but she was no damsel in distress, and I was enjoying seeing her in action. Perhaps a little *too* much.

"You're in no position to threaten me. You have nothing." Katrina tried to break away, but Irena's nails dug into her skin as she leaned closer.

"Correction: I lost everything, but gained so much more in the process. I suppose I should thank you for fucking Daniel. If you hadn't, I wouldn't know how much better I could do."

Was I the better she was referring to? Probably not.

Did I run with it, though? Hell fucking yes.

A heavier set of footsteps broke their stare off, and the douchebag of the century rolled in, in an unbuttoned white shirt and pants tight enough to cut the circulation off his legs.

"Irena, let go of her," he yelled as if he was the lead in some Marvel movie.

Madness exploded hot and thick inside of me when *he* gave her an order, but I held off for the perfect moment.

As if just now realizing that she was still holding on to Katrina, Irena released her. She wiped her hands on the backs of her thighs while the Russian figure skater stumbled back as if she'd suffered a bullet wound. She clutched her wrists and whimpered as Douchebag—that was his official name now—closed in on them, hugging her from the back and shooting laser beams at Irena with his eyes.

Irena shook her head. "What a shitshow."

"Why are you here?" Douchebag demanded.

"Well, certainly not because I missed you, you can rest assured." Irena shifted her weight to one foot and crossed her arms.

"Stay away from us," Katrina huffed, a whole viper acting like a wounded animal. She reminded me so much of Farah, the urge to squeeze her little neck overwhelmed me. And since I couldn't act on it, I allowed myself to get off on the imagination.

"Wrong person, love. Your boyfriend is the one in need of a tighter leash," Irena corrected her, and despite being outnumbered, she was having fun setting the record straight. She was too calm to be faking it. It was like watching a cat toying with mice.

"Stop spewing bullshit, Irena. How much more delusional can you get? I only contacted you because I wanted my hoodies back."

Right.

That got me walking.

He texted and called her because she was suddenly unavailable, and his interest sparked. He wanted to see if he could pull her back in, stroke his ego by thinking of himself as irresistible.

"Well then, invest in some scuba gear, and you can collect them from the bottom of the Atlantic Ocean." Their gazes hooked on me as Irena finished her sentence.

Katrina's glazed over with confusion and piqued interest. Douchebag, on the other hand, managed to recognize me from the get-go—I must've made quite an impression because last time he saw me, it was extremely dark—and once he managed to pick up his mouth off the floor, his nostrils flared, and he squared his shoulders as if he actually believed he could cause some damage.

My knuckles were itching for some action, but I simply wrapped my arm around Irena's waist, who startled but relaxed when she heard my voice. "Littering? Not a good idea, babe. You should've burned them instead."

Her pretty pink lips formed an O as she stared at me, and she straightened ever so slightly, regaining some confidence. She matched my smirk and got my strategy immediately.

"That takes too much energy. I thought I'd give the bare minimum in return as well."

"And who might you be?" Katrina addressed me.

"Wouldn't you like to know?" I examined her from the tips of her Nikes to the blonde strands on her head.

"I'll have you both thrown out for harassment if you don't leave," Douchebag, who had seemingly lost his tongue up until that point, sputtered with renewed energy.

Irena laughed under her breath like she knew something we didn't, and I raised a brow, staring the tool down. "I'd like to see you try."

"I'd *love* it," Irena played along, and I smoothed my hand down her spine, spreading my fingers over her hipbone and pressing her closer to me.

He opened his mouth, and I cocked my head sideways, waiting for his response, but it never came. His face turned red as a poppy, and his girlfriend felt inclined to defend his honor.

"You have no right to talk to him like that."

"Who's gonna stop him? You?" Irena quipped, and Douchebag's new girl forgot all about her supposed injuries as she took a threatening step forward.

Irena didn't need my protection, but I still pushed her behind me and took center stage. I wasn't above a good troll, but these two were so thick it meant I had to spell it out for them. Patience was no virtue of mine, and they'd find it was best to stay on my good side.

"I'm only going to say this once, so you better listen." Douchebag's slicked-back hair was so ridiculous I almost wanted to cause him bodily harm for that alone. Still, he took a step back when I advanced forward, and I thought maybe he had a little sense left in him. "If you take Irena's name in your mouth again, I'll remove your tongue and shove it so far down your throat you'll never be able to make another sound. This goes for both of you. All right, Regina George?"

I wasn't so sure blondie got the reference, and I didn't care so long as they heeded my warning. If it was up to me, I would've destroyed both of them already. Taking the high road just led you to nothing but regret. Facing our problems head-on was the way to go, but since Irena hadn't learned that lesson yet, I did as much as I could with as much freedom as I was given.

Katrina's lips twisted in disgust, and she turned to her boyfriend, who was perfecting his blank expression as he tried to figure out how he would play this. She tapped her foot on the floor and pointed at me. "Are you going to let him talk to me like that?"

Already fed up with our past encounter, that was all the ammunition Douchebag needed to run his mouth, puffing up his chest like a peacock—about to be stripped of its feathers.

"We'll do whatever we fucking pleas—"

My control disintegrated, and I was not escaping spending the night at a police station.

I didn't let him finish.

As if on auto mode, my arm propelled forward, and I heard a crunch as I punched him flat in the face. His skin rippled from the force, and blood spread over my closed fist.

My knuckles throbbed, but I went in again for a second punch, needing him to learn his place.

Karma had finally caught up with him, but like the coward that he was, he continued to run. The shocked cries around me were nothing but faint background noise as I focused on driving my fist at his face.

By the third punch, though, he dropped like a sack of shit, hitting the floor with a thump.

I paused with my fist mid-air, rage and confusion constricting my chest. I had half a mind to follow him down and bring even more pain to his moaning ass because few things felt better than an orgasm, and knocking a piece of shit out was one of them.

"Killian! No!" Irena attached herself to my back, speaking quietly, as if screaming would have no effect on me right now. She managed to make me turn halfway, smoothing her hands down my biceps. "Stop, please. There are cameras everywhere."

"Daniel? Babe?" Katrina kneeled beside Douchebag, cradling his face in her hands, and when he didn't reply, she spoke in a lower voice. "Get up! *Stop embarrassing me.*"

Wow.

True love right there.

When I remembered how anxiety-ridden Irena was back in New York when I forced her hand on releasing those screenshots, a primal kind of rage smothered me at the damage these two had managed to cause, even though Irena was a pro at hiding it most of the time.

I moved on instinct, stepping closer once more, but Irena walked backward, dragging me with her. I resisted, hooked on the blood dripping down his chin and the exertion of my breaths. I was running high on adrenaline. Fighting used to be a hobby of mine, an unhealthy one, albeit it worked for me.

"Let's go. Now." I heard Irena's voice hiss in my ear, and she physically had to get behind me to force me to go down the opposite side of the hallway. I reluctantly started moving my legs when I heard her huffing and puffing. My blood was still boiling, but putting her in another difficult situation made me no different from her ex.

"We're gonna sue you for this. You're gonna get what's coming to you!" Katrina shouted, and I almost turned around.

"Let her talk." Irena gave me a shove. "I'm gonna handle this."

"How?"

"I know a guy that works at the control center. He's gonna wipe the footage." We turned the corner, despite every bone in my body screaming at me to go back and finish what I started. "Just keep walking and stay calm."

"I am calm," I snorted, then glanced down at her to find the color had disappeared from her face.

Fuck, I'd really done it this time.

Irena pulled her phone out of her pocket, scrolling through her contact list as I held open the double-sided door and let her go first.

"Of course, you bloody are. *You* knock someone out, and I'm the one that's worried," she muttered.

An ugly feeling I couldn't quite place crawled through my lungs and made its way up my throat, forcing me to blurt out, "About *him*?"

The scent of jealousy was so heavy in the air we both paused in the middle of the road. There wasn't any traffic at this hour, and the lot was mostly empty. She stared at me like she was trying to solve a complex math problem, and I poked the inside of my cheek with my tongue as I waited for her answer.

I wasn't proud of my little outburst, but I was owning it. She could fuck and like whoever she pleased once we were done, but for as long as she was in this arrangement with me, I was the only one whose touch she'd tremble for. If she needed a refresh, I had no qualms about making her bend for my punishment.

"About you, you *buffoon*," she exploded, her body shaking in revulsion that I would even suggest that. I was having a hard time wrapping my mind around her statement, so she went on, surprising me further. "I don't want you to get in trouble for me."

It was foreign to me, having someone worry over me. Someone other than Saint and Luca occasionally. I had friends and even went through a social butterfly phase in the past, but they were all meaningless when most of them were in it because they wanted to fuck me or for the wild parties I used to throw.

Irena averted her gaze when I continued staring at her like she was a puzzle I was trying to decode. In an impulse reaction, I palmed her cheek to regain her attention. Her blue eyes were as dark as the night sky, calling to me, coaxing me in to find out what sort of nightmares they carried. If I could, I'd eradicate them all because she was too good, too pure-hearted to lug that sort of weight around.

"Protecting you is no trouble. It's my duty, Irena. When I agreed to help you out, that made you mine in every sense of the word. Mine to touch. Mine to taste. Mine to fuck. And mine to keep safe." I heard the catch in her breath, and a torrent of heat shot straight to my dick as a result. "I don't ever want you to think of yourself as a burden, okay?"

We both swayed closer, seeking, while she looked at me like I was the only thing existing in the world. A weird tingling sensation spread over my limbs at the glimmer of trust I found there, and I attuned myself to the tempo of our breaths and the crackle in the air, signifying that something was changing...*shifting* as our situationship of sorts started to take shape.

"Yes," she breathed out, and I swallowed hard.

I couldn't take it.

I couldn't take one more second of her staring at me like I hung the moon without the urge to take her long and hard on the fucking asphalt overwhelming me.

And so, to avoid a different kind of scene, I patted her ass and motioned to my car. "Good. Now, get moving."

CHAPTER EIGHTEEN

KILLIAN

"Tell me something," I started to distract myself from the passing streetlights illuminating her chest and taking my attention off the road.

She was a driving hazard in that white shirt of hers. It had a sweetheart neckline, and it was so tight on her, the tops of her breasts almost spilled out of it. Not to mention how that baby pink short skirt she had on did wonders for her long legs. Keeping both hands on the wheel was a hard fucking task.

"What?" She glanced up from the email she was drafting for her manager.

It turned out her plan had worked a little too late, and the producers of Stars on Ice had offered her a ridiculous amount of money to appear in the season's finale and stir shit up for the next season. And if I'd gathered something from spending so much time with Irena lately, it was that she didn't let a grudge go, so she showed up to turn them down personally.

I was sure they could've offered her millions and she'd

still refuse just to see the disappointment and anger on their faces.

She was determined like that. Even on things she sucked at, she pressed harder until she nailed them, like driving, for example. She passed her test on the third try—her last one—so it struck me as odd that I'd never really seen her driving anywhere this past year.

Could it be that she finally gave up? If so, I'd start believing in miracles.

"How come you never drive?"

"'Cause I like being driven."

"Irena..."

"*Mylicensewasrevoked.*" She said it so fast I didn't catch anything past *My.* There was also an asshole that wasn't allowing me to overtake him, so I put our conversation on the back burner as I turned my left indicator on.

The BMW driver—figures—immediately veered left with no indicator on, and I changed direction at the last minute, overtaking him from the right. My hellcat's whine was so loud, Irena dropped her phone, and I was fucking glad because she'd been hooked on that thing since the second her ass made contact with my red leather seats.

"What?" I asked, and she grumbled, patting the area around her legs with no luck. Her cell had to have slid to the back. I was going eighty miles an hour. You could say I was in a bit of a rush.

"My license was revoked, okay?" she admitted in a hushed tone, slumping back in her seat when the seat belt wouldn't let her lean forward anymore. "But it wasn't my fault an old lady chose to cross the street when the light was still orange. She was going too slow, I was going too fast, and well, it just happened."

It just happened?

What exactly had happened?

I looked over to her, catching her pained expression, and matched it with one of my own. "You ran an old lady over? Orange lights are there to warn us to slow down, *not* speed up."

I mean, I knew she was bad, but not this bad.

"I was in a rush," she justified, twiddling her thumbs to avoid my judgmental stare. "And I managed to break in time. I didn't *run* her over. I just gave her a little nudge. She was fine," she went on in a whiny voice.

I couldn't control my laughter at the absurdity of her statement. In fact, I couldn't believe she was still walking free right now. I was sure some hush money was involved, but whoever helped her out was smart enough not to want to do it twice.

I *tsked* at her. "Good thing you're not allowed behind a wheel anymore."

Her left eye twitched when I stopped at a red light and gave her a *see? That's how it's done* look. She pursed her mouth like she was debating what to say or do. In a move that I wasn't anticipating, she unbuckled her seat belt, leaned in my direction, and whispered, "All right, Mr. Perfect, let's see how you do under pressure."

Placing her hands on my legs, Irena slid her body over to sit sideways on my lap, her legs lying over the center console. I raised the hand brake and released the clutch, putting the car in neutral as I adjusted to make room for her.

"What—Irena, what are you doing?"

She threw her hair back, her spine digging against the door, and her minty breath splayed over my face when she huffed as she tried to get comfortable, wiggling her ass over my lap. I grabbed her hips as a result, steeling her in place because my poor dick was suffering beneath the thick material of my pants.

"Seeing how fast you manage to get us home." She shrugged, her wandering fingers toying with the collar of my shirt. She lowered her eyes, taking in my body fully before hitting me with the full force of her coy gaze. "Killian, I have a confession to make."

My teeth clenched under her perusal, and I hated but also loved where she was taking this. She was trying to make me eat my words by seeing how I performed under a heightened kind of urgency to get home and fuck the living daylights out of her.

The line of cars moved a bit, and a horn alerted me to it. I cursed under my breath and shifted to first gear beneath her legs, crawling forward at a snail's pace.

"If it's probably going to cause us to crash, hold it in until I'm not driving anymore."

Her amused giggle rolled over my skin, and goose bumps spread where she touched. Irena burrowed her face in my neck, her lips brushing against my strained tendons. I punched my foot on the accelerator a little harder, praying we got to the next stoplight soon.

"Watching you punch the living shit out of Daniel was one of the hottest things I've ever seen." She rolled her hips, and I faltered, shifting to the wrong gear and making the car jolt. Like the car crash veteran that she was, Irena didn't even flinch. She breathed a laugh, biting into my skin like a savage. "It made the urge to fuck you even bigger than before if that's possible."

My cock was painfully restricted as it tried to grow but

couldn't. It was already swelling, desperate to break past my clothes and get inside her cunt less than an inch away.

I damn near breathed a sigh of relief when the stoplight looming ahead switched from green to orange. I hit the brakes way sooner than I should've, but I couldn't find it in me to give a shit right now.

Finally free to use my hands, I let the wheel go, threading my fingers through her hair and holding the back of her head as I hovered my lips over hers. I wanted to swallow down her little excited breaths and tattoo her mouth on mine.

"You're mistaken, Lilith. I'll be the one doing the fucking." I punctuated my sentence by slamming my lips over hers, prying them open with my teeth like a brute as I hunted down her tongue, caught it, and tangled it with mine.

Her sweet smell filled my nostrils, and I barely let her up for air, addicted to the crushed roses-like aroma.

I was such a fucking goner for this girl. Her games made me crazy. I'd built this up—*her* up—so much, my peace of mind was fried the past few years I was forced to stay away. Now that I was given a chance to sample the finest wine of them all, you best believe I wasn't letting one sip go to waste. By the time I was satisfied, she wouldn't be able to walk.

I kissed her deeper and pulled her closer, pursuing her by dragging her bottom lip out and then diving back in again to play with her tongue, silently demanding she take everything I gave her because it was all hers anyway.

I was hers.

The thought made me grow a little cold and weary, because the fact that *this was temporary* flew over my head, but I couldn't find it in me to break the kiss. Not when she whimpered, as if asking for more. My entire body throbbed from the feel of her, and I was so fucking tempted to slide my hands in places I wasn't going to want to let go of. It took several honks and cars zooming past to make me break away.

Chest heaving and nostrils flaring, I kept my hand on her head as I tried to drive with only one hand. It was a fucking challenge, but still feasible.

Trees whizzed past us, indicating that we were out of the downtown area and approximately thirty minutes away from home, so I kept my foot firmly pressed on the gas pedal.

"Is that so?" Irena went back to taunting me by nibbling beneath my ear. "And when, pray tell, will you do that?"

I punched into sixth before reaching down to adjust my swelling dick. For the first time in my life, I wished I had one of those self-driving cars—you never knew when they'd come in handy, like now, for example.

"You'll get your pussy filled the second we step foot in my apartment," I rasped, but apparently, my answer wasn't good enough.

"Hmm..." Her tongue darted out, gliding over my skin like velvet, licking and then kissing my neck and trailing kisses across my cheek, eating me up like a damn dessert. "I don't think I can hold off that long."

"Lilith," I hissed when she started leaving tantalizing little pecks over my lips. I retracted, but she came looking for more. "Our first time will not be in a car."

The sky fairy was testing my patience today because the next thing the vixen did was push against my chest, grab her shirt's puffy sleeves, smile, and look me dead in the eyes before she did the unthinkable.

She pushed her top down to her waist and threw her hair over her shoulder, exposing her breasts.

My exhale came out as a wheeze when I darted my gaze to her tits, and the fact that I couldn't touch her made me want to crawl into a hole and die. All satin-like skin, with hard pink nipples, not too big but enough for me to feast on. My mouth watered as a result, and taking my eyes away from her was a challenge. There would be no time for anything else tonight. She was only getting my cock, in seven different ways.

I blinked slowly, fucking hating her for a split second as she fanned herself and said, "Is it hot in here? I'm starting to feel really hot."

"You really are a demon," I rasped, swallowing hard.

"I *need* you, Killian," she said, thrusting her tits in my chest. Her pebbled nipples poked through my shirt, and I veered slightly off the road as my hand automatically went to touch them.

Cursing, I gripped the steering wheel again.

"Irena, please." I found myself begging. Something I never fucking did. It made me uncomfortable and reminded me of all the times my pleas were ignored. My tone cooled as I went on. "This is a manual car."

I could only drive with one hand on the highway, and seeing as we were nearing the end, it wouldn't be a wise choice to continue to do so.

"Your hands *are* free, aren't they?" she taunted.

"Fucking witch." My voice came out too whiny for my liking, so I cleared my throat, feeling a flush crawl over my cheeks.

First begging and now blushing.

What else would this woman pull out of me?

"I thought Lilith was a demon." Even now, she found the time to sass me.

"She was a witch too in a Netflix show."

"I'm sitting topless on your lap, and you're talking about a Netflix show? I have to up the ante."

The blood in my dick raced when her fingers wandered downward, fiddling with my zipper.

"Irena, don't," I warned, and she didn't unzip it.

What she did do, though, was nudge my hard-on with her ass and moan like a fucking porn star. "You feel fucking incredible."

I knew I was done for when she threw her head back, looking like a picture straight out of a *Playboy* magazine with her vibrant strawberry blonde hair that clashed perfectly with the fairness of her skin.

My self-control was a goddamn joke, and the logical part of my brain went missing around the same time my moral compass did.

I couldn't resist her.

"Fine. Fine. You win." I gave in, but this was far from a loss. "Keep your hands where I can see them, or I swear to God, we're not walking out of this alive, and I'm not dying without experiencing your cunt around my cock."

"Priorities." Irena laughed, and with all the shifting around she was doing on my lap, my cock was practically begging for her warmth. "I can't wait until we get home."

"As if I can." I blew out a frustrated breath, taking a left down a nondescript road with an incline. It was out of our way, but it led to a nice secluded place with a view, and it would do. "Three years of being unable to stop thinking about you, and you're going to make me fuck you in a car."

I was in the wrong gear and trying to climb uphill as fast as possible. Still, I didn't care because she was pressed even tighter against me as a result, and she was the one feeling fucking incredible now.

Irena sucked in a breath, like an expert actress. "You couldn't stop thinking about me for three years?"

"As if you didn't already know." I rolled my eyes, then smirked at her. "I bet you wanted me even longer."

"True, I wanted you the second I saw you." She owned it, but my breath still caught in my throat.

I didn't pay much attention to her back then, other than some teasing conversations here and there, mostly because I saw the interest in her eyes, and she was two years too young for me. That might not seem like much, but I felt it. She had grown up to be a force of nature, barreling through anything that stood in her path with steel determination.

Her nails massaged my scalp as she went on. "I wanted to run my fingers through your beautiful hair. I wanted to kiss your full lips." Her mouth ghosted over mine, and I claimed her lips even as I tried to drive, fulfilling her wish. "Feel your body moving against me, on top of me, and below me," she finished when I let her up for air.

I could've cried when I finally spotted the little pocket by the road's edge. It was hidden away by big red maple trees. It was so easy to miss. No car would be venturing out here this late into the night, so I veered to the right and set the parking brake before I had even properly slowed to a halt. You could see the whole city stretching out beneath you from up here, but I only had eyes for the devil on my lap.

I was pretty sure I looked like a starving animal as I set my chair all the way back and said, "I'll give you anything you want."

She kicked off her heels, properly straddling me, her skirt

bunching up at the waist and her tits begging me to take them in my mouth. "Are you clean?"

"Except that." I grimaced, and she paused her mission to free my dick from my slacks, staring at me in confusion, so I clarified, "I am clean, but I'm not doing anything without a condom."

I unbuttoned my shirt all the way, unwilling to compromise. Still, my resolve quickly melted as if dunked in boiling hot water when her warm palm wrapped around my aching dick. She pumped me twice and stopped, taking the shape of my sweetest form of torture.

"But I'm on the pill," she whined, and I closed my eyes as if I could resist the temptation if I couldn't see her. Her words still pierced through me, though, finding the weak spots in my shield with little ease. "Please, Killian, you said anything I wanted, and I want to feel your bare skin inside of me."

Irena's fist tightened on my cock, as if to prove a point, and I weighed the pros and the cons.

Well...there were no cons, except for being forced to come to terms with my past. I'd never slept with a woman without a condom on, not by choice, at least. I couldn't even remember what it felt like. I'd blocked that part out of my brain.

But it was different this time.

This was Irena Fleur we were talking about, the most maddening and tempting creature in my life. She was safe, even though it didn't feel like it with the way she was seeping past the cracks of my defense with little effort.

"Now, how can I say no to that?" I asked, deciding to go for it, and struck like a viper out for blood. Grabbing her hair at the back of her head, I pulled her neck back and took a handful of her ass in my other hand before taking her nipple in my mouth and saying, "I wanted you in a bed. I wanted to kiss every square inch of your body first, sink my tongue into your wet cunt, and then plunge my dick inside of you, but *no*, we're cutting straight to the chase."

Her body shook with shock at my assault, and she gasped, slowly surrendering in my arms. She moved her ass over my hard-on, and when flesh met flesh, my eyes rolled to the back of my head. Of course, she was wearing no panties. Everything about this woman was designed to seduce. I was so painfully turned on it wasn't even funny.

"I always liked jumping straight to the main course, anyway," she whimpered when I bit and sucked everywhere, trailing my hands all over her, squeezing and yanking her hips, hitting me with the two words that drove me past the point of return. "Sir, please. I need something solid to replace the nothingness I've been clenching around this entire time."

I rolled my window down to allow for some fresh air in and clear off some of the lust in the atmosphere, but there was no such luck. Her scent was still the only one registering in my brain. The sweet musk of her cunt mixed with her body lotion and perfume swarmed my senses until there was nothing else but her.

I popped her nipple from my mouth, glancing down to see she had already done all the work for me. My dick was free and pointing up like a flagpole toward her cunt like he was already aware of the final destination.

"You undo me, Irena. Fuck," I breathed out hard, and she accommodated me by positioning herself over my dick. I captured her hands and placed them on my chest when she made to work me into her tight body. "This is going to hurt, baby. I don't have the patience to go slow."

Her nails sunk into my skin, eyes closed like she was in pain. "Please, do it. How much longer do I have to beg for it?"

We both gasped when I crowned her, and I took in her cinched waist and beautiful breasts, my cock throbbing a mile a minute before slamming her down on it so hard she screamed, her voice echoing into the woods around us. My eyes clamped shut, and my muscles flexed as I held my breath the moment our bodies connected, lost to the aimless, sensual slide of my dick entering her pussy. Irena felt like fantasia in the flesh, vibrating beneath my hands and begging to be directed.

She released a heavy sigh as she tried to adjust to my length, and I plunged in and out one more time, almost experimentally, getting used to this new feel of fucking without a condom on.

"Shiiiit..." she hissed out, and as a result, her face directed toward the roof of the car.

It might seem like a brag, but I was so big most girls couldn't take me in fully, let alone all at once, so I kept still for a few seconds, making sure she was good to go. "Are you okay?"

"I think I died and went to heaven," she moaned, and tried to get some traction by rolling her hips.

A throaty grunt escaped me as a response, but I held her still. She had set the tone for the entire evening, and I was taking whatever freedom I had left.

I fisted the tips of her hair and brought her face down to mine, our foreheads touching as I growled out, "The ride has just begun, baby, so you better hold on tight."

Her answering moan was loud and heady. I didn't need any more of an invitation to begin thrusting into her again and again like a man possessed. I slid against her insides, relishing in the sensation of her inner walls closing around me and filling me with jolts of static. I went in so hard, the dirty sound of our skin slapping and joining together echoed around us, accompanied by broken gasps and lusty moans.

She was so fucking tight.

I collared her neck with my free hand, bringing her down harder, and pushing my hips up faster until the car rocked with us. My thighs hardened as slivers of pleasure shot from my stomach and thighs, all leading inward to my groin.

"I can't believe I'm having sex with my sister's brother-in-law," she said hoarsely, like I was fucking the energy out of her and she could barely use her voice.

"Jesus Christ, Irena," I croaked, not needing a reminder, and tightened my hold on her neck. "Give me your mouth."

I didn't have to tell her twice as she reached my lips within milliseconds. Her tongue sought mine, twirling and tasting. Our teeth and tongues clashed as she deepened the kiss, finding a way to establish her own dominance even while I was the only one controlling the movement of our bodies. She was fierce, passionate, and merciless, feeding me all the frustration she felt at being able to look but not touch, speak but never utter what truly plagued her mind.

I answered back in kind, grabbing her ass in my hands, pulling her hips back, then slamming into her repeatedly, blowing past all the red tape and warning signs. This moment was worth every scandal undoubtedly coming our way if anyone ever found out how deep our attraction went.

Sweat and other bodily fluids coated my skin, in particular where we connected. I got an ego boost from how easily I was sliding in and out of her. She was so wet; her essence ran down my balls and made a mess on my seat. Thank fuck they were leather. Otherwise, the stain would've been hard to explain.

"Your sloppy cunt is dripping all over my pants," I groaned when she clenched around me.

Goddammit, I hadn't realized how much sex with a condom dulled the sensation. It wasn't bad by any means, but it didn't compare to going bareback. Doing it wrapped up was like watching the most beautiful sunset ever...on a TV screen. Without one, you got a front-row seat and watched the colors slowly fade from the sky live.

If she was taken aback by my choice of words, she didn't let it show as she inquired, "Are you complaining?"

"Never." A fiendish grin took over my mouth. "I doubt you'll ever get this wet for anyone else."

"And I doubt you'll ever get this hard for anyone that's not me." She chuckled, knowing her worth.

My lower abs burned from all the effort I was putting in, and I welcomed it. Fighting exertion only added to the overall feel. Irena's face was a picture of bliss as I brought my hand down on her ass, the crack of my palm connecting with her skin making precum seep from my cock.

If I kept up this pace, I wasn't escaping an orgasm, so I dialed it down a bit, pressing her back against the steering wheel and looking at where we connected. It was quite possibly the most erotic thing I'd ever seen, having her greedy cunt eat up every last inch of my cock.

I massaged her butt, spreading her cheeks, before sliding my hands forward and digging my fingers into her thighs.

"Grind on it, Lilith," I ordered, my voice grave, mesmerized by how fluidly we moved together. "Make it worth my while."

"Your wish is my command, sir."

Irena held on to my knees and rode me with abandon as her eyes collided with mine, staring into my fucking soul while she let loose. She circled her hips, grinding her wet heat into my body so every tight inch of her rubbed off on me. She bounced on my cock, harder and harder, going for pressure over speed, rocking back and forth against me every time she came down. Her body glistened with sweat as she took what she needed, riding me like I was her fucking sex toy.

"Holy shit." I snapped my teeth at her, my muscles bunching and twitching. "You took that to heart, huh, baby?"

"You don't like it?" She flashed me a grin.

"You know I fucking love it." I squeezed her pliable flesh, feeling the urge to eat her up alive as I leaned forward and kissed and sucked her tits like I was starving.

"God, those hands of yours are gonna leave some bruises," she said breathlessly, yet her tone held no notes of complaint.

"Am I hurting you?"

The motion of her head was a mix of a nod and a shake. "A little, but it's a good kind of hurt."

Irena stopped rolling her hips altogether, purely bouncing up and down on me right now, showing me just how good it was. I squeezed my eyes shut, bracing against her excitement. *Shit.* Blood flooded my cock, but I didn't want to come yet, so I had to tackle her release first.

"What about this?" I applied pressure on her clit and grazed her nipple with my teeth. "Is this better?"

"Killian..." She stilled for a second as if not wanting this to end and exhaled a moan. "Oh..."

I retook control when she faltered. I thrust between her thighs, arching my hips up in rapid fashion, impaling her on my cock. I fucked her deep while rubbing my thumb over her bundle of nerves at the same time.

"Come, Irena," I urged, wanting to bring her over the edge first. "I need you on the hood and the fucking back seat of my car. We're taking advantage of all available surfaces, baby."

"No, please, I don't—" She cut herself off with a gasp as I sucked on the flesh of her breast but continued with an urgent whisper. "I don't want to come this early."

"It'll be your first orgasm of the night, Irena, not the last," I assured. "Listen to me, and *come*."

I changed the angle at which I was penetrating her, and it seemed I hit the perfect spot when she froze up as if unable to function anymore, and she started vocalizing her satisfaction.

Another gush of wetness coated my dick as her muscles tightened and squeezed around my cock while her orgasm moved through her, and I let my head drop to her chest, constricting every muscle in my body to hold off my release.

"Jesus Christ," Irena cried, still in her high, and I took it personally.

"Nah, baby, stop rewarding him for all my hard work." I wrapped her hair in my fist, twisting once, twice, and bared her neck to me, running my tongue and teeth up to her mouth. Fucking her like she was a stripper and I was getting my money's worth, I said, "Go on, scream *my* name."

I didn't know if it was possible for a woman to have a second orgasm a few minutes after her first, but I could've sworn her inner walls tensed around me again as her arms enveloped my body. Chills spread down my back when her nails dug into the back of my neck.

"Killian!" Irena moaned even louder than before, and I ate up the remainder of her words with a hard kiss.

My mouth and breaths consumed hers as I took everything she had to offer. The cinnamon on her tongue. The warmth of her body pressed against mine. Her sheer strength, her sweet disposition, and untamed side. I wanted it all.

How are you going to tire of this in a month? a little voice in the back of my head taunted. It chipped away at the pure delight that ran through my veins, but I buried it down deep, throwing in layer after layer of soil to keep the doubts out and let me relish the moment.

Irena's breathing slowed, and she slumped against my chest to regain some of her power. I was still sheathed deep inside her, and I put a pause on the frenzy that consumed me to appreciate her beauty. Her hair stuck to her temples, eyelashes fanning her cheeks, bathed in a healthy flush that gave her an angelic sort of glow.

If I could take a picture of this moment, I would, but I doubt Irena would find that particularly appealing.

"You're so gorgeous, sitting on my dick like it's your goddamn throne, but I need you below me," I told her, popping open my door after removing my shirt and shaking off my pants. It had to be around fifty-five degrees, but I felt like I was still on fire.

"Whatever you want," she mumbled, resting her head on

my shoulder as I sat up, holding her by the waist in order to lift her out of the car and around the door.

The air was heavy with the scent of petrichor, and I could spot flashes of light past the rocky edge of the cliff over Astropolis. The wind kicked up a notch out here, and Irena shivered as I placed her on the hood, wrapping her legs around me to borrow some of my warmth.

"It's cold," she complained, and I pecked her pout.

"Just for a few seconds. I'll warm you right up." I backed up my statement by pulling entirely out of her, then pushing back in, sheathing myself to the hilt. Irena's head fell on the hood as she groaned, hyper-sensitive after her orgasm. I mirrored the sentiment after doing it again.

A loud clap of thunder sounded, shaking the ground and the car, and Irena held on to me, her concerned gaze bleeding into mine. "It's going to rain."

No less than five seconds after her observation, the sound of pouring rain came first, and I braced my elbows on either side of her, shielding her body from the shower that followed, heralded by dazzling claps of thunder. The water acted like a soothing balm against my burning skin, coming down on us with a ferocity that made me think it was trying to wash away our sins.

Even though I enjoyed it, Irena shivered in my arms, her back lifting off my car to avoid contact with the water that slid from the roof onto the hood. I started my assault back up again to distract her from the hostile environment and make her focus on the heart of her pleasure...*me*, humble as always.

"Despite being the sweetest thing I've ever tasted, you aren't made of sugar, Lilith."

Lightning illuminated the sky over the trees, bathing us in light. Irena's eyes flashed, almost the exact same electric blue, at my praise. The distance between her legs widened, and she tilted her hips up every time I slammed home, meeting me thrust for thrust.

The rain raged on, but it didn't impact us. Yes, we got drenched to the bone, though neither of us cared, seeing as we were otherwise occupied.

I drove into her so violently she groaned in both pleasure and pain. My fingers kneaded her ass as strange sounds came from both of us, guttural groans that no sane human should have the ability to make.

We were both pure animals right now.

I couldn't stop pounding into her with frightening intensity. My lungs were starved for air, but my body begged for more of her.

"Most girls dream of getting *kissed* in the rain, not railed," she said in a broken whisper, and I bent further down to claim her mouth with mine. The kiss was sloppy, as we were way past the point of being able to uphold any technique.

"You get both," I replied, gulping down her irregular exhales. "How does it feel to be the chosen one?"

"Aghhh..." Her lashes were adorned with droplets of water, and they rolled down her cheeks like tears of happiness when her eyes closed. She mumbled some incoherent nonsense when her clit rubbed against the base of my dick.

"Aghhh," I mimicked, raising a brow. "What an eloquent answer."

"I hate you," she cried out.

I stood tall in front of her, smoothing my palm from her neck to the valley between her breasts to feel her erratic heartbeat. It was pounding faster than the speed of light, the telltale signs of a lie. It probably was because I was pounding into her with no reprieve, but I rolled with it.

"You're a beautiful liar, Irena." My hand closed in around a breast, and I squeezed as I kissed my way up from her navel, licking some of the water that had pooled in her belly button all the way before closing my mouth around her puckered nipple, whispering against her skin, "But that's okay, I'm having the best time fucking the lies right out of you. My work here will be complete only *after* your screams turn louder than the crushing thunder."

Hours passed, or at least it felt like it.

The rain stopped, and the wind settled, but my appetite for Irena Fleur was as raging as ever. Usually, I would have given in by now. She'd come two more times, and her voice had turned hoarse from all the screaming.

My rhythm was a mix of gentle and wild, not wanting to hurt her because she had to be super sensitive by now, but the little minx kept asking for more after a few slow thrusts, and I couldn't contain myself. We went through a few alternating positions. I arranged her on the side, which gave me a lovely view of her perky ass that called for my palm to leave marks all over her pale skin. And with her legs over my shoulders, embracing her thighs as I raced across a track with no finish line in sight.

My eyes turned heavy-lidded as I neared my release, and I struggled to keep them open, not wanting to lose a second of this. Of finally claiming the girl that lingered on my mind for so long, stepping out of my comfort zone, and enjoying sex way more than I normally did because she forced me to unload some of the weight of the past.

"Come with me, please," Irena begged, and I spread her knees, encircling her waist and holding the back of her head as I pressed my cheek against hers, inhaling the salt on her skin.

"Even if I wanted to fight it, I can't. Your pussy is too tight, too wet, too fucking perfect."

My whole body shook as we stayed locked in an embrace. She came first with a throaty sound that triggered my own release. My balls tightened, and my back jerked in a straight line as I drove into her with wild, deep thrusts.

There was no doubt in my mind that we were a match made in hell. She felt nothing short of heavenly, but God knows she was built for sin. I emptied inside her for so long that I didn't think it would end. When we came down, it seemed like an eternity had passed, and I paused all movement, my energy at an all-time low.

"No one has ever complimented my pussy directly," Irena mumbled, slurring out a laugh that got caught in her throat when I pulled out.

Watching my cum dripping out of her cunt was an experience unlike any other. It was a rare first for me, as I always insisted on wrapping it up, so I gathered some of it on my fingers and, in an impulse reaction, pushed the milky white consistency back inside Irena, but stopped once I heard her pained hiss.

It was probably wise to let her recuperate for a few hours.

"That's a shame. She is phenomenal, in my opinion."

I dragged her down from the car's hood, not allowing her feet to touch the wet ground as I raised her in my arms, carrying her tired body to the back seat so she could have a little nap while I drove us home.

I set her down, straightening her skirt over her legs—even though it was beyond repair, it would do until we went through the lobby—and grabbed her shirt from the front. She batted me away when I tried to get her to sit up, but I urged her to wear it nonetheless and used my shirt to wipe between her thighs.

I'd be going shirtless, but oh well; I put so much work on my body I might as well show it off.

When I made to get out, she held on to my arm and said, "Killian, you're so much more than I could have ever imagined."

My throat dried up, and I licked my lips, letting my gaze roam over her, appreciating all the small details like the freckle above her upper lip and a tiny cut on her hairline. No matter how much I fought it, I finally reached out, tracing the scar with my thumb.

"So are you, Irena." Her eyes closed, and she rested her cheek in my palm, looking content and ready to fall asleep right there, but unfortunately, I had to crush her plans. "Now, let's go home. I leave for work at seven in the morning, and that means we get"—I checked my watch, noting that we had been here for two hours—"nine more hours of me fucking you over and over again."

"Nine more hours?" Her eyes snapped open, a pleading quality to them. "Killian, I'm already spent."

Poor thing.

She was used to *wham, bam, thank you, ma'am* situations.

To be honest, I usually didn't go this hard, but I was making use of every little bit of time we had together. Our schedules were always packed, and with a deadline looming over our heads, sacrificing a bit of sleep was necessary.

"That's too bad." I nipped the top of her breasts. "But we'll build up your stamina."

CHAPTER NINETEEN
IRENA

"I can't believe you woke me up at the ass crack of dawn to walk your fucking *cat*," Killian complained in a gruff voice.

I ran my eyes down the rest of his body, examining the faint scratch marks that started underneath his hair and disappeared beneath the black neckline of his shirt. I lit bright red when we woke up and realized he couldn't hide them under his clothes. Still, he'd chuckled and said that my artwork deserved to be displayed and insisted I add some more when he rolled over me to give me a proper good morning, as he called it.

Unfortunately, it had to end fairly quickly. Dusty had already spent the night alone, and I'd feel guilty if I didn't take him on his morning walk, as he enjoyed them thoroughly. His fluffy tail was stuck high in the air, and he pranced before us on the park's pathway, scanning the fall orange leaves for insects or birds.

"Dusty is a scaredy cat—any type of noise will spook him —so I take him out before anyone wakes up," I said, but

Killian didn't seem all that keen on listening to my explanation.

"This is the first time I've seen anyone walking a cat," he went on, correcting himself once he saw how far ahead Dusty was and how much he was pulling on his leash. "Well, a cat walking his owner."

"I feel like he gets bored in the apartment all the time." Not only dogs but cats should go outside as well, in my opinion. "I got a bird feeder to keep him entertained, but I could tell he needs more mental stimulation, so I trained him to go on walks."

"Looks like he was a lousy student," Killian observed him as I stopped walking because Dusty decided to roll on a patch of grass.

"Cats aren't like dogs, smart-ass. They like to take their time." I turned to him with a raised brow. "Besides, haven't you heard the phrase, *stop and smell the roses?* You could learn a thing or two from Dusty."

"He's eating one right now."

My head snapped back in my cat's direction, and indeed he was pulling on his extendable leash, running toward a rosebush by the side of the pathway. He took a yellow flower in his mouth before I could stop him.

"Dusty!" I yelled, and he paused like he was aware he was in trouble, yet still went on a few seconds later as if he hadn't heard me. *This fucking cat.* I was convinced he had a death wish most days. "No! Those could be poisonous."

I picked up the pace and ran the short distance, but Killian and his long legs beat me to it. Crouching to his knees, he picked up Dusty, laughing when my cat grunted in protest. Killian cradled him to his chest, and a hot guy holding a cute cat almost caused my ovaries to explode.

I bit my lip as he scratched behind Dusty's ears. Killian's eyes flicked to me, recognizing where my thoughts had wandered, and he groaned, "God, I could be eating *you* out right now."

"Like a breakfast-in-bed type situation? We can still make that happen," I replied, all too eager.

"No, we can't. I work in an hour."

"You work too much." I deflated like a balloon. He had two fucking jobs, and I barely got to see him as it was. I wasn't sure I would get my fill of him with our time crunch.

"I like what I do, so it doesn't bother me much."

"It bothers *me*. We only have so much time. I want to monopolize all of yours."

He gave me an unimpressed stare, setting Dusty on the ground again when we returned to the walkway and away from the roses. "You're one to talk. Aren't you flying to Milan for, like, three days?"

"I'm helping out Aria with some suppliers. Saint couldn't go, and we didn't want to leave her alone. I also get to drown my sorrows in limoncello and eat my anxiety away in cheesy pasta, so it's a win-win."

"What do you have to be anxious about?" He dusted some of the cat hair off his shirt—my least favorite part about having a cat; their fur got everywhere.

"I haven't heard back from any networks after Amani pitched my show idea," I sighed dejectedly.

I used to avoid my problems any way I could. I excelled at placing them in the back of my mind until I couldn't ignore them anymore. Still, the thought of failing at something as important as this haunted me every second of the day.

"Isn't that a lengthy process? It's only been two weeks."

"Yes," I grumbled.

"But you're impatient?" he concluded, and I couldn't do anything but confirm.

"I *am* impatient. I can't help it."

"You know you remind me of a cat: you're cute but vicious, you have random bursts of energy, you make your distaste clear when you don't like someone, and you want everything done your own way."

The tips of my cheeks turned ruddy at his evaluation of me. Cute but vicious was a description I could get behind, but I didn't think I was ever outright rude to anyone.

I sped up my pace to keep up with his long legs and asked, "I make my distaste clear? Whatever do you mean? I'm polite to everyone."

"Really?" He raised a dark brow. "Didn't you tell me you never got along with Katrina because you didn't like her vibe?"

I rolled my eyes at his example. "She started it. She tried to sabotage me every step of the way when we were younger."

"So you liked her before that?"

"Well, no, she acted like a little golden child. She was always after the coach's praise, and whenever anyone else got a compliment, she glared at them like they'd pissed on her breakfast. I steered clear of her."

"Okay, *she* really is something else." Killian shuddered. "What I meant was, the second the people you used to be friends with showed their true character, you shed them off like second skin. I had the laugh of my life when one of them called you, and you shut the phone right in their face."

"That just means I'm not stupid or gullible. Of course I'm not going to entertain assholes that talked shit behind my back." I faced forward again, matching Dusty's gait and walking along with my hand held high.

Killian's arm looped around my waist, a brand of hard muscle pulling me closer to his side. Those ever-present butterflies in my stomach took flight again when his amused stare bore down on me as he said, "As you shouldn't. Most people wouldn't be so blunt with their disregard, is all I'm saying."

Staring at his ocean eyes was unnerving. Killian had a quiet calm that could send you running, so I didn't know why I found myself wanting to delve deeper into the intensity of his gaze.

Like it usually happened with us, it took zero point five seconds to go from a normal conversation to wanting to tear each other's clothes off. Seeing as that was quite impossible in a public park where more people had begun appearing, holding on to their morning cups of coffee as they headed off to work, I took it upon myself to keep the conversation going.

"Point made." I gulped, getting rid of this dryness in the back of my throat. "You know what kind of animal you would be?"

The left corner of his mouth lifted like he couldn't wait to hear it. "Enlighten me."

"An elephant," I blurted out, sucking my lips in my mouth as I prepared for the chaos that would ensue.

Men and their fragile egos.

Like clockwork, Killian's smile dimmed, and he huffed.

"Really?" he asked incredulously.

"Listen..." I pinched his side, rushing to explain. "You maintain your cool so well, no one sees you coming. It takes a lot for you to lose your temper, but when you do, good luck to the ones that wronged you."

A quiet killer.

That was what he was.

It was my understanding that it didn't always used to be this way for him, judging from the stories I'd heard of his youth. He had worked on himself and perfected the art of striking when people least expected it.

"That explanation makes me feel *this* much better." Killian held up his thumb and pointer finger, pinching them together until a sliver of space remained. "What happened to a lion, a wolf, a shark? Anything but an elephant?"

"It's not you." I raised a shoulder as I set off at a quicker pace, leaving him a few feet behind. "Embrace your inner elephant, Killian. It's who you are."

"I'll show you an elephant," he groused, and with Dusty leading the pack, we set off on a run. Killian was chasing me and Dusty, a squirrel that had the misfortune of walking in front of us at that very moment.

My lungs burned as I laughed and jogged at the same time. Killian let me get ahead, giving in to the thrill of the chase if the soft laughs under his breath were anything to go by.

There was a lightness in my heart, and it was mirrored in Killian's demeanor today. Whatever had passed between us yesterday had eased some of the nerves that were ever-present before and bonded us tighter together. Even if it had been less than twenty-four hours, Killian had turned more playful, opening up little by little every second.

"Got ya," Killian gasped as my back slammed into a tree trunk, and he pressed against my front, the smile on his face as dazzling as the stars in a night sky.

I breathed in deep, struggling to speak while I got my heart rate under control. "I let you win."

"Oh, I think I won you over a long time ago, Fleur." Killian cradled my chest, smoothing my hair back, and leaned down for a toe-curling kiss, his full lips claiming mine with the same urgency that led to a ten-hour-long sex marathon.

I was sore as hell, but when he pried my lips open with his teeth, and his tongue invaded my mouth like it was unclaimed land it sought to conquest, I felt like I could go on for ten more hours. The possessiveness in his kisses made my heart beat a mile a minute and a steady pulse thump between my legs.

"Perhaps." I sucked in a breath when we disconnected, refusing to put all my cards on display.

My fingers toyed with the blond strands of hair caressing his nape as Killian placed his forehead on mine and closed his eyes. I followed suit, soaking in the sounds of nature: leaves rustling in the wind, birds chirping on tree branches, and Dusty meowing at them from below.

"You make me feel like before—" Killian's chest brushed against mine, and I could feel his heartbeat elevate when he stopped his sentence abruptly.

"Before?" I urged.

"Before life turned so complicated," he filled in. Still, the words were hollow, like he hastily put them together as he rephrased his original thought last minute. "Like I'm thirteen again, and my only worry is if the girl I'm so infatuated with will let me under her skirt or not."

I swallowed down my need for answers, accepting his statement as it was. I liked to believe that one day we would reach a point when he'd be completely comfortable discussing anything with me, but out of fear that it was just wishful thinking on my part, I spoke to drown out my doubts.

"*Infatuated*—what a lovely word." I smirked. "Do tell me more."

"Your mouth was the first thing that got my attention, painted berry red and spewing a thousand words per minute." The glint in his irises turned wicked as his thumb pressed over my lips, smearing my lip gloss and turning my cheeks about the same crimson color as he pressed on. "Your hair came next, shining in the sun like molten metal, then those lovely eyes of yours as deep as the ocean yet as clear as a lake, and finally, your body with all that honed muscle that melted under my touch like a candle set ablaze."

My mouth dropped open at his description of me. For the first time, I realized Killian didn't just draw with his hands but his thoughts as well, painting pictures so vivid, his mind constantly found new things to get excited by.

"Were you an author in a past life?" I asked rhetorically. "No one has ever talked about me like that before."

I sucked his thumb in my mouth, and he rewarded me with a masculine grunt as he watched my lips wrap around his finger with hungry eyes. The hair along my arms stood when he dragged out his digit slowly, leaving a trail of wetness in his wake as he circled his large palm around my neck.

"No," he breathed harshly. "I am too obsessed with you in this life, and probably some past one, if they exist. I wanted you for so long. I fear it's in my blood, my genetic makeup."

"You have me." My response was automatic.

Desperation welled in my throat when he shook his head and said, "For a limited time only."

Hope made my chest puff out slightly, and I let my hands slide down his pecs, his heartbeat beating almost in sync with mine as I asked him, "What are you saying, Killian?"

There was a second where the sincerity in his eyes outshined the cool image he was constantly trying to project, and I saw a myriad of emotions swarming behind his blues. Need, affection, longing, and one that caught me off guard...*fear*.

Of the unknown?

Of the consequences of pursuing whatever this was between us further?

I didn't know, but I was going to find out.

I opened my mouth again to voice the questions in my mind, but it was like a switch went off inside him, and that rare look he allowed me in his head was ripped away, replaced by that concerning vacancy.

Killian was many things, but an open book he was certainly not.

"Dusty is currently making a head start toward the pond," he intercepted what I was going to say, removing his hands off me and taking a step back, his voice hoarse as he continued, "Get to running, Lilith."

A curse that would make my mother die a thousand deaths ripped from my mouth as the moment vanished, and I realized in my lavender haze I'd let go of Dusty's leash.

So I did get to running, knowing in the back of my mind that this discussion would be brought up again.

CHAPTER TWENTY
IRENA

Four weeks went by as fast as a rushing torrent. Much to Amani's dismay, modeling jobs came flooding in after word got out that I was offered my old job back, and with the work came more money than I'd ever made from ice skating. Because of my pre-platform and the attention my name brought, clients were willing to pay big bucks. Despite my increased earnings, I didn't allow myself a single splurge, save from donating to some of my favorite charities.

I had to hold on to the money in case no network picked my show up, and so far, it was looking pretty bleak. My dad almost blew up when I told him I was planning on investing all my savings to make Sting of Ice a reality, but I knew I could make it work. My drive and determination reached new heights every time Katrina and Daniel tried to ruin me. There had been plenty of attempts ever since Killian bashed his face in.

With no evidence, of course, because I had that wiped in no time. Fooling the world through a cell phone screen was easy, but not the people who got to witness what pieces of shit they were through daily life. Promo for their new season wasn't going well either—I suspect that was why I was called in—and they tried to salvage it as best as they could.

I didn't fan the flames any further. I was busy portraying a picture-perfect life. Obviously, there was no such thing as perfection, though some would say living next to a six-foot-tall sex god that made sure you got no fewer than three orgasms a day was pretty close.

Killian's and my relationship was mutually beneficial: I got my revenge, and he got *me*. It was strictly sexual...or, well, that was the agreed-upon term. We never bothered to set any more rules, so this past month, understandably, lines got blurred. The fact that we got along outside of the bedroom as well didn't help matters.

Even mundane things we did together brought me joy, like grocery shopping or driving me around whenever I had any errands to run. I was making a conscious effort to eat more home-cooked food. Still, when Killian witnessed first-hand what a disaster I was in the kitchen after I almost cut off the tips of my fingers several times and nearly burned myself with hot oil, he took over. It sort of became a tradition of sorts every night—us eating dinner that *he* had made because I couldn't be trusted.

I did get ahead of myself sometimes, like when I offered him to spend the night at my apartment so he didn't have to leave immediately after sex like usual. He promptly reminded me that cuddling wasn't part of the deal. At that moment, I wanted the earth to open up and swallow me whole, but I kept my ground and sarcastically stated we'd never agreed on anything like that. He shut me up by saying that I should've paid attention to the fine print.

From that night on, I grew colder, even though I had no

reason to. I'd agreed to this voluntarily after all, but I got carried away by all the increased attention he was paying me. Killian enjoyed my company and body, but unlike me, he hadn't forgotten that *we* could never happen. As much as I hated admitting it, he was right.

We couldn't happen, and some distance during this whole ordeal, no matter how minuscule, would benefit us in the long run.

Still, the fact that he was right didn't prevent me from acting petty. I hadn't seen him in three days, claiming I was super busy with work, and I didn't invite him to the Halloween party Bea was throwing. It was partly because I was embarrassed as hell and because he could've been kinder with his delivery.

The Astor men weren't famed for their empathy, but we Fleur women didn't take any shit either.

So fuck him.

"Hey, babe, mind taking this to the dining table?" Bea handed me a silver plate filled with fries that somehow looked like severed human fingers. Even though they reeked of ketchup, they seemed so realistic I shivered.

"Of course," I replied, squeezing past people to head to the living room.

Bea brought her A game every Halloween.

It was her favorite holiday, and since her family didn't celebrate Christmas, she went all out with this one. Her two-story home was decorated from top to bottom with all things spooky. There were Ouija boards framing the walls, skeletons by the front door, spider webs everywhere, carved pumpkins in every other corner of the house, and an abundance of fall candles making the whole place smell like a pumpkin spice latte factory.

Her costume was out of this world too. She pre-planned them months in advance, and this year she was dressed as a vintage Playboy bunny with a suit that cost three grand. It was well worth it, though, as it clung to her body perfectly. Halloween was that one time of the year when you could dress as a slut and no one would bat an eye, so why not take full advantage of it?

I had.

In the previous years, I'd embodied every redheaded fictional character possible since I despised wearing wigs. They were always itchy. Merida, Ariel, Poison Ivy, Natasha Romanoff, Jessica Rabbit—you name it, I'd dressed as it. So my choices were limited this year.

And that was how I found myself in a floor-length black dress with outrageous cut-outs, a plunge between my breasts big enough to reveal my belly button and require double-sided sticky tape to keep my boobs from spilling out. I had a cross hanging from my neck, devil's horns on my head, and fake blood running down the sides of my mouth.

I was Lilith in the flesh.

It made sense to come as her since I heard that nickname every day, plus I could taunt Killian with the fact that he never saw me in this costume.

"Looking great, Fleur," a gravelly voice echoed behind me, and I twisted at the waist to see who it was.

My eyes widened when Christopher Nolan took up my field of vision, his impressive bronze chest exposed in his Tarzan getup. Bea was better at keeping up with our old high school friends than I was, and a ton of them were invited tonight. I let my gaze roam over his body before smiling at him.

"Christopher!" I dusted my hands off as I approached him.

It had been a minute since I'd seen him...live, that is. I saw him on TV all the time. He'd made it big after he got drafted by an NFL team straight out of college. He was bulkier than I remembered, and he'd let his curls grow as opposed to the faded buzzcut he used to sport.

"A *you look amazing too* would be greatly appreciated," he joked as I hugged him.

"Your ego gets inflated daily. Why would I add to that?" I chuckled when we came apart because there was always an onslaught of thirsty comments wherever his name was mentioned.

His almond eyes crinkled at the corners as he examined me from head to toe, and I squeezed his biceps, retreating a step. Chris had always been the overly flirty type, but I was proud to say I hadn't succumbed to his charms. Not because he wasn't attractive—because he was abnormally so—but he was way too complicated for me with a new girl on his arm every day. Casual, I could do, but when you went through so many people, jealousy was bound to follow.

He never stopped trying, though, and even now, years later, I saw the determination in his face as he examined me and flicked his tongue over his bottom lip. The doorbell rang before he could say anything, though, and I patted his hand, heading for the foyer. I was on door duty while Bea finished up in the kitchen.

"Let's catch up later," I offered.

"You bet your ass we will." He gave a little whistle as I walked in front of him, and I rolled my eyes at the action. Another reason why I hadn't given in? He was way too eager.

It seemed like emotionally unavailable men that pretended to dislike you were more up my speed.

I grabbed a plastic pumpkin bowl filled with candy. The house was already packed, and I doubted Bea had invited anyone else, so there had to be trick-or-treaters.

I opened the door only for my smile to freeze when I gathered who was leaning against the foyer, arms crossed in a thin black sweater and distressed black jeans with a metal chain attached at the waist. My grip on the bowl loosened when I reached his face, beautiful as always, with stormy blue eyes and a square jaw that made him appear angry even when he wasn't. His blond strands caressed the top of his forehead, overdue for a haircut.

I thought embodying Lilith and having Killian miss it would be a punishment all on its own, but he had to one-up me by showing up. And he was currently undressing me with his eyes, eating up the view like a man starved.

My first reaction was to overreact as I opened my mouth, but I thought better of it, biting my tongue and shifting my feet. That was what he wanted—he always got the upper hand somehow, so I decided to play it cool.

I squared my shoulders, taking up more space and blocking the doorway as I asked, "And what are you dressed as?"

His pupils dilated at the sound of my voice, yet he didn't give anything away as he said, "Myself."

"Really? And here I thought you were a clown," I spewed my vitriol before I could contain myself. "*Dressed* as a clown, I mean."

An infuriating half smile took over his lips, but he refused to take the bait. "Your passive-aggressiveness is only succeeding in giving me a semi."

My gaze dropped instantly, but I made a point of blinking slowly, as if to act like I wasn't trying to confirm or deny his claim.

After grabbing a lollipop, I set the candy bowl by the foyer table. I had this annoying tendency of chewing on my lips whenever I felt anxious, so in an attempt to keep busy, I unwrapped the sucker and swirled my tongue around it, eager to watch Killian squirm for once.

He latched on to the movement, but I didn't give him an extensive show. I shoved the lolly on the inside of my cheek and made to close the door. "Being hard for no reason is nothing to brag about. You should see a doctor."

His palm prevented me from doing that, spreading flat against the wood as his expression showed he didn't tolerate nonsense. "There is a reason, and she's standing right before me."

I sighed, popping the lollipop from my mouth. "Why are you here, Killian? You weren't invited."

"I was. He's my plus-one." It wasn't Killian that responded. Another man appeared behind him, smoothing his hands down the lapels of his suit, the white shirt underneath it drenched in what I hoped was fake blood. His hair, a darker shade of blond than Killian's, was longer than most and slicked back, making him look like Patrick Bateman from *American Psycho*.

The newcomer had a *got ya* type of grin on his face, and I recognized him as Nicolas from that day at the club with Killian and Luca. Bea had kept in touch and hadn't told me anything. That was a first.

Slightly salty, I said, "This isn't a wedding. There are no plus-ones."

His smile got bigger, and as if on cue, the song in the

background changed to "Hip To Be Square" by Huey Lewis and the News. Goose bumps spread down my back, a sense of danger wafting in the air at the amused look on his face when he stared down at me like he wasn't used to people questioning him.

"Not when you come dressed as a groom," he argued, as if I didn't know what he was actually dressed as.

I raised a brow, crossing my arms. "And Killian is the bride, I'm assuming?"

"No, he's the second groom. Get with the times." He snapped his fingers, and like he had more important things to do, he brushed past me, not bothering to wait for my response. "Now, if you'll excuse me, I need to find your friend."

I huffed, fixing my hair over my shoulder after it got swept back, and Killian shrugged, enjoying this thoroughly.

"You're unbelievable," I spewed, but there was no point in pursuing this any further. Killian always got what he wanted. Spinning on my heels, I left him at the door. "Whatever. Have fun, I guess."

It clicked shut a few seconds later, and I felt a presence at my back, looming over me like a ghost. I stopped abruptly at the end of the corridor, and he slammed against me, propelling me forward. His hands on my waist stabilized me, and I clenched my teeth as I threw him a glare over my shoulder.

"Have fun somewhere far away from me." I removed his hold from my body. Still, he completely bypassed anything I said and started up a conversation like he hadn't made me feel like a cheap whore the last time he saw me.

"You dressed as Lilith."

"It was just a clever costume idea. It had nothing to do with you."

"I'm sure it doesn't," Killian replied, his tone thick with irony.

"Stop following me." I shut down an argument I wasn't going to win before it started, pointing at him as I walked down the rest of the hall.

I expected him to disregard me once again, but was pleasantly surprised when he didn't and instead went toward the direction Nicolas had disappeared to.

I needed some time to forget what had happened, and he robbed me of that by showing up tonight. It probably wasn't that deep for him, but it was for me, and he had to understand it. He was used to discarding girls as soon as he had his use of them. I liked aftercare and cuddling, though, so he'd have to make do.

Killian blended in better than I thought with Bea's and my friends.

Until that moment, I'd never really seen him in a social setting. I had this view of him not getting along with other people because he was always so demanding, had little to no empathy, and was ready to step on everyone to get his way.

Turned out I was wrong.

I tried hard to ignore him, but I couldn't help tracking him with my eyes as he made the rounds, meeting new people. All of them were enamored, especially the girls, giggling and talking to him longer than I would've liked.

I thought he'd flounder without my attention and, of course, he had to go and prove me wrong.

So, wrapped in a cloud of jealousy, I headed toward the backyard to get him out of my sight. It had proven difficult to ignore him.

It was cold as balls out, but there was a bonfire burning, a Halloween tradition. We gathered around when the party died down a little every year and told scary stories. I'd heard most of them already. People tended to forget the stories they'd told a year ago, so I didn't get scared.

The only one that could still affect me was Marcia, another friend from high school. She always had a thing for paranormal stuff, wore all black with heavy eyeliner, and went to work as a ghost tour guide in Salem after we graduated.

She was low-key cool, if you omitted the fact that she found scaring people fun.

A group was already gathered around the fire. It wasn't the traditional sort, with big wooden planks sticking out of it. Bea had a crystal fire pit a few feet away from a kidney-shaped pool. At the end of the evening, we voted on who told the worst story with a show of hands, and whoever lost had to jump in fully clothed.

Now, that wasn't a fun punishment at the end of October.

I usually sat next to Bea, but she was in a gray love seat with Nicolas. That would just be awkward, so I plunked my ass on a large sectional next to Christopher, who had a big enough coat to fit both of us. There were around ten people, and one of them was already speaking, so they didn't pay much attention to me when I sat down.

Chris welcomed me with a smile, and I pointed at his coat and whispered, "Mind if I scoot in with you?"

"Of course not." He shook his head, ripping it off his

shoulders—his very *naked* shoulders. "Here, you can have it."

Although he was pure muscle, I doubted he could survive in this cold topless without his nipples freezing off, so I attempted to put it back on him. "No, no, I don't want you to be cold."

"I've been forced to play in the pouring rain and while it was snowing. I've gotten used to cold temperatures," he insisted, but I wasn't relenting.

He was sitting down, not exercising every muscle on an open field. It wasn't the same. We went back and forth a few more times, earning a few shushes, but our argument was put to rest a few seconds later.

"I've got it," said none other than my sister's brother-in-law, who apparently, I was only supposed to be fucking but also got extremely jealous whenever I talked to another man that wasn't one of his buddies. I could hear it in his tone. A vibrato said *you do not want to fuck with me.*

My back stiffened when he scooched in next to me at the end of the couch. I didn't turn to look at him. This man could decode me faster than I could open up my mouth and speak. I didn't want him to see the satisfaction on my face that he had indeed come after me and didn't stay to chat with those girls.

I wasn't as oblivious to him as he tried to portray, after all.

"Do you know him?" Chris asked, not intimidated easily, seeing as he was twice the size of Killian.

I replied with an "unfortunately" at the same time, Killian said, "I'm her boyfriend." I whipped around, half tempted to remove my shoe, and hit him upside the head with it. He pursed his lips as if keeping a laugh in because he knew I couldn't dispute his statement.

I regretted asking for his help in the first place with each passing second.

"I didn't know you had a boyfriend," Chris stated antagonistically.

"Now you do." Killian nearly leaned over me to stare him down, shoving *his* jacket on my exposed chest and removing the one Christopher had haphazardly managed to throw over my shoulders.

I was sure these two would go at it all night—you could cut the tension with a knife—but Bea's obvious cough put some space between them. Killian wasn't backing down, and Christopher was too proud to concede without having the last word.

He took out his wallet, dropping his business card in my lap. "If he gives you any trouble, call me, and I'll take care of him."

I nodded, my fingers curling around the edges of the card, and Killian snorted like he deemed it impossible. I didn't bother throwing on his jacket, preferring to turn numb from the cold than give in to his caveman behavior. I scooted away from him when Chris removed himself from our bullshit and curled up next to an available blonde at the other end of the couch.

Killian took the balled-up jacket from my hands and held it up. I shivered, yet still didn't make a move to cover up, leading him to hiss out, "If you value your ability to walk straight, you will put this on."

"And what if I don't?" I asked haughtily.

"That can be arranged." The heavy-lidded look he gave me portrayed his blinding desire to steal me away from here and ram his dick inside my cunt as punishment for leaving him celibate for three days.

"Um, excuse me." Our little battle of wills was paused when Marcia addressed us, her onyx-black hair shining in the night. "I'm not jumping in frigid water because you were too distracted to listen to my story."

My cheeks flamed as this was the second time I was being put on the spot, so I fumbled to find something to say. Eventually, I settled for, "You could never lose this game, Marcia."

It was lame, and I sounded like a true ass-licker, but as long as it got them off my case, I was good.

"True." She shrugged before she dismissed us. "But pay attention."

Killian was on the verge of speaking, most likely to tell her he could do whatever he wanted, so I snatched his damn jacket, hating myself for the deep inhale I took when his woody fragrance wrapped around me as it almost engulfed me whole.

We were too stubborn for our own good.

Settling back, I wiggled around as I tried to get cozy. Marcia was going on and on about a true story of a boy that got lost in the woods—one of the reasons why she always won, in my opinion, was because her stories weren't fictional, which made them even freakier.

It wasn't hitting as much today, though, it probably had something to do with the overbearing man next to me, subtly shifting closer and closer until his breaths hit the base of my neck, hence my inability to focus.

"What did she mean by jumping in frigid water?" Killian's question tickled my ear, and I tilted my head sideways in an attempt to ice him out.

"Every one of us has to tell a scary story, and the person with the lamest one has to jump in the pool," I explained coolly.

I was aware I was acting unreasonably. Perhaps if he hadn't shown up today, my anger would've died down by tomorrow, but in classic Killian fashion, he wanted to force my hand, and I wasn't going to let him weasel his way into my good graces without a proper apology.

"That doesn't seem too bad. Drink enough alcohol, and you won't feel a thing."

"I'd rather freeze for a few minutes than puke my guts out in the morning." I sliced my gaze sideways when he extended his hand to me, holding a tissue. "What's this?"

"For when you start to tear up. I noticed you crying when we watched *Hereditary*." He dropped it in my lap when I made no move to take it.

I was a bit surprised he had noticed that when I'd tried to hide it by immediately wiping away the few stubborn tears that managed to escape from the corners of my eyes. I liked watching scary movies, but my body wasn't in the same boat, seeing as I would tear up at even the lamest YouTube ghost videos.

"Are you trying to get back into my good graces?" I balled the tissue in my fist. "If so, an apology would work better."

"Never realized I had something to apologize for," he answered drily.

"You have the emotional intelligence of a toad," I snapped, and received some dirty looks in return.

Blowing out a big breath, I let the matter go for now, and thankfully, Killian gathered that this wasn't the time or place to talk about this.

The circle went on, one after the other, and when my turn came, I was so out of the loop, I went the basic route and talked about a mysterious woman that appeared in your bathroom mirror at midnight if you said her name three times and slashed your throat. My first clue that I was going to lose was when everyone groaned when they realized I was talking about Bloody Mary. The second one was when they laughed when Killian asked what would happen if multiple people called her name at the same time?

He was digging his grave in deeper.

I gritted my teeth as he took over, talking about a man who lost his wife and decided to remarry. The new stepmom was beyond creepy, showing a profound interest—the negative kind—toward the two oldest brothers who tried to warn their father, but he was too blinded by her beauty to listen to them. The abuse went on and on until they decided to end their lives and haunted the rest of their family that chose to ignore their pleas until they went mad.

Killian didn't disclose whether this was based on actual events or not, but it didn't matter. He narrated it in such a way he had enraptured everyone and even managed to make me cry. He patted my hand as if to say *there, there* when he was done, and his reassuring presence stood right behind me when I got voted to jump in the pool after a show of hands.

"Do it, do it, do it, do it!" Bea started to chant, and they all soon followed the more I stalled.

I dipped my toe in, testing the water, and pulled it out like the pool was filled with lava instead. After being warmed by the fire and Killian's jacket for the past hour, the change in temperature was going to be a shock to the system.

"Come on, I'll jump with you. It's not the first time we've

gotten wet together," Killian threw in an innuendo, and I'd rather smash a pickle jar on the floor and eat it, glass and all, than accept his help. If it wasn't for his little comment, I wouldn't be standing here.

"Don't pressure me, Killian. I'm going in at my own pace."

"The rules say you have to jump in the pool, sweetheart, not get in slowly."

"Always a stickler for the rules." I turned to him. He was bathed in a blue hue from the pool lights, and that unperturbed attitude of his was crumbling the more I fought him.

Good.

I wanted him to see I could affect him just as badly as he could me.

There was a flicker of indecision in his eyes before they hardened, and he started taking determined steps forward, breaching the gap between us.

One second, my feet were firmly planted on the floor. The next, I was thrown over his shoulder, staring at the rest of the guests' amused faces before Killian jumped, and we plunged, clothes and all, into the pool water.

A bit counterintuitive, but my first reaction was to scream, which resulted in massive amounts of chlorinated water rushing down my throat. Every crevice of my body was flooded with cool liquid as we sank. Killian had partially slid me down his body so his shoulder wouldn't dig into my stomach, and all the places where we connected made the temperature drop a tiny bit more manageable.

I coughed as my lungs filled with water, and that resulted in me taking in *even more* water. I managed to slide off Killian's grip after thrashing around, and the space around me was filled with a million bubbles when I opened my eyes. I didn't spot Killian until I calmed down and closed my mouth. My cheeks puffed up like a pufferfish.

I should've swum to the top, but I had half a mind to drag him further down with me and see who could survive longer without oxygen.

Me or him.

Killian's blues clashed with mine under the water, flashing with concern when he saw that I was still under. So, he swam to me, his palms clasping my waist as he dragged both of us up.

I sucked in air like I was starved once we broke the surface of the water. Through my peripheral vision, I could see that the small group of people that stood there before had expanded, and they were all laughing and cheering like we were in fifth grade again and somehow this was considered an awesome prank.

With fury racing in my veins, I sought out Killian, getting even madder when I beheld how gorgeous he looked, drenched wholly. Because how could this man do something and not look like a supermodel at the same time?

"You fucker." I kicked my legs underneath me, swimming closer. "I'm going to kill you, Killian!"

"That sounds funny." He wiped at his face, unfazed, and pushed his hair back.

Bea, sensing the brewing storm, had managed to steer people ever so slowly back into the house. I was way past the point of caring what people thought about me, though. I was usually careful, but when the switch inside me flipped, it was difficult to get me under control again.

"Ugh!" I groaned, deciding not to put a cap on my craziness then. Teeth chattering from the slight wind, I made a little triangle with my hands and propelled water toward

Killian's direction until he was drowning in my artificial mini waves.

I heard him coughing, and it only urged me to go harder until he was forced to get closer to me, despite the gallons of water being thrown at him, and capture my wrists in his hands so I would stop.

I didn't, though.

I squirmed as Killian tried to get me under control, pressing me into the side of the pool. The back porch, which was filled with snickers and whispers until a few minutes ago, fell quiet, alerting me to the fact that my best friend had left me alone with *him*.

"Irena," he bit out when I almost kneed his balls, his grip tightening so much it felt like a rough band of calloused fire. "Calm down."

Those two words somehow resembled telling a woman in the street to smile in my mind, so they had the exact opposite effect of what he intended them to.

"Don't tell me to calm down. First, you humiliate me, then you push me in a pool all in the span of a week." My high-pitched tone scared some of the birds in the trees across from us as I heard some of them suddenly taking flight.

Killian's brows met his hairline as he said, "Humiliate you? When the fuck did I ever do that?"

"Are you playing dumb, or are you actually dumb?"

"Is this about not cuddling after sex?" He hit the nail right on the head with a cruel twist of his lips. "You knew what you were getting into, Irena. I warned you beforehand."

The water made it easier to slide from his grip, and I slithered away from him as fast as I could, heading for the stairs to climb out of the pool. I wasn't as cold as I thought I would've been, and I suspected it had something to do with how Killian raised my blood pressure through the roof.

"I did, and I made a mistake for ever pushing your precious boundaries, but you didn't have to be such an asshole about it," I shouted over my shoulder, only to find out he was trailing close behind me.

"Where are you going?" he asked.

"Away from you!" I retorted.

"No, you're not," he pressed, giving me a pause. "I listened to you. You're going to have to listen to me."

I sighed, exasperated, as I clasped the railing but didn't lift myself out of the water. I loved Halloween, and he had already ruined my night, so I guess hearing him out one more time wouldn't hurt anyone but my pride.

Hugging the metal to regulate my body temperature, I told Killian, "Well, speak before I get pneumonia."

He tried to corner me again, but I held up my hand, keeping him at a distance. It was like my body short-circuited when he was close, and all my resilience went out the window at the lamest excuse, so I needed to keep him at bay if I wanted to be able to think clearly.

"Your wit, the way you go after what you want, and the way you are not afraid to talk back to me were the qualities that made me go nuts over you long before you came to me with this fucking proposal and long before it would be deemed appropriate in most people's eyes." His admission made my throat close up, but I didn't dare interrupt him, so he went on, speaking fast, like a man on a mission. "That night you called me out about avoiding you and told me how you used to sneak out your bedroom window to let stupid fucking teenage boys touch you, I saw red. And it didn't make sense 'cause I've done far worse. I felt the urge to slap my name on your ass and let every asshole know you were off-limits."

"So you *were* avoiding me," I muttered dumbly, because I didn't know what else to say to that.

My blood had warmed up to imperious levels, and I was feeling all fuzzy inside, like he had just handed me the world.

He'd told me exactly what I wanted to hear: that I wasn't alone in my crazy fixation with him, that he had been thinking of me for as long as I had him. My jealousy wasn't one-sided whenever I thought of him with *Mia*, and as toxic as that sounded, I was glad he shared the sentiment. It meant he cared enough to want me only for himself.

"Are you listening to what I'm saying?"

Killian swam closer, and this time I allowed him access to myself, my anger dying down as a different sort of heat enveloped my bones. He gripped my chin between his forefinger and thumb, pulling my gaze to his and smoothing a drop of water under my lips.

"I was already so far gone for you when you were virtually nobody to me. The more this goes on, the more I fear who I will become when this"—he pressed a feather-soft kiss on my lips, groaning low in his throat—"stops. Cuddling with you, spending the night together is just gonna add to the pile of things I won't be able to part with."

When this stops.

Indeed our expiration date was looming ahead, and my stomach was twisting in knots at the anxiety that knowledge brought forth.

He was being smarter than me, one step ahead.

But that still didn't stop me from wanting more, *needing* more.

"Get drunk with me," was my lackluster reply, but I needed some giggle juice to get rid of the evening's funk.

Killian leaned back to look into my eyes, confusion laminated over the lines on his forehead. "What?"

"Let's forget who we are for just a night." I burrowed my head in his wet chest as I spoke, ghosting my lips over his heart. "Let's just be Irena and Killian. Do all the things we fucking want to, and forget all of them come morning."

Killian pecked the crown of my head as he thought it over for a few seconds before ultimately giving in. "You've got yourself a deal, Lilith."

CHAPTER TWENTY-ONE
IRENA

I woke with a start.

It felt like someone was sanding off my face, and my ass was on fire while I was being suffocated under a weighted blanket simultaneously. I shifted around, trying to get comfortable under the *really* heavy comforter, but I just sunk deeper into the mattress and got very hot.

I rubbed a hand down my face to get rid of the sensation and accomplished nothing when a few seconds later, a rough surface of some kind shifted toward rubbing against my chin. I was floating between the land of dreams and reality, and hearing that familiar low engine-like purr brought me back to land.

Dusty.

I had to feed Dusty.

Head pounding from the light pouring in from the windows in my room, I froze when I saw a male's head spread over my waist, tucking me against a warm body that I realized was the reason I was overheating under the blankets. Last night was a blur, but a little bit of Killian's pine scent broke past Dusty's horrible breath as he shoved his face against mine, so I relaxed once more.

Duty called even if I was disoriented and barely able to sit up straight, so I untangled myself as gently as possible from Kill's arms and shushed Dusty when he began meowing, like he always did when I was about to feed him.

He didn't listen to me, of course.

Impatient little shit.

My head didn't stop pounding after I gave him his food, and I was so out of it I didn't even remember how I ended up peeing with a toothbrush in my mouth at the same time. The slight burn between my legs indicated it had been an eventful night, and the soreness of my ass cheeks sealed the deal.

I had to talk to Killian about his little slapping kink.

Even though I enjoyed it, he had to loosen up on the force because it was uncomfortable to fucking sit.

Curious as to how inflamed my skin was, I lifted his black T-shirt and turned my back to the mirror to look at my ass after brushing my teeth and washing my face. Surprisingly, I was met with nothing but smooth, pale, and *bare* skin, seeing as my panties were having the time of their life hanging from the ceiling fan. I faced my phone toward my left cheek and nearly dropped the damned thing when I spotted something unusual.

Block letters.

Sixteen of them, and an apostrophe.

Writing on my skin.

There was writing on my fucking ass cheek.

Okay, okay...I need to relax.

There was no way this was real.

I rubbed at it, but all it did was send my heart racing

when it didn't come off and also a shot of pain through me. As if I was submerged in beetroot juice, I turned flaming red when my slow-processing brain came to a realization.

A tattoo.

One worse than a tramp stamp.

"What the fuck?!" I screeched and immediately went back for a second look, zooming in. Sure enough, it was still there after I rubbed my eyes twice, too, to ensure I wasn't imagining things.

Oh, no.

Oh, no, no, no.

"Killian, Killian!" Panic mode settled in, and I stormed out of the bathroom, into my adjoining room, seeing the culprit of it all still sound asleep. My blood boiled, and I threw the blankets off him, not even taking a second to admire his full nudity. I shook him awake, full-on yelling, "Killian, wake up!"

He rolled on his back infuriatingly slowly, hair sticking in all sorts of different directions, eyes open only for a couple of milliseconds as he visibly fought against sleep.

"Wha-what?" Killian managed to mutter, scratching the top of his head.

"I have a tattoo on my ass!" I was too fired up to wait for him to wake properly, so words fired out of my mouth faster than fucking Eminem. "And it says—"

"Slow down." He cut me off with his gruff morning voice, glancing around to gauge his surroundings. Killian yawned loudly, resting his weight on his elbows, and squinted at me. "Let's drink some coffee first."

"No, we will not drink coffee." I nearly stomped my foot on the ground, irritated beyond comprehension and in disbelief at what came out of my mouth next. "I have a tattoo on my ass that says *Killian's Property* on it!"

"Ah, shit!" He shielded his eyes when a ray of light shone directly on him as the sun lowered over the sky, not hearing me at all as he asked, "Fuck, can we at least close the blinds?"

"No, I'm leaving them *wide* open," I screamed, and he winced at my volume. Slamming my hands on the mattress, I said, "Focus, Killian."

He blinked a couple of times, fighting to keep his eyes open, and I had to bite my cheek to not voice out how adorable it was. In a time like this, the only thing I should be thinking about was how incredible it would be if I chopped him up into fine little pieces.

"Sorry." He yawned loudly once again before giving me his undivided attention. "You have a what, and it says what?"

"A tattoo on my ass that says"—I gave him my back, modesty out the window as I lifted his shirt to show him— "Killian's *Property*."

The fucking horror.

This was demeaning in so many ways that I'd run out of ink if I tried to list them.

Killian's Property.

Killian's fucking Property.

I still believed there a possibility I'd taken some weird mushrooms last night, and all of this was a figment of my imagination. I mean, surely the effects could carry on to the next day. That was some strong-ass shit.

There was a beat of silence while Killian caught up to the gravity of the situation, and then the rustling of sheets as he sat upright, leaning in close like he couldn't believe his eyes.

"Jesus fucking Christ," I heard him mutter. He had the same reaction as me and tried to wipe it off. Tingles spread where his thumb rolled, but I crushed them into fine powder. This was so not the time.

He moved closer after coming to the same conclusion as me, that the tattoo wasn't going anywhere, and repeating, *"Holy crap, holy crap, holy crap,"* over and over again, making me feel like...well, *crap.*

I let my shirt drop. Killian had already seen me naked and had explored every part of me already. I wasn't comfortable enough to expose myself in front of him for long periods of time yet, though.

"Mind telling me how that got there?" I fought to keep my voice steady.

He clutched his left pec over the blanket, glancing down. "I think I have one too."

I gnawed on my bottom lip and regretted ever asking him to get drunk with me last night. I didn't remember much past changing into some dry clothes Bea had on hand for us when we walked in her house dripping wet. The rest of the night was a blur of shots, laughter, and flesh and lips meeting. I could vaguely recall a sour candy contest, mostly because I still carried the taste of it in my mouth even after brushing my teeth twice.

It was a freeing experience, touching and kissing in public without the fear of having anything leaked, because no one knew him at the party besides Bea and his friend.

Having him permanently inked in my body, though, and vice versa? I could cry.

"A tattoo?"

The comforter fell to his hips at my question. After taking a quick minute to appreciate all the rolling abs and tan skin, I gasped when I beheld what he was pointing at. Two blue butterflies with fluttering wings sporting intricate designs on them sat over the space where his heart was, the color so vibrant it looked like they were about to fly off him any second.

His tattoos were concentrated on his arms, so except for a word in Latin I'd noticed inked along his hipbone, his chest was free of any of them, save for this fresh one.

"Blue butterflies?" I studied them, marveling at the shading underneath and the black edges of their wings. "That's what you said that night I found you nearly passed out drunk outside your door."

"Oh, no," he exclaimed, staring at me as if seeing me in a new light before lunging for his phone on the bedside table. I got an eyeful of his crotch when he abandoned the blankets completely, and my mouth watered when his hard length pointed at me, even in a time such as this.

Morning wood, coupled with the fact that I wasn't wearing anything besides his tee, had to have an effect.

Killian scrolled through his phone, impervious as to where my gaze had strayed and pulled at this hair, mumbling, "Shit, shit, shit."

I set my perv thoughts on probation and sat on the bed, knees first. "Mind filling me in?"

"I—" He pulled at his hair harder, and I reached up, capturing his hand with mine.

My emotions had settled a little now that I knew we were in this together. Sure, my tattoo was on the extreme side, but those butterflies had to be in relation to me since he had linked them to my nickname before.

Killian was usually harder to figure out than a whole-ass maze, and somehow reading the frustration on his face as clear as day had me kissing the back of his hand to provide some relief, never mind the war that was still raging inside me.

His cheeks were laced with pink, and I couldn't believe my eyes. Was that a blush I was seeing? Sensing my renewed interest, he interlocked our fingers together and dragged me next to him so I got to peek at the text conversation he was reading that had him flushing like a ladybug.

Ray: Go easy with any physical activity today. You don't want to pull on the new tattoo too much.

Ray: And tell your little friend to avoid sitting down too much, and keep the kinky shit light.

Ray: Although, with the way you wouldn't let me tat her last night and kept repeating, you'd be the only one that got to see her ass, I doubt it.

It was my turn to flush crimson red from the very top of my head to the tips of my toes. My body adopted a second pulse at the mortification of how we'd acted last night. I could hear my heartbeat in my ears.

So it was a tattoo.

And not one of those stick-on that peeled after one wash.

"Oh my God, tattoos are permanent." I dropped the phone like it was made out of lava. It fell on my lap, then rolled on the carpeted floor, but Killian's attention was on me as I squeezed my face between my hands and went on a rant. "What am I going to do? I can never model for underwear now. People will be able to see it through my figure skating tights. I can't even go to the beach. *What is my future husband going to think?"*

Killian's face was somber until the last question, but in the flip of a second, it was like every bit of his guilt disappeared. I was sure his inner caveman would make a resurgence, but my concern was very valid because the day when we would stop playing house was fast approaching.

"He can choke for all I care." Indeed, his inner green monster peeked his head out. I gave him a stern glare, and he cleared his throat, rephrasing, "I mean, a tattoo is hardly permanent, laser removal exists, or you could cover it up with another tattoo. Also, it's small enough I imagine it won't be much of a pain to Photoshop away after your shoots, and you can wear undies that are a little more conservative."

He touched my hips on either side in an attempt to get another look at the tattoo, but I scooted back.

"Keep your hands to yourself," I voiced, different solutions and problems wheezing past my brain at the speed of light. "I'm serious, Killian. What propelled you to write something like this?"

"I was drunk out of my mind," he reasoned, shrugging. He wetted his bottom lip, gaze turning heavy. "Besides, who wouldn't want to brand their name on your lovely ass?"

"This isn't funny," I voiced sternly.

"I know it's not," he sighed. Humor was his default response to alleviate the awkwardness, but it wasn't cutting it this time, so he surprised me with a dose of vulnerability. "The butterflies are kind of your brand on my body too."

"How so?" I tilted my head.

He placed his fingertips lightly underneath his tattoo, drawing my attention as he went on to explain. "I don't just call you Lilith because you both have red hair and you act like a she-demon." A flash of a smile decorated his lips, and it was so dazzling I couldn't find it in me to debate him. "They say a sign that you're being pursued by Lilith is when you see a blue butterfly following you that can reportedly seduce anyone who looks at it. And in the weirdest turn of events, the first couple of times—way too many to be considered a coincidence—I saw a blue butterfly a few minutes before or after meeting you. It has never happened to me with anyone else."

A layer of goose bumps coated my skin, and the hair on my nape prickled as I digested what he admitted.

I was the first to scoff at any paranormal activity video and call bullshit on it. Still, there was an unsettling feeling deep in my bones that stopped me from questioning the validity of his statement. My very blood roared in my ears, my body buzzing like a live wire, a euphoric sort of haze filling me, reassuring me and telling me to trust the process.

"That *is* creepy. How come I never saw them?" I raised a brow, placing my fists on either side of his legs as I got on my knees.

The fact that *I* was etched over his heart had misplaced possessiveness twisting me up in knots. My little freak-out session was put on pause, placated by the fact that we both shared the same struggle, and he didn't seem too torn up about it, quite the opposite.

Killian's thumb brushed beneath his pec, as if finding comfort in the new addition to his body.

"'Cause you were the one trying to seduce me, *duh*." He rolled his eyes, and I took the opportunity to lay him flat on his back when he was distracted.

Cold air rushed up my stomach as I kneeled over him. His heated gaze strayed directly to the space between my shirt and chest and then to my ass, perched in the air, his *brand* on me on full display as I stared at him through hooded eyes.

"I kind of like my nickname now. I wasn't aware that you were capable of having such deep thoughts," I taunted, pressing a featherlight kiss on his abs.

He tensed, raising a brow. "Surely you shouldn't be making fun of me now that you're my property."

My property.

I had the weirdest reaction to that statement. On one hand, it pissed me off so much, if it was possible, I would have steam billowing out of my nostrils. On the other hand, it sent a rush of slickness down my thighs when his dick twitched from his own words.

"Don't even joke about it." I bit down on his skin, hard enough to make him hiss. "At least my 'brand,' as you call it, is cute. Yours makes it look like we're stuck in the caveman era. What am I going to do about it?"

The blue in his stare darkened as he looked at it again, unable to help himself. "I say keep it. Seeing my name on you makes me harder than I ever thought possible."

I glanced down at his jutting erection, pointing toward my chin like it was begging for some action, veiny and big, so fucking big it burned when he stretched me out.

"I can tell." I twisted my lips in a mocking smile. "You'll pay for the removal once we go our separate ways."

He matched my energy with a simple, "As you wish."

There was this weird tension in the air whenever either of us mentioned how short our future together was. Since he admitted how much it would hurt him when *we* ended, I was able to spot the signs of his agitation more clearly, like the drum of his fingers along my thighs and him licking his lips as if trying to keep words from escaping.

I placed my hand on top of his beating heart and lay down nearly completely. His cock was nestled between my boobs as I traced the dips and valleys of his stomach with my lips. "You never told me what the rest of your tattoos mean."

"Not all of them have meaning. Most of them are there because they look cool," he replied, on edge as I got my tongue in the game, sucking and licking my way down.

"But some of them do?"

"Yes."

"Do share."

I reached his waistline, marveling at the way his head fell back in anticipation, at the power that I held over him, then turned to the ink along his arms, wanting to know more about the stories he had drawn on his body.

A few years ago, he had only five, but the more he withdrew from his family as he gained his independence, the more he added. There were some small ones, like a few diamonds on one hand, and a flock of birds on the other near his wrist with lines so fine I was impressed by how the ink hadn't bled yet, that decorated four of his big designs.

He started by pointing at the bloodiest one of them all over a bejeweled set of bull horns. It was a heart—not a cutesy one—a legit *human* heart, dripping with blood and spewing it out of its cut arteries and aorta as well. The veins along the middle were engorged, the bright red pops of color made it look healthy, but there was an underlying melancholy in it too.

"That one represents the saying, *the blood of the covenant is thicker than the water of the womb*, which means that bonds that you've made by choice are more important than the people that you are bound to by the water of the womb—the exact opposite of how we use it."

I stroked his side with my thumb, rubbing soothing circles on him. "I hate your family for making you feel less than and neglected. You're the smartest of them all."

He shook his head, and as many strides as he had made to combat his father's daily criticism about not amounting to anything, I could tell he held his reservations and fought harder every day to prove *him* wrong when the only one he should be thinking about pleasing was himself.

"Saint is the smartest of us all, and the only one I actually *feel* is my family."

"Saint is business savvy, but very blunt. He doesn't have the emotional intelligence you do. And I'm glad you were there for each other when no one else was," I restated my point.

All these days together, I'd witnessed Killian read people like they were an open book. Like that day he took me to a meeting with the landlord of the store space he ended up renting and got him to drop the price by two grand, just with an easy chat about some football team he likely had no interest in. Killian had targeted his weak spots like a pro, with his hands in his pockets and an easy smile on his face.

"What about this one?" I nodded at his other hand when he didn't fight me on it, massaging my thighs with his hands, getting impatient.

The tattoo was of two men, one leaning down and smashing a hammer over a scythe, the other standing right next to him, holding a matching one poised over his shoulder.

"It's a matching one I got with Luca. It's supposed to be the two of us," he clipped. A short answer that didn't invite room for more questions, so I let it go, noting that he and Luca must have quite the history together.

"And this one?" I asked yet again for the Latin phrase on his hip, hungry to know more about him. It was a quote, so it couldn't be pointless.

Libet volare, pro cadere.

I licked it when he hesitated to answer, and he groaned. I could google it, but I would only be provided with a translation, not what it meant to him.

"Don't you have more clever uses for your mouth rather than talking?" He quirked a brow, wound tighter than a gnat's ass, not ready to reveal his secrets yet.

I let it go, mostly because my core had started hurting from not having him inside me—*yes, it was a thing.* It was like I hungered to be filled up nowadays, a weird sensation that had never happened to me before. I found other people attractive, but no one I physically *ached for* except for Killian.

"Prickly, prickly, prickly," I murmured, palming his hard length and watching as his eyes rolled to the back of his head when my breath ghosted over it. "But not here. Here you're always smooth and hard. Ready for me."

The instances where Killian surrendered completely were few and far between, but today was one of them.

I wrapped my mouth around his cock in one go, and he lounged against the pillows like a god, his expression a painting of pain and pleasure colliding as I laid my tongue flat against his dick and took him in deep.

I could never fit the whole of him inside my mouth, not unless I wanted to throw up, so I rolled my hand over his base, stroking him over and over. His fingers tangled in my hair in an automatic response, but he simply held them for me, needing to look at my face as I took my own pace.

It wasn't fast and hurried. Sometimes, I preferred taking my time and savoring him slowly and torturously, keeping my gaze hooked on his like I knew he liked it—*correction, loved it.*

Killian loved watching my cheeks hollow as I drew him in, my lashes fluttering up at him. Innocence wrapped in sin. He adored the idea of tainting me, and being ruined by him sounded like my idea of a good time.

"You're a goddamn vision, Irena Fleur," he gasped, a frown line appearing over one brow. "Sucking on my dick like it's your job, those tits peeking beneath your shirt, and my name on your ass."

My shirt had ridden up, hanging beneath my shoulders now, and I made use of the tattoo's short lifespan, putting on a show for him, arching my back, and propping my lower waist higher in the air.

I tightened my lips around him, sucking harder, my chest puffing out with pride when I extracted an actual shout from him. He stilled the movement of my head, pulling at my hair when made to swoop down again, so I retreated, swirling my tongue around the sensitive head of his cock before letting him go with a pop.

A coy grin tugged at my lips as I told him, "I might as well ruin you for all others when you walk away from me. I'm toxic like that."

The thought of him with anyone else had me breaking out in hives, sadness and disappointment rolling into one and getting stuck at the base of my throat. That day Mia rang my doorbell was one I didn't have any particular interest in reliving.

I was running away.

As soon as this was done, I would be moving out because I couldn't keep living opposite him if he brought any other girls home. And he would, because that was the only way either one of us could move on.

His eyes shone like sapphire stones as he bent toward me, controlling the movement of my body by my hair. He tugged up, so I straightened, then he twisted my head around, and I faced the opposite way. Killian positioned himself behind me, pushing on my shoulder until I had no choice but to submit and fall over.

I had barely gotten on my hands and knees when he pushed inside me in one go, sliding into the hilt. A shuttered exhale escaped me at the intrusion, and I fisted the sheets when he wasted no time thrusting in and out of me. Doggy style wasn't a preferred position of his, but I suspected the newest addition to my body had something to do with his change of heart.

"I might not let you go after all." He twisted my hair in his fist, and my heart hammered in my chest. "That's *my* toxic trait. I want what I can't have, and I'm willing to take down the whole world to gain it...*you*."

My pulse went wild, and my ears rang as he stretched me out.

I felt like I was being pulled in all sorts of different directions at once, and I couldn't believe what I was hearing. It was so at odds with the Killian that insisted on sticking with our deadline, on distancing himself as much as he could so he wouldn't break it.

Maybe, this was all an illusion or a fever dream. Anything sounded more plausible than Killian tossing any scrap of independence away.

It could've also been the sex. Boys always thought with the head between their legs first.

"Killian—" I started only for a moan to steal the rest of my words when he pumped me hard, rolling his fingers down my back and grabbing onto my hips to force himself down harder. I gulped, seeing stars, but still needing to clarify the meaning of his statement. "Wha—What do you mean?"

"I mean, I want you, baby," Killian didn't hesitate, a growly quality in his voice as I met his thrusts by driving my body back with force. "Not for a week, not for a month. Hell, I don't even think I'll be satisfied after ten years of having you around."

My chest swelled, and his shadow loomed over my head when he leaned down to press a kiss to the base of my spine, rubbing his nose there, too, in an endearing manner that contrasted everything about the way he was owning me right now.

"Your sweet cunt wrapped around my cock, my tongue in your folds..." He pulled out long enough to taste me and moaned under his breath like I was the most delectable thing he'd ever had. "My teeth sinking into your ass," he continued, following up on his words, and sinking his sharp teeth in my tender skin before pushing back in and delivering a smack on my ass that would sting for days on end. "I need this every day, all fucking day."

He pressed his body against mine, and I twisted my head until our lips met. The kiss was a hot, frantic clash of teeth and mesh of tongues, gasps, and moans. He was as inside me as one could get, in my body and in my heart, yet I craved to have him closer, hold him to me forever and take down anyone or anything that tried to tear us apart.

Killian's smiles made my days brighter, his frowns ruined any chance of peace I had until I found out what was wrong and tried to cheer him up, and his touch made my heart sputter like a fish out of water. Any activity I did with him, I enjoyed it ten times more than I would have with anyone else, even my sister and my best friend, for fuck's sake.

It was clear to me I had fallen in love with him for a while now, but there was no way I was saying it first and for a good reason. He only enjoyed the time we spent fucking from his answer, and while I was crazy about our chemistry in the bedroom, I appreciated all the other things about him too.

"So you just want me for sex," I panted when we parted, and he made a face that said he thought I was stupid.

"I need your sassy mouth that is not afraid of telling it like it is." He leaned down to nip my lip and accidentally nicked it as his vicious thrusts propelled us forward, the bed even shifting from its previous post. A salty taste bloomed in my mouth as the scent of iron bloomed in the air, and he chased down my blood with his tongue in my mouth, resulting in an open-mouthed kiss that turned my brain to jelly.

"Your ruthless and brilliant mind that is brimming with all sorts of plans and ideas," he continued, pressing his lips to my temple, and I felt like crying when he cupped my heart under the shirt that he had somehow not ripped to shreds. "And your beautiful heart, capable of so much empathy and good, you make me feel like I'm in heaven when I simply step near you."

A watery smile spread on my lips from hearing his opinion of me, and I was sure if someone took a picture right now, the goofiness on my face would be almost comical, considering the position we were currently in.

But I was floating on cloud nine. Any other concern was forgotten as the high I was experiencing with Killian made me forget there was such a thing as purgatory, and sometimes your waking life could be transformed into it if you upset the wrong people.

I had my sister's blessing, though, and that was all that mattered to me.

"You're going to make me cry," I complained, eyes brimming with unshed tears.

Killian pushed me back further, spreading my legs wider, and this new angle had my belly quivering and chills spreading all over my body. He hit a spot inside of me that turned my vision white. My inner walls tightened around him, and a mix of a gasp and a groan escaped him as he repeated the motion, getting me on the edge only to go slow again.

"Good, another thing to cross off the bucket list, making a girl—*my girl*," he corrected, and my mouth opened in a silent scream. *Did he just say what I thought he did?* His breath tickled the base of my throat as he whispered in my ear. "Cry happy tears in bed."

"Oh," I moaned when his talented fingers dipped underneath my body and found my clit. Every part of him aroused me—his muscles brushing against my back, his cologne encompassing me, the timbre of his voice, and his weight on top of me. Getting to keep all of that, not having to compromise what we'd built in such a short period of time, felt like God was finally smiling down at me after a period of constant heartache. "I need you—"

"No." He stopped me before I could finish my sentence,

before I could admit how much I needed him too. "Don't give me an answer yet. Not before you know my whole truth."

His whole truth.

I wasn't shocked by the knowledge that he was keeping things from me. Daily there would be little triggers, questions he was wound up too tight to answer, parts of his life he would omit from ever mentioning, that gave me the perception that there was more to know about him.

"Whatever it is, it's a part of you, and I want it," I said, and heard him grit his teeth like he had difficulty trusting that I would accept him, flaws and all.

You couldn't love just one side of a person, though. Even the jagged pieces, the rougher sides held beauty that helped paint a bigger picture. They helped shape the person he had become today, so to me, they were beautiful as well.

"Later, Irena." He pressed his face against my hair, inhaling my scent, chasing that momentary distraction. "Just feel the moment."

"Oh, I'm feeling it, all right." I wiggled my ass as he pumped his hips over and over, his fat cock rubbing the muscles deep inside me. "All eight inches feel glorious."

"Greedy girl, with a greedy cunt, taking it like a fucking champ." He pinched my clit, and my hips bucked. It was like I was a loaded grenade and I would explode the second my pin was pulled. Killian held all the keys to my release, and he was driving me to it, slowly but surely, milking the ride. "You're built for me, Irena, with the most perfect apple bottom ass and the perkiest tits I would love to see bound and clamped."

I all but melted into the mattress when he reached for my chest with his other hand. It was an erogenous zone for me, but no one ever paid them much mind because they weren't big. Killian put a stop to that, though, as he taunted me by circling his finger over my nipple.

The act sent pins and needles rushing over my body, and I screamed so high, I bet Colin heard and put two and two together, realizing why I avoided him, as my first orgasm of the day rolled through me. It was like standing on shaking ground, afraid to fall, but once you did, you realized how much you enjoyed the vibrations of the earth against your body.

My lower body convulsed and quivered, and I was pretty sure my slickness was rushing down the backs of my thighs. That was how hard I'd come. The slaps of Killian's skin against mine turned louder, a filthy music that harmonized with my whimpers.

I grew impossibly tight, but Killian refused to come, even though I was gripping him to death. I didn't know how he did it, maintained his composure despite growing impossibly hard inside me. He kept thrusting without faltering his pace, and as a result, the tension from my body never disappeared. That sleepy high never came, as I'd grown accustomed now to not relaxing after one orgasm and prepping for the next one.

"I-I didn't know you were into that sort of stuff."

"There are a lot of things you have yet to find out. This is still the beginning of our story, Lilith." There was a dark promise laced in his statement.

"I do know one thing." I grinned over my back at him.

He looked like a freaking god, staring down at me, a pained expression on his face like the pleasure he was experiencing was too much, sweat running down his temples and concentration laced on the lines of his forehead, like caring for me was the most important task of his life.

"Yeah? What's that, beautiful?" Killian gave me a curious brow lift.

"My tattoo unlocked a new favorite position for you."

"It sure did," he immediately groaned, pushing in deeper and deeper at the reminder. "What I wouldn't give to smack your lovely ass red right now, but we gotta make sure you heal properly," he said with the most devoted voice ever, like he was talking to an obtuse client.

"I can't believe you're giving me tattoo care advice while we're having sex." I laughed breathlessly, shaking my head. "Only you, Killian, only you."

"Are you not my property, baby? I gotta make sure you're as healthy as one can be." He licked the side of my neck, then clamped his teeth on my shoulder, marking me, proving a point. Electricity sparked inside my veins, flowing directly to my groin as his mouth prevented me from rocking forward.

"I am," I cried out, my feminism flying out the window.

"You are what?" Killian demanded, letting go of my shoulder and driving his hips forward so hard I lost none of the pressure. "Say the whole thing."

"Yours," I whimpered, reaching the edge of the cliff again, my very bones shaking with anticipation at the impending drop.

"Nah, I think you can do a little bit better than that. What are you?" He squeezed my breast and pressed down on my bundle of nerves until I saw stars, galaxies, the whole fucking universe.

"Your property," I called out, then repeated it, my urge to please taking over any sensible thought in my mind. "I'm Killian Astor's property."

"Damn right you are." He bit and kissed my back, my neck, my cheek, and my lips over and over again like he couldn't get enough, like he wanted to eat me alive, swallow me whole. "Mine."

"And you're mine," I sobbed against his mouth, every nerve ending beneath my skin on fire and about to combust.

"And I'm yours," he echoed.

When we came together, it was a silent affair. A pleasure so deep, so raw, the very foundations of the entire fucking building shook. Neither of us could speak as this wave rolled over us. Bursts of every color in the rainbow went off behind my closed eyelids, and I could've sworn a different sort of liquid had escaped from between my legs.

It was thinner, runnier, and sent relief spiraling through every corner of my body. If I didn't know any better, I would've thought I'd peed, but the unparalleled sensation of rupturing delight that accompanied the act made me realize I had just squirted all over Killian, who was laughing in joy and cocky male pride after a second of confusion before he too registered what had just happened.

"Oh my God, I can't believe I just did that." My weak voice shook with embarrassment as the orgasm subsided.

An exhausted Killian dropped right next to me, still fully inside me, his smile brighter than the sun as he cupped my face and kissed me sweetly, saying, "Well, believe it, because I'm going to make sure it happens again."

CHAPTER TWENTY-TWO

KILLIAN

My thumb was about to fall off.

I'd been scrolling through my phone for the better half of an hour now when Luca gave me a break by dialing my number. The picture of Irena in her bikini I was ogling disappeared as his call came through. I was never a big social media fan, but I'd created an account to see what Irena was posting.

The result?

Liking all of her pictures like an obsessive creep and gaining a raging hard-on in the process.

I didn't know what was going on. The tightly held control I clung to snapped like a Lego, and I had no control over what I said when she was around. Clinging to stupid rules like not spending the night together was laughable after what I'd promised her two days ago.

An indefinite extension of our deadline.

It was reckless and stupid, but the anxiety that rushed over me whenever she'd mention us going our separate ways left no room for doubt. I had bitten the bullet. I did what I swore would never happen to me; I got too attached to Irena Fleur. I was desperate for her time and attention. So much so, I was willing to put my relationship with my entire family on the line if it meant keeping her.

Uncertainty ran through my veins as I accepted Luca's call—another wave, a tidal one, in need of tackling.

"You're going to tell her?" His voice lacked the usual joking undertone, transporting me to a few years back when we were both vulnerable teens trying to pull each other from quickly absorbing quicksand.

I pushed the driver's seat all the way back, but despite the cushion under my ass, it felt like I was sitting on pins and needles. Working up the courage to ask him to bring a third person into a secret only the two of us shared for the longest time had me on the verge of throwing up the Thai food I had for lunch.

"I think so, yes." I released a long breath through my nose, listening to the pitter-patter of the rain beyond my building's garage, hoping it would calm my heart rate. "I wanted to run it by you first. It's as much your story as it is mine."

Luca's consent was important to me. I couldn't go forward with it without getting his blessing first. I texted him that I wanted to tell Irena about my past right after I got out of work, and have been waiting in my car for him to call me ever since I drove home, knowing that Irena would be waiting for me upstairs.

"Can't you keep me out of it?" he asked, and I thumbed the steering wheel's red stitching as I thought it over.

I totally could.

Learning the same bad thing had happened to more than one person solely served to make an already bleak story darker. There would be important details I would have to omit, though. Irena wasn't unreasonable; she would understand even if she, later on, found out I kept things from her, but I wanted to be done with it. As selfish as it sounded, I wanted to tell my full truth to the one person I trusted who wouldn't see me as a victim but as a survivor.

"I can, but I wanted to give her the whole truth. I won't, though, if you don't feel comfortable," I compromised.

I could faintly hear a roulette spinning in the background, and loud voices, ones glazed with drunken delight, chatting and gossiping. I immediately knew he was working. The shady deals he made sure went through always took part in a casino, most possibly with a leggy blonde placed on the target's lap to persuade them to sign their soul away faster.

There was shuffling on his end as he most likely stepped outside, gathering that I was being serious, and this needed his full attention.

"Are you sure about her? I mean, last time we talked, you were set on it being a short-term thing."

I wasn't an indecisive person. When I set my mind on something, I did it regardless of how much of my energy or willpower it sucked. And meeting Irena halfway had only served to solidify her permanent position in my life. One I would jump through flaming hoops to maintain.

"Yeah, I was being deliberately obtuse," I admitted, and he snorted.

"Happens a lot," Luca commented drily, right after a door slammed shut and quietness followed. An image of him in the back alley of the casino, a cigarette hanging from his lips as he glared at the overcast New York sky, painted in my head.

I let his comment pass, considering living in rat-central punishment enough for him.

"Telling my family is going to be a shitshow, but they could launch a full smear campaign against me, and I wouldn't give a shit."

It wouldn't be anything new anyway. My father had been busting my balls since I was old enough to talk.

"You're that determined, huh?"

Was I determined enough to endure all the sick jokes people would make at our expense? All the scrutiny that would follow?

I genuinely couldn't care less what any rando said about me, but the people I cared about most were involved, so that complicated things.

The more the barriers crumbled between Irena and me, though, the harder it became to deny the truth. Like how much I enjoyed falling asleep next to her every night after a lifetime of feeling no such urge and always leaving a girl's bed like a thief in the middle of the night. Even waking up to a manipulative Dusty purring louder than a motor to get his breakfast extra early was fun.

Going back to the *void*, the emptiness that plagued me before Irena forced herself beyond my walls, sounded as appealing as pulling out a tooth.

"It's gonna sound fucking crazy, but it just feels *right* whenever she's near. All my worries melt away, and I'm just in the moment, enjoying life. It wasn't until recently that I realized I was carrying a dark cloud over my head. It fades away the more time I spend with her, and I don't even feel the need to drink anymore."

His sarcastic laugh pierced through the silence as he said almost incredulously, "So that's the answer, then? I need to find another woman to erase all the trauma a *previous* woman caused?"

It sounded counterintuitive, I'd give him that.

"It doesn't have to be a woman. It could be a friend that reminds you how good life can be if you don't let your baggage define you," I argued, turning into a fucking shrink. I didn't mind it for Luca, though. "I would love for that to be me; you're like my brother, man, but our history is too intertwined for me to be able to provide you with that feeling of escapism."

Despite perseverance and strength, we would forever remind each other what had happened because we had been in it together.

"You're like a brother to me too, Killian," Luca shared the testament, sounding more somber than he ever had. "I want nothing but the best for you, so feel free to tell her anything you wish. I trust your judgment."

My chest clenched tightly when he gave the go-ahead, and I found it hard to breathe as I said, "Thank you."

"Just do me a favor."

"Anything." My response was immediate.

"Tell her after my visit next week. I don't think I can bear to look at the pity in someone else's eyes."

You and I both.

I understood what he was saying better than anyone, and secretly I was pleased to buy myself more time. I acted the opposite, though, hoping to inspire something in him that triggered his last vein of wanting a happy ever after. Because Luca was on a suicide mission daily, and maybe a person to ground him, give him something to fight for would help.

"You will eventually have to. Don't even think about ghosting me afterward," I warned.

He snorted. "You're not getting rid of me that easily, *stronzo*. I know I have to, but I'd rather put it off."

"Okay," I sighed, understanding that feeling as well as probably ninety percent of the population.

The sound of a lighter igniting alerted me that he was on his second dose of nicotine already, as he laughed mockingly while blowing out a breath. "*Dio mio*, it only took you like what? Two months to become totally pussy whipped?"

"Shut up, Mietitore. Your time will come, I'm sure. And then I will be the one making fun of you." I fixed my coat, taking a quick snap of my parking number because I was the type of person that forgot where the hell I'd parked the night before, so I needed photographic evidence.

"Nah, single for life here, baby. My job doesn't allow for such attachments," he shot back, and to an extent, he was right.

It would take a really fucking brave woman not to be intimidated by Luca's lifestyle. But out of eight billion people in the world, one had to be out there somewhere.

"Bullshit," I fought him just because.

Our back and forth went on for a little bit longer until that sinking sensation disappeared now that I had Luca on my side like he always was. Even though he didn't like to admit it, he *was* attached to his little sister, despite whose blood ran in her veins.

This line of work—the path his father had already paved for Luca since he was a toddler—I could only see it going one way, and I would take measures to stop it before he ended up nine feet underground.

"We're going to eat chocolate-covered strawberries while staring at the full moon reflecting over the Atlantic?" Irena gushed as she settled back on an assortment of throw pillows I stole from her home when she was out, flashing me a teasing grin, her pearly whites shining in the night. "Who would've thought you were such a romantic at heart, Killian?"

I'd borrowed Ray's RAM pickup truck to celebrate starting construction on my tattoo shop. I hadn't told my boss yet I was leaving because the store wouldn't be ready for a good year—plenty of time to complete my apprenticeship. The place was a fixer-upper, but I wasn't complaining about the price we'd gotten it for. Ares certainly delivered on his promises. We'd knocked down a wall today, and I was assisting wherever I could. Even though I was no professional, I could swing a hammer, especially if it got Irena all hot and bothered, as she claimed when she came to check on the progress after her work.

"Let's keep it between ourselves. I've got a reputation to uphold, Lilith." I winked at her and scooted right next to her, hogging most of the very small space, my ankles hanging over the sill.

I'd gotten one of those ready-made picnic baskets with some weird jams that weren't *my* jam—*pun intended*, cheeses, crackers, and a bottle of red. Irena had gushed over them, though, especially the strawberries, coupled with the full moon shining down on the surprisingly mirror-still waters, and she was putty in my hands.

I hadn't even brought out the main course yet, her favorite if her posts were supposed to be believed.

I cradled her against my chest, rubbing my hand down her arm to warm her up. It was slightly windy, seeing as we were close to the edge of a cliff, but nothing we couldn't handle.

"Thank you, baby," she sighed, her body going soft, and a sense of unparalleled peace gripped me as she stared at the view, enchanted, and I stared at her.

"I like that," I said, kissing the crown of her head. She turned her face upward, and I took the opportunity to peck her lips too.

"What?" she murmured against my lips.

"You, calling me that word."

"Baby?" Something in my gut tightened when she said it again, and I nodded. A smile spread across her face. "Why, you keep surprising me, Killian Astor."

I winked. "I live to keep you on the edge of your seat."

I could sit there and hold her to me forever, but her stomach growled, alerting me that it was time to feed the beast. Otherwise, Irena turned into the very definition of *hangry*.

I slapped her hand away when she reached for the strawberries, and she glared at me, calling me the fun police when I insisted that dessert came last. She brightened when I pulled two plates of *pastitsio* from a second basket, though, and grabbed it from my hands before I even got a chance to pull the plastic off.

"Ah, Greek food." She shimmied her shoulders, taking the fork I handed her. "The way to my heart."

"I didn't see the appeal at first," I started, and disbelief ripped across her face, but I shrugged. "Most of the recipes had too much meat, but this one seemed nice."

"The mainstream ones, but there are a ton of other dishes that are so good without being overkill, *gemista, tourlou*—looks nasty but tastes great, and the spinach pie my *giagia* makes is out of this world."

She took a bite and moaned so loud the sound traveled straight to my cock. I rolled my shoulders and dug in, too, placing the plate on my lap, and the béchamel sauce, mixed with the thick pasta and minced meat, was a combination made in heaven. It was so good. I was glad I got two servings.

"Is that why Saint gained a couple of pounds after visiting Crete?" I asked, and she nodded.

"Most definitely. My grandma is something else. She will chase people around the house with food, telling them to eat because they're too skinny, and if you don't do what she says, oh, it's personal then."

"Sounds like a lovely woman." I chuckled.

"She's the best. She radiates so much warmth, even Grandma Chloe turns polite around her."

"The one from your dad's side? The one you ran from that day you crawled down your bedroom window?" I raised a judgmental brow. She made me lose five years of my life that day.

"The one and only. Risking my life in order not to see her should tell you all you need to know. She's the one that arranged Saint and Aria's marriage in order to save her fortune after getting into business with the wrong kind of people. It worked out in the end, but if it hadn't, you best believe I would never allow her back in our home again."

That was my girl, always sticking up for her people. The fierce loyalty was admirable when it was directed toward the right people because there were plenty that would seek to take advantage of it. And they had, like her douche of an ex, but she proved she could stick up for herself, and I would happily provide any assistance along the way if needed.

As we finished the rest of our food, Irena told me more about what life was like growing up. Her grandma Chloe seemed like the perfect case of a mother too obsessed with her own son to ever like anyone he picks as a partner, so it understandably led to some tension along the way, but from what she told me, her mother didn't back down. A dynamism I could certainly see in both Irena and Aria, albeit their father's creativity had stuck with the older sister, whereas Irena got her stubbornness and unwillingness to let things go from her mother.

It was weird because, from what she told me, people always thought she took more after her father, and maybe it was true looks-wise. Her character was a copy of her mother's, though.

"I think Aria knows about us." Irena dropped the bomb after finishing her serving of *pastitsio* while munching on a breadstick. I paused with a cube of Parmesan cheese between my fingers, my heart picking up its pace as I sliced my gaze to her. "No, that's a lie. I don't think so. I *know* so. She might have even set us up now that I think about it with this coincidental neighbor thing, and she even insinuated that Saint could come around if we were really serious about this," she rambled, but stopped when I held my hand up in the air.

"Irena, breathe," I ordered, finding the blue hue her skin had taken on concerning. "When did this happen?"

Irena explained what Aria had said when they were trying on lingerie—a detail I didn't miss—and once the initial shock wore off, my lips twitched by the cunningness my sister-in-law had displayed. I didn't think she set out to set us up, but she probably suspected there was something brewing between Irena and me, based on how much Saint was busting my balls about it, and decided to test that theory out.

If that was the case, I would forever be grateful to her, and it took some of the stress off our family finding out if she already knew. If there was anyone that could pacify Saint's anger, it was her.

"I'm just telling you in case you backpedaled on the whole *I might not let you go, after all* comment a few days ago. I'm sure it's going to be hard to break the news, but our siblings love us too much to stand in our way." Irena completed her breakdown with a doubt-filled voice, shoving the rest of the breadstick in her mouth and avoiding my gaze.

My brows rose at her conclusion and the fact that she thought I'd backpedal so quickly on my promise, and I tugged the pillow she hugged to her chest away, recapturing her attention.

"I have not changed my mind about anything. I want you more and more every fucking day," I responded a little harshly, but I didn't like the second-guessing and doubt she was filling her head with.

She chewed on her lip, those eyes of hers shining brighter than the moon. "Then why haven't you told me your truth yet?"

"Because I'm fucking scared, a wimp, whatever you want to call it." I faced forward, raking a hand through my hair as I listened to the waves crashing against the rugged cliff. I wasn't mentioning Luca yet, not until after his visit.

Irena shifted closer, placing the food on the side, her soft cheek making landfall on my pec as she whispered, "What are you scared of?"

I glanced down at her, her mere presence and proximity calming my volatile emotions. She kept my gaze, her palm smoothing over my stubble as she encouraged me to go on.

"You, running for the hills when you grasp the amount of shit I carry and how that might possibly impact your life as well." I loosened out a breath, my arms snaking around her waist as I pulled her to my lap as though I wanted to keep her glued to me forever.

"If you think I'd do that, then you don't know me at all."

"I know you." I tightened my hold and leaned back to get a good look at her. Her chin was up in the air and defiant, and her nose wrinkled with distaste until I said, "You're fucking brave, strong, and loyal, always going to bat to protect your people. I just need some more time to work through things."

Her expression dissolved into a softer one as she rested her forehead against mine. Our breaths mixed, hearts beating in tandem as she nodded. "I don't want to pressure you, Killian. You can take all the time you need. I simply wanted to see if we were still on the same page when it comes to this being together thing."

"We are, Irena. I never want you to doubt that."

I kissed her until her frown turned upside down. When she pulled back for some air, her lips were wet, and her eyes were glossy with desire. I suspected that had partly to do with my erection pressing into her delicious behind, and she confirmed it by glancing down and licking her lips.

The vixen played hard to get, though, and asked, "Good. Can we have dessert now? I can smell the strawberries from here, and my mouth is watering."

I reached for the basket again after placing Irena next to me, took the tin box out, and handed them to her. "They're all yours."

"You're not in the mood for dessert?" Her forehead wrinkled as I scooted down the truck bed and jumped on the soft ground beneath, leaning half my body over and grabbing her ankles.

"I am, but first, you need to lay flat." Leaning half my body over and grabbing her ankles, I tugged so her back flattened on the surface. She parted her legs, her wide eyes peering at me through the space between them. I cocked my head and smirked. "And scoot to the edge of the truck, so I can feast properly."

Another squeak escaped her as I did just that, throwing her legs over my shoulders after spreading them with no resistance. Her dress bunched under her ass, and she lifted her hips when I flicked my chin up.

Her black panties didn't last long, but I shoved a strawberry in her mouth to distract her before throwing them over my shoulder and into the Atlantic. I was on a mission to get rid of as many of her underwear as possible; they were a nuisance on most occasions, and I'd prefer if she didn't wear them at all.

Red liquid ran down the side of her mouth as she spat the stem out, and maybe it was because I had her bare pussy on display and her beautiful lips parted with a gasp when I ran my fingers through her slick folds, but I found the action so incredibly erotic, my dick fought to be freed from the constraints of my pants.

"You and your insistence on doing it outside, Killian." She tried to complain, but tensed as I got down to eye level with her cunt, her knees pressing into my ears in anticipation.

I nudged her clit with my nose, inhaling deeply, intoxicated by her musky scent. The first few times I did it, she nearly passed out of embarrassment, but going down on her was one of my favorite pastimes, and her natural fragrance was one of the biggest reasons why I was so addicted to her cunt. I wanted her to embrace her body and love it as much as I loved worshiping every part of her.

I groaned as I swiped my tongue over her a couple of times, spreading her juices and making her wetter at the same time. Pussy didn't usually taste like anything, but it had a slightly salty undertone you became addicted to, especially if you were as fucking obsessed with the person it was attached to as I was. Those sexy little whimpers she voiced every time I feasted on her replayed in my mind until the next time I got to have her.

"At least I don't take you to any busy places, so you can scream as loud as you like when you come on my face." I grinned at her, and she watched in fascination as my face gleamed with her essence while I added my fingers to the mix and inserted two inside of her at once. They slipped in with no resistance, her inner walls enveloping them like they were good ol' friends.

"How considerate of you," she breathed, her head kicking back, those light red strands spreading over her like a crimson halo. Her back arched, chest puffing when I wasted no time, letting her adjust to the intrusion, and I began thrusting my fingers inside her, my thumb caressing the sensitive strip of skin between her vaginal opening and anus.

Irena turned tighter than a drumstick as I prodded her

asshole, eyes snapping open and elbows shifting underneath her to prop up her body in record time to watch what I was doing. I decided to push in there as well, keeping my gaze locked on hers as I explored more viable land ready to be conquered.

"Oh fuck," she mewled, her voice husky and cracking with desire. She wiggled her ass to get comfortable, but I dug my fingers into her thigh to stop her from moving around. I was the one setting the pace, the one she had to listen to, and the only one able to provide her with the relief she craved.

"You had doubts, and I'm about to eradicate them." My breath ghosted over her clit, and at the prospect of getting my mouth on her again, she came alive like a flower blooming beneath the sunlight, her entire body relaxing and submitting to me. I gave it a little tug, pure lust clouding my brain at her sharp inhale. "If it gets too much, start counting the stars I make you see."

She panted as I used both her holes at once, punching inside both her anus and cunt with cold precision as I scissored my tongue over her tender bud. Judging by the surprise written on her face when I first ventured to her asshole, she had never been touched there, and the thought of claiming a first of hers made my cock weep with happiness.

It would take a while to get there. I couldn't very well shove myself inside her anus without stretching her out first, no matter how much I wanted to, so we'd start with fingers and progress to butt plugs when she felt ready. My impatient mind was already conjuring up images of fucking her sweet little cunt on all fours while a red jewel that matched her hair and the lingerie she'd wear from me shone as we worked up a sweat.

An irrational anger lit at the thought that she kept those

pieces from me, so I shoved in a little faster and a lot harder until her eyes gleamed with unshed tears at the delicious stretch in her ass, and I elicited a high-pitched cry from that full mouth. Echoes stretched into the night, and I chuckled when her elbows gave out, and she fell back down with a thud, struggling to get a pillow under her head so she wouldn't miss a single second of the show.

"And then when we get home, you'll put on that lingerie you bought and give me a show," I spoke, giving her a minute to adjust. Her watching me with twin flames in her eyes only added to the pleasure. "Tomorrow, I'm giving you my card, and you're going to buy some more."

"I have my own money," she argued, despite being at my mercy, that backbone of hers forever present.

"Oh I know, but I doubt you'll appreciate spending so much money on them, only to have me rip them right off you."

"Killian, that's such a waste."

"Nothing ever spent on you is a waste, baby. You're the biggest prize of all." Irena whimpered, her body curling upward as I pressed a kiss on her mound before launching my assault on her senses, lapping her up like she was the sweetest, ripest strawberry of them all.

"I could eat you out for hours and still die a starving man. You taste like fucking nirvana." A growl rumbled up my chest as her taste embedded into my soul, nearly stealing my vision. She was so goddamn addictive. I was going to make this last as long as I could, not only for her, but for me as well.

"Killian," she begged. "Use your teeth again, please."

"Like this, Lilith?" I asked, before sucking her clit in my mouth and lightly grazing my teeth over it. Her mouth dropped open as she nodded and gave further instructions.

"You can bite harder." I did, positively exhilarated at finding out she got off on the sting of pain. Then again, I already knew, given how much she liked donning my finger-prints on her hips and my teeth marks on her neck.

"Perfect. Fucking perfect," Irena praised, and pure male satisfaction rushed through me.

I kept up the pace, occasionally rubbing against the extension of her clit inside her cunt. She went wild when I did that, her body stiffening like she was harboring a huge weight on her shoulders, and me getting her off would get rid of it. I missed it on purpose, though, finding my own satisfac-tion in showing her how much of her pleasure was in my hands and how I controlled the way her body reacted.

I also liked seeing the euphoria clearly depicted on her strained facial muscles and the precipitation coating her body and dampening her clothes despite the cold-ass temperature.

"I know I am." I smirked.

"Humble too," she bit back, even while fighting to regu-late her erratic breathing.

"Why shouldn't I be when you'll be calling me a god in three." I added my ring finger inside of her, too, stretching her so much I felt myself through the skin separating her anus from her pussy. I curled them upward, and her lower belly started to convulse. "Two," I counted down before using my tongue to apply the perfect amount of rolling pres-sure on her clit.

She was so wet, the vulgar sounds from where I was penetrating her overpowered the roaring of the wind and the crashing waves of the ocean. A sob ripped from her mouth as she neared her climax, and I delighted in hearing it. As much as I could anyway since her thighs pressed harder against the sides of my face and every kind of noise turned muffled, save for her heartbeat pulsing wildly through her whole body.

"Jesus," Irena yelled when she finally broke, her voice breaking as a scream released from her throat. The blissful tone bled into my name, and I nearly creamed my pants like a fucking teenager when she proved me right. "Oh dear God, Killian."

Her eyes rolled, and she shuddered so violently one would think I was exorcizing a demon from her body. I ate up the sight because while Irena was incredibly attractive in a—she could rock a trash bag, and everyone would still be mesmerized by her—type of way, she radiated a sort of heavenly energy one could only dream of when she came.

The noises that burst from her mouth as I kept up the pace were unrestrained, her voice heavy with all-consuming bliss. It lasted for what felt like hours—this high of hers—and I ate up every second of it, figuratively and literally.

"You didn't even let me get to one." I struggled to catch my own breath after keeping my mouth glued on her, extracting the maximum amount of pleasure possible. "Such an impatient little girl."

Irena was on her back, eyes half shut as she heaved, her hands still clutching the blanket beneath her into a vice grip. I crawled my way up her body, and she studied me curiously as I ran three of my fingers over her lips. Like the good girl she was, she opened her mouth and sucked them clean.

"See how perfect you taste? How could I ever give this up?" Her legs locked around my hips, greed pooling into her blues when my erection poked at her entrance. I set her mouth free, clutching her sides, and flipped us around, with me on my back and her spread over my chest.

"I swear you could make me come by talking dirty to me alone, Killian," she mumbled into my shirt, and a laugh worked its way up my throat.

I gripped her hair into my fist, stretched her neck, and kissed her damp brow, my thumb rolling over that lovely tattoo on her ass, reminding her who she belonged to. "We can certainly test that theory out."

CHAPTER TWENTY-THREE

IRENA

I got two of the happiest news of my life on the same day. The first one was that my idea had finally been picked up by a streaming company, not a TV network, which was even better in my book. They wanted to start production as early as February if we moved fast enough with the casting and contracts.

That was like moving at the speed of light in the TV industry, but I understood that they relied on the recent drama to lure the viewers in.

I didn't see it then, but I knew now Daniel cheating on me was one of the biggest blessings I'd ever received. He was essentially dead weight, holding me back from realizing my full potential. How much better I could do.

There were many moving pieces still—the future was unclear—but I'd never felt so at peace before, like I was where I belonged, with *who* I belonged.

Bea was picking me up from a photo shoot when Amani called to tell me the news, and I screamed so loud she nearly hit the car in front of us. And then she cursed me out when it happened again a few minutes later when my dad called to tell me that Aria had gone into labor.

God, I couldn't believe it.

There would be a brand-new member joining our family. My sister was going to be a mom, I was going to be an aunt, and I was pretty sure every paper in town would dub Saint as the latest hot guy in town to join the DILF club.

Tension running high, Bea and I power walked to the hospital's entrance. I was buzzing with excitement at the thought of holding my new nephew or niece, and I was fucking glad we were finally going to find out the baby's sex. I didn't know whose bright idea it was to wait until the very last moment, but I was so impatient that it could've never been me.

The scent of antiseptic hit me straight in the face as I scanned the white walls and reception for a nurse I could harass for my sister's room number because no one was answering my texts.

It turned out I didn't have to, though, when my mom rushed through the entrance a few seconds after Bea and me. She didn't see us at all, her gaze laser-focused forward as she plowed past us, holding two Starbucks cups in her hand.

I shared a confused look with Bea before we ran after her.

"Mom, Mom!" I whisper-yelled because it was a hospital, and I didn't want to disturb anyone.

"Mrs. Fleur!" Bea had no such qualms, though, and shouted my mom's name so loud she stopped in her tracks, and the people around us did double takes.

I smiled apologetically at them, giving Bea the stink eye as we reached my mom, who had stopped in the middle of the hallway. Her hair was windblown, she was in jeans and a hoodie—an outfit she wouldn't be caught dead wearing in different circumstances—and her face devoid of any makeup as opposed to my full glam. Perks of coming here straight after a photoshoot. I couldn't wait to get cute pictures with my nephew or niece.

"You are late, Irena." She tapped her foot on the floor, scanning me from head to toe when we reached her. She didn't acknowledge Bea, but I doubted she minded, given the situation.

"Sorry, I was at work and didn't see the phone calls until I was done with the photoshoot. How far along is Aria?"

"When she almost chewed my head off asking for a coffee, they were about to inject her with an epidural. Your dad told me she just started pushing, so it could be an hour, or it could be twelve," Mom answered, leading us to the elevator.

I breathed a sigh of relief as we entered the elevator, and Bea asked, "She's going to drink coffee while in labor? Is that recommended?"

Mom shook her head, pressing our floor's button and the silver doors slid closed. "No, she's having it afterward. I got her an iced one. We just need to store it in the fridge."

"Both of them?" I raised a brow.

"The other one is for me. I need caffeine if I have to deal with Saint's mother for one more minute." She downed about half the cup after saying that. "You know she really had the gall to say she'd babysit *my* grandchild every week-end? As if I would ever let that happen."

Bea giggled next to me, aware of the chaos that was about to ensue in the waiting room because when my mom didn't like you, she made it known. Her track record with Celia wasn't the best either. I only hoped they would think of Aria and not get into it.

"Aria's in-laws are here?" I wrung my hands together, a sudden nervousness blooming in my belly. Like they would take one look at me and somehow know I'd been fucking their youngest son at least two times a day.

"Just Celia, not the husband. Thank God for silver linings."

Indeed.

Being in Noah Astor's presence and trying to act polite while imagining chewing his head off for how he treated Killian—*Saint, too*, was going to be tough.

I guess there was a reason he wasn't invited at all. The elevator pinged when we reached our floor, and the steel doors slid open to reveal a waiting room chock-full of people, so ridiculously attractive I took multiple double takes.

We walked in, and I smiled at Eliana and Serena, the brunette and blonde best friends my sister had formed a close bond with last year. They waved at me from their clear plastic seats under the TV.

Their husbands were conversing with my dad a couple of feet away. Their presence, one more imposing than the next. Leo had a classic Mediterranean look about him, with tan skin and sage-green eyes. While Ares was like a book bad boy come to life with his leather jacket and hazel eyes combo.

"And Killian? Has anyone notified him yet?" I inquired when I didn't spot him next to his mom, standing off awkwardly to the side as she had no one to talk to.

Bea pinched my side, most likely telling me to lay off with the questions or I would raise suspicions, but my mom was too consumed by the moment to notice anything.

"Yeah, Saint did. Just like you, he wasn't picking up. I'm not sure if they got through to him yet. We spoil you younger kids way too much."

"Tell me about it, Mrs. Fleur. My little sister got the sweeter end of the deal, I swear," Bea was quick to jump in, reminding me of how much she used to complain about her little sister stealing her clothes and her mom taking her side because sharing was caring when she still lived with them.

"The first kids are the experiment, dear. We learn as we go."

I rolled my eyes as we neared the group, but didn't argue. *Look but don't touch* was a perfect phrase for Saint's friends because you couldn't ignore their presence in a room. When I was younger, I used to attend some of the boring-ass parties Saint threw just so I could ogle them for hours on end, and years later, I still flushed red when they muttered their hellos at us. One glance at Bea made me feel better, though, because she wasn't faring any better.

"Daddy," I greeted as he enveloped me in a half hug, his gold hair combed and styled to perfection like the meticulous freak that he was.

His cologne tickled my nose, and my nerves calmed at the familiar scent. They'd put us all and Aria in adjoining private rooms. Only a few people were probably allowed in. Much to my surprise, Celia also approached us, and we all formed a little group outside of the passing nurse's path.

"Is Killian inside?" On my second time bringing him up, Mom did stare at me weird.

Maybe he had shown up while she was getting coffee, though. I just wanted to be sure. It seemed unfair for him to miss this when all of us were gathered here. He would've liked to be present.

"No, he is not replying to any of his calls." Ares frowned as he pulled out his phone, most likely to try again.

"I'm sure he's just busy at the company. He'll come after," Celia butted in, standing right off the corner next to Serena.

"What company?" I tilted my head, my brows bunching.

"Falco and Fleur? He started working there at the beginning of the year," she was happy to inform me, and my blood boiled.

"He resigned a month ago," I answered drily, crossing my arms, because what mother was so out of touch with her child's life? One month was plenty of time for her to have caught on.

No one spoke for a couple of seconds as my bitchy tone allowed for a wave of awkwardness to roll in. I was sure many of the people here wondered why I'd stuck up for Killian when we were virtually nothing, but I couldn't find it in me to care. They'd find out soon enough, anyway.

"I'm going in." Rolling my shoulders, I broke away from the group, not waiting for Celia's reply, and started for my sister's room, with Mom following close in my heels.

"I'll wait out here," Bea said, and I winked at her over my shoulder in acknowledgment.

The nurse at the door moved away when we walked in. I remained as quiet as I could, as if making any noise would spook the doctor between my sister's legs, but it didn't matter. Saint's head snapped toward us like he had a built-in radar, his body tense, ready to kick out anyone that disturbed Aria.

I smiled at him, and he relaxed by my sister's head, his hand clasped in her white-knuckled grip as she listened to the nurses and doctor, laid out on the bed and panting lightly in between pushes.

"Irena!" my sister cried when she spotted me. A layer of sweat covered her body. Her hair was up in a ponytail with a few strands sticking on her temples, and from the waist up, she was covered in a blue hospital gown. "Good, you're finally here."

I shuffled over to the other side of her bed, avoiding looking at what the doctor was doing in contrast to my mom, who hovered behind her like she could do a better job.

"Whatever you do, don't let her hold your hand," Saint mouthed at me over Aria's head, and the death grip she had on him turned even tighter, judging by the wince on Saint's face afterward.

"I heard that, you asshole. It's your fault I'm in this situation right now, so I'll bloody squeeze your hand as much as I want to. You're not feeling even an ounce of the pain I'm experiencing," she yelled, squeezing her eyes shut as another contraction hit.

"I'm sorry, Spitfire," he parroted like he was used to being called out this evening and simply smoothed her hair back when she was instructed to push.

"I'm never having sex ever again," Ariadne breathed, and panic seeped into Saint's expression.

I didn't know whether to laugh or cry. Part of me was slightly amused, and another hurt for the pain my sister was clearly experiencing. Deciding to forgo Saint's advice, I extended my palm to her, and she wasted no time wrapping her hand around it.

I hissed under my breath and said to one of the two nurses, "I thought it didn't hurt that much if you got an epidural."

"It dulls the pain. It doesn't take it away completely. It also works better on some than others," she informed, a polite smile on her face, acting like this was completely normal and she saw worse on a daily basis.

"Ariadne, I need you to push a little harder," the doctor instructed.

"But I am pushing hard already," Aria nearly sobbed.

Saint pressed his lips to her forehead, muttering, "Come on, my love, just a little bit more."

"Okay, okay." Aria nodded under his encouragement, silent tears running from the corners of her eyes as she kicked her head back and gave it her all.

Three minutes, five, ten passed, and still nothing. My dad peeked in a few times to see how it was going and winked out just as quickly, not equipped to handle stuff like this. Mom tried to be encouraging by informing us that only the first pregnancies were like this and the second one would be much easier. Aria nearly bit her head off for already thinking about a second baby when the first one wasn't even here yet.

I smoothed my thumb over the back of her hand, providing any type of comfort I could, but internally I was freaking out myself. If this is what women went through to bring another human into this world, I wasn't sure I wanted one. Adopting another cat, on the other hand? Now that sounded like a good idea.

"It burns," Aria sniveled.

"It's because the baby's head is stretching the birth canal. The feeling will only last a few minutes," a nurse said in an infuriatingly positive tone. "Can you take a few deep breaths for me? Try to pant while pushing to reduce the chance of tearing."

"Saint," she called out, and her husband was nearly on her at this point, worried to death and kissing the side of her face and head at any given moment. Whether he was trying to calm her or himself down, I couldn't tell.

"I'm right here, baby. It'll all be over soon," Saint encouraged, and as if his words gave her strength, she huffed and puffed, pushing and releasing deep groans right after, like she was running a marathon.

"The baby's head is crowning. A couple more contractions to go now," Doctor Ghauri (according to her name tag) notified, and everyone held a collective breath as we readied to welcome a new life into the world.

It turned out a couple more contractions lasted an hour longer, during which Killian was still a no-show. Worry bloomed in the back of my mind, but I hoped he was just busy and hadn't gotten around to checking his phone yet. Nevertheless, I chose to get lost in the excitement of the moment and not dwell on it.

It was nine PM on the dot when my nephew released his first cry and my sister a relieved sigh, a sweaty heap on the hospital bed, as they rushed to clean her baby up, patting him with a towel and suctioning fluid out of his mouth.

It was the first time I saw Saint so torn about who to care for first. He kept whispering reassuring words to Aria while his eyes tracked his son with a fierce desire to protect him. I was sure he would destroy the entire building with my two hands if something happened to him.

"Hey, little angel," Aria smiled down at her baby boy when he was placed on her chest, and his cries subsided at the sound of her voice.

We all hovered over his head, and he stared, mesmerized. Saint extended his index finger toward him, and his son wrapped his palm around it, so tiny, so breakable, Saint sucked in a stuttered breath, and I already knew the little man would be more well protected than Fort Knox.

"He's adorable," I cooed, unable to keep my eyes off him.

"He has his daddy's eyes," Aria commented, caressing the baby's soft cheek and staring into his innocent liquid gold gaze.

"And his mom's beautiful hair," Saint echoed, leaning down to give both of them a kiss on their heads.

"What's his name?" my mom asked next to me as the doctor stitched up Aria between her legs.

My sister and brother-in-law glanced at each other, and in one voice, they said, "Arsène."

CHAPTER TWENTY-FOUR
IRENA

The first sign that something was wrong was when Dusty didn't greet me at the door when I walked in. He usually was by the door before I even got out of the elevator, meowing at me to feed him.

The second?

The living room light was on, and I didn't think I had forgotten to switch it off. At this point in the day, though, my brain was fried, so I went with the flow. The door was working perfectly fine. There were no signs of a break-in, just my hyperactive mind creating all kinds of scenarios.

I walked to the bathroom first to wash off my makeup. It had turned disgusting after such a long day, did my business, then went on the lookout for Dusty. His fatass sometimes got trapped behind the TV console, and he slept there for hours until I got home and freed him.

As I entered the living room, though, I found him happily munching on some dry kibble that was half spilled on the floor, half in his bowl. He gave a little grunt of acknowledgment, and my throat ran dry when I spotted a lump on my couch.

A man—Killian, I recognized when I tiptoed closer—was sleeping on his stomach, clothes rumpled, arm slung over the edge of the couch, his face buried in a turquoise pillow. I cocked my head when I inhaled, and the scent of alcohol was so strong it burned down my nostrils.

"Killian?" I asked, but he didn't budge. "Killian," I tried one more time, but no such luck.

I sat on the edge of the couch beside his legs. I could tell he was intoxicated immediately when the smell got even stronger as I touched his back, shaking him awake. "Killian? Killian, wake up."

He grunted as if telling me to bugger off, so I shook harder until he moaned in annoyance and flipped on his back, blinking rapidly, his eyes red as he tried to focus on me.

"Lilith?" he croaked, reaching out to hold my hand like he couldn't believe it was me.

Worry twisting up my stomach in knots, I looped my fingers through his and made to clear the confusion that was swirling in my brain. "Killian, what are you doing here?"

Where were you today?

Why are you drunk out of your mind?

Why do you look like you have been crying for hours?

I had so many more questions at the tip of my tongue, but I held them in, wanting to get to the bottom of whatever was going on as gently as possible. My bones were screaming for me to lie down, but something else rooted me on the spot, like a sixth sense that realized something terrible had happened.

"You're home?" He glanced around as if he was just now remembering where he was.

"Obviously." I squeezed his hand to regain his attention. "What's going on?"

"It's still Friday?" Killian inquired, horror seeping into his expression when I simply nodded as if a three-headed demon dog had materialized behind me. "So, this is not a dream?" He suddenly sat up, only to slump against the couch again like his whole world was spinning.

I reached out to stabilize him when he swayed. "What's not a dream? What's going on?"

He didn't reply immediately, his eyes growing hollow, like he was recounting what led him to drink the entire liquor store by the likes of it. His jaw hardened, and the temperature in the room dropped by a few degrees as he dug through his pockets and pulled out his phone.

I watched, clueless, as his grip turned white-knuckled the longer he stared at the phone, like he was willing it to self-destruct. Whatever he was seeing had shaken him badly enough to miss all the other texts from all of us at the hospital.

"He must've—" He cut himself off with a sharp inhale, his blank stare meeting my face. Killian's next words sent a chill down my back. "He must've wanted to end it after I asked him if I could tell you the full story. I never should've done that."

End it?

There was only one way one could interpret the combination of those two words, which wasn't good. Goose bumps spread over my arms, and a tightness enveloped my chest, making every breath I took labored. It didn't take a genius to figure out that whatever news he had received had messed him up pretty badly.

"Killian..." I wrapped my palm around his forearm, but he didn't look at me. I gulped, pressing forward. "I'm a little lost here."

"I never should've asked him." Killian shook his head, repeating himself. The sheer shock in his expression, like the skies had opened up as he kept reading a sentence over and over on his phone screen, which made me want to rip it out of his hands.

I searched for whatever gentle bone remained in my body, though, and motioned toward the cell in his hands, asking, "May I?"

Clearly, he wasn't in any position to form coherent sentences right now, as he was still a little drunk and in shock, so it was better that I saw whatever was troubling him myself.

He didn't exactly give me the go-ahead to get his phone, but he didn't resist either when I pried it out of his fingers. Dusty, who had finished eating up all that extra serving of food, settled near Killian's feet, keeping a watchful eye on us like he could sense that something was amiss.

The first thing I noticed was that this was a text conversation with Luca, and all of Killian's missed calls and texts over the past three days that were never answered until early this morning...were not from Luca.

I shifted uncomfortably, scared to read on because I was aware that Luca and Killian were tight. Anything that happened to Luca would undoubtedly have lasting emotional effects on Killian.

Luca: Killian, this is Yazmin.

My palms turned clammy from how tight I was clutching the phone, but I steeled my shoulders and read on.

Luca: I saw your text pop in yesterday, and unfortunately, Luca will not be able to make it. He got in a car accident three days ago on his way to you and was rushed to the nearest hospital, but they couldn't save him, and he passed away last night.

Luca: The funeral is in five days. You're more than welcome to come. I understand that this is a lot to digest. I'm devastated too. I'll text you my number, and I'll be here if you ever need anything.

If I wasn't already sitting, I would've collapsed on the floor.

A wave of heat crawled up my neck and into my face, most likely turning my skin red as the silence turned suffocating, the weight of the news crashing into me like a tidal wave. I breathed in deeply but ended up wheezing my exhale out as oxygen got stuck in my throat.

"Luca's dead?" My whisper echoed around the room as if I'd yelled the question into a loudspeaker.

Killian blinked slowly, his dilated irises like a thin ring around the black of his eyes. The phone clattered on the floor when he nodded, and he folded his arms over his stomach as if nausea was making a mess of his insides.

"I was hoping I had imagined the conversation with Yazmin," he breathed.

I knew from past conversations that Yazmin was Luca's sister, and my heart bled for both her and Killian as I saw him grapple with the realization that his best friend was *gone*.

I struggled to keep my mouth from dropping open. My mind couldn't process that a young man, one as ambitious and successful as Luca, was gone when he had so much left to live for. Killian couldn't process it either, given that his first response had been to get blackout drunk and then crash at my place.

"Killian, I can't believe it." In an attempt to make it even a little better for him, I settled myself on his lap, threading my fingers in his hair as I squeezed him in a hug. His arms remained limp by his sides, but I wasn't offended. I couldn't imagine what was going through his head at the moment.

"That makes two of us," he mumbled into the crook of my neck, his voice still a bit slurry. "I called her afterward to confirm, and the pain in her voice couldn't be faked. I lost my best friend, and she lost her brother."

The sandwich I had after letting Aria and Saint enjoy their first day with their baby found its way up my throat, and I had to swallow a few times to get it back down again.

There was no handbook that stated how to help a person process devastating news, and I was no pro at consoling anyone. I was like a fish out of water, so out of my element, it wasn't even funny. The only thing that kept me talking was my need to alleviate Killian's pain even the slightest bit.

"But it was an accident, right? What did you mean by '*he wanted to end it?*'"

"That's what they say, but Yazmin wasn't convinced, nor am I." He drew a ragged breath but went on like he needed to get this off his chest. "Luca has been flirting with suicide for a while now. He never really got over what happened to him. To both of us, but mostly him because he had to live with her."

"What happened?" My hands shook in his hair, unsure if I would be able to stomach more terrible information tonight.

So much had already happened. The excitement of my new TV show deal had worn off before I could even share it with anyone, and I had a feeling that not even Arsène joining our world could salvage the situation.

"I was planning on telling you after his visit, but I guess it doesn't matter now," Killian admitted, his arms finally wrapping around my waist and molding our bodies closer together, almost like he didn't want me to pull away from whatever he had to say.

I didn't.

I squeezed him tighter, resting my cheek on the top of his head, and stared at the sparkling city lights outside the window in an attempt to calm my hyperactive mind down.

No amount of mental prepping could have prepared me for what was about to follow, though, because when he uttered that first sentence, my blood ran so cold it was like someone had buried me under an ice cap.

"His stepmother would touch him inappropriately when he was too young to retaliate, gaslighting him into thinking it was normal."

Ever since Killian said he had to tell me something before we could take the next step together, my curiosity had run wild, and my imagination took the reins, coming up with every possible story under the sun. There were plenty of turns this could have taken with his negligent parents and his history of violence. Being bullied at school and forced to act out was my most likely contender.

But this? This was like the worst-case possible scenario come true.

And Killian mentioned it happened to both of them, so he was spoon-feeding me information little by little. My chest squeezed painfully as I put the math together, and the longer I stayed silent, the tenser Killian's body turned beneath me.

"She did this to both of you?" I forced myself to get some words out, but it wasn't nearly enough.

"Yes, but he got the shorter end of the stick," he supplied, and I felt his heart race under my ribs as he launched into explaining his past. Or it could've been mine. I wasn't sure at this point. "Farah was friends with my mom and visited us pretty often. She spent the night at our place one time, and I was unconscious when it first happened. I imagine she must've slipped something in my drink because when I woke up, she was touching places she shouldn't have."

She was touching places she shouldn't have.

A queasiness came over me, and Killian's hold on me only made it worse. I was a mess of epic proportions fighting off the feeling of pity because, as far as I was concerned, both Killian and Luca were survivors, not victims. The need to spread Farah's insides on a string and watch her bleed out also roared in my veins.

I was fiercely protective of the people I loved, and if whoever hurt Killian was still walking free today, I would go above and beyond to change that.

It had gotten so hot I was sweating bullets at this point, so I combed Killian's hair back and looked down to find him surrendering to my touch as I pressed our foreheads together and reluctantly asked, "How old were you?"

"I was eight," he offered, and his answer was like a shot

to the heart. "It went on for three more years until Luca and I started hanging out and realized she was doing it to both of us—*him on a daily basis*. I was luckier because she would only visit us once or twice a month, and if I learned she was coming beforehand, I made myself scarce."

I swallowed one more time, but there was no fighting the bile that had accumulated at the base of my throat or the burning of my eyes.

"How did you—" I started, but stopped to take a deep breath. "How did you stop her?"

"We didn't for a while. We didn't think anyone would believe us. Our culture teaches us that men love *any* attention we get from females, and we should be grateful to have an older, beautiful woman even glance at us. We were young and dumb, and we didn't know how to deal with it."

Understandable.

What kid would know what to do at that age?

The adults were supposed to, but not only had they failed spectacularly, they'd invited the wolf into their own homes.

"But you did, eventually?" I pressed, needing to know what happened to Luca's stepmother, if she was still out there.

"Luca. He managed to convince me to go to the police after months of thinking it over, but a few days before we actually *did* go, she died from cardiac arrest. It was like fate had finally given us a break, and the situation died down without anyone finding out," Killian explained, his lips coming up in a humorless smile. "But maybe they should have. Maybe someone else could have incentivized Luca to seek out therapy more than I ever did, and he wouldn't be—" He cut himself off, like he couldn't bear the truth, but eventually powered through. "He wouldn't be *dead* now. It could have all been prevented."

"Killian." I cupped his cheeks, forcing him to look at me. The devastation in his eyes was so raw it made me tear up. No kid should ever have to go through what they did. "There is nothing I want more than to have a time machine and prevent anything like that from happening to either of you, but Luca's death was an accident."

From what I had gathered, he had asked Luca's permission to tell me their story, and now he was blaming himself for what happened because Luca might've not been as on board as he initially led on. It was really far-fetched, but shock wasn't synonymous with rationality, and I was sure the effects of alcohol still lingered.

"I have to go to New York, be there by Yazmin's side, and find out what actually happened," Killian said, and shifted underneath me like he got a sudden dose of energy.

I slid my hands to his chest and pushed him back down. "And *we* will, but it's twelve o'clock in the morning. There isn't much you can do right now."

Neither of us was in the right state of mind to handle the five-hour drive to New York, and there was no way I was letting him out of my sight. We could travel first thing tomorrow morning when he wasn't intoxicated, and my need to vandalize a grave had subsided a little.

"Men aren't supposed to cry, right?"

It was the first time since I met Killian that I'd heard him sound so weak, and it broke my heart into a million pieces. There were a lot of ways toxic masculinity fucked men up, and this was one of them, feeling like they had to bottle up their emotions or they weren't *"manly"* enough.

"Men can absolutely cry. You aren't made of steel, my

love. You just lost your best friend." I stroked his jaw, and he blinked, a couple of drops spilling over.

"I can't believe it, Irena. I still can't believe it. It feels like I'll wake up tomorrow, and all of this will be a dream." There was no sobbing, no gasping for air, just silent tears sliding down his cheeks, triggering mine as well, for the loss he was experiencing and for the way someone else managed to fuck up his childhood so profoundly.

I was shaking, reeling over the information he had shared.

"I know, baby, I know." I leaned in close, kissing his tears away and wrapping my arms around his neck. "I'll be with you every step of the way. We'll figure everything out together."

He let out a sigh as if he needed to hear me say that, and we melted into each other, working through the distress and heartache in each other's arms. There was no more space for talking because nothing could really fix the situation except for time.

CHAPTER TWENTY-FIVE
KILLIAN

Grief was the most peculiar thing.

It was like a blast of wind had knocked a window down, and cold air seeped in, leaving me helpless in the face of it. I expected it to close a little each day, but the hole only got bigger every time I picked up my phone to call or text Luca, only to remember that I couldn't do that anymore.

News traveled fast, so I spent the five days leading up to the funeral dodging calls from concerned family members, mainly Saint, and spent whatever savings I had left on top-shelf liquor.

I had never lost anyone close to me.

Then again, I never let people get close to me except for a select few. I realized now it was a defense mechanism. They couldn't hurt me if I never allowed them to have that kind of power over me. It took Luca passing away for me to learn that.

The morning after I received Yazmin's text, I woke up with

a pounding headache to find Irena waiting for me with a cup filled to the brim with black coffee. My whole body hurt as well since we'd fallen asleep on the couch, so whatever she was telling me wasn't registering as I tried to get my bearings straight. The name Arsène caught my attention, though, and I learned that my little nephew was born the day before, and I'd missed it.

They'd all been at the hospital except for me, and as much as that added to my already gloomy day, a spear of sunshine drove past the overcast clouds. I felt excited for about five seconds before I remembered who I'd lost the same day another life joined the world.

Arsène Astor.

The name breathed new life into our family, one of new beginnings. I was sure Saint was sweating bullets. He had never imagined himself as a father, responsible for another's life, but I knew he would do great. He was more of a father to me than ours ever was.

I was dying to meet the little guy, but it would have to wait. Feeling even an ounce of excitement translated into betrayal in my mind, since Luca wasn't even underground yet.

Guilt ate me up inside whenever Irena was near me and made the pain ebb away as if I deserved to feel the full force of it. It was a natural reaction to be at peace when I was with her, and I wanted to selfishly chase the escape only she could provide.

I couldn't very well cling to her forever, though. She was more than willing to follow me to New York, but I couldn't ask her to abandon her responsibilities and come on a four-day trip with me. I didn't want her to. There were some things I was supposed to do on my own, and wallowing in my hotel room for four days straight until I couldn't avoid the inevitable anymore was one of them.

Luca had kept hush-hush about his life over here in New York, and I understood why as I got in the elevator at his uncle's house. My surroundings dripped with opulence, marble floors, open spaces, expensive art hanging from the walls, and chandeliers in the ceiling so big they could crush you in two.

It wasn't anything I wasn't used to. I grew up around tools that would compete about who had the bigger house. Until I looked a little deeper and noticed how heavy the security detail was.

A guard with a semi-automatic greeted me at the door when I walked in, and my Uber driver couldn't get out of there fast enough. If I had driven, I was sure someone would've been searching my car. There were cameras in every corner, some even disguised as everyday objects, and guards stationed at nearly every door on the first floor, keeping a watchful eye over the grieving relatives. The term *blood money* played like a loop in my head, but I was too buzzed to really feel any sense of danger.

After climbing the stairs to the second floor, I walked down a long hallway, stepping on a red Persian rug, and didn't even think to knock before sliding the door to Yazmin's new room open. It escaped my mind, but thankfully her back was to me, and she was standing in front of a window, staring at her uncle's expansive land.

Her hair was still dark brown, but it reached her waist now as opposed to the shoulder-length haircut I was used to seeing her in a couple of years ago. It almost blended in with the black dress she was wearing. Her typically tan skin looked paler than I'd ever seen; maybe it was the combination of colors washing her out, or she hadn't been eating well. Judging by how tiny she looked, it would have to be the latter. Yazmin had always been a small kid, but her weight was unhealthy, even for her short stature. Her joints poked out, and her collarbones were so sharp it was concerning.

"Still haven't grown an inch since the last time I saw you, kid." She still hadn't noticed I had entered her room, so when I spoke, she startled.

Hand pressed over her chest, she spun around, and her mouth dropped open when she spotted me at the threshold. Yazmin squinted her eyes as I stepped closer, occupying myself by shutting the door to keep the thoughts of Farah at bay.

She was her mother, after all. They were bound to look alike, but I was taken aback by how many features of hers she had inherited. The long and straight nose, strong jawline, and high cheekbones were all Farah. I found solace in the fact that she had the same gray eyes as Luca, albeit a shade darker, and nearly identical lips, with a pronounced cupid's bow and thinner bottom lip.

"Killian?" Her voice came out weak as she scanned me from head to toe, her mouth curling downward when she noticed my matching black suit.

"Hi, Bee," I greeted, and unshed tears filled her eyes immediately at the nickname. Luca and I used to make fun of her because of a yellow dress she was obsessed with when she was a kid, and the name just stuck long after she outgrew it.

I opened my arms, and she crashed into them, an onslaught of bottled-up tears rising to the surface as soon as I embraced her. She was skin and bones, and her sobs were so hard we both shook. It didn't matter that I hadn't seen her in nearly a year. A sense of familiarity hung between us. Yazmin was a tough cookie. This had to be the first time she was letting her true emotions out, and a lump grew in my throat when I thought about what life had in store for her now.

Luca was her last immediate family member that was alive, so now she was stuck living with her uncle. While he was kind enough when I met him downstairs, his choice of occupation left much to be desired.

"It's all right. It's going to be all right," I reassured her, not quite believing myself.

Was it really? She was still a teenager, for fuck's sake. She shouldn't have to be going through any of this. There were a million different scenarios as to how this could play out, and only a handful were favorable.

One thing was for sure, though: I would be commuting to New York a lot more often. Looking after Yazmin would be the thing Luca would've wanted me to do.

"No, it's not. He's dead, Killian. *Dead.*" She tore away long enough to let me get a glimpse of her teary cheeks and puffy under-eyes. "I have no one left."

"That's not true. You'll always have me," I said, and I meant it. I tugged her over to sit at the edge of her bed. "And I met your uncle outside. He seems to love you very much, and Luca believed in him enough to entrust your life to him."

She fiddled with her fingers, wringing them over in her lap, clearly uncomfortable with the idea of living in this fortress. I didn't blame her. No one would've liked living under a constant state of surveillance.

"His wife doesn't like me. Her face screws up every time

I enter a room. I don't think she wants me living with them," Yazmin admitted reluctantly, and my jaw hardened.

I hadn't considered the second part of the equation. How not everyone on the other side of the coin might've been as excited for the new addition to the family. The house was large enough you could get lost in it for days, though, and I doubted the wife had to lift a finger, considering the army of butlers downstairs. They weren't short on cash either. She was just being a cunt.

"His wife can suck it." At my words, the gray in Yazmin's eyes hardened, like she shared the sentiment. I told myself not to worry *too* much because, at the end of the day, she was raised by Luca, and if there was one thing he instilled in her it was his ability not to take any bullshit. "Listen to me. She gives you *any* trouble, you call me, okay?"

Yazmin nodded, then sighed, lingering on some empty picture frames decorating the cream wall across from her bed, like she couldn't see the point in putting any photos up.

"Why can't I come live with you?" she asked quietly, then picked up speed before I could reply. "It'll only be until I turn eighteen in three years. I'll be so silent, you won't even know I'm there. I'll even work and pay rent."

I didn't know whether to laugh or cry. I was so numb, I did neither. The day had barely commenced, and I was already treading on thin ice. I didn't want Yazmin to feel unwanted, so I broke the news as gently as possible.

"You can't, Bee. I'm sorry. The state would never allow you to move in with me. I'm not married, I'm young, and in the eyes of the law, we're virtually strangers."

Her eyes filled with unshed tears again, and I threw my arm over her shoulder, cradling her head to my chest. She was the closest thing I had to a little sister, and the responsibility weighing on my shoulders was heavy.

"You'll get through this. I believe in you." My thoughts weren't snappy, so I couldn't think of anything better to say as I drowned in my own sorrow.

"Do you, really?" Yazmin sniffled. "You're drunk as a skunk right now. You probably don't even know if *you'll* get through it."

"I forgot how perceptive you are."

"I'm not perceptive; you literally reek," she complained, detaching herself, and I took a discreet sniff at my chest.

Yup, she was spot-on.

I did smell like I'd bathed in a pool of Jack Daniels.

I blew out a breath, sticking my hands in my hair. I'd grown accustomed to always having Luca there. He had been a part of my life for as long as I could remember. It would be difficult to unlearn what I'd become used to and let go of a person I was so dependent on.

"You're right," I relented, my arms dropping by my sides. "I don't know if *I* will be able to push through, but I am sure you will. You've already lost so many people that were important to you at such a young age and prevailed."

"None of them mattered as much as Luca did. My mom was..." I held my breath as Yazmin paced before me, burning a hole through the white fur rug at her feet. "Let's not beat around the bush. She was a bitch. I think she always secretly despised me simply because I was born a girl and Dad... I liked him, but I barely got to see him because he was busy all the time."

Farah was disturbed on many different levels. I was sure she was disappointed she missed the opportunity of having one more person to torment, not for the reasons Yazmin thought. I never wanted her to find out, though, and Luca shared the sentiment. She already had enough to deal with already.

"Luca *was* my brother, so that makes you my sister by default. You can always count on me," I promised, and my words weren't filled with hot air. "I'll visit you as often as I can, Yazmin. I'm only a short plane ride away."

I could probably even buy a helicopter with the money Luca had left me in his will. His fortune was to be split in half between Yazmin and me, but I wasn't keeping it. I would be giving it to her as soon as she turned eighteen. This life...the one Luca was forced to work in by birthright, it wasn't one he wanted for his sister. I would make sure to provide her with a way out.

"I wish I could talk to him one last time." She stopped in front of her vanity, looking at a picture of them she had stuck in the corner of the mirror. "I was there when he passed, but I never actually got to say goodbye because he never woke up."

"You and me both, kid." The world spun when I got up, but I managed to stand next to her without stumbling and studied both of them.

The photo was taken before they left Astropolis, with a younger Yazmin on Luca's back and a gappy smile on in front of a heavily decorated Christmas tree. Even though he hated being at home when Farah was there, he would always rush back on December first because Christmas was one of Yazmin's favorite holidays, and he'd promise her they would decorate the house together.

Luca hated the glimpses of Farah he saw in his sister, but that didn't take away from how much he also loved her. He never let her lineage dictate his affection for her.

"He would burn down the world for you, though." I kissed the crown of her head. "Never forget that."

Her attention lingered on the picture, her eyes red like she had been crying for a week straight—which wasn't far from the truth. She squared her shoulders, though, bit her lip, steeling her spine, and turned toward the door, saying, "We should go."

"Yazmin?" I caught her wrist before she could walk past me, and she raised a brow. "Promise me something."

"What?"

While it was true that she got a lot of traits from her mother, I also saw Luca in the stubborn set of her jaw and her tendency not to sugar-coat things. I didn't manage to save him, so the least I could do was put in the extra effort for Yazmin. Seeing her go down the same road as her brother would be the final nail in *my* coffin.

"Study really hard in school, and go to college as far away from here as you can. Whichever one you want. Don't even think about the money. I will take care of it."

Yazmin sucked her cheeks in as she thought over my proposal, but shook her head a few seconds later. "I don't think I can promise you that."

"Why not?" I asked, and she glanced around.

"Even the walls have ears in this home." She started for the door again, but I pulled her closer and leaned down so she could whisper whatever it was that held her back in my ear, and she did, causing my heart rate to speed up. "I don't think Luca's 'accident' was *actually* an accident. I've told you that before. Plenty of people would've benefited if he was gone."

She *had* told me that, but that was a well of never-ending questions. Irena was right. My decision to talk to her about our past hadn't influenced Luca in any way, given that a car had crashed into him from the opposite side. There were no survivors, no one we could grill to find out any details, but Luca never failed to mention how high-risk his job was. Losing him had always been a possibility, but not one I thought would ever come true.

"That's not your cross to bear, Yazmin. If they did it once, nothing is preventing them from doing it twice," I rebutted, but that determined glint in her face remained as she shook me off.

"I'll try really hard in school, okay?" She tried to pacify me.

"That's still not a promise."

"It's the best you'll get." Yazmin turned her back on me.

CHAPTER TWENTY-SIX

IRENA

There was a heavy cloud of fog covering rows of gravestones, some mold-ridden and weathered with age and others fresh, a beacon of recent losses. The sky was overcast, and the soil was wet, making for a slippery, mulchy ground. I had the brilliant idea to wear a pair of black heels today and the sole of my shoes sunk down, defeating the purpose of being able to see what was going on over other people's heads.

I wasn't alone, though.

Saint Astor stood tall next to me, his football-built body allowing him to tower over everyone else. Luca was an attractive young man that used to live in Astropolis, so the news that he passed away spread like wildfire in our little community. Saint rushed to see how his brother was doing after finding out, but Killian had already left for New York without informing anyone, so the both of us settled for the next best thing—showing up to Luca's funeral uninvited.

I didn't know where Killian had stayed for four days since he wasn't answering his phone, but fortunately, I'd found out where the funeral would be taking place online. Saint was definitely worried, considering he hadn't bothered asking me why I insisted on coming along. The cat was nearly out of the bag, though, now, and there were far more important things to deal with than the repercussions of what would happen if people found out we'd been fucking around behind everyone's back.

"Do you have any painkillers on you?" Saint whispered as the priest held his brief service. It was an intimate one, with friends and family only, so we stood at the back as we tried to blend in with everyone else.

I wasn't sure what company Luca kept, but I'd spotted men with guns, talking to their sleeves a couple of times now, and I gathered we wouldn't be so welcome if anyone noticed us. Saint was unbothered, though, and I fed off his energy, hoping the phrase *fake it till you make it* actually worked this once.

"Why?" I whispered back as I rummaged through my black clutch. There were some essentials I always kept on me, and Advil was a must when I spent long hours talking to people, so he was in luck.

I handed him two as per his request, and he swallowed them dry, explaining, "Cemeteries freak me out. I get a headache every time I step foot in one."

It was a field of dead people, so it didn't strike me as odd that it could make people uncomfortable. It did make an impression on me that *Saint* was affected. My sister's husband was the definition of an all-American alpha male with his background in professional football and put-together looks. He was literally dubbed as *the* golden boy by traditional media, so any sign of weakness took me by surprise.

I took a painkiller myself to combat the anxiety that swirled in my belly and stood on my tiptoes to get a glimpse of Killian, but I had no such luck.

"What's he doing now?" I asked Saint.

"Exactly what he was doing five seconds ago." He rolled his eyes. "He's standing solemn-faced in the front row next to Luca's little sister. If something changes, I'll tell you."

I cinched the waist of my coat tighter, not impressed by his attitude. "Well, all right."

"I don't get why we're hiding."

"We're not hiding. We're just standing in the back," I reasoned, and the side glance he threw my way spoke plenty.

"I don't get why we aren't *standing* next to Killian," he rephrased, and I bit the inside of my cheek.

When we first set out to come here, I failed to mention that I hadn't told Killian we were coming. Then again, if he had picked up the phone, I could have, but he never did. So here we were, unable to get close to him but present nonetheless in case he needed us. There was this pressure in my chest, telling me to seek him out and make sure he was okay, but I remained rooted in place.

"We kind of showed up uninvited," I said reluctantly. "I told Killian I would come down with him, but he left like a thief in the middle of the night and hasn't picked up any of my calls ever since. I've been worried sick."

Saint stroked his five o'clock shadow, mouth set in a frown. "Did he leave *your* bed in the middle of the night?"

I could see the hole in the ground where the casket was placed clearly from my vantage point. I held my breath when Killian, along with three other men, began shoveling the crumbled-up soil back in. It was the first time I'd seen him in four days, and I ate up the view.

He was as devastatingly gorgeous as ever, albeit with deep black circles under his eyes, unruly hair like he'd pulled at it one too many times, and a heartbreaking look on his face, like he was present but barely surviving as he buried his best friend—brother, even of so many years.

The visual was so harrowing even Saint stiffened beside me, and I threw him a side glance. "Is that really what you want to discuss right now?"

"Why is everyone painting me as the villain?" He sighed like he was tired of having to defend his position constantly. "I care for both of you, and I didn't want to see either of you hurt."

I softened at his explanation, my frustration sometimes leading me to forget that his intentions were good. "No one's painting you as the villain. You can just be a ballbuster sometimes and never accept that some things are outside of your control. You cannot bully free will out of people."

We shared a glance where I saw some of his defenses crumble as he let go of whatever vision he had built up in his head. Being who he was, though, he defended his opinion until the end. "Free will is overrated. The world would be a better place if everyone listened to me."

It was my turn to roll my eyes. "Don't bring anything up around Killian. I don't want to upset him even more."

"I'm an asshole, not heartless." Saint fixed his tie. "Besides, what's done is done. There's not much I can do to prevent you two from getting together now."

"You're being uncharacteristically chill." I narrowed my gaze, suspecting that Aria might have had something to do with it. "Did my sister coach you beforehand?"

"I've barely slept a wink these past few days between caring for Arsène and worrying about Killian. I'm picking my battles, baby Fleur."

All right, that made more sense given that he fell asleep as soon as we got on his private jet, and then had a tall black coffee to tide him over for the rest of the day when we got in the car.

"Wise man," I commented.

He shook his head. "Tired man is more like it."

An elderly couple that stood before us threw us judgmental glares over their shoulders, and even though our whispers were barely louder than the whistle of the wind, we zipped it for the rest of the service.

Tremors ran up my fingers when the gathered crowd started dissipating after the priest finished up the ceremony. Luca was fully underground, and despite only having met him a couple of times, a cloud of sadness floated over my head at the young life lost.

Any minute now, Killian would spot us, and my body was all wired. As if fine-tuned to his surroundings, Saint took my shaking hand in his and gave it a reassuring squeeze. We stood off to the side as people fleeted past us, and my stomach flipped when Killian and Yazmin appeared in my field of vision.

He was staring at his feet as he walked, and it was Yazmin that noticed us, her nose red either from the cold or all the crying. Her gaze bounced over us at first as she went on to scan the lined-up cars by the side of the road but came back just as fast, doing a double take at Saint. Her footsteps turned brisker, and she veered slightly off-path to get a closer look.

"Saint?" she called to confirm it was really him, and Killian's head snapped up at his brother's name.

"Saint?" Killian repeated, an expression I couldn't quite name overtaking his face when he saw both of us. It was a mix of relief and despair, like he wasn't used to having his family by his side in his hardest moments.

"Hi, Yazmin." Saint greeted her with a kind smile, and I could've sworn her sad eyes brightened a little, and a faint blush marred her cheeks. "I'm really sorry for your loss."

"Thanks." Her answer was clipped, but in no way rude. More like she'd gotten tired of hearing that particular sentence again and again. She lifted her chin in my direction. "Is this your wife? I heard you got married a few years ago."

A gurgling noise came from Killian's throat. I'd forgotten Saint was still holding my hand, so I shook it off me as a shiver worked its way down my body. Don't get me wrong, Saint obviously broke the hot-o-meter, but he was also my sister's husband, and that sent immediate disgust roiling through me.

"She's not," Killian intervened; at the same time, I said, "Oh no, I'm Irena, his wife's sister."

At the sound of my voice, Killian scanned me from head to toe like he'd missed the view over the four days he'd been away, his gaze running like a balm over my skin. Save for the concern that plagued me about him, I was able to name another emotion that had kept me tossing and turning at night: *fear*. I'd had other boyfriends in the past, but no one I was terrified of losing, and this level of attachment brought a sense of danger and discomfort along.

Yazmin picked at the dead skin around her nails, clearly out of her element at the charged atmosphere her question had created. Saint's left eye twitched despite him trying to play it cool, Killian's stance challenged him to say something, and I crossed my arms, hoping they held off on the inevitable explosion for a while longer.

This wasn't the time or place.

"I'm really sorry for your loss, too," I told Yazmin, subtly elbowing Saint. She gave me a forced smile, and neither of us mentioned how pleased we were to meet each other. It would've been an obvious lie under these circumstances.

"What are you two doing here?" Killian cut through the small talk.

"We're here for you. If you got into the habit of checking your phone every once in a while, you'd know all of us have been worried sick about you." Saint ground his molars, failing miserably at this whole gentle approach thing. I got where he was coming from, though. I got where both of them were coming from.

"Saint," I warned under my breath, and he reluctantly pulled his gaze away first, the veins on his neck straining as he faced Yazmin again like he wasn't used to backing away first.

"Let me walk you to your car, Yazmin," he offered her, and she eagerly took his elbow to escape the impending confrontation. She waved at me as Saint led her away, and I dipped my head in a sketch of a bow.

I imagined being left to my own devices with Killian would've calmed my nerves a little bit, but the silence that followed had the opposite effect. My pulse sped up when he shoved his hands in his pockets. No hint of that longing I spied on his face not too long ago.

"He knows?" Killian asked simply.

"He put two and two together when I insisted on coming along."

"And he doesn't care?" A corner of his mouth pulled up in mock humor. He already knew the answer to that, but I preferred his sarcasm over regret. The fact that he had none pulled a sigh from my lungs.

"I'm sure it's a tough pill to swallow, but he doesn't get much say in the matter. Plus, he's willing to give you a pass after the week you've had," I supplied, stepping on a concrete pathway to salvage whatever was left of my heels. Killian tracked my every move with hazy eyes and slumped shoulders. "You look..."

"Like hell?" he filled in.

"Like you've been through hell," I corrected. Killian could never look like hell. His worst was most people's best. I wrapped my arms around myself to fight the urge to embrace him. I missed him, but his standoffish attitude had me worrying that he would brush me off. "What have you been up to the past few days?"

As if the concern in my voice loosened something in him, Killian stepped up beside me, his arm brushing against mine. The briefest touch filled me with heat, and I subconsciously leaned toward him as he expertly avoided the question. "Look, I'm sorry for ghosting you—*all of you*. I needed some time away."

He didn't have to tell me anything. I could *smell* what he had been up to.

"You don't have to apologize, Killian. A text back would've brought me some peace of mind, but I understand." I breathed in deeply, going for the kill. "I booked a hotel room at the Marriott, and I'll be here until Tuesday in case you need me."

He hadn't told me whether he was coming back or not, but after seeing him tonight with Yazmin, it was clear he wouldn't. They had the same vibe Saint and I did, perhaps even closer, and I was certain he would linger a couple more days for her.

"You're too good for me, Irena."

"I'm no—"

Killian's voice was barely a whisper, but it carried enough weight for me to slam my mouth shut mid-sentence. "But you should go. I'm going to stay for at least a week longer to help Yazmin out."

A coppery tang filled my mouth as my teeth sunk into the edge of my tongue to keep my words at bay. I usually made the mistake of speaking before I could think, and I was wound up so tight I was at a really high risk of saying the wrong thing at the wrong time.

"Did I do something wrong?" I asked, sizzling heat fanning up my chest and spilling into my face. I didn't get why he was shutting me out. "Are you still blaming yourself for—"

He looped his fingers through mine and brought the back of my hand to his lips. They were rough and cracked, but I welcomed the sensation anyway.

"I'm not, and you didn't. You did everything right, but you shouldn't have to put your life on hold for me."

"I don't mind, Killian. I—" I took a deep breath, cutting myself off.

My palm turned clammy in his hand. I couldn't believe what I was about to say. I couldn't believe it took me a mere two months to reach this point. The point of no fucking return because this was the first and likely the last time I would ever feel this all-consuming desire for another person.

It might've sounded naive. I myself would've laughed at my inner monologue a year ago, but my very soul ached at the thought of staying away from him for a day longer. My skin was addicted to the feel of his rough fingertips and the pressed indents of his teeth. My mind had gotten attached to his dry humor and wit. And my heart literally burst at the faintest hint of his vulnerability.

He was my dark fairy tale in the flesh, and together we made for a twisted fantasy I would've never imagined would come true.

My chest expanded with an inhale as I went on to rip the Band-Aid off. "Sometime during these three months we spent together, I fell in love with you, Killian. The kind of love that rejoices in your highs and sticks with you through your lows. In such little time, you managed to become one of the biggest parts of my life, and without you in it, it's bleak, as if all the color was robbed. I cannot go on like everything is normal because when you're sad, I'm sad, and when you're hurting, I'm hurting. I want to be there for you *always*, not only when it's convenient."

They said the hottest fires burned blue, and his eyes the moment I blurted out the L-word was no exception. They shone as bright as a raging wildfire, scorching through tissue and bone.

His lips pressed together tightly, leaching of color. Emotion rippled across his face, but it was too much and all at once for me to decode his state of mind. Hope sparked in my chest when I thought I spied that reciprocated affection I so craved, but it was gone just as quickly as I watched him literally come apart like broken glass.

He was fighting an inner battle from what I could see, as his hold on me got impossibly tight before he forced his fingers to open. Killian's palm stayed flat across mine for a heartbeat. The knots in my belly constricted painfully when he took a step back, all those shifting emotions settling into a frosty expression that rooted me in place.

My heart was beating so fast it could've flown out my chest in any given second, but then he replied with a curt, short sentence that caused it to shrivel up and drop to my stomach.

"I need some time to myself, Irena. I'm sorry."

Rock, meet bottom.

I took a step back.

My jaw slackened.

I took another step back and blinked rapidly to combat the stinging in my eyes.

I had just told him I loved him. I'd told a man other than my father that I loved him for the first time in my life, and the response I got was that he needed time.

There was no mistaking the anger that swept over every inch of my body, but it fizzled out as quickly as it rushed in. There was no doubt in my mind Killian loved me back. I simply had to remind myself that he had just lost his best friend and didn't know how to process his feelings. It was too early. His grief was too raw.

"I see." I tried my best to keep a neutral expression and clasped my hands over my clutch. I was like an open book to Killian, though, as he honed in on the tremble of my chin before I could squash it. The regret portrayed in the half step he took forward didn't do anything to reassure me. "In any case, I'll be here until Tuesday if you change your mind."

I threw an olive branch, but the best he could do was nod in acknowledgment.

Lingering for a second too long, I committed his features to memory, scanning every inch of him before spinning on my heels with a heavy heart. It went against everything I had in me to leave him like this.

Every stride I took was reluctant. I was dragging my feet all the way to Saint, who had dropped Yazmin off and leaned against his black Escalade, pretending to be busy on his phone. The kernel of optimism stayed with me until I reached my brother-in-law and forced him aside, slipping into the passenger seat before anyone could see my crumbling expression.

He hadn't called out my name, and I couldn't bear even a look back. I could feel his gaze still boring into me, but it meant nothing when he let me go.

"He's not coming?" Saint asked as he slipped into the driver's seat.

"No, he said he wants to be alone for a little while." I fumbled with my seat belt, my voice shaky.

"He's grieving, Ina, don't worry." Saint helped me out by strapping me in and patting my arm afterward. It did nothing to reassure me, but I gave him a closed-mouth smile. "He'll come around. He wouldn't have defied me if he didn't have some deep feelings for you."

CHAPTER TWENTY-SEVEN
IRENA

I was on top of the world...or at least I should've been.

It had been two weeks since Luca's funeral. And two full weeks without a word from Killian, save for a few brief text replies. I fought with myself initially, unsure whether to reach out to him after our last meeting, but my concern got the best of me, and I asked him how he was holding up. The answer was always the same: *fine*.

Fine. Everything was always fine.

His bold-faced lie *was* my reality, though, because finally, it seemed as if all the chips were falling into place. I'd signed my streaming deal, and the amount they were offering me was beyond anything I'd ever dreamed of. Bea was the first person I brought along the Sting of Ice ship, and I was excited to be working with my best friend. I was having so much fun visiting my new nephew as he was the cutest baby I'd ever fucking seen (and no, I was not just saying that because he was my blood), and my petty side took over, and I thoroughly enjoyed the meltdown both Daniel and Katrina seemed to be experiencing oh so publicly.

So why was I feeling so hollow at the same time?

All my dreams were coming to fruition, and I was not enjoying them as much as I was supposed to.

"Look, it hasn't been a week of Stars on Ice being aired, and they're already considering dropping it." Bea shoved her phone in my face, and I let go of the papers I was shifting through to read the article she showed me.

The words blended in together, and despite my best efforts, I couldn't read past the headline: **Trouble in Paradise? Things don't seem to be heading so well for the beloved figure skating duo.**

I got a sense of what it was about, though, so I didn't need to read more of the trashy column. I pushed the phone back to her and straightened in Bea's spinning chair. I'd started spending a lot more time at her place because the longer the apartment opposite me went vacated, the worse my mental state got.

"What?" I asked, perplexed, grabbing a slice of cucumber from the healthy charcuterie board Bea had made before we gathered to go over some prospective skaters for the show.

We'd pulled out all our contacts and printed out the top thirty we considered the best of the best. We would have to shave off ten more, and then from the twenty that remained, only ten would make the cut. It all depended on their availability and the network's willingness to work with them. I would provide the prospects I thought were the best choice, but I wasn't the ultimate decision-maker.

"Allegedly." Bea threw her dog a bite-size of chicken as he waited patiently for snacks next to the glass dining table. "The first episode did well, but viewership has dropped drastically since then, and apparently, there is some internal conflict between the cast and the producers that is costing the network more money than they're willing to spend."

"Interesting," I mused, scratching Cory's—her black lab's —head.

Bea raised a brow. "Really? You seem anything but interested."

I puffed my cheeks out, holding in a sigh as I stared back at the spread of papers on the table. We created profiles and printed them all out, and yet going through them felt like a chore when I should've been over the moon.

My mind was otherwise occupied, obviously, and after everything that happened this past month and everything I'd learned, it was getting difficult to pretend like I had that many problems of importance. So I got cheated on, and a girl was mean to me. I wasn't the first or last person that had happened to. It was embarrassing when I remembered how Killian would listen to me complain about them for days on end while he had gone through what he'd gone through.

I had to move on eventually.

"I'm over it, to be honest," I admitted. "They lost the public's credibility and are in a loveless relationship. I, on the other hand, got my happy ever after."

My face was set in a frown, and Bea swirled the sweet tea in her glass, judging me with her eyes over the rim as she took a sip before saying, "Then why have you been moping around for the past few weeks?"

Good question.

The answer was obvious, but that didn't mean I was going to admit it out loud. It was one thing for me to know how much Killian's well-being affected my mood, but I wasn't ready for other people to find out.

"I haven't. Work has been keeping me busy." My excuse was followed by a blank stare on her part, and I faced away. "Please don't push me on it. I'd rather not talk about it yet."

I grabbed yet another vegetable slice—carrot this time—and munched it slowly. Eating was a stress relief sometimes. I was also craving a glass of wine, but after seeing how Killian handled Luca's loss, I hadn't drunk a sip of alcohol. It numbed you, and growing too attached to that feeling was the last thing I needed.

"Dear Lord, he must've done a number on you," Bea commented, and I crossed my arms, silently asking her how long this would last. She held her hands up and said, "Fine, fine, let's change the subject. Have you thought about what you'll be doing for your birthday?"

I blinked in surprise. "My birthday?"

She tilted her head. "Yeah, it's less than two weeks away? Don't tell me you forgot your own birthday."

Fuck, of course. It was December first tomorrow; my birthday was on the tenth. It had totally slipped my mind, but honestly, I wasn't so sure I even wanted to celebrate it. I mean, what was the point of celebrating getting one step closer to death?

"Of course not," I lied. "But it's too early to plan."

"Since when? You used to do it months in advance."

"Well, the excitement wears off the older you get."

She rolled her eyes at me. "Bitch, you're turning twenty-two. That's hardly old."

"Tell that to the white hair I found on my head the other day," I rebutted, but that one probably had more to do with stress than aging.

"How about we go to Miami for the weekend?" She ignored me, shimmying her shoulders in excitement. "It says it's gonna start snowing around that time, and I'd rather not be here for that."

"I do miss the hot and humid weather." Said no one ever. I hated the heat, but I had to throw Bea a bone, or she would turn relentless. "But I can't leave, not now."

I shook my head, not explaining any further, but she got it. I couldn't leave even for two days without any closure with Killian. I wanted to be here in case he needed me.

Bea sighed in understanding and stole another sip of her sweet tea. "Fine. But I'm taking over the party planning."

KILLIAN

If I could've prolonged my return to Astropolis any longer, I would have.

I stayed by Yazmin's side for nearly a month. She was more stubborn than a mule, and whatever the antonym of Zen and relaxed was. The anger in her called to me, but there wasn't fucking anything we could do and not end up in a ditch.

If you'd told me a couple of years ago I'd be the one providing guidance to another person, I would've blown a plume of weed straight into your face and then laughed my ass off. But here we were. I'd checked in with her *thrice*, and I'd been back for only a day.

Losing Luca wasn't something I'd be able to get over any time soon, but helping Yazmin out gave me purpose and took my mind off things. Also, it weirdly felt like I was close to him through her, and as selfish as it sounded, I planned on taking full advantage of the fact.

"Some would believe that other people are ranked higher on your roster, yet here you are, visiting me on your first day back. I feel special," Ares heaved, resting against the boxing ring at his home's gym.

I'd come back to town yesterday as I couldn't hold off on the work that still needed to be done in my tattoo shop. It would've been Luca's wish to see it up and functioning. I also still fully planned on paying back the loan he'd given me, but Yazmin would be the beneficiary. I was going to set everything up so a way out will be waiting for her if she ever wants it.

I hadn't worked up the courage to go to my apartment, though, and instead crashed at Ares's for the night. He didn't hover, and he didn't ask unnecessary questions. It was also Saturday today, and he had enough time to go through a training session with me.

Saint, Ares, and I used to always do so together until they expanded their families and bailed. Their friend Leonardo Bianchi was the first to peace out, and then they all followed soon after.

I didn't mind. It only told me that I should find friends my own fucking age.

"I needed a sparring partner and thought you might need the exercise after spending the better part of the year at home." I jugged some water. "I was right. You've grown rusty."

He waved off my insult, rubbing his sweat off with a tiny towel. "What you need is a distraction, although I don't see why you're here when you have the perfect one literally in the apartment opposite you."

Didn't I know it?

But I couldn't pile my shit on her plate when she should've been focused on her new show deal. I'd come across the article during *isolation,* as I called it, and I was so fucking proud of her for reaching her goal. When she told me she loved me, I wanted to shout it back, scream it from every rooftop in the city, but not at the expense of overshadowing such an important moment in her life.

"Irena is worth more than me using her like that," I argued.

"You might want to let her know at some point." Ares's lips didn't move when the words came out, and I spun toward the entrance of his home gym, catching my brother roll through them like he owned the place. "She was barely holding in her tears on our drive back to her hotel."

"What the hell?" I asked, my gaze shifting between him and Ares. The latter had the sense to look guilty as Saint pinned me with an unimpressed glare and rested his shoulder on a weight-lifting machine.

"Hello, brother," he greeted, and I glared at Ares as he jumped out of the ring.

He took note and raised his hands in an *I surrender* motion. "Sorry, man, I had to let him know you were here. He was worried about you."

I cracked my neck from side to side. It was like my system was short-circuiting, and I didn't know how to behave around him. He was my *blood* brother, and his concern was valid, but I didn't know what to expect from him now that he had found out about Irena and me.

"He can take your spot. I imagine there's some pent-up aggression he wants to release after finding out how close and personal I got with his sister-in-law."

The words flew out before I could stop them. I went into the defensive as the walls closed in around me. So many things happened in such a short span of time I was having a hard time keeping up.

My brother's gold eyes glittered with rage for a split second before the emotion shifted into something worse —disappointment.

"Do you think I'm that much of a douchebag?" he asked quietly. "My little brother lost one of his best friends, and I'm gonna chastise him about who he chooses to bone?"

I ground my molars together, hating myself. Saint could be a ballbuster, but he cared for me before anyone else.

"Right, I'll take that as my cue to leave." The awkward tension between us led Ares to back away slowly.

Saint ignored him, and I did too, for forcing me to tackle a tidal wave I wasn't ready to. Saint wasted no time getting into the thick of it and started me down. "Is that why you stayed at a hotel last night, or why you haven't bothered to even ask how your nephew is doing 'cause you thought I'd be mad you and Irena fucked?"

My heart rate sped up at the mention of Arsène. I'd officially hit rock bottom. Nothing said you were a world-class loser more than ignoring your nephew's existence because you didn't want to deal with your brother's bickering.

"How did you know I stayed at a hotel?" I neither confirmed nor denied.

"I'm always keeping tabs on you, Killian, *always*," Saint stated hoarsely, and I could've sworn I saw the faintest hint of red in his eyes, but he blinked before I could make sure and stared at a white speck on the dark wood floor. "I don't show it nearly enough, but you're my little brother. I love you, and your safety will always be a priority of mine."

"You really don't care?" My jaw locked. He'd gotten so defensive about his opinion on the matter in the past, I truly believed he'd excommunicate me for even breathing her way. "About Irena and me being together, I mean."

He shook his head. "The kind of together that bothered me differs from yours. I thought you'd hook up a couple of times, and then our relationship with the Fleurs would turn even more strained than it already is. But I witnessed first-hand it was much more than that. She would go to bat for you. I hope you know that."

"I would too. I-uh—" I nearly blurted out the L-word but held it back just in time. Irena should be the one to hear it out of my mouth first, so I settled for the next best thing. "I really care about her. I never saw it coming. It did start out as something casual, but I didn't prove to be as unaffected as I thought I would."

"What's holding you back from telling her so?" he inquired, and I climbed the two short steps down, plunking my ass on the edge of the ring. I rested my head on the elastic behind me and glared at the ceiling.

"Everything and nothing at the same time," I said, not much of an answer, but the best he'd be getting for now.

I didn't want to weigh her down with my baggage at such a happy time in her life. The disappointment on her face when I didn't share the sentiment killed me, but I was only acting with her as a top priority in my mind. Saint joined me and sat next to me, sighing when he realized I wasn't going to expand on my half-assed explanation.

There was a mirror opposite us, and for a second, we looked so freakishly alike it was unsettling. Beyond our physical attributes, both of us had deep black circles under our eyes and had lost a bit of weight. It was the first time my brother presented himself in a less-than-perfect way, and my gut twisted as a result, recognizing that it was my fault.

Like Saint could read my thoughts, he slapped my back and caged my neck. "Just because Luca is gone doesn't mean you're on your own, Killian. I know you two bonded under tough circumstances, and it was a special friendship, but I'm *your* blood. I can be a cunt sometimes, but don't take it to heart. I'll always be here when you need me."

My cold heart warmed at his words. I never depended on anyone, but knowing that the option of having someone to fall back on was there understandably made things a whole lot better. There was one thing that gave me pause, though, and I hooked on to it.

"What do you mean by tough circumstances?" My forehead bunched, and I transitioned from staring at him through the mirror to meeting his gaze head-on. He didn't shy away, his eyes telling me he knew something I didn't, and his folded hands and smaller stance betraying that he wasn't in his element right now.

"What did you mean by tough circumstances?" I repeated, louder this time.

"Do you remember when the first year after I moved out, you used to ask me if you could stay over at my place all the time?" I nodded, and he cautiously continued. "At first, I thought it was to escape the *troubled souls,* for lack of a better term, that raised us, but it kept happening more and more, and I started getting suspicious. You'd also gotten really jumpy and would subtly flinch whenever a door opened abruptly."

"You spent Christmas at home that year when you'd rather shoot yourself than live with our parents again, even for a short period of time," I remarked, my blood roaring in my ears as I sensed the direction this conversation was taking.

"It was to observe you," Saint confirmed, lighting another fire on top of the five hundred that were currently wreaking havoc in my life. "Everything started falling into place when Luca visited one day, and his stepmother accompanied him. You were both really uncomfortable around her and shied away from her touch, and I don't know, I just had this inkling, especially after I caught her trying to corner you in the bathroom." His hands tightened into fists as he relieved the memory. "So I had her followed and had a P.I. look into her. He did a background check and found out she was charged as a sexual predator when she was twenty-two and living in Florida. It all clicked then."

It was like an atomic bomb detonated right before my eyes, as everything I thought I knew turned out to be a lie. The little bubble I had protected—Luca and I had protected all this time—burst like it was nothing more than a gum bubble. I debated whether I heard him right, whether I'd done it and drunk too much, and now I was permanently drunk.

It never occurred to me that someone else might've figured it out.

That they cared enough about me to look deeper than most people.

"All this time..." I shook my head, but it did nothing to stop my world from spinning. "All this time—you-you knew?"

Guilt etched on his face as he cringed, wringing his hands together in his lap. "I couldn't prove anything shady was going on, and frankly, I wasn't going to sit around and wait to gather proof. I was already late in recognizing the signs as it was. I didn't want to keep failing you."

To keep failing you.

My throat bobbed with a nervous swallow, all that hidden anonymity I held toward my family unraveling. Technically, it wasn't their fault I never spoke up, but I always hoped one of them would pull me out of the murky waters I was forced to swim and drown in.

"What did you do?" I shifted my whole body toward him.

"Farah Mietitore didn't actually die from cardiac arrest, Killian," he said coolly, meeting my gaze head-on. "Her husband shot her in the head when he caught her cheating on him with another man and then shot her lover too. I was the one that tipped him off and waited at the motel's parking lot until I heard the shots."

Another blast went off as a second bomb dropped. My fingers trembled, and my whole body felt numb, like I was suspended in thin air between reality and fiction. I wouldn't believe what he was saying if I hadn't witnessed him admit it firsthand.

I took a ragged breath that shook my entire body. "But no, why would they say—"

"You're telling me you've been friends with Luca for nearly a decade and didn't find out what sort of business his family was involved in? They had the means to clean everything up." He cut me off with the perfect explanation.

"Why didn't you say anything?" I tugged at my hair as I tried to wrap my mind around the fact that my brother had indirectly ended someone's life for me. His hand smoothed up and down my back as I lost it, slowly but surely. "Why did you never say anything?"

"I didn't know how to approach you about it. I was in college. I couldn't say anything to Mom and Dad for the same reasons you never entrusted them either, I'm guessing." Saint released a shaky breath. "I did my best keeping a close watch on you ever since, and as you grew older, you never brought it up either, so I assumed you weren't so keen on anyone finding out."

"This is a lot to process." I pressed my palm into my stomach, fighting the urge to hurl.

"I'm sorry. I'm sorry it took me so long to figure it out." Saint's hoarse voice echoed with regret. "I'd give anything to turn back time and have you never go through something like that. I would've shot the cunt myself if I had to."

I didn't know how much time had passed, but the next time I felt somewhat relaxed, it had started snowing outside, and Ares's entire backyard was covered in a thin layer of white powder. I wasn't proud to admit I shed a tear or two for the second time, but Saint did so as well when I opened up again about what it was like during that time. A kind of otherworldly lightness filled me when I was done, since the secret I carried for so long left the cavity of my chest, and the extra empty space allowed me to feel lighter.

He proceeded to apologize a thousand times over, even though I reassured him it wasn't his fucking fault. It wasn't anyone's but Farah's, and Saint had been a kid himself. Eighteen and twenty were hardly old enough to have the mental capacity to deal with something like that. Besides, as soon as he was made aware of what was going on, he got rid of her in the most brutal way possible.

I was seeing my brother in a new light, slightly terrified of the lengths he'd go to and happy I wasn't one of his enemies. In my wildest dreams, I'd never imagined him capable of doing something like that, but as far as I could tell, he had no regrets and no second thoughts. At the end of the day, he didn't actually pull the trigger. He only fueled the fire.

Sometime during our conversation, Ares poked his head in to make sure we hadn't killed each other and left laughing when he saw that our lazy asses had taken to laying down on the blue mats along the floor, too emotionally exhausted to remain seated.

Saint yawned, the aftermath of having a newborn, and I followed suit because I'd barely slept a wink last night while not being able to see Irena even though we were in the same city.

"Killian," he started, and I perked up. "I hate to spring this on you now, but please reconsider keeping Irena waiting any longer. That girl is fucking miserable without you. This separation it's not doing either of you any favors."

"It's her birthday tomorrow," I started as an observation, not a question.

"It is?" he asked.

"Yes, and I'm going to need your help to set it all right." I nodded, something warm spreading in my veins as my mind conjured up a plan most people would deem insane, but I wouldn't do a lame love confession. I was going to go all out.

CHAPTER TWENTY-EIGHT

KILLIAN

L ast night was eventful, to say the least.

After Saint and I got a much-needed nap in Ares's gym, he tried to talk me out of my plan multiple times. Still, I didn't listen, even though my very soul trembled at the mere thought of following along with it. I was more of an acts-of-service guy. Words of affirmation seemed like nothing but a bunch of hot air to me, so despite shaking in my boots, I went ahead with it...and nearly jumped behind some thorny rose bushes when Irena's father answered the door.

All my bravery fled out the window when I was finally forced to face the task at hand, but in the end, I pushed through.

I'd gotten to know Mr. Fleur during the brief amount of time I worked at Falco and Fleur. He was an all-around nice guy—fiercely protective of his daughters, though; an aspect of his character I got to witness when I told him I was seeing his youngest daughter, which was serious. His smile instantly turned upside down, and I was sporting a black eye for touching his little girl.

Thankfully, Saint was able to vouch for me, and once he realized that I was serious about her, he calmed the fuck down. Irena's mother stared at me with a knowing grin the whole time we spent at their place. From what I gathered, she'd already figured out that something was off during Aria's labor.

Perhaps I should've consulted Irena before visiting them, but the only way this plan could work was if she remained clueless. I didn't want to hide anymore. The truth about us would eventually come out, as I wasn't planning on letting her go any time soon. In an attempt to get ahead of the curve, I figured her parents would appreciate it more if they didn't learn of our relationship with the rest of the world.

Afterward, Saint took me to see my nephew. He was in a blue ball with a head full of curls like his mother's. I thought newborns weren't supposed to have a lot of hair, but Arsène proved to be the antithesis of that rule. He was much too young and much too small to tell who he took after more, but judging by the Michael Phelps lungs he had on him, his temperament aligned more closely with his father's. Saint could blow the roof off a place too when he was *hangry*, like little Arsène when his mother took too long to feed him.

Arsène *Luca* Astor.

When they told me his middle name, my heart squeezed, and I didn't know how it was possible, but I fell in love with him even more. He was the fucking cutest kid I'd ever seen, and I wasn't so easily impressed by the little terrors, as I called them. I was already planning on getting a tattoo to commemorate Luca, and I thought it would be perfect if I incorporated Arsène in it too. A man stepping into the light, the meaning of both of their names combined. Saint didn't have any tattoos on him, but as soon as I told him my idea, he decided to get rid of another first and join me.

I didn't go home that night, either. Part of me was very insecure about whether Irena still wanted anything to do with me after nearly a month of radio silence. I went to the person that would have all the answers—Bea. And after cursing me out for ten minutes straight for making her best friend sad, she put me out of my misery and told me that Irena thought about me every day. I wanted to kick myself for letting it get this far, but I was planning on straightening things out soon. Bea had been against me since day one. She softened up, though, when I asked for her help the next day and bid me goodbye with a strongly worded warning.

"How do you think she'll react, buddy?" I patted Arsène's back, trying to get him to burp after feeding him a bottle and letting Aria and Saint get some much-needed sleep while I helped with the little munchkin.

Arsène's answer only served to fuel my nerves as he barfed over my shoulder, letting me know he had no confidence in me whatsoever. I cringed, holding him under his armpits and away from me, when the warm liquid dripped down my shirt. He kicked his feet in the air, gurgling happily at the expression on my face.

"That bad, huh?"

IRENA

"Mind your step," Bea instructed, but I couldn't see a single thing with the fucking blindfold she forced me to put on and tripped over some twigs on the floor.

"Bea, where the hell are we?" I held on to her arm so tight I was most likely cutting her circulation off, and sniffed the air. "It smells weird, like that fertilizer my dad uses on his vegetable garden all the time."

If I could go back in time, I wouldn't have let her blindfold me, but it was my birthday today, and I didn't want to ruin her surprise. She said it was going to be a close ride, but we drove for two hours straight, and I started to get antsy.

"Would you stop complaining? We're almost there."

A tree branch rubbed against my shoulder, clueing me in that we were somewhere with vegetation, although the sun wasn't too intense, so I was still in the blue.

"As much as I love nature, I'd much rather spend my birthday partying than hiking. Please tell me we're not doing any outdoorsy stuff." I tried to trick her into telling me, and when we came to a stop, I thought I'd succeeded.

"Here," she huffed, and I was ready to remove the cloth she'd wrapped around my eyes until she referred to me in the third person. "Dear God, she hasn't stopped talking since I put that blindfold on her."

My brows bunched. "Who are you talking to?"

"Good luck," Bea said, and I got further confused.

Good luck for what?

"Bea?" I gave her one more chance, but I heard shuffling like she'd left me alone in the middle of nowhere. "Hello? I'm taking the blindfold off," I threatened, and when she still didn't reply, I did.

My head was slanted downward as I loosened the knot, and I didn't have the patience to work it all the way out, so I simply let it drop around my neck. An unnatural amount of light flooded my vision, and it took me some time to adjust. I was standing on a pathway, though, I noticed that much, and colorful flowers started where the paved stone pathway ended.

"Really? A garde—" I started, blinking to get used to the brightness that attacked my retinas, but shut up once I saw it wasn't Bea I was talking to. A six-foot-tall man cast a shadow over me—*no,* not just any man, *my man,* dressed in a suit and tie, way more dapper than I'd ever seen him, but just as handsome as ever. "Killian?" I asked in a stunned voice, not trusting my blurry vision.

He gave me a closed-lip smile, and while my entire body lit up like a live wire from being in his presence after a month, I didn't dare approach him. I was excited but scared of a second rejection. There was hope in his eyes, but heartbreak still lingered in the droop of his shoulders.

"Not just any garden, an enclosed butterfly garden." His sultry voice wrapped around my body like a snake, and I preened, having missed even hearing his voice. "The largest in the entire East Coast. So many species are currently at risk of extinction due to habitat destruction and climate change, so they figured, why not create a space where they can flourish?"

I didn't want to remove my gaze from him, but I had to see what he was describing for myself.

The room was moist and nearly blistering, with a dome-like glass ceiling that allowed for light to flood the lavish, wild plants that stretched all around us. We stood at the very heart of the garden. Aside from the vegetation that surrounded us, little rustic benches were placed at various points across the expansive plot, and arbor-covered bridges stood over mini artificial ponds with moss growing along the heavy gray stones that bordered them.

The real attention catcher was the thousands of butter-flies swarming around us. They came in all different shades and patterns. White, blue, orange, yellow, dotted, and striped. I even spotted one whose wings seemed transparent save for a brown border around them.

I twirled in place as I surveyed one particular orange one adorned with symmetrically perfect black dots. It beat around me happily, and I went very still, like I was getting ready to draw an arrow, my body hardening into stone. The butterfly rested on the tip of my nose, its little wings clapping together as it settled. I crossed my eyes comically to watch it.

"And we get to come and look at them. It's a win-win," I voiced, mesmerized.

I'd never been surrounded by so much beauty before. I followed them with my eyes, and a red one with black-edged wings nearly settled on me, but I moved aside just in time and bumped into Killian, who caught me by my arms. It was a knee-jerk reaction because I found them fascinating to look at, but in the back of my mind, I remembered that they were classified as insects and freaked.

"Exactly." Our gazes met and held for an agonizing second where I craved to hug the shit out of him because having his warmth pressed against me was the most at peace I'd felt in a while, but I took a step back, giving him the space he'd asked for.

"How are you holding up, Killian?"

"Much better now that you're here, Lilith." He gave me a

crooked grin, in much better spirits than the last time I saw him, and my breathing deepened.

I kept the excitement that rushed at me at bay, not trusting this change of heart, and asked, "How did you find this place?"

"I did some digging on the internet. They keep close track of the butterfly population here and have had a tremendous amount of success. They encourage donations, and in return, let you name one of their butterflies, and after they die, give you a frame with the preserved body."

Oh, that was so clever, and such an amazing thing to do to help preserve endangered species. It would also make for a really unique gift, with a deeper meaning considering our history.

"Did you name one?" I breathed, slightly giddy when he nodded. "Oh, did you take a picture of it to show me?"

"I didn't have to." His gaze fixated on a spot over my shoulder and instructed, "Turn around."

I did so slowly so as to not spook the butterfly that would clearly be there, and my body hardened into stone when a majestic blue one stood perched on a tree branch three feet away from me, its little wings clapping together occasionally as I approached it. Goose bumps prickled my skin when Killian's words about how he used to see them right after meeting with me came back to haunt me.

Were they really an omen? It certainly seemed that way, when even in a garden full of butterflies with colors more diverse than the rainbow, this particular one found its way to me. A long, muscular arm stretched behind me, as Killian's front brushed against my back. I gasped quietly, my pulse stuttering like it was struggling to stay confined in my body.

"This particular species loves following you around, and

they currently only have one of them." His hot breath curled around the shell of my ear as he extended his finger toward it, and the butterfly stepped into his awaiting hand like it was a paid actor.

"Oh my God, it's so beautiful," I muttered when he brought it closer to me. The color shone like pigmented ink on its membrane-like wings. "How can you distinguish it from other species with blue wings?"

"The orange bands inside the blade border. One of the workers told me only Karner blue females had them."

So it was a girl, then. That explained why it jumped to his arms so willingly. Miss Blue and I shared a mind as my throat bobbed from having him so close to me, that ocean-light scent messing with my hormones.

"This is the one that always appeared after we met?"

"Yes."

"What did you name it?"

"Lilith Blue," he supplied, and the air between us became thick and charged. Lilith crawled up the back of his hand like she knew we were talking about her. "You might think I'm way too superstitious, but some things are too strange and too strong to be coincidences."

"I don't think that." I shook my head and regretted it instantly when Lilith Blue fluttered away, spooked by the sudden movement. It swirled in circles, joining the rest of the dancing butterflies around us, until it rested atop a leaf, hanging over our heads like mistletoe.

"I didn't only bring you here to show you the butterflies. I also wanted to show you what *you* mean to me." He barricaded past my already weakened defenses with words that melted the winter wasteland my soul had turned into after a month of no contact.

Somewhat secure that he wasn't trying to break up with me as gently as possible tonight so Saint wouldn't get on his case, I turned to face him, placing both my palms on his hard chest. I held off on any words when he puckered his lips like he had more to say, his palms closing around my wrists in an attempt to keep me there.

"Before you, I was stuck in a cocoon of distress and unhappiness. I can't count on one hand the number of times I considered just ending it all. Life had no meaning and no purpose; the days blended together like my life was on a constant loop. But then you appeared on that window and started chipping at the protective layer surrounding me every time you got the chance. I was too scared to find out what was on the other side, so I constantly pushed you away. But the progression had already started, and before I knew it, you'd swept me off my feet, and for the past few months I've been with you, it felt like I was soaring above overcast clouds with a pair of colorful wings."

My breath hitched, his confession reverberating around me and filling me with so much joy and hope you'd think he'd gathered the stars from the sky and handed them to me. His heart raced beneath my palm, mirroring mine, as I desperately tried to keep my emotions in check while we worked a few more kinks that needed to be addressed.

"But why would you shut me out if that was the case? When I could've helped alleviate your pain?"

"Because I didn't want to drag you down with me, Irena. Losing Luca shifted the entire perspective I had on life. I didn't know how I would react. I didn't know if I could handle the loss, and I didn't want to hurt you as I figured things out."

"Killian, when I told you I loved you, I didn't mean parts

of you, I meant all of you." I said it again. The L-word. The same shock I spotted the first time zinged through his eyes, like he couldn't quite grasp the concept of someone accepting him unconditionally. "You hurt me more by robbing me of the ability to be there for you and care for you."

"I realize that now, and I'm sorry. Letting someone else pick up the pieces is hard when you've been doing it on your own for as long as you can remember." His hold on me tightened, and the gushing wound over my heart started healing slowly, stitch after agonizing stitch.

"Don't do it again, please. I don't think I can handle you going radio silent on me ever again. I was up most nights wondering how you were doing and then randomly crashed through the day because my body couldn't handle the exhaustion."

Pain rippled across his expression when I explained what it felt like having him choose to numb his feelings with alcohol. The anxiousness that plagued me was so raw I had to put on two layers of concealer to hide the evidence of the troubled nights I was experiencing.

"I promise, never again." The sincerity in his tone left no room for doubt, and I nodded, my tense body softening up.

I refused to make the first move this time, as this was something *he* had to make better, and he gathered what I was waiting for as I looked at him from underneath my lashes. He caught my drift and dipped his head, his mouth closing in on mine. I went limp in his arms at the first taste of him after so many weeks, and Killian gathered me to his chest, strong and resilient, steadfast.

"Is this my birthday present, then?" I licked my lips when we came up for air.

"One of them." His beautiful lips curled with a smile.

"There's more?" My eyes widened, and I bounced on my heels.

He nodded, the humor in his expression bleeding out as a more vulnerable uncertainty took its place.

"The first time I saw you, Irena, I knew I was screwed." He tucked a strand of hair behind my ear, his fingertips caressing the sensitive spot underneath it until I caved in and rested my cheek into his palm. "You were my brother's sister-in-law, and here I was, noticing the way your lips curved when you talked or smiled, and how your eyes sparkled in the sun and darkened when you were angry. How you flushed the prettiest shade of red when you were anxious or turned on and how you bit the inside of your cheek every time you lied."

"What? I don't," I denied it and automatically did just that right after and cursed. "Fuck."

Killian's smile lit up the room when I proved him right, but he went on as if I hadn't spoken.

"I wasn't ready at first, but the best kind of love is unexpected, and I am madly in love with you, Irena Fleur."

I closed my eyes, relishing the word as it rolled off his tongue. I already knew it. Even though he'd never said it, I felt it emanating from him. I slid my hands up his chest and palmed his cheeks, giving in to the urge to get impossibly closer to him. As if reading my mind, he wrapped me in his embrace, his arms like steel bands around me.

"Timing and circumstances didn't matter. You are meant to be mine, and I'm meant to be yours. Despite my best efforts to fight it, you were like a magnet for me. I got lost in your orbit, but I didn't feel lost at all. You feel at home, like that familiar street where a warm house waits, and I will never give you up. Even if one day you decide you're tired of me, you'll always be the only woman, fuck, *human* in my heart."

"Never. I will never tire of you, Killian. You're the only one for me too. Words can't describe how much I love you and how far I would go for you."

A broken noise escaped his throat, and he clutched the back of my tulle, baby blue dress that I'd particularly picked out this morning because of how much it reminded me of his sparkling eyes as we kissed hungrily. Wherever Bea had disappeared off to, I hoped she couldn't see us, because I was ready to tear my man's clothes off right here, right now, and give the butterflies the show of their lives.

Killian interrupted my thought process by asking, "Then what do you say we make it official, Lilith?"

"How?" I heaved, trying to regulate my heartbeat.

He distanced himself from me, and confusion raced across my mind when his comforting heat was robbed from me. Killian's glistening lips tipped up when I followed after him, but he held his left hand up and I stopped in my tracks.

"We've only been together for three months, but you owned me way before that, sweetheart. Our souls were meant to find each other." His other hand fiddled with something in his pocket, and when he got a little black box out and got to his knees, a feeling of breathlessness shimmered through me, tingling my limbs. When he popped the question and opened the box, I nearly disintegrated. "Will you do me the honor of marrying me, Irena Fleur?"

Disbelief shot at the top of all the emotions cycling through me, shock following close by. They all churned together like a broken washing machine until my brain emptied out of all thoughts, and one question kept repeating over and over: *Is this really happening?*

A thrill ran through me when I opened and closed my eyes several times and he didn't disappear. Killian remained in place, his right arm outstretched and holding an emerald-cut, blue sapphire engagement ring with a diamond frame I had to do a double take on when it seemed suspiciously familiar. When it clicked and I realized it was exactly like the one my dad had bought for my mom, my knees went weak.

"Killian, is that my family's ring?" My voice was hoarse, and he shrugged.

"I asked for your hand yesterday, and Bea covered the black eye your father gave me with makeup today so I looked good in our engagement pictures," he admitted casually, as if he had not just set my world on fire. I gasped, my chest falling and rising sharply, but he went on like it was nothing. "But he agreed in the end. I figured I'd make the decision easier for you if you knew you had your family's approval."

The expression on my face could be described in only two words.

Utterly flabbergasted.

I had so many thoughts launching in my brain like erratic ping-pong balls, I blacked out for a good few minutes. To get them back under control, I had to let them have their moment one by one, arranging them into a straight line like a person suffering from OCD arranged their pantry.

Killian loved me enough to want to bind himself to me forever.

My parents approved, despite initial resistance.

They gave him our family ring to give to me.

Both Aria and Saint were on board.

Bea had helped Killian set this whole thing up.

Everyone was getting along and allowing us to live our love to the fullest.

It sounded like a dream come true.

Too good.

Too perfect to be *my* life.

"Baby," Killian addressed me, as if reminding me of his existence. My ocean-eyed, golden-haired man looked so handsome on his knees for me. "I don't mind waiting on my knees forever for you, but ants are crawling up my pants. If you could give me an answer, I'd appreciate it."

"Yes." There was no hesitation as I launched myself into his arms. We both went tumbling to the ground, him on his back and me pressing kisses all over his face like a lunatic, as I literally felt my love cells multiplying in my chest. "Yes, yes, yes, a thousand times, yes."

Whoops of joy and celebratory laughter coming from somewhere in the back of the garden made it past our little bubble. I paused my assault, raising a brow at him from above. "Who else is here?"

"Our family." He smiled, his face flushed with joy as he spread his arms, surrendering fully. "I told them to bugger off, but they insisted on coming."

I shoved my face in his chest, squealing from embarrassment that they got to witness me almost maul him. Killian's chuckles vibrated through me until I, too, started laughing at the absurdity that was my life.

"You're the best thing that ever happened to me, Killian." I pressed light pecks across his jaw.

He slid the ring on my finger. "And you're my entire world, Ms. Soon-to-be Astor."

EPILOGUE

KILLIAN

Six Years Later

"Who is this?" A little curly-haired demon tugged at the bottom of my pants, his liquid gold eyes hooked on the marble headstone rooted in the ground about four feet away from us.

I knelt on the ground so I was at eye level with my nephew standing in front of his mother's legs, a near picture-perfect copy of Aria, much to Saint's delight. I tried to tease him about the fact that his son looked nothing like him our first night at the cabin we'd rented for our annual Christmas trip to the Catskills. He put me in my place by telling me he thought Aria was the most beautiful woman in the world, and if their kid took after her, that was a win in his book.

It was only supposed to be Irena and me at first. We had a short-lived engagement and got married in a shot-gun wedding on Christmas Eve in Vegas, much to everyone's disappointment. We weren't so set on having a big ceremony, but we did go all out for our honeymoon with a trip to the

Bahamas, where we got our own little private villa so I could set Irena's bikinis on fire and have her swim and walk around naked during our entire time there. I joined her, of course.

Good times.

And we made a pact that no matter how packed our schedules got, we'd treat our honeymoon as a yearly thing, not a one-time occasion. Somehow, our siblings caught wind of it and came along one year. We decided to spend it at the Catskills, ruining all the fun ideas I had on how to utilize the jacuzzi to the maximum with Irena.

I made the mistake of being too much of a great host because they'd never stopped coming ever since. So a tradition was born where the girls would much rather spend time with me while my workaholic brother worked, even while on vacation.

"This is my brother." I hooked my finger toward Luca's resting place, watching as Arsène's eyes widened in confusion.

"But my dad is your brother." He poked his bottom lip out as he contemplated what I'd told him.

"Saint is my biological brother. Luca is my found brother, and I love him as much as I love your dad," I explained.

"Like you and Alexander, my love." Aria fixed a stray curl back in place, referring to Ares's son. He and his sister, Penelope, were born a year before Arsène and had taken quite a liking to each other since they were close in age.

"I don't love Alex. I only keep him around because I love his *sister*." Arsène squinted at his mother as he dropped the bomb.

My wife's melodic laugh echoed around me like wind chimes harmonizing in the late summer breeze. She looked like a wet dream and like the cutest person in the world with her red mittens, an oversized coat, and a nose and cheeks redder than her strawberry blonde hair.

She patted her nephew's shoulder and said, "Would you look at that? The Astor gene is strong with this one."

I curved a brow at her, but let the sly comment pass when she gave me a smile promising to extend my naughty list by a mile before Christmas tomorrow. Instead, I gave some friendly advice to the youngest member of our family. "Well, maybe don't admit that so openly, bud, especially not in front of Uncle Ares."

"Why not?" he asked, his stubborn streak shining so bright, I had to agree with Irena. Even though he looked nothing like his father, he was all Saint character-wise.

"Because it would hurt Alex's feelings," Irena explained, her answer differing drastically from the one I had in mind. *Because he would bubble-wrap his daughter and never let you step foot in their house again.* "How would you feel if someone befriended you just to get close to your sister?"

"I don't have a sister," he answered simply.

"He's got you there." I chuckled, because this kid had an answer for everything.

"Arsène, what you said is not nice. Don't mention it again." Aria used her firm voice on him.

"I don't like your tone." He frowned at her, and both Irena and I had to puff out our cheeks to keep from bursting out. One thing was for sure, these little trips had turned a lot more fun once he was old enough to join.

"I have my work cut out with you, huh? Let's take a walk and give Kill some privacy, okay? Come."

"Shout if you need me." Irena pecked me on the lips, and

I took the opportunity to squeeze her lovely ass before she batted me off, giggling as she took after her sister.

She was still fit as ever, but had gained some extra meat on her curves the past few months, and I loved it. I guessed it had something to do with her sitting season six of Sting of Ice out.

The show had gone on to perform unprecedented numbers on the first season partly because people wanted to hear her side of the story after Douchebag broke up with Katrina when Stars on Ice was not renewed for another season, and everyone realized how full of shit they were. And *primarily* because of our relationship, which made every headline one could imagine. Speculation ran rampant for the first two years. To this day, we still heard disgusting rumors about family orgies or Saint and me swinging out our wives. People had too much time on their hands, so we didn't pay that shit too much attention.

Life still had its ups and downs, but for the most part, I was deliriously happy and disgustingly in love. If only eighteen-year-old me could see me right now, he'd be running for the hills.

"Don't think I don't know you had a hand in this," I spoke out loud, swiveling toward Luca's grave. It was a rare sunny December day, and I plunked myself on the ground in front of Luca as we got our monthly chat in. "When you died, it was like someone took my heart out and cut a part of it off, then shoved it back in my chest all botched," I reminisced.

It was so many years ago, but the pain never dulled. They said time healed all wounds, but I begged to differ. Mine was still as fresh as it was the day I found out, and what added to the ache was that I never got to say goodbye.

So here I was, attempting to heal my trauma by talking to a grave. There was no guarantee that Luca could hear me, but coming here was therapeutic, so I did not miss a meeting.

"But weirdly, it's like I can sense that part that is missing, and it's never too far away. It's like you're watching over me, and the more time passes, the more I believe that given how fortunate and blessed I have been in my life." The wind rustled, some crunchy leaves spinning in a circle around his tombstone, and there it was again, that sense of a pair of eyes trailing over my body. "I got the girl, and I got my dream job, all thanks to your encouragement and help because if you'd never helped me get my head out of my ass and go after Irena, I don't know where I'd be today. And without your monetary help to open my shop, I'd be surviving off food stamps and Ross shopping sprees because I was too proud to ever ask my family for anything."

I unwrapped the plastic foil off a slice of some store-bought Panettone I'd bought—one of Luca's favorite Christmas desserts—and left some in his resting place, knowing the birds and squirrels would have a field day the second I left.

"I don't know what life after death holds, or if it even exists at all, but I'm hoping the whole heaven and hell story is real, even if I get sent straight to purgatory after I take my last breath. So long as you find the sense of peace you lacked in *this* life, I'll be happy even chilling in hell with other asshats like me."

Pebbles poked my knees as I got up. Despite how fucked up it sounded, I took it as a sign of acknowledgment to soothe my inner need to be able to communicate with Luca in some type of form.

"I love you, brother. Forever." I tilted my head toward

the sky, scanning the clouds like if I looked hard enough, I'd be able to spot him flipping me the bird from above. "Thank you for looking out for Irena and me."

We had a lot to do today, as it was Christmas Eve. Hence, I kept my visit short when I considered the two and half hour drive from the city to the Catskills, but I still felt more relaxed than ever. A one-sided conversation with my best friend was still quality time spent with him, and no matter how sad it sounded, it helped soothe me.

Leaving Luca's resting place, I jogged toward the direction Irena, Aria, and Arsène had disappeared in, just in time to hear Arsène ask a question that would certainly have Irena blushing the deepest shade of red in existence.

"Mommy, what are those dark spots on Auntie Irena's wrists?"

"What dark spots?" Aria's eyebrows met, and she turned around so fast she caught a glimpse of the bruises before Irena could hide them under her sleeves. Her gaze grew perplexed, but it was like a light switch flipped in her head when I caught up with them with a cocky smile plastered on my face.

"I-I—" Irena started, not noticing me yet, too preoccupied with finding a plausible excuse. "In my rush, I tried to stop an elevator door from closing the other day, but it caught my wrists, and they bruised pretty badly."

"You tried to stop it with both your hands?" I voiced my confusion with a dark laugh, and she jumped when she saw that I'd made it back.

Her arctic blues could freeze me over with how frigid they were, which was bizarre given how much *fun* she had acquiring those bruises...handcuffed to the head of our bed.

421

"Yes, I did." Her elbow met my stomach, and I coughed, her pointy ends doing some damage.

"You two are something else." Aria shook her head, and with a near-silent voice, added, "And please move that bed of yours away from the wall. Some of us actually like to get some sleep throughout the night."

Irena, who'd permanently adopted a beetroot hue, nodded rapidly, her hair catching the sun's light with the motion, and nearly sagged with relief when Aria let the topic fly, walking a few steps ahead with her son. I opened my mouth to intervene, but as if fine-tuned to all my movements, she turned before the first vowel could even escape from my mouth and intercepted whatever I had to say.

"Did you talk with Yazmin?" she asked, triggering the part of me that I like to keep buried way deep inside—the anxious one. "Why didn't she come? She always joins us when we visit."

"I did. She told me she had a school project she couldn't miss." My cool demeanor betrayed the fact that I knew her reasoning was nothing more than an excuse and was fucking infuriated there wasn't much I could do about it save from forcing her to meet me after half a year of only talking on the phone. I could tell something shifted recently in her life, and it must've been bad enough that she didn't want me to find out.

"I worry about her. That foster mother of hers is easily one of the worst people I've ever met. I don't get why she still chooses to live with them when she has enough money to buy a penthouse on billionaire's row if she wants to," Irena wondered, and even though I had an inkling that started with *Lu* and ended with *ca*, I chose not to share it. The less Irena knew, the safer she was.

"Yeah, I worry about her too." I shared the testament, and Aria took a right that led us back to the driveway. Her pace compared to ours was comical due to the height difference. Four steps for her was one stride for me and two for Irena. "She keeps postponing our monthly meetings, but now that I'm here, I'll track her down. She won't escape me this time."

Irena bit her lip, staring at me like I'd uttered the single hottest thing a man could say. And I tilted my head, giving her *that* look. The one that made her damp and had her begging me to spank her at three AM, after multiple rounds already. She used to be the one that found it hard to keep up, but the roles were starting to reverse as of late as she'd turned insatiably horny.

She shivered and dropped my gaze first, like she was actually scared she was going to fucking jump me right here, right now. She bent over, plucked a fallen leaf from the ground, and twirled it in her hand to keep busy. The trees in this cemetery were so tall and full, leaves fell the whole year round except for those three short summer months.

When she spoke again, I didn't expect what came out of her lovely mouth.

"Did you know that after seeing how good you were with her when I joined you on your trip to the Big Apple the first month of our engagement, all my worries about how you'd be as a father disappeared?"

"You mean you ever doubted me?" I pursed my lips, going down the funny route, although a light sparked in my chest at the prospect. Both terrifying and exhilarating at the same time.

"No, not you. Your hothead tendencies." She fiddled with the brown leaf, slowly tearing it apart like a used napkin. "But you were so kind with her, so patient and loving, it made my baby fever spike."

"Hmm." I tapped my chin. "I've never thought of myself as a dad before, but I guess you're right. I would excel at it like I usually do with everything."

"Keep that conceitedness in check, Lucifer. You wouldn't want our baby to be picking up on that," she teased.

"Why not? There's nothing wrong with being a little proud. It just means you love yourself." I threw my arm over her shoulders, this baby talk working up an appetite for her. I didn't particularly want any soon, but I was open to the prospect if it meant I got to witness Irena's belly round-up with my kid.

"Dear Lord." Aria threw her long chocolate locks over her shoulder, stopping so abruptly, if she was driving right now, someone would've rear-ended her. I was about to ask what was wrong when the soles of her heels created mini indentations on the dirt path below as she spun in place, and pointed a finger at me, then at Irena. "She has said the word *baby* a thousand times, and you still haven't gotten the message?"

"What message?" I inquired, genuinely lost as the two of them gave looks that didn't tell me shit other than they knew a secret I didn't. "What message?" I repeated, and Aria scoffed.

"Men are clueless. I don't know how they'd survive in this world without us." She gave me the two cents I never asked for, tapping her foot on the floor, causing an equally confused Arsène to do the same, learning from his elders.

Irena, who had been uncharacteristically quiet, sucked a

quick breath before delivering the news quickly and efficiently, like ripping off a Band-Aid. "I'm pregnant, Killian."

The whole world suspended when that sentence came out of her lips, and for a minute, I wondered if my ears were playing tricks on me. Regnant, remnant, stagnant... There were plenty of words I could've misheard, but none of them fit in that sentence.

"You're what?" I staggered back.

"Pregnant," she said, slower this time, like she was talking to a child. "We're going to be having our own little baby in six months."

Like a dam had broken, all the sounds came rushing back, and I went from not being able to hear anything to getting irritated by even the ruffling feathers of the birds flying from tree to tree over us.

"No—" The fuller tits, the increased sexual appetite, the increased appetite in general—the dots started connecting one after the other, and I nearly hurled. "How?"

"You want me to explain how I got pregnant?" She tilted her head, and I got the sense that she thought my question was stupid, gaze slicing to Arsène. "Right now?"

"What is *pregnant*?" Arsène couldn't help but pipe in again, but his mother shushed him, and he listened to her for once.

"No, I mean—" I started, cutting myself off, not knowing how to articulate my thoughts and feelings. "We were being safe, Irena."

"No contraceptive is ever one hundred percent foolproof," she reminded me, picking at the dead skin cells around her nails, the first sign of apprehension I most likely caused.

"And you fuck like rabbits," Aria added to her answer after covering Arsène's ears with her palms.

"Are you not happy?" I cracked at Irena's whispered inquiry, and shook my head so hard my brain rattled.

"I am, I am," I repeated in an attempt to convince myself, but found out I didn't have to because part of me *was* genuinely excited to see what the by-product of the two of us would look like. "But I'm also scared shitless."

"You'll do great, Killian. You got the rundown with Arsène and know all the basics. Not many first-time parents can say that," Aria intervened, not realizing it was different when it wasn't your child, and it was easier when sharing the responsibilities.

"When did you find out?" I scrubbed my palm down my face, chilling it with the freak-out because I was working Irena up too.

She was growing a baby in her belly, *holy shit.*

She was growing *my* baby in her belly, holy *fucking* shit.

I wasn't totally opposed to having kids, not one of those people. I was married with a stable life. The timing wasn't terrible, just unexpected.

"Aria forced me to take a test last night after I missed my period for the third month in a row." Her palm curled around her belly, and an unnamed sort of emotion gripped me when I realized I'd helped create a new life with my favorite human in the whole world. "When I saw those two lines appear, I was as shocked and scared as you are, but if there's something I'm a hundred percent about, it's the ability to succeed in anything in life with you by my side." Her fingers laced through mine, and I rested our hands on her stomach that would start showing soon.

In an unexpected turn of events, a pang of excitement hit

me, albeit late. However, I'd take it over the vomit-inducing concern I had about my child's upbringing when it was still the size of a peanut, if not smaller.

Everything would be fine.

Everything was always okay with Irena beside me.

"Don't forget about us too," Aria piped in. "We'll help out as well."

Irena gave her sister a thankful smile before her blues clashed with mine again, her devotion toward our family a raging wildfire growing taller by the second. "We have all the support, financial security, and most importantly—"

"Love," I finished for Irena and dropped to my knees in front of her flat tummy, bearing people's curious glances as I kissed my unborn baby that I was terrified to mess up but couldn't wait to meet. "Unconditional love."

THANKS FOR READING!

Enjoyed Sting of Ice? Please consider leaving a brief, honest review!

Join my newsletter! Be the first to receive exclusive content, announcements, giveaways and more!

Scan the code to join:

ALSO BY CLARA ELROY

City of Stars Series

Kiss of War #1

Vow of Hell #2

Lick of Fire #3

Sting of Ice #4

Blue Bloods Series

Drowning in Secrets #1 (02/24/23)

Swimming in Lies #2 (08/19/23)

FIR #3 (TBA)

Scan the code to read the books:

ACKNOWLEDGMENTS

To my readers—Thank you so much for the love you've shown the City of Stars series. If it wasn't for you and your encouragement, I wouldn't have been able to complete this world. My life has changed drastically since I first published Kiss of War and you're the reason why. I adore you.

To Jessica—Thank you for keeping me sane and always knowing what to say. If it wasn't for you I would've gone crazy a long time ago.

To Erica—Thank you for your keen eyes, and putting up with me and my tight deadlines. You are amazing!

To Ariel, Mia, Libby, Claudia, Fab, and so many other wonderful readers I'm forgetting right now—thank you for being with me from the start, and not hating me much when I forget to reply to messages.

To Salem—you are one of the biggest reasons this book took so long to publish, by distracting me with your cuteness, but I love you anyway. Thank you for the snuggles and laughs.

To Books and Moods and Kristy Sill—Thank you for being so incredibly talented. I love my covers so much!

Forever grateful,
Clara Elroy

ABOUT THE AUTHOR

Clara Elroy is an Amazon Top 100 best selling author of romance novels that make your heart clench. Her love for reading began when she was a young girl, and would lose sleep because she wanted to read "just one more page."

Clara lives for reading and writing about flawed and relatable characters. She loves making sparks fly between stubborn men and the badass women that make them kneel.

When Clara's not typing away at her computer, you can find her with her nose buried in a book or writing biographies in the third person.

Yeah, she's cool like that.

Visit claraelroy.com for more!